Under the Perigean Moon

Olivia Richardson

Under
the
Perigean
Moon

ISBN 979-8-9993341-0-7 (Paperback Edition)
ISBN 979-8-9993341-1-4 (eBook Edition)

Library of Congress Control Number 2025913934

Characters and events in this book are fictitious. Any similarity to real persons, living or dead, is coincidental and not intended by the author.

Cover Design created via Canva.com
Printed and bound in the United States of America
First printing July 2025
Quechee, VT 05059

Table of Contents

For Cooper

In Which it All Begins

A wail cleaves the night sky in two. A second follows and then a third. The fourth, however, is drowned out by a cacophony of church bells formally announcing the birth of a new royal. Citizens from all over the kingdom of Sephiroth lift their voices in toasts and well wishes for the health of the new baby.

King Jasper and Queen Clarice celebrate the birth of their daughter with much quieter fanfare, but no less joy. They cherish their three sons to the ends of the earth, but they have been hoping for a daughter for many years. The queen suffered through several miscarriages and two stillborn children before being able to carry another to term. That she is a healthy baby girl is even more of a reason to celebrate. Though it is not considered proper, the king and queen lie together on the delivery bed and adore her.

"What should we name her?" King Jasper's voice is soft. Labor was not easy for Queen Clarice, and he can easily see the exhaustion etched in the lines on her face.

"I was thinking we should call her Eleanor."

The king swells with pride. His great-great-grandmother Eleanor was the last queen by birthright in Sephiroth for several generations. Her rule saw the longest stretch of peace and prosperity for the kingdom and the fruits of her reign still served them today.

"If we are naming her Eleanor then her middle name should be Clarice after her mother." King Jasper gently brushes the sticky strands of his wife's bangs out of her eyes and marvels at her. Three times before she has brought life into this world and yet he still finds it amazing. "Princess Eleanor Clarice of Sephiroth. Welcome to the world."

The two bask in the rosy glow of welcoming their new bundle of joy into their lives, oblivious to everything beyond the canopy bed they lie on. Outside the full moon hangs low in the sky wreathed in a light so bright it rivals the noonday sun, trying to catch a look at the new baby. They listen to each and every breath baby Eleanor takes, giving thanks for her strong lungs and her even stronger will. They count her small fingers and toes and brush at the wispy auburn curls already forming at the nape of her neck. Mother and baby are safe, and all is right in the world.

Far off in the night, another birth is celebrated. The seventh son of a small island nation is born on a night with the moon at its absolute zenith, the waves singing his praises as they crowd the shores. Though much humbler than the grand palace in Sephiroth, the Manor House is elegant and cozy. Members of the royal family join together to sing the ceremonial welcome songs and dance for the prosperity and long life of the new prince throughout the halls and verandas.

All throughout the kingdom, the people lift their voices in song as they welcome the newest addition to the royal family. They dance through the streets, festive ribbons and paper chains trailing behind them as their feet follow the familiar trails along the cobblestones. Musicians are on every corner and bakers hand out sweet cookies and rolls to anyone who stops near them.

Baskets sit along the front stairs of the manor house and the townspeople make the journey throughout the night to fill them with small gifts, scraps of parchment well wishes for the family, and bright blooms of fresh flowers. Pink and yellow frangipanes, delicate rounded rose mallows, and spiky strelitzia cascade from the baskets and tumble down the stairs in a delicately perfumed current. As one, the nation comes together to welcome the new baby into his place in the world.

The prince himself sleeps, oblivious to the festivities being carried out in his honor. He snores softly in his hand-carved cradle as the moon begins to fade and the sun rises, the sound of waves whispering soothing words in his ears.

$$\cdots \,) \cdot \bigcirc \cdot (\, \cdots$$

The woman sits wreathed in moonlight. Hands resting gently on her knees, she tries to block out the sounds around her and find peace. She is distracted tonight, finding it difficult to ignore the sounds of the waves lapping the shores far beneath her and the calling of the insects from the grass around her. An unsettlingly loud croak next to her left knee scares her sideways as a mammoth toad hops past.

Closing her eyes again tightly against the moonlight, her breath comes out in a frustrated huff. She must observe silent meditation before joining her people in celebration tonight or she will not be able to perform the necessary rights.

With measured breaths, the woman looks inwards again. A prickling spark starts behind her heart, and she nurses it gently, feeding it until it becomes a flame. The flame serenely flickers once, twice, three times, and then floods through her with a heat that leaves her breathless.

Everything around her goes quiet for a moment and then the sounds flood back in, but they are muted in a way. The woman exhales in relief. She's done it. Opening her eyes, there is now another woman made of the purest moonlight sitting at the side of the cliffs and waiting for her.

Knees creaking even in her corporeal form, the woman stands and steps away from her physical body. Though she cannot fall in this in-between world, she is still overly cautious as she joins the woman at the cliffside and turns her face to the stars.

"It's a beautiful night tonight, Aurelia." The woman's voice is a lilting harmony, soft and assertive all at once. "Are you preparing for a wedding?"

"A baptism," Auralia says, readjusting her skirts beneath her. "The parents hope that you will choose their child as the next Wisdom."

"And what do you think of their hope?"

"She is not yet three months of age. It is difficult to know just how she will grow."

The woman of moonlight bows her head thoughtfully. "Her life force is strong and her presence commanding. We shall see if she blossoms into a natural leader by her tenth birthday, but I do not believe it is yet time for you to take an apprentice. You still have much to do in this lifetime."

They lapse into silence, watching and listening to the world around them. Aurelia glances over her shoulder at her physical form sitting in the grass behind, and shudders gently. It is always unsettling seeing herself like that, face serene and swirling tattoos glowing purplish blue. Even after all these years entering the in-between, she has never grown accustomed to the sight of her body waiting for her to return.

"Is there more you would like to discuss?"

"There is a child born this night to the Koralans," the woman says thoughtfully, "and another born in Sephiroth. They will journey here."

"Together?"

Aurelia cannot hide the surprise in her voice. It is rare enough to have visitors from Korala in their village, but to know they are to receive someone from the kingdom of Sephiroth? Unheard of.

"Together, and separate," the woman muses. "He will arrive first in six months' time; however, they will not come together until many years beyond that. Look for them for they are instrumental to the future of our peoples."

"Of course, My Lady."

"There is one more thing we must do on this night."

"Whatever you require of me I shall do." Aurelia bows her head in deference to the woman of moonlight.

"Join with me. We must create a binding spell before it is too late."

Aurelia craves to know why it must be done this minute but wisely chooses to keep her questions to herself. It did not do well to question the Moon Goddess.

"For whom?"

"A woman named Belladonna."

Chapter 1

In Which the World Ends

Nora

I'm on fire. It's deep within my belly, spreading too fast to control. Warm tendrils course through my veins and each time he touches me they spark and fizz under his fingertips. I will burn for this man.

Hands grip my waist and move to the laces at my back. Clumsy fingers struggle with the slippery ribbon before sliding upwards and into my hair. We move in perfect harmony, giving and taking in turn as we tease the other.

He's tracing constellations down my neck when I feel those same hands sliding under my skirts and up my leg. Hold on now. This is new territory, left uncharted and unexplored for a reason. Gripping his wrist, I halt his progress as best I can. If he didn't have me backed into a wall I'd move farther away.

"Teddy, we have to stop."

The words grate in my ears. Gods I hate having to say them. I'm always the one drawing the line and stopping us before we go too far. It would be nice if he was the one to put an end to things for once instead of me always having to be the responsible one. Because no matter how desperately I want to go farther than I allow, I am always the one to say no more.

Teddy pulls back from my neck, eyes unfocused, and blinks at me. Our breathing is heavy and rapid, chests heaving in time as we surface. A small grin slides across his face and Teddy nuzzles back in, gently kissing and teasing the soft skin beneath my ear.

"Oh, come on." His breath is light as a whisper and goosebumps prickle along my neck and arms. "Just a little longer."

With concentrated effort, I push him far enough away I can wriggle out from where he has me pinned against the wall. Little by little my breathing slows as I take in the familiar sights of the long unused nursery. Tucked in its own corner of the palace halfway between the family quarters and the servants' quarters, the nursery makes a perfect place for me and Teddy to meet discreetly without anyone knowing what we're getting up to. That's the idea anyway.

"You know I can't. Mother requested we have a private breakfast together and I can't be late for that. She'll never let me hear the end of it."

Teddy groans and dramatically flings himself across a sheet wrapped chair. "I don't understand why you can't be a few minutes late. You're just going to the green drawing room. That's not exactly private."

Abandoning my attempts at straightening my decidedly rumpled appearance, I toss a long deserted stuffed bear at him and laugh as it bounces off his pale hair. "You know why. Mother only has breakfast with me when she needs to discuss something she considers important and if I want to skip a lecture I need to be on time. How do I look?"

Teddy greedily looks me over and I shiver under his gaze. My lips feel swollen and bruised and goosebumps begin rising on my arms again. It's not fair that he can get my heart racing with just a look. No one should have that kind of power over another.

"You look as beautiful as ever." He rises and gives me a brief hug. "You'll be fine, Nora. I'll be here if you need some moral support."

I pull him down for one last kiss before slipping out the door to the hallway. My hands slide over the satiny fabric of my skirts and fruitlessly attempt to smooth out the worst of the wrinkles. Hopefully, Mother won't notice. Ugh. A private audience with Mother is never a good sign, but the sooner I'm there the sooner I'll be able to leave. Better just get this over with.

• • • ☽ • ◯ • ☾ • • •

"Marriage?" I recoil back in my chair and actively fight to keep my eyes from rolling. "Can I at least finish my breakfast before you start talking about ruining my life?"

"Oh, come now, Nora, don't be so dramatic."

Mother looks at me calmly as she sips her tea. Like she didn't just tell me I have to get *married*.

"Dramatic? You think this is being dramatic?"

"Yes, I do actually. It's been six months since your birthday. You know it is customary that, once a princess turns twenty, she begins the search for a husband. Be thankful it's no longer sixteen."

"Yes, how comforting." Mother's eyes narrow at my sarcasm. Uh oh. If Mother can sense my insincerity, I need to try much harder to hide it. "And as I told you and Father when you brought it up on my birthday, unless I am able to marry Teddy then I have no interest."

"Theodore is unfit to become a prince." I can hear the clear disapproval in her voice.

"What's so wrong with him? He's kind and charming and hardworking. According to our latest etiquette lesson those are all valuable traits for a royal to have."

"You know very well what's wrong with your plan." Mother bites off her words, the strain of being polite beginning to wear on her already. "If you are unwilling to accept the answer and cooperate in the search to find a husband then your father and I will move forward with selecting one ourselves."

"So not only would you force me to marry, but you would also subject me to an arranged marriage."

My appetite gone, I carelessly toss my fork and napkin over my plate and huff back in my chair. I know I really am too old for this behavior, but it's hard not to act like a petulant child. Especially with Mother treating me like one. Before I can change my mind about finishing breakfast, one of the many servants pressed against the gilt patterned wallpaper swoops forward and removes my plate. *There goes that I guess...*

"Marriage is not the end of the world, Dearest," Mother says softly. I can hear the effort in her voice as she tries to remain soothing. "I know you have many strong, ahem, opinions about it, but there are still traditions and duties we as the women of the family must uphold. Part of that duty is for you to marry."

"I don't want to marry."

"I know. I admit I was unsure if I ever wanted to marry when my partnership with your father was arranged, but I could see what I could do for my family and my own country by making the alliance." Mother's voice turns wistful, her eyes far away in a distant memory. "Over time the alliance turned to respect, respect turned to friendship, and friendship to love. Your father and I have been happy for many years. Give it a chance, Nora, and the same can happen for you."

I scoff quietly. Everyone can see that my parents are meant to be together. They're clearly two halves of the same coin and complement each other perfectly. To try and convince me that my experience with an arranged marriage will be the same is foolish.

"I know you don't believe me," Mother murmurs.

She gestures offhandedly, and one by one the servants blending into the wallpaper slip out of the room until we are truly alone. The soft snick of the door closing prompts me to sit up just that much straighter. Mother never dismisses the servants.

"In truth we do not have the luxury of postponing any longer. The High Counsel is demanding you be married by your next birthday."

A shiver crawls up my spine. Even though Father is the king, the High Counsel has a lot of sway in the running of the kingdom. Made up of the patriarchs of the prominent leading families throughout Sephiroth, the High Counsel are emissaries for the people. They spread news, uphold the laws in their respective guilds, and bring the fears and concerns of the common people to Father when they themselves are not able to attend Grievance Hours. If there's ever a group of people you don't want to make angry, it's the High Counsel. Father has ultimate say in decisions made, but if these men decide that he is no longer performing his duties correctly they can very easily stage a coup and replace him with any one of his children. Provided his children cooperate, of course.

"I don't understand why though. Hayden, Ren, and Samael are all in line for the throne before me and they're all unmarried. Why is my sole purpose as princess to be married off to become someone else's problem? Shouldn't their efforts be directed towards Hayden and ensuring he produces the next heir?"

Not for the first time I feel a pang of resentment towards my older brothers and their freedoms. All my life I've trailed after them as they enjoy the advantages that come with being male. Just yesterday, Ren and Samael took off on a trip to Ailona just because they can. When I had asked to join, Mother had put her foot down and refused to even let me know what ship they were sailing on so I couldn't even make a good attempt at stowing away. She claimed it was too dangerous or some such nonsense.

Lately Hayden has been embracing his role of Crown Prince and taken on some of Father's responsibilities as he becomes more integrated into the High Counsel. He shadows Father regularly throughout his duties to help prepare him to step in when Father eventually steps down. Tradition aside, why isn't he being hounded to find a bride and pop out royal heirs?

Mother just pinches the bridge of her nose and exhales slowly. "Your father and I have taken great pains to make you an equal of your brothers. We have ensured you can hunt, defend yourself, ride, and receive the same level of schooling as they did. In some ways, you surpassed your brothers, and, in some ways, they surpassed you. I know you want the same freedoms they have, but that is not the reality of the world we live in."

I sit quietly and just watch. It's obvious Mother is struggling to find the right words to try and convey what she truly means. While she can give a lecture or rousing speech off the cuff, it's often harder for us to find the words to communicate clearly.

"You are one of the strongest women I know, and I am proud to call you my daughter." Mother's voice catches and she pauses a moment to steady it. "In many ways I wish you had been born first. If you ever got the opportunity to become the queen, I know there would be great prosperity and advancement throughout Sephiroth.

"The High Counsel is pushing so hard for you to be married, I believe, partly out of fear. They know you are strong willed, and our people love you. In a revolt to overthrow the line of succession there is a good chance that you would be the one selected to take the crown and not your brothers. That fear is driving the High Counsel to insist on your marriage to try and remove that threat."

The sweet temptation to roll my eyes washes over me like a hug and I struggle not to react. If Mother doesn't want to give me the actual reason why I have to do this then fine. At least have the decency not to lie to me though. The chances of me being considered first in line to replace Father are slim to none. Actually, they're worse than slim to none.

"Can't Father just overrule them or something?" I ask carelessly.

"He has held them off for the past three years. They wanted to have you married by your eighteenth birthday, but we stopped that from happening. They are becoming stricter each day. Several credible threats have been brought to our attention that risk us losing our position and possibly our lives. An unmarried princess has remarkable political power for both her allies *and* her enemies. We need the full endorsement of the High Counsel and if that means you need to be married within six months time to ensure their support then so be it."

It's like all the air leaves my body. I slump back in my seat, attempting to understand what Mother is saying. So many questions flood my mind, and I struggle to find the right ones to ask. What threats? Why didn't they tell me sooner? Am I to be nothing more than a pawn in a larger game my entire life?

Mother watches me with eyes the same shade of blue as a warm sunny day that wraps around you and holds you close. While I had inherited my red curls from her, my eyes are the same hazel green as Father's. My distress must clearly show on my face because Mother reaches across the table and gently takes my hand.

"I wish we had the luxury of allowing you a love match," she says gently. "The High Counsel will not accept Theodore even if your father and I do. We cannot risk their wrath, not right now. Many of the surrounding kingdoms have eligible young men for you to choose a husband from. I wish you would be involved in the selection process, but I understand if you would prefer to remain separate."

I shake my head slowly, not wanting to meet Mother's gaze. If I look at her, I'll probably start crying and that's the last thing I want. I'll save my tears for Teddy. For when he can comfort me.

The thought of choosing a husband raises a bile in my throat that I struggle to swallow around. They might be able to force me to sign away the future I want, but I am definitely not going to help make it easier for them.

"Can you do it, Mother?"

Chapter 2

In Which a Plan is Made

Queen Clarice watches Princess Eleanor over the abandoned remains of their breakfast table. The princess sits hunched in her chair, nose twitching the same way it has since her youth when she was trying hard not to cry. Clarice loathes seeing her children upset. It is even harder when she knows that she is the reason for it.

She wishes to reach out and comfort Nora, but knows that the princess needs time to be on her own to process through her own feelings before accepting any help from someone else. Truth be told, Clarice doubts she will even be the one to offer that comfort when it is finally wanted. Nora stopped going to her a long time ago.

Pushing back from the table, Clarice silently pads across the plush carpeting of the drawing room and out into the hallway. The guards on either side of the door half-bow briefly and return to their statue-like countenance, their faces frozen in the blank stare servants and military seem to have mastered.

Sighing, Queen Clarice straightens her skirts and lifts her chin. She sashays her way down the hall, around the corner, through the library, and into King Jasper's private study.

"I'm not interrupting anything am I?" she asks as she pushes through the heavy wood door.

Jasper startles briefly from his papers and blinks at her a few times before a smile breaks out across his face. "Of course not, My Flower. Is everything alright?"

Clarice hovers awkwardly between the heavy stuffed armchairs before the stately mahogany desk Jasper sits behind. She fidgets with her skirts and forces herself to bury her hands in the hidden pockets near her bodice, so she doesn't wrinkle the fabric. Her tailors will demand her head if she ruins yet another gown with her worrying.

"I spoke with Nora." That simple string of words speaks volumes and Jasper's face falls. A small twitch of anger at the corner of his mouth is the only indication of how he really feels. "She took it as well as we had hoped. She asked that we oversee arranging the marriage."

"It's probably better that way," Jasper intones grimly. "I imagine she is not happy."

"It's hard to know the extent of just how Nora feels. She's trying to hide how upset she is, but she will not talk to me and most likely will refuse to. I left her in the drawing room to give her some space."

Jasper hums absently as he shuffles papers around on his desk, pulling packets from drawers and leafing through them. He is very aware that Nora has always hated crying in front of others, and it is always better to give her space when she needs it. They both are hyper aware that they are the cause of their daughter's pain and struggle to accept that they can do nothing at this moment to fix it.

"Did you tell her why?"

"I told her the High Counsel is pushing for her marriage before her birthday. I also told her that they would not allow her and Theodore to marry."

Jasper nods thoughtfully. "All truth. Good. Did you tell her about...?"

"No."

"Clarice, we talked about this. We need to tell her. She deserves to know."

"I know."

Jasper gives Clarice a knowing look and she begins to fidget again. In a whirl of anxious energy she paces a familiar path back and forth across the study — fourteen steps to the window overlooking the gardens, turn, fourteen steps back to the chairs, a brief moment weaving between them, twelve steps to the bookshelves on the far wall, turn, and repeat. Jasper remains behind his desk, hands steepled under his chin as he watches her restlessness.

"I know she deserves to know. I just don't know how to tell her, and I can't bear the thought of what happens if we don't succeed. It's hard enough for me to agree to marry her off and pull some poor boy who doesn't know any better into this mess as well! What would his family think of us if they knew?" Clarice pauses in front of the window and buries her face in her hands. "No mother should be put in this position. If we tell her the truth, we risk her interfering and then we lose her anyway."

Tears slowly track down Clarice's face, slipping through her fingers. Her shoulders hitch as she cries. Jasper ventures out from behind his desk and pulls Clarice into his arms. Clarice resists at first, but after a few soft words she sinks against Jasper's chest, burying her face into his shoulder.

"It's going to be okay," he croons softly. "Trust me."

Jasper's doubts catch hold and overwhelm him. His own tears threaten to fall into Clarice's soft hair as he holds her close. The chiming of the clock on the mantle cuts through their shared sorrow like a knife and they separate briefly, trying to discreetly wipe away the wetness that stains their cheeks.

"Now," Jasper says, his voice carrying only the barest hint of emotion, "we do have some prospects to sort through. All upstanding young men from good families with many children. While it will be painful for their parents to separate from one, they will not be left without heirs. The High Counsel and I have made some preliminary selections. Would you like to see?"

Clarice nods. Jasper weaves back around his desk and returns to rummaging in one of the many drawers. Pulling out six sheaves of paper bound in leather; he lays them across the worktop and gestures for Clarice to join him. She stands across from him, leaning with both hands on the polished desktop while Jasper flips open the packets and presents them to her. On the top pages are names, ages, kingdoms, and brief descriptions of who they are.

"How did you get these?" She asks incredulously.

"I put word out for Nora's birthday last year for any and all traveling emissaries to take back a message to their monarchs to submit an official profile of an eligible son for a possible alliance."

"Very clever indeed. How many sent one back?"

"Thirty-seven in total. One family even sent two, but we opted to choose the youngest son for consideration due to his age." King Jasper slides his hand across the desktop and covers one of Clarice's with his own. "Would you like to go through them together?"

The day marches slowly onward with only the occasional interruption of servants bringing food and tea to disrupt the search. Jasper and Clarice comb through the packets on the eligible grooms and weigh pros and cons for each one. They consult maps and charts for proximity to their home countries, books to determine compatibility with goods and services trading, and the submitted dossiers to try and judge personalities from the little information provided.

For most of the day it seemed that Prince Azar from Heyanth was leading the pack of eligible bachelors. A partnership with Heyanth would strengthen Sephiroth trade routes and provide access to their Apatite mines. His ranking dropped dramatically around lunch when they consulted with the Heyanth emissary and discovered Azar had entered into an agreement with another princess and was no longer eligible for marriage. Why he did not withdraw his name from the selection process sooner is a mystery that not even the Heyanth emissary was able to solve. Jasper unceremoniously doused the now offending dossier in the dregs of his soup bowl and it was carried away with the rest of the abandoned lunch dishes to be disposed of.

The afternoon stretches before them as if it cannot be bothered to move any faster. Names, countries, trade routes, and opinions swim between Jasper and Clarice until they become an unintelligible stream of words and symbols.

After many hours hunched over papers, Clarice stands and stretches her creaking back as the clock happily announces the five o'clock hour. She selects a shortbread cookie from the long-abandoned tea tray sitting on the side of the desk. The study is chaos incarnate, papers and books haphazardly strewn around the room where they were forgotten.

"I believe Prince Alon of Korala is our best choice." Retrieving his messy packet from the side of the desk, she holds it out to Jasper to review again. "He's the youngest son of an island nation. Rich and stable economy, but no real defenses to speak of. They're not considered the highest-ranking nobles, so I doubt any of the children have been able to make strong alliances with any of the other nations."

Jasper nods agreeably as he sorts through the same papers they had looked over so many times already. "I agree, My Flower, he is a fine choice. I will alert the High Counsel that a candidate has been chosen and dispatch an emissary to Korala at once. We will do everything we can to make up for the loss of their son."

Chapter 3

In Which an Agreement is Reached

Alon

Water swirls around me in blue and aquamarine bubbles as I dive into the surf. Bright colored fish scatter and crabs and lobsters scuttle away across the sandy floor. Ahead of me, Ryo cuts through the water towards the flag perched jauntily on a small pile of rock. The rhythm of the waves on the surface set the fabric moving in lazy ripples that almost make it look like it's blowing in the wind.

With smooth strokes I follow Ryo, circling around to the far side of the flag. Cove and Hanale should have known this would be an easy win. They'll have a much harder time getting around Caspian at the top of the east wing to claim ours.

Ryo snags one corner of the heavy canvas and I take the other. Together, we kick off the rocks and heave it to the surface. The water laden fabric screams its protest and threatens to drag us back down to the sandy depths, but the combined strength of me and my brother are enough to raise it into the sunlight. Gulping in fresh air, we shake saltwater from our hair and faces.

"Ready?" Ryo grins at me over the waves, the familiar lines and planes of his face crinkling together.

"Let's do this."

Flipping to our backs, we pull the flag taut across our bodies and try to raise it completely out of the water. It protests loudly as it leaves the sea, but another good tug and it begrudgingly allows itself to be raised above the surface. We backstroke towards the shore, making sure to stay parallel so we don't risk the flag sinking and dragging us back down. Sand scrapes along our necks and grates across our backs as the surf pushes us through the shallows and up onto the beach.

"C'mon!" I sputter, trying to gather as much of the flag in my arms as possible. "Get that side!"

Ryo collects the rest of the loose fabric and together we run haphazardly through the sand. Thankfully, we're able to avoid the steep rock steps cut into the side of the cliffs and head directly through the port town. All around us merchants and various workers yell and curse at us as we barrel through the wooden maze, scattering birds and children alike. It doesn't take long before we leave the busy port and town behind and start to climb the hill leading to home.

Air stings my tired lungs and my muscles ache from the exertion, but Ryo pulls ahead, and I struggle to catch up. We climb the front stairs in leaps and bounds, our breath coming in fits and spurts. The front door is already hanging open and we slide inside, our feet unable to find purchase on the cool marble.

Baba is in the front hall like he always is when we play capture the flag. This time, however, he's talking to a portly man standing with his back to us. I barely notice his well tailored suit before we're dropping our sodden mess at their feet.

I double over, clutching my sides as I try to catch my breath. Ryo crows in excitement and an echoing call answers from elsewhere in the manor. Caspian must have seen us coming and is en route from the east wing.

"Please forgive my sons, My Lord," Baba intones. He shoots us a withering look. "Her Majesty and I have been encouraging some friendly competition."

"Quite alright, quite alright," the man sniffs. He adjusts a pair of tiny wire rimmed glasses and assesses Ryo and I like cattle at the market. "I will admit I did not expect them to be so...wet...at our first meeting."

"Why don't we move onto the veranda and I will have some refreshments brought out." Baba gestures for the man to go first. Once his back is turned, Baba winks at us and whispers, "well done! Go get changed and come down with your Mama and the rest."

"Who do you think that was?" Ryo asks as we climb the stairs to the upper floors.

"No idea, but he didn't seem to think very highly of you."

Ryo sniggers and shoves me with his shoulder. I shove back and we race headlong to the fourth floor where our bedroom is. Mama and Baba had converted the uppermost floor of the Manor House to a dormitory style room for me and my brothers before I was even born. As we grew and needed more privacy, they erected movable walls that could be pulled around our beds to get some respite from the others. For the most part the walls would stay pushed out of the way and we would cohabitate peacefully, but the Great Sock Debacle a few years back definitely put some wear and tear on the partitions.

It had gotten so bad that there was even talk of moving us into separate rooms on the lower floors to put an end to the fighting.

Windows line the west wall and beds line the east, a small space left bare to allow the door to swing open unimpeded. The partitions are tucked discreetly to the sides and out of the way, but still within easy reach if they're wanted. A set of double doors and a balcony at either end of the room allow fresh air in at all hours. I inhale the salty sea breeze and make my way down the room to my own cot in the back corner.

Kalani and Atlas are already dressed and making last minute adjustments to their hair in front of a shared mirror. Mama scolds Cove as she straightens Hanale's jacket. A few minutes later Caspian puffs up the stairs, out of breath from running in from the east wing.

"There you are!" The usual calm and rolling notes in Mama's voice are pulled taut. "Why are you all wet?"

Cove and Hanale guffaw behind her, quieting immediately when Mama gives them a look.

"Alon, get changed quickly. We need to do something about that hair."

"Mama, we both know that's hopeless." I shrug. My hair has just enough of Mama's curl to give it a mind of its own and, so far anyway, no comb nor paste has been able to tame it. "Besides, it's wet. What does it matter anyway?"

"Because the emissary from Sephiroth arrived today and wants to speak with us!"

All noise in the room ceases. Several pairs of eyes bore into me as I pretend nonchalance. "So?"

"So, if he is here, it means something is happening." Mama clasps her hands on my shoulders and hugs me briefly. "If they chose you or Ryo, Starfish, then this could be the answer we have been looking for. This could mean good things for us."

A small tendril of fear swims its way up my spine, and I try to keep my breathing steady so it can't spread any further. After several potential matches for my elder brothers fell through, it was no secret Mama and Baba were hoping for an alliance with Sephiroth. Being a small island nation definitely has its perks, but attracting strong neighboring kingdoms with which to forge mutually beneficial partnerships is not one of them.

We're not large enough to be able to create a true navy for protection and rely heavily on merchants from neighboring kingdoms for many goods. Sephiroth is one of the biggest merchant kingdoms and, if we can strike an alliance between our nations, we have a real chance for protection and prosperity we wouldn't have been able to achieve ourselves. It's why both me and Ryo had been submitted as possible suitors for their princess.

"Everything will be fine, Mama." I try to give her a reassuring smile, but my face feels stiff and unmoving.

She nods and turns to continue fussing over the others. Ryo and I exchange worried looks across the room as we busy ourselves with drying off and changing. I had agreed to have my name put forth as a possible suitor when Mama and Baba had asked because I honestly thought it would mean nothing. Who would want the seventh son of a dinky island nation who, to be perfectly frank, didn't really bring much to the table? She is a princess of one of the wealthiest and most prosperous kingdoms around. I guess I figured she'd be married off to a first or second son of an equally strong nation.

Once changed, Mama tuts over us like a nervous hen for a few more minutes, smoothing hair and shirts alike. One final nod of approval and we fall in as Mama leads us back downstairs and, inevitably, to the veranda Baba and the emissary are waiting on. While the trip upstairs was loud and boisterous, the walk back down is silent and heavy. Our funerals are more fun than this.

I nudge Ryo sharply and whisper, "cut it out before Mama sees you."

He shoots me a look but manages to stop pulling on his ear. He only does it when he's nervous and I smile to myself. I can see Caspian clenching and unclenching his jaw while Kalani's normally smooth gait is stilted and awkward. I realize that all my brothers are nervous, not just me and Ryo. Our success at a match with Sephiroth could open doors for my brothers to pursue education, escape, and their own chances for alliances. Somehow that helps put me at ease. with their nerves there's no room for my own.

Baba and the Sephiroth emissary sit on the veranda drinking glasses of sparkling wine. I can tell by the color that Baba insisted on one of the finer bottles be brought up from the cellars. Mama and Baba value hard work and humility regardless of station, but they are definitely not above putting on a bit of a show to make sure people don't think we're poor and helpless. That's all this is though. A show. The influx of piracy over the last few years has wreaked havoc on what little export business we have, and it's begun to make it even more dangerous for the local fishers to venture out. We desperately need an alliance with Sephiroth, but we don't want them to know that.

"Ah, here they are now." Baba rises and takes Mama's hand to present her to the man. "My Darling, this is Lord Archer from Sephiroth."

The usual bowing and nodding and ceremony that happens every time visiting nobility arrives happens just the same. If I'm lucky

I'll be able to slink back behind my brothers and escape notice. I glance at Ryo, and he looks like he's about to hurl.

"How nice to meet you, My Lord." Mama smiles so brightly I can see Lord Archer blink once or twice, faintly stunned. Mama does tend to have that effect on people. She gestures back to us. "These are our sons: Kalani, Cove, Atlas, Hanale, Caspian, Ryo, and Alon."

Lord Archer bows to us in turn and we nod back. Kalani and Cove study the dignitary with open interest, but Atlas, Hanale, and Caspian seem mildly bored. Tension radiates off Ryo next to me and I'm sure he can feel my nerves just the same.

"With all due respect, Your Majesties –" the short vowels and clipped consonants make the familiar words sound alien to my ears "– I would like to request an audience with Yourselves and with His Highness Prince Alon."

The gust of relief from Ryo hits me like a gale force wind and I struggle to remain upright. *They chose. Why did they choose* me? The importance of my family's hopes and dreams truly settles onto my shoulders. And it is a terrifying weight.

"Of course," Baba says amiably. "Boys you are dismissed. Alon please join us."

My feet move heavily across the floor towards one of the open seats. I sit, just catching myself before total collapse. Ryo is the only one that lingers after the dismissal. He's always worn his heart on his sleeve and his relief and guilt play across his face like sunlight on the waves. I look at him and smile. *Talk later*, I mouth.

"We are on a bit of a schedule so I will be direct provided that is alright with Your Majesties," Lord Archer begins. A gesture from Baba encourages him to continue. "As you know, Their Royal Majesties, King Jasper and Queen Clarice of Sephiroth, gathered dossiers regarding potential suitors for their daughter, Her Highness

Princess Eleanor. Their Royal Majesties have chosen His Highness Prince Alon as the groom.

"If agreeable –" he pauses briefly to cough into a scrappy handkerchief and hand several papers to Baba "– Their Majesties are willing to provide the following as a dowry to the Kingdom of Korala in exchange for the union: a yearly allocation of funding for infrastructure and defense, six armored warships and crew to begin the development of a navy, agriculturalists to assist in the development of usable farmland, and advisors, if accepted, to assist with further growing Korala into a well established nation for merchants and trading."

My eyes tear themselves away from Lord Archer's face as a sharp intake of breath from Mama briefly distracts me. She sits next to me with her hands in her lap, but I can see the bright glassy look in Mama's eyes, and I know she is trying hard not to cry. This is everything Mama and Baba were hoping for from an alliance. I can see how much they both want it.

"Additionally," Lord Archer continues, "Their Majesties will ensure that his Royal Highness Prince Kalani and all six of their Highnesses, the Princes of Korala, are welcomed at the palace and universities of Sephiroth for any additional training or education they choose to participate in. They may become members of the court if desired and Their Majesties hope that His Royal Highness and Their Highnesses, the Princes and Princess of Sephiroth, may do the same with Korala.

"There are more specifics outlined in the documents –" Lord Archer nods to the papers Baba holds "– but those are the things Her Majesty Queen Clarice requested I specifically mention in this meeting with Your Majesties today."

Mama and Baba nod mutely. I can see the shock written on Baba's face and in Mama's fidgeting hands. Neither of them knows what to say.

"Thank you, Lord Archer," Baba says with as much grace as he can manage. "When will you require an answer?"

"It has been decided that Her Highness Princess Eleanor must be wed before her twenty-first birthday in just under four months' time. I ask that you provide me with an answer within the week to ensure there is enough time to relay the news back to Their Majesties and to ensure proper provisions are put in place. If you wish to accept, we will need to set sail for Sephiroth as soon as possible so we have ample time to return to the palace and make preparations for the wedding."

"Thank you," Baba nods, "I believe we have much to dis —"

"I accept the offer." The words tumble out before I can think better of it. All eyes turn to me. "I mean, *we* accept the offer."

"Alon," Mama says softly, "I think we should talk about—"

"With all due respect, Mama, there is nothing to talk about." I turn back to Lord Archer. "I accept the terms laid out. We should be able to set sail for Sephiroth within the week."

"I shall alert the staff to make preparations to leave immediately," Baba says, spearing me with a look before turning back to Lord Archer. "My Lord, may I have you escorted to one of our guest rooms? It has been a long journey and I'm sure you are in need of a good bed."

"Much appreciated," says Lord Archer, coughing into his handkerchief again. "I barely slept on the crossing over — if I wasn't seasick, I was being tossed around like a dandelion in the wind!"

Mama and Baba rise with the Lord, accompanying him to the hall. I hear Mama stop one of the servants and ask her to escort Lord Archer to the Emerald Rooms on the third floor.

I'm already in motion before they finish their polite nothings and turn back around. If Mama and Baba try talking to me about this, I'm going to change my mind, and I can't do that. I can't. It's everything we need, arranged marriage or not. So instead of acting like the newly engaged prince of almost twenty-one years that I am, I flee from the veranda out into the sunshine like a child and head towards the water. I need to think.

Chapter 4

In Which a Moonlit Tryst Comes to Pass

Nora

A soft tap comes from my bedroom door.

"Nora? May I come in?"

Abigail looks at me questioningly in the mirror and I give a small sigh and nod. She opens the door and then returns to braiding my hair. I watch in the mirror as Mother stands uncomfortably in the center of the room, hands worrying her skirts into endless wrinkles.

"Your father and I heard back from the emissary sent to Korala. They have accepted the terms of the engagement. Prince Alon and his family will be arriving about a month before the wedding."

Internally I cringe at her words, but I try to keep my face passive and expressionless. I don't want Mother to see how much this upsets me.

"Thank you for telling me, Mother."

My words are thick with unshed tears, and I know she can hear it. Mother reaches out a hand towards me but then seems to think better of it and buries it back into her skirts.

"Did you need something else?"

"No. That was all."

"Well, then. Thank you for letting me know." My voice is airy. Pretending at nonchalance that I wish I actually felt.

Mother must have decided it wasn't worth trying to continue a conversation because she turns abruptly and leaves, the door closing behind her with a sharp snap. The resounding silence is deafening. It seems that all we mean to each other lately is closed doors and unspoken words hanging heavy between us.

Tears try to rise to the surface again, but I quash them down. I don't want to cry again. I *won't* cry again. I have already spent too much time lately crying over this boy I have never met. I have grieved for the loss of my freedom and the loss of the future I crave. Because it doesn't just end once I'm officially married. As soon as the proverbial ring is on the finger, I am sure there will be the expectation from him to 'settle down' and start popping out babies as quickly as possible to produce an heir or six for him. I can't imagine a worse fate for a woman.

My pity party is cut short as another knock echoes from the door. Abigail harrumphs quietly and goes over to see who it is. A few moments of silence and then the door closes again. Abigail sets a small paper elephant on my vanity and discreetly excuses herself off to straighten my bathing room. Bless her, she knows what it means. Only Teddy sends me notes like this.

Carefully unfolding the elephant, I read the words scrawled in Teddy's familiar writing:

My Sun,

I heard that a suitor has agreed to the marriage. Meet me at our place tonight at the usual time. I need to talk to you.

T

"Abigail, draw me a bath and lay out my riding habit please."

Abigail nods and pulls the bell rope to summon more of the maids. They arrive quickly and without fanfare, curtsying briefly to me before withdrawing to fetch warm water from the kitchens. It will take a moment for a full bath to be drawn, but there's nothing I can do to make it go any faster. Checking the clock, I have just over an hour to bathe, dress, and sneak out. Not as much time as I would like, that's for sure.

• • • ☽ • ◯ • ☾ • • •

"Nora?"

The call is soft through the darkness, floating gently above the other noises of the night around me. I straighten on the hard stone bench I had slumped onto earlier when I arrived and peer through the gloom.

"Teddy?"

Appearing from the trees at the edge of the clearing, he leaves a trail of footprints in the frost on the stone pathway. Teddy pulls me up from the bench and wraps me in a warm hug. Under the trellis archway, that all too familiar prickle of tears in my eyes rises again and I can't fight them back this time. They fall onto Teddy's chest as I inhale his familiar scent of cinnamon and spice.

"Shhh it's okay. Don't cry. I'm here." Teddy gently rubs my back and sways like you would to calm a cranky toddler. "I'm here."

After a while, my tears slow and I'm left with horrible gaspy breaths as I try to calm myself down. Teddy helps me sit back down on the bench and pulls a flask of water from his side, carefully uncapping it before offering it to me. The cool water helps soothe my throat and calms me the rest of the way.

"How did you find out?" My words come out in a rasp.

"My father told me today after the Counsel met. He was surprised Korala had agreed. I thought they had finally given up on this. Why now?"

"I thought so too." I hiccup briefly. "I already told you that the High Counsel has been pushing to have me married by my twenty-first birthday. Mother said there were threats made towards my family and our ability to remain its rulers if I didn't marry."

"That doesn't make any sense. My father hasn't said anything to me about threats to overthrow the king."

I shrug helplessly. "Maybe someone knows something about us and doesn't trust your father not to say something. Maybe he's not telling you to try and protect you. Maybe he's not...not high enough ranked..."

I can see how my words hurt Teddy. He stiffens slightly and forces himself to relax again. It has always been a sticking point that his father, Lord Moore, is considered one of the minor lords on the High Counsel and his ancestral property is smaller than most. It is a title and property Teddy is set to inherit when his father passes and is something he both craves and resents.

"Can we make an appeal? Lords and Ladies have married into the royal family before. Why can't we appeal to have you marry me instead of a foreign prince?"

"Mother said the High Counsel would never accept you as a candidate."

I wince as the words hang between us, colder than the chill in the air. Anger flashes across Teddy's face and he tries to keep the fury from his eyes. Even with only the poor light from the lantern I know they would be the same gray as the clouds after a rain. Teddy's eyes change like the weather and even after all these years I sometimes struggle to understand what they're saying.

"There's nothing we can do," I say softly, looking at the stars. "I am trapped in this mess and there's nothing we can do to change it."

Teddy pulls me close again and I sink into him. He's so warm and comforting and *home* that it hurts to think we won't be able to have this forever.

"Maybe it doesn't have to change that much."

"What do you mean?"

Teddy blows out a breath, billowy white in the night. "Plenty of kings and queens have lovers. Who's to say that I couldn't be your consort?"

"Teddy, that's ridiculous. There's no way we could get away with that."

"Why not?"

"For one, there's no way a man would allow me to have a consort. For another, something horrible could happen to you if we were ever caught."

"When did you ever allow a man to tell you what you can and cannot do?"

Teddy's eyes glint mischievously at me, and he leans down to kiss me hard and fast. His soft and humorous lips are fueled by a passion and fire that leaps onto mine and spread through my body to my toes. I don't want him to ever let me go.

Teddy's strong arms wrap around my waist and pull me off the bench onto his lap. I let out a brief grunt at the flash of pain as my knees bang into the bench on either side of his hips, but a quick shifting adjustment and I settle into his lap. The skirts of my riding habit pool around me and cascade down his legs. His hands wander across my body, stroking, caressing, comforting, and exciting.

"Can I?" He murmurs against me.

"Yes!"

Teddy kisses across my jaw and down my neck, leaving a trail of stars to match the ones above us. My fingers work furiously on the topmost buttons of my bodice and Teddy pulls one side away to bury his face against my bare shoulder. I run my hands along his arms and up into his hair, pale locks glowing in the faint moonlight from above. I hear Teddy groan, the sound echoing from deep within my own body.

Teddy places both hands on my hips and pulls me even closer to him. There's no mistaking his hardness against the inside of my thigh and my breath hitches.

Wait. No. We can't do this. Not here. Not now. Once again, I have to be the one to stop us. To draw that line in the sand and say no more.

"Teddy," I gasp. He's struggling to undo more buttons with one hand while kissing his way back up my neck. "Teddy we can't. Not this."

Placing both hands on his shoulders, I push him back. He reluctantly straightens and we stare at each other. Our heartbeats are erratic, chests heaving in unison. After a moment, he carefully shifts me back to the bench and kneels before me.

"Teddy," I warn gently.

He nods silently and pulls me forward to the edge of the bench to hug me again. His face nestles against my exposed chest, in the hollow beneath my throat. We remain there together. Silent. Once my heartbeat returns to normal, Teddy pulls back and kisses me softly once more.

"I know I will not be allowed to marry you, Nora –" he brushes a piece of stray hair from my face "– but I still want to be with you. Even if that means risking my life and always ducking into dark corners."

Teddy stands and gives me a small, sad smile. He retraces his steps from before and disappears back through the trees and gloom the way he had come. The only evidence he was even here in the first place is my disheveled appearance and the footprints on the frozen ground. *Maybe a consort wouldn't be that bad...*

The sounds of night flood into the silence around me. They emphasize just how alone I really am and how cold the air is out here. Abigail had wanted to escort me through the gardens with the promise of keeping a respectful distance, but I had forbidden her from coming. Now I regret my choice. It turns out the last thing I want is to be alone right now. Buttoning up my riding habit, I strike out on the familiar winding paths back to the palace and back to my warm bed.

Chapter 5

In Which a Path is Chosen

Alon

"Don't run off now," Baba instructs as he helps Mama down from the carriage. "We are supposed to have dinner with the family in just a few hours. I'm sure Mama wants to go over some etiquette with you and your brothers."

My enthusiasm for our arrival in Sephiroth has already begun to wane and it hasn't even been a full day. The journey over was uneventful, but after so many weeks stuck in the confines of a ship with only my family to interact with, it was nice to stretch my land legs again. I had been hoping to do just that when I jumped down from the carriage, not waiting until the footman opened the door. Apparently, Baba had other plans.

"Oh, leave him alone." Mama slaps playfully at Baba's arm. "The boy has come this far without embarrassing himself. Let him get his land legs back and then we'll worry about making sure he uses the correct fork in front of his future bride."

I laugh away the pang of nerves and bow to Mama before turning back to the palace before us. While some would describe it as stately, I guess, I would categorize it as more severe or even a bit tacky. The towering roofs, broad stairs, and small gargoyles perched along various windows and ridgelines loom in front of me. For the first time since leaving Korala, an emptiness swallows me whole. The front entry is a cacophony of sounds, smells, and voices and I back away from the chaos before a porter lugging one of my brothers' trunks can accidentally run me over.

"Is there access to an open space? Somewhere to take a walk?" I ask the blank faced guard at the bottom of the stairs.

"Of course, Your Highness. There are the gardens" His words are stilted and unsure, like he's not used to being addressed. "Around the gatehouse and through the door with the ivy. It's usually kept unlocked during the day, but if there is an issue, come back to the gatehouse and we can unlock it for you."

I smile a thank you and amble off in the direction he gestured. A well-kept path meanders between the guardhouse and the side of the palace and out beyond. The further I go from the front entrance the quieter it gets, and calmness washes over me like the tides. Nothing like a bit of freedom and nature to help center me and make me feel like my life isn't spinning completely out of control. *You did sign up for this after all*, I chastise myself. Still, leaving everything to marry a complete stranger for the good of my family doesn't exactly come easily.

It doesn't take more than ten minutes to find a beautifully carved doorway in a tall fence. Climbing ivy has swallowed most of the walls, but the door itself is well maintained and mostly clear. I lift the latch, and it swings open easily on oiled hinges.

Breathing deeply, I can smell earth and a wild tangle of plants. The wind sings through the trees above me, and small critters and birds chatter away. A sense of longing fills the space behind my heart, and I step through into the wildness before me. *Maybe being here won't be so bad after all...*

A veritable maze of pathways leading in every which way intersect and branch off in seemingly no discernable pattern. Some paths are named and so wide a wagon could easily pass through, but others are barely more than a deer trail and hard packed earth. I decide to listen to the longing behind my heart and choose my path at random. There's no way I can accidentally leave the gardens with the walls surrounding them so what's the harm in getting a little lost?

Time seems to have little meaning as I wander through the lush gardens in full bloom. The only thing I care about are the sights and sounds and smells of this new place, so comforting in its similarities to the wild spaces back home and yet so completely foreign it leaves me mildly off kilter.

Turning down yet another unmarked path, I find myself at the edge of what can only be described as a true wild space. It was probably once an outlying garden, but it has been left to its own devices for so long it has truly run amok. The resulting tangle of flowers and greenery creates a beautiful mess that clearly hasn't seen a gardener in many years.

Myrtle and daisies romp side by side together and cover the ground in a thick carpet. Dandelions and even more daisies sway delicately together between large slabs of slate that were laid out to create a pathway to the center of the clearing. Brightly colored stones fit together in an exquisite jigsaw of a patio that reflects the sunlight like glass. Honeysuckles and roses twist and braid themselves together along an arched trellis, their wispy tendrils gently reaching down to frame a simple stone bench of carved white marble. Then, I see her.

Too old to truly be called a girl, the woman sits in the shade of the trellis reading a thick tome. A mass of barely restrained red curls spill over her shoulders and fall halfway down her back. Her dress is as deep as the sea on a stormy day, setting off her red hair and pale skin in sharp relief.

Even sitting, I can see her athleticism in how she holds herself. Every muscle is in place, hinting at the control that comes from regular exercise. Her neck curves gracefully as she reads the book propped her in her lap, fingers absently twisting a loose curl near her temple.

Behind my heart, the longing I felt earlier explodes in my chest and becomes a hard nub. It's almost like it has taken the shape of a flower bud waiting to bloom. The sudden warmth flooding through me knocks the wind from my lungs and leaves me gasping like a fish. I want to talk to her. I *need* to talk to her.

My lungs expand erratically as I take a few deep breaths to try and steady myself. Stepping out from the shaded border onto the dull stones of the pathway, I make sure to stay on the slate as much as possible to try and preserve the wildness around me. Last thing I want to do is mar the beauty around me.

Halfway to the patio, a chipmunk darts out of the mass of wildflowers and scurries beneath my feet, nearly toppling me in the process. I bite out a curse and manage to right myself with as much dignity as possible. She's watching me now, like a hunter watches its prey. Who's truly the hunter and who's the prey is still to be seen.

"Who are you?" She demands, her voice curt. Her entire demeanor has changed and what was once soft and graceful now stands hard and calculating before me. "What are you doing here?"

"My apologies." I make a small bow. Without knowing who she is or her station here at court I figure being overly polite is better than possibly insulting her. "I was wandering through the trails at random and found this place by chance. It seemed inappropriate to leave without introducing myself. I am —"

"You can't be here." Her words come sharp and fast. "These grounds are private. You need to leave."

I blink, surprised. Apparently, I had erred and let my eyes cloud my judgment of her character. That feeling when I first laid eyes on her was indisputable, however. I can't ignore it.

"Please forgive me..." I wait a beat or two to see if she supplies her name. She does not and I push on the best I can. "If you would be so good as to act as an escort and show me the way back to the palace, I would be greatly appreciative."

It's clear she doesn't want me to be here nor have anything to do with me. Why did I ask her to escort me? Apparently, I'm not the only one thinking that.

"No."

The word is complete and said in a way that does not invite argument. She purses her lips and glances back towards the treeline, around the clearing, and, finally, back at me.

"This is my first time visiting the royal gardens. Would you be so kind as to at least point me in the direction of the palace so that I may take my leave?"

"Take the path to the left. Follow it until you reach the beech tree with the horse fountain and take the right fork. You will be able to see the palace from there and can find your own way."

"Thank you." I smile. I try to put on a little more charm than usual. "If I have any problems I shall scream for you to come rescue me."

The woman rolls her eyes, clearly annoyed by my attempt at a joke. I bow once more for good measure and pick my way back across the clearing. Thankfully, there are no wild rodents to test my balance this time.

Back on the trail, a flash of red catches my attention. Scouring the leaves, I see a man standing amidst the treeline and trying hard not to be noticed. His pale hair reflects the sunlight, his height and brown clothing making him seem like one of the many saplings growing among the more established trees. If it wasn't for the loud red of the family crest on his tunic I might not have seen him at all.

Pretending not to notice him anyway, I follow the woman's instructions and practically dance a jig down the pathway. Sephiroth is promising to be more interesting than I had originally hoped. *Now I just need to get through this dinner and –*

Reality comes crashing back down around me with an unwelcome reminder. Dinner. Tonight. Where I'm supposed to meet my future wife. Gods damn me to hell.

Chapter 6

In Which Introductions are Made

Nora

The anxiety in my stomach sits like a viper ready to strike at the slightest provocation. Ever since that man almost discovered me and Teddy earlier in the gardens, it sank its fangs into me and refused to let go. The bite only gets worse as time inevitably marched onwards through the afternoon hours.

Teddy had been less than pleasant to be around this afternoon. His normal carefree attitude was gruff and blustery as a winter day. He spent most of our time together complaining angrily about how his father doesn't trust him to manage certain aspects of their ancestral home and nothing I could say or do helped convince him that he didn't need to worry. I could tell Teddy felt bad about his churlishness and did what he could to hide it, but we were both on edge and ended up cutting our meeting short. Neither of us can ignore the fact that our time together is very quickly running out.

It definitely does not help that the delegation arrived from Korala today. I am fairly certain the man from earlier was part of the group – his thick wavy hair and darker skin fit what I know of the people of the island nation. Thinking about him brings a pang to my chest and I absently rub the space over my heart. He had looked at me in such a way that sent a spark of...*something*...coursing through me. What exactly it was I couldn't say for sure, but if I had to guess it would probably be fear. I usually run to the gardens to try and avoid visitors after all. It's a safe space for me.

Now I don't have a choice. Mother has gathered us all together in the same room with the intention of proper introductions before dinner. Hayden and Father relax in matching armchairs in front of the fire, discussing political issues in hushed tones. The weariness Father carries around with him these days is concerning. The earlier whispers have turned into rumors of revolution and Father has started quietly investigating to see if there is any weight to the words. I had tried to ask Teddy earlier if he had learned anything new, but he was such a bear about everything else he brushed me off completely.

Mother sits next to me on the sofa, quietly working on a needlepoint of wildflowers. My own needlepoint lies abandoned next to me as my hands are too jittery with nerves to hold the needle without stabbing myself. Ren and Samael lounge on the sofa across from us with the disinterested look only men have the freedom to adopt when talk turns to marriage and heirs. That familiar jealousy for their freedom flashes through me, and I bite my tongue so as not to say something I will regret.

"Eleanor, stop fidgeting." Mother eyes me carefully. She's acting like I am going to fly out of my seat at any moment and hurl myself from the window.

I instinctively flinch at the use of my full name and tuck my shaking hands under my knees, trying to keep my foot from tapping impatiently. A rumbling from deep within my stomach reminds me I had missed tea because I had been out in the gardens with Teddy. And supper has been delayed in order to accommodate our visitors. A brief knock comes from the door and Marshall, the butler, opens it and slips inside.

"May I present Their Majesties, King Hemi and Queen Ululani of Korala." His voice rings through the room, snapping us all to attention, and he bows low.

The man and woman that walk through the door are not what I expected. He is shorter and a bit round in the middle, with an air of joviality that sparkles through his eyes. His dark hair and dark bronzed skin mark him as a native Koralan. She stands a few inches taller than him, with unmatched grace and elegance. A mane of light brown hair is caught up in an stylish, jeweled net at the nape of her neck, giving away the fact that she is not a native Koralan herself. Queen Ululani married into the royal family from another island nation. Much like me I guess you could say.

They are dressed in matching blue – him in a well-cut silk suitcoat and her in a floor length velvet gown with tiered skirts. Silver stitches edge their garments and dainty needlework in plump flowers shimmer in the light. While the fabric is rich and the clothing well tailored and well made, the designs are fairly simple. My own hunter green dress Mother had insisted I wear is considered modest for our courts and it makes more of a statement than the queen's.

Clearing his throat, Marshall continues. "And may I present His Royal Highness Prince Kalani, His Highness Prince Cove, His Highness Prince Atlas, His Highness Prince Caspian –" *good grief, how many are there?* "– His Highness Prince Ryo, and His Highness Prince Alon."

Six practically identical young men troop in and assume almost a defensive line behind the king and queen. They are definitely all related to each other and all children of the two nobles standing at the front. I send up a silent prayer of thanks that the man I saw earlier from their delegation is not part of the group. Now I just have to figure out which one of these is my husband...

Mother and Father rise to greet them.

"Welcome to Sephiroth," Mother says graciously and moves to kiss King Hemi's and Queen Ululani's cheeks. "It's so wonderful to finally meet you."

Father and King Hemi have already excused themselves from the crowd and retreat to the desk in the far corner to talk quietly over snifters of an amber liquid. The princes come crashing together and then splinter off into smaller groups, talking and laughing and elbowing each other as introductions are made and small challenges are issued. Only Hayden and the eldest Koralan prince (*Kalani I think*?) remain in a serious and somewhat stilted conversation near the door.

"Queen Clarice, the honor is all ours," Queen Ululani says. "We are so grateful for your invitation and the alliance this union will bring for our two nations."

"Please, call me Clarice. I believe we are missing one of your sons? I only counted six."

"Yes, please forgive us. Alon —" my ears perk up briefly "— is running a bit behind. He got lost in the gardens this afternoon and — here he is now! Alon, come say hello!"

The viper in my stomach sinks its fangs even deeper into me as the seventh son blusters into the room and takes up sentry next to his mother.

"You!" I half shriek. It slips out before I can stop it and heat climbs across my shoulders and onto my neck as everyone turns to look at me.

"Have you already met?" Mother asks. I can see her trying to reign in her own embarrassment from my outburst. When I fail to answer in time she prods further, "Nora?"

I'm attempting to come up with something to say that doesn't incriminate myself further. Admitting I was with Teddy would start a fight I don't want to have, but Alon breezes ahead without a care in the world.

"We met briefly in the gardens earlier although neither of us realized who the other was. Her Highness was gracious enough to point me in the right direction back to the palace after I got lost."

"Well, isn't that lovely." Queen Ululani smiles warmly and brushes something off Alon's shoulder.

"Quite." Mother chews on the word like she can't decide if it is truly lovely or not. "In that case, please allow me to formally introduce you to my daughter, Princess Eleanor."

I rise from the couch and make an awkward curtsy. Prince Alon makes his own bow and the four of us stand in a small pocket of uncomfortable quiet in an otherwise boisterous room. The clock on the mantle chimes happily seven times and falls silent. Mother and Queen Ululani converse in quiet whispers for a moment and then Mother claps her hands twice to settle the room.

"I believe dinner shall be ready in a few minutes," she announces. "Why don't we all start making our way to the dining room?"

The gaggle of men disentangle themselves from their various activities and perches, tumbling across the room and through the door in staggered groups all while still talking and laughing. It's very similar to the cattle lowing to each other as they come in from the pastures to feed and I can't help but giggle. From the corner of my eye, I see Alon smirk as he watches me.

"Why don't you two take a few moments to introduce yourself," Mother says, laying a hand on my shoulder to keep me from leaving. "I will send someone to fetch you shortly."

"No, Mother, that's not necessary." I try desperately to come up with a reason to not be left alone with him. "It would be rude if we were late."

"No need to worry." She smiles at me. It's a warning. A smile that says this is not a battle I can win. "I believe a demonstration has been prepared for our guests before the meal truly begins. I will smooth any ruffled feathers at your lack of participation."

Resigning myself to my fate, I sigh and sink wearily back to the sofa, my stomach letting out another grumbling protest at being even later for dinner. The bitter taste of defeat and ill will rises like a bile in my throat. Prince Alon escorts our mothers to the hall and Marshall slips out behind them, closing the door with a soft snick. *And then there were two...*

"Please forgive me for —"

"They wanted to get us —"

We both stop. The silence between us stretches deafeningly after all the noise from our families earlier. Alon gestures for me to go first.

"Please forgive me for my rudeness earlier in the gardens. If I had known who you were I would have behaved differently."

"Thank you, but the apology is unnecessary." Alon bows. "From what I gather I disrupted you in a private moment and it is I that owes you an apology."

I nod in acknowledgement. "What should I call you? Constantly addressing you as Your Highness will be difficult."

"Alon is fine. And you, Eleanor?"

"Nora," I correct automatically. "Only Mother calls me Eleanor when she is displeased with me."

I watch a smile spread across his face. If I hadn't been so set on disliking him from the start I might have found a friend in him. It's a shame really.

"In the spirit of our marriage starting in honesty and truth, there's something I feel I need to tell you." I flinch slightly at the word marriage and Alon watches me intently. "I need to be up front about the fact that I will not love you."

Several unreadable emotions flash across Alon's face and he turns slightly away from me to look out the dusky windows at the far side of the room. I take the opportunity to look a little closer at him.

He stands a few inches taller than I, sharing the same deep brown skin and dark hair as his brothers. Unlike his brothers, however, his hair is less straight and carries much more curl like his mother's does. His shoulders are square like King Hemi's and his nose has the same small bump as Queen Ululani's. His hands are calloused, but not rough. It's clear he is used to working with them, but it's done out of want, not out of need to survive. A well tailored coat in the same blue as his parents hugs his torso and hints at a trim waist and well-proportioned frame.

"That seems to be a grand statement when we only just met. You do not even know me."

"I already am in love with someone else. He was believed unworthy by the High Counsel; therefore we are not allowed to marry. You were chosen in his stead."

"And what allows this High Counsel to make these decisions?"

"They are advisors to my father and representatives for our people. They are powerful men that we do not wish to make enemies of."

"I see." Alon turns back to face me. "And there is no chance that you could grow to love me."

It's stated as a fact. Not a question. I answer in kind.

"No. This marriage is one of alliance and to fulfill a duty, nothing more. Your kingdom reaps the benefits from mine and the High Counsel has no reason to try and overthrow my father as king." Alon's face grows cloudier. "I will provide you with an heir if required, but there will not be a freestanding invitation to join me in my bed."

"How do you —"

"I'm not finished." I hold up a hand to stop him. The words I had prepared to say jumble together and I fight to straighten out my thoughts. "You are free to bring whomever you choose into your bed so long as you are discreet and I will do the same. I understand that there are requirements for our presence as a married couple, however I intend to spend much of my time here in Sephiroth continuing my studies and assisting my family. You are welcome to join me here or you may return to Korala."

"So, you intend for us to be married, but to not actually be married." There is a humor in Alon's face that I do not appreciate.

"You are correct."

"May I ask what I have done to deserve such a life?"

"You are complicit in robbing me of my freedom and neither allowing me to marry the man I want nor to pursue the life I had hoped for."

"You paint me as your enemy and make it sound so simple, but you seem to forget that I am also making sacrifices for this union."

"And my plan allows us the freedom to live the way we want with minimal interruptions while fulfilling our duties."

"So that's all I am to you? A duty?" Alon asks. He rubs a hand across his face and suddenly looks exhausted. "I don't think —"

A tap comes from the door and a maid enters, bobbing a curtsy. "Beg pardon. Her Majesty requests I escort you to the dining room for the evening meal."

I rise from the couch, my head held high, and follow her from the room. I don't even bother to look back to make sure Alon is following. His footsteps trail after us like an echo to my own.

Tension begins to slowly loosen its grip on my body and my shoulders haltingly sag, the breath huffing out of me in quiet bursts. That had gone much better than expected, but I have a horrible feeling this will not be the last time we have this same conversation.

Chapter 7

In Which the Plot Thickens

Boar

"So, the rumors we heard are true then. The Koralan's arrived today."

My face is a hard mask of neutrality. Hopefully, it's hiding my disgust and not giving anything away. I gaze around the table before me, taking in the men sitting sloppily in their chairs. Their soft features and well-manicured hands betray their youth and lack of experience with working in the real world. *Keep it together*, I remind myself, *you need them*. For now, anyway.

A nervous energy clings to them like bad perfume. Despite my frequent warnings, most didn't even bother to change from their finer clothing and wear their family crests half hidden beneath dark cloaks. Idiots every single one of them, but idiots I need to use.

"I move that we table the discussion of the, ahem, foreigner problem for the moment and congratulate ourselves for disrupting the grain deliveries." Lion raises his tankard and toasts the ceiling with exuberance. "Those stores will come in handy when the weather turns cold and there's not enough food for the commoners!"

Loud agreement from all around echoes high above us off the damp stone ceilings. I rub my temples, a poor attempt to dissipate the pain pulsing behind my eyes, and slump even further back into my seat. Of all the things I could be doing right now this is definitely not where I want to be.

I *should* be working out the next step in our escalation plan, tracking trade routes and sowing dissent between the commoners and their representatives on the High Counsel. Or I could be figuring out how to get rid of the complication that is the princess's betrothed. Hell, I would even rather be waiting in the ditch on the side of the road to commandeer two measly wagons of grain again. Instead, I'm stuck in this long-forgotten basement cave drinking slightly colder than room temperature ale and listening to a bunch of idiots preen. How charming.

I know they say a great kingdom isn't built in a day, but hell I'd hoped we'd be a little farther in dismantling the monarchy by this point. We've already spent a year building the foundations for gods' sake. Rumors and angry people are one thing. An entire overthrow of government is another beast entirely.

"Oh c'mon, Boar, don't be like that. This is a celebration!"

Gods, I regret letting them choose code names.

"You know what? You're absolutely right, Wolf. We should celebrate." I stand, lifting my tankard in mock salute. "Come let us drink to our meager victory in commandeering two wagons of grain away from the royal reserves to our own pocket! Let us drink to the family of foreigners who sup in the royal dining room far above our heads and threaten to undo all our hard work! By all means let's drink!"

I down the rest of my ale and slam the tankard on the table in front of me. The heavy bottom bounces off the pockmarked wood and the whole thing skitters off and over the side. The heavy clank as it hits the stone beneath us sings dully as the tankard comes to rest several paces away.

They all stare at me, eyes wide and mouths frozen somewhere between smiles and fear. Good. They need to understand exactly where we stand.

"Does anyone else have something they'd like to drink to?" Deafening silence descends over the table like a blanket. "Good. Then instead of celebrating every teeny tiny insignificant step we make that gets us closer to rebellion, how about we figure out a way to remove the threat that is the foreign princeling. If he weds the princess, we risk everything falling apart. Does anyone have any brilliant ideas they'd like to share, or must I do everything myself?"

Chapter 8

In Which Attention is Ignored

Alon

There are so many events to attend and plans to finalize before the wedding can happen that I lose track of all semblance of time. The weeks bleed together in an abstract parade daring me to try and keep track of it all. Mama works tirelessly with Queen Clarice to get things ready for the wedding and Baba is often with King Jasper finalizing plans for the alliance between our two nations. Hayden and Kalani frequently join them for long hours spent hashing out farming techniques and strategies for navy training.

The rest of us are left mostly to our own devices, provided we follow a regime of training and studies that is. Eleanor, no *Nora*, joins in most days and trains fearlessly alongside the rest of us. While she refuses to spar with me, Nora has taken on every one of our brothers with a fierceness and determination that is both admirable and terrifying.

Though she loses more matches than she wins, it is very clear Nora is knowledgeable in hand-to-hand combat and is decent with short-ranged weaponry. She even manages to disable Cove with a clever maneuver that uses his own body weight against him. The last time Cove was bested he was fifteen and Hanale had gotten a lucky shot. I wish Nora would agree to spar with me, to be able to feel her closeness and strength, but each time I ask she refuses.

My afternoons are most often spent either with Baba and King Jasper or roaming the grounds trying to bump into Nora. She has been doggedly determined to avoid me as much as possible, however, and sometimes goes to the extremes to keep her distance. I have discovered she likes to spend much of her free time in the gardens or the library and so I am now a ghost haunting these spaces and hoping to see her. I read more books in the days leading up to our wedding than I think I have in the past four years just so I have an excuse to be in the same room as her.

I can't seem to break the icy facade Nora's put up. I've attempted various tactics to try and get her to open up and talk to me, but nothing works. More often than not she rolls her eyes and huffs annoyedly when I flirt, dismisses me with a distracted wave of her hand when I attempt to approach her in the library, and blatantly turns the other way when I see her outside on the palace grounds.

Several times I've caught her sneaking off into the gardens with the same man I saw before at the edge of the clearing, but I always lose them in the maze of pathways. It's fair to assume that he is the man she claims to love. I don't know if it's jealousy clouding my judgment, but he must have a stellar personality or be great in bed because appearance-wise he doesn't have much going for him.

The two of them roam the grounds as part of a larger group with a seemingly never-ending rotation of young male courtiers. I didn't think the larger group really paid any attention to me when we crossed paths around the palace, but I've caught a few of them lingering outside our rooms. They skitter off like scared dogs when I try to approach them to talk, though.

I casually mentioned it to Mama and Queen Clarice, but they seem unconcerned and dismissed it as members of the court being interested. I just can't shake the odd feeling of being watched, though, and always double check to make sure my bedroom door is locked before I fall asleep.

• • • ☽ • ◯ • ☾ • • •

I inhale deeply and try to ease some of the tension in my shoulders. The most daunting task to face by far has finally arrived – I am being presented to the High Counsel for evaluation. It doesn't quite make sense to me seeing as how King Jasper and Queen Clarice have already made the decision for me and Nora to be wed, but I figure it's not really my place to argue. Nora seemed worried when she mentioned her father being overthrown as king, and I want to make sure I don't contribute to that in any way.

It's obvious as soon as I enter their meeting chamber that the High Counsel has already been in session for some time. Tea trays lay scattered across the vast table and various scrolls and maps wade between them like the oceans between islands. The chatter dies down as my entrance is announced and I come to port just inside the door, unsure of where I should go.

"There he is!" booms King Jasper from the far end of the table near a fireplace so large a man could practically walk inside it. "My Lords, may I present Prince Alon of Korala. My future son!"

He says it with such warmth I can't help but smile. It takes enough of the edge off my nerves, and I relax just a bit under the multitude of eyes staring at me from around the room. Taking my place in the proffered chair, what follows is the fiercest cross examination I have ever experienced before in my life. They quiz me about my family, what I know of Sephiroth (thank you, endless afternoons in the library!), and my opinion on various topics they are currently discussing. After an endless barrage of questions and a briefly whispered discussion among the Lords at the table, a sour faced gentleman stands up and bows to King Jasper.

"The High Council agrees with Your Majesties' decision with His Highness Prince Alon as the groom to wed Her Highness Princess Eleanor. The date shall be henceforth in four days — one week before Her Highnesses' twenty-first birthday."

King Jasper beams his approval at me, and I am free to excuse myself from the chambers.

$$\cdots \,) \cdot \bigcirc \cdot (\, \cdots$$

I survey the elegantly decorated green drawing room and try to catch Nora's eye across the table. She is intently focused on her roast carrots and refuses to look at me just like always. She's going to have to talk to me eventually and, unfortunately for her, I have nothing but time and patience.

From the other end of the table, King Jasper loudly proclaims my triumph with the High Counsel to the rest of the family. Mama and Baba listen with rapt attention and cheer in turn. I should be the one proudly sharing the accomplishment, but I don't have energy to do more than just answer the occasional question thrown my way.

When King Jasper announces the official date for the wedding, Mama gasps, "they have the same birthday!"

Nora's head snaps up and she stares at me across the table. Mama and Queen Clarice start chattering away about how our marriage is fated and they need to plan a birthday party for us and "oh they won't mind returning from their honeymoon for a day to celebrate their birthdays would you dears?" It's painfully clear our opinions are irrelevant, so Nora and I smile politely and return to staring at the food on our plates.

· · · ☽ · ○ · ☾ · · ·

The morning of my wedding dawns clear and blue skied. There's an air of mystery and adventure in the wind and the energy is catching. Unlike at home, my brothers and I have all been given separate rooms in the palace, as is custom for Sephiroth. Our rooms are all clumped together along a long hallway and Mama and Baba share a suite around the corner.

The solitude of my own space is greatly welcome. Especially today of all days. My body stretches and releases, shaking the sleep from each joint and muscle as they bend and contract. *This is it. This is really happening today.*

My quiet is quickly disrupted by several maids carrying large buckets of hot water and filling the tub in the small bathing alcove on one side of the room. As quickly as they appear, they retreat, and I am once more left in silence. The steam wafting up from the tub is too inviting to ignore and I sink beneath the surface, my body tingling from the sudden shock of warmth.

Mama had hung my wedding suit on the changing screen yesterday and I inspect it from afar while I soak. I had wanted to wear more traditional Koralan clothing, but Mama had insisted I wear a Sephiroth suit to 'do it the right way' whatever that meant.

Queen Clarice had been more than happy to have the palace tailors create something for me, and it is clear they are well skilled in what they do. The suit is a rich green as deep as the dried seaweed we snack on back home. The fit and cut are complementary to my body and, lining the hem and cuffs, small golden fish bounce along the edges. Dark green pants and vest and a stark white shirt complete the ensemble.

A soft tap comes at the door while I'm toweling off, eying the breakfast tray left by one of the servants. I quickly throw on a robe and tie it tightly shut to make sure I'm completely covered.

"May I come in, Starfish?"

Mama. I gladly open the door and there she stands, wrapped in a plush robe, breakfast tray in hand. I take her tray, setting it down across from mine, and happily accept her hug. Together we take our seats and dig in to the delicious food.

"How are you this morning?"

"Nervous."

"And excited, I hope? You are getting married after all."

I nod noncommittally. If I knew Nora cared for me the same way I do for her then I would be a bit more enthusiastic about my wedding day. But Mama doesn't need to know that.

"You can't fool me, child. I see the way you look at her. It's the same way your Baba looked at me when we were married."

My chest leaps in protest and I absently rub the place above my heart. It's taken on a dull ache ever since I first saw Nora. "Is it that obvious?"

"If one knows how to look. To anyone else all they would see is a sparkle."

"I'm not sure that sparkle is shared." I haven't told anyone about my conversation with Nora that night, but I'm still not entirely sure why. "Mama what if it never is?"

"Give it time," she says encouragingly. "Love sometimes comes in bright flashes, but other times it is a slow building flame that you must nurture and grow. The loves that last are the ones that are tended like a garden — remove the weeds, grow strong roots, and understand that love changes like the seasons. Each stage in life is different and the balance between the two of you will shift and change. It will be hard sometimes, but it doesn't mean it's not worth it."

A lump settles in my throat and I struggle to swallow my breakfast around it. Mama always knows exactly what to say.

"Now," Mama says brusquely, all business again. "Eat up, Starfish. We have a wedding to attend."

I can't help but laugh as Mama toasts me with her teacup. We finish our breakfast together in easy company, chatting about everything and, seemingly, nothing.

Chapter 9

In Which a Wedding Occurs

Nora

"Nora? Are you up? It's time to get ready."

Mother's voice floats through my door and cuts through the fog settling in my mind. I can hear her barely contained excitement. It's my wedding day. Hooray.

Sighing, I haul myself out of the cozy nest I had made among the pillows and blankets in my bed and open the door. Mother stands before me, her arms full of silk, while Abigail hovers behind with a breakfast tray. I step aside, opening the door a bit wider, and they parade inside. Abigail sets the tray down on the table in the corner, bobs a curtsy, and then leaves again. Mother hangs the dress up on the side of the changing screen. The better to admire it, I guess.

"Come," she instructs, "eat. We can't have you going through today on an empty stomach."

"I'm not really hungry," I say as I dutifully sit down across from her. I spoon some fruit and a muffin onto my plate and push it around absently. "How long do we have?"

"The wedding starts in three hours. Just enough time for breakfast and then to get you dressed."

I sigh heavily. "There's nothing I can do to change your mind?"

Mother looks at me, really looks at me, appraisingly. "Nora. Sweetheart. I know you feel like your life is ending but trust me when I tell you it's not. This is just the one path you had not considered when planning your life out when you were ten."

We share a small smile. My life plan at ten was full of big dreams that included such fantasies as becoming a pirate and swimming with mermaids. Somewhere along the way I went off track and never really found my way back.

"There is also the matter of tonight –" Mother clears her throat nervously "– that I wanted to discuss with you. About what occurs. Between a man and a woman."

"Oh, Mother please—"

"Nora this is not easy for me to say, and I ask that you just listen. Tonight —"

"I already know." Heat rises along my shoulders and neck. I try not to look guilty.

"What do you mean you already know?" Mother's voice is sharp. She stares me down with the same look she uses to intimidate someone when they disagree with her. "If you and Theodore —"

"No! No, nothing like that."

"Then how do you know?"

"The maids," I say simply.

Several years back I had overheard the maids talking amongst themselves about a roguish stable hand and what they wanted to do with him. It didn't take much to bribe them with some of my pin money to tell me the rest.

"They should not have done that." The ice in Mother's voice is mirrored in her eyes. "Promise me that you never did that with Theodore. This is important, Eleanor."

My shoulders automatically rise at the sound of my full name. "I promise, Mother, we never did. I wouldn't let it go that far."

Mother studies me with a critical eye. She can tell when I'm lying the same way I can sense her fear and anxiety running beneath the surface excitement. As much as I'd like to think otherwise, we are very similar. Satisfied that I'm telling the truth, Mother lets out a breath and sits back in her chair, resuming her breakfast.

"All right then. I was thinking we should do your hair the same way we did for the Harvest Tide celebration last Autumn. It was very becoming."

I nod, grateful for the change in conversation, and continue to move my breakfast around my plate. Once I've eaten enough to convince Mother I'm not going to faint at the altar, she sweeps me unceremoniously into a bath Abigail had overseen being drawn while we were eating. Her hands move with steady reassuring strokes as she proceeds to wash and perfume my hair. Peonies float amid the scented water and I sink into it without protest. I had snuck out yesterday and gone riding through the back fields with Ren as one final bid for freedom. The warm water soothes my aching muscles and worried mind.

By the time the bath has grown cold, and all traces of dirt are gone, I have almost been able to forget I'm getting married today. Almost. I rise, wrapping myself in a thick robe, and Mother parks me in front of my vanity.

Shooing Abigail and her own Mistress of the Hair away, Mother brushes out my locks herself. The whole time Mother brushes, curls, pins, and loops, she chatters about everything and nothing. I receive detailed instructions about where to stand at the church, order of events for the day, how to walk, and *"remember to use the correct fork with luncheon, Dearest, we are not uncivilized after all,"* amidst bits of gossip she has learned from various aunties, cousins, and friends that have come to stay for the week to partake in the wedding festivities.

In seemingly no time at all, my usual mass of red curls have been tamed into an elegant chignon full of swirling seed pearls and promise. Mother watches me in the mirror as I turn this way and that, assessing her work.

"It's beautiful," I breathe. "Thank you, Mother."

Her eyes flood with unspoken sentiments and she smiles. "It's time to get dressed."

Moving away from the vanity, I position myself in front of the floor-length mirror and watch as Mother and Abigail remove the dress from the hanger and bring it over. I step into the skirts and wait as they are tied at the base of my spine. The corset top fits like a second skin, the embroidery a true testament to the skill of the tailors. Roses, greenery, and birds are stitched in pale pink, blue, and green threads. They accentuate and hide in turn to give me the appearance of a true waist and hint at a possible, although nonexistent, hourglass figure. If anyone has doubts about our tailors being proficient all they have to do is take one look at me in this dress and they will be convinced. I gently run my hands over the butter soft skirts as Mother sniffles behind me.

"You look absolutely radiant, Nora." The telltale thickness in Mother's voice that signals tears are on their way hangs heavily between us. "There's just one more thing."

I turn and watch Mother bring out a small leather-bound case I've never seen before. She motions for me to turn back to the mirror, and I grudgingly comply. Behind me, I hear a soft click and the faint protest of old hinges as the case is opened to reveal its hidden treasure. Stepping up behind me, Mother carefully places the most beautiful tiara I have ever seen amidst the few loose curls in the front of my hair. She expertly secures it, straightening a few locks she had knocked out of place, and then steps back to let me take it all in.

At first glance, the tiara is simple — just bands of thin gold braided together into a half circlet. When you look closer you see the seed pearls and opals expertly woven in among the delicate gold strands. Each one shines as brightly as any diamond and demands attention without eclipsing the other. They wrap delicately around my forehead and highlight the matching gold and blonde strands amidst all the red in my curls.

"It's beautiful, Mother. Where did you get it?"

"It's mine. From Ailona. My mother, your Amma, gifted it to me on my wedding day. Now, I gift it to you."

A hollow sadness grips my heart, and I fight back tears. No matter how much I have resented her these past few months, I know deep down that my mother loves me and has done everything she can to protect me. She's not perfect, but, then again, neither am I.

"Oh, don't cry! You'll make me cry!"

I wrap my arms around Mother and hug her as tightly as I can. "Thank you, Mother. You have no idea how much this means."

I take the proffered handkerchief and dab at the tears threatening to spill over once again. So many tears cried over just one day. After all of Mother's careful primping I don't want to spoil the effect of her hard work. A soft tap from the door, and Lady Wimple steps inside.

"It's time," she announces.

I look at Mother one more time, gather my skirts, and make my way out into the halls. This is the last time I will ever leave my childhood room, and I pause just outside to take it in. The comforting familiarity beckons to me like an old friend. I want nothing more than to run back inside and lock the door and never come out. But instead, I give myself a shake, square my shoulders, and walk away down the hallway.

••• ☽ • ◯ • ☾ •••

My arrival at the church is more complicated than we initially expected. Crowds of people flood the streets, and our carriage is delayed several times with well-wishers. Mother tries to hide her distress, but I can see it in her strained smile and furrowed brow. I take her hand, squeezing gently, and continue waving to the crowds on all sides.

Thankfully, we arrive with minutes to spare, and we dash up the steps to join the end of the procession just as Alon's father escorts his mother into the church. Mother kisses me once more and then takes her place at the front of the line to enter next with Hayden. Father hands me a bouquet of pink roses wrapped in ribbons, eyes glassy at the sight of the tiara in my hair, and gives me a tight hug.

"You look beautiful," he whispers gruffly.

The music picks up as we slowly shuffle forward. At the appointed time, and once they've been signaled by one of the men servants, Alon's brothers escort their partners into the church. The broad backs of the men before me dwindle one by one as the music continues to build in preparation for my entrance.

Finally, it's my turn. I step through the doors, and my breath rushes out of me in complete awe at my surroundings. The church is dressed in swags of white silk with flowers displayed on every surface. Mother must have raided the hothouses several times over to make sure there were enough. Huge garlands of pink roses, baby's breath, and maidenhead ferns line the aisles and walkways and every spare surface that is not covered in silk. Colorful ribbons of the same pinks and blues and greens embroidered in my gown are delicately woven among the flowers in braids and whorls to make it seem like the flowers are alive.

Father and I start down the wooden floored aisle together, trying hard not to disturb any of the blossoms crowding in. All around me, family and friends watch as we make our way to the front of the church. There are even a few teary eyes and damp handkerchiefs among the pews. *Teddy must be so happy. This is better than we could have ever dreamed of.*

About halfway down the aisle, I catch sight of Teddy in one of the pews. He looks absolutely miserable in his stiff formal suit. *Wait, that doesn't make sense.* Teddy is supposed to be —

My gaze snaps to the front of the church and reality comes crashing back in with a vengeance. Teddy isn't waiting for me. *He* is. Alon. The person I'm *actually* marrying today.

He stands watching me with such wonder and warmth in his face that my heart cracks apart, the fissures growing deep. Not him. It's not supposed to be him. This is something Teddy and I are supposed to have. Together.

Father and I come to the end of the aisle at the front of the church and there's nowhere else for me to go. Nowhere to run. I struggle to keep the sadness and disappointment from my face.

Kissing my cheek, Father places my hand into Alon's and retreats to sit with Mother. Taking a deep breath, I turn to face Alon. Here we go, I guess...

Chapter 10

In Which Life Changes Unexpectedly

Alan

Nora lets out a huge sigh as she collapses into a chair. "Thank the gods that's over."

I study her discreetly. "I take it you did not enjoy our wedding day?"

She snorts. "What do you think?"

The wedding was beautiful. Mama and Queen Clarice had really outdone themselves and created quite the event. I'll admit I don't remember much of the ceremony. The church was stiflingly hot, and the priest spent much of it droning on about the burdens of marriage. Apparently Sephiroth chooses to focus on the hardships of a union instead of the blessings.

The one part I do remember quite clearly is the kiss. Or rather, Nora's attempt at avoiding it. We finally got through the sermon and the vows and then the priest intoned the symbolic 'you may now kiss the bride.' I leaned in to kiss Nora, but she turned slightly at the last minute, so I kissed her cheek. Nothing beats starting your marriage off with a good dose of avoidance.

The reception luncheon had gone off without issue and we spent much of the afternoon greeting courtiers, thanking guests for coming, and dancing when Queen Clarice put her foot down and insisted. Nora humored me with two dances to be polite but refused any further advances. I think I danced more with her mother and her few female relatives than I did with Nora herself.

We had been dismissed off to our "honeymoon suite" for the night. Smaller than most suites, it consisted of the sitting room we were now in, a small bathing chamber off to one side, and the en suite bedroom. In the morning, we will be setting out for her family's summer house on the coast for the week before returning for the joint birthday party Mama and Queen Clarice are planning for us.

A knock from the door announces the arrival of a small army of servants carrying platters and carafes of unknown liquids. They quickly deposit their wares on the table and bow their way out with only minor giggling and pointed looks. Wonderful. Nora helps herself to some of the food and shoots me a look of such vitriol when I make a move to join her at the table that it's clear the sofa is the safer perch.

"How would you like to handle tonight?" I ask casually.

"If you are asking whether we will share the same bed or not then the answer is no."

"Surely you don't intend to have me sleep on the floor?"

"Of course not," she says flippantly. "You can sleep on the sofa. I told you before that I would give you heirs. That does not mean you may join me in my bed whenever you so choose."

This is officially ridiculous. Rising from the sofa, I cross the room to where Nora sits at the table and pull her chair around so she's facing me. Nora protests loudly and makes like she's going to move from her seat. Placing one hand on either side of the chair so she can't slip away, I lean down, making sure to look her in the eye.

"Are you sure," I ask huskily, "there's nothing –" I blow gently on her neck below her ear "– I can do –" I move slowly to the other side and blow in the same place "– to convince you –" I hover mere millimeters from her lips, our breath mingling "– to share with me?"

I am so close I can hear her heart skip briefly and feel warmth as it rushes through her body. My own heartbeat answers in kind and the ache behind my heart flares again. Of course it's for her. How could it not be?

Nora slides two hands up between us and tries to shove me backwards. It's not actually enough force to move me, but I choose to step away anyway. I clearly caught her by surprise.

"No."

I shrug casually. It's not particularly surprising that it didn't work. Surveying the crammed table, I spot a familiar carafe of wine sitting on the far side. It's one of the ones Mama brought with us from Korala.

I reach across the table and easily snag the handle, lifting it up and over the piled dishes. Popping the cork out, I inhale deeply. The familiar comforting smells of home are full of promises and possibilities.

"You should try some of this." The liquid sparkles in the light as it tumbles into my cup. "It's my favorite from home."

Nora nods noncommittally and I retreat back to the sofa that is apparently going to be my bed later. I can't wait.

The wine is cold and clear as it slips down my throat. There's a faint taste of something running beneath the surface, but I can't put my finger on it. That's odd. Maybe the seal broke, or it spoiled somehow on the journey over. It would be unusual, but not impossible.

I sip absently, watching the fire. There's a dull ache in my chest and I try to reach for it, but my arm hangs limply next to me. I can't even move my fingers. *That doesn't make any sense.*

My lungs struggle to expand as I breathe, reluctant to change in any way. I force the air in and out of my body, but it's sticky and slow moving. It fights to remain separate from me, but once I inhale it clings to my nose and my insides like tar.

"Are you alright, Alon? You've gone all red."

I can't seem to answer. Nothing is working right. I am no longer in my body, and I see myself lose control, swaying dangerously across the sofa. The fire shrieks and chatters at me as if through a tunnel. My eyes roll back in my head, and my heart ceases its frantic rhythm in my chest.

Chapter 11

In Which Poison is Found

Nora

"Oh, c'mon Alon don't be so dramatic. This isn't that big a deal."

I roll my eyes at his slumped form on the couch and go back to my dinner. A wet thump pulls my attention again and Alon's cup now sits in a puddle of spilled wine on the carpet.

"Come on, seriously? Mother will have our heads for getting wine on the carpet!"

Still nothing. Fine. I guess I have to do everything myself just like always. Harumphing, I stand and cross the room, skirting around the couch. Kneeling in front of the soaked carpet, I go to pick up the glass.

"This is really not funny, Alon, at least get off your –"

A strange, strangled keening leaves my throat as I scramble backwards from Alon's unmoving form. I would have ended up in the fireplace if a harsh crackle from a spitting log didn't warn me to stop moving. Erratic heartbeats pound through my body and my palms are slick with sweat. Gingerly, I approach the couch again.

Alon is immobile, slumped over the couch with his limbs akimbo. His mouth is twisted into a harsh grimace and his eyes are wide and unseeing, like two orbs staring into nothingness.

He's dead. The words rattle around my head like the glass marbles I used to play with Ren as a child. He's dead. What the hell do I do now?

As if in a dream, I stand and go into the adjacent bedroom. The silk bellpull is half concealed by the canopy but gives easily as I tug. I just pray Abigail is the one dispatched to the room. She should be coming soon anyway to help me prepare for bed, but that's not for, how long? One hour? Three? What time is it anyway?

I take my place back at the table, shoving my plate and the rest of the food as far away from me as possible. My back is stiff and unyielding, ramrod straight in the stupidly uncomfortable chairs mother insists match the table and just watch Alon. Logically, I know he's not going to move, but there's something incredibly terrifying about having a dead body *right there*.

The door opens with barely a sound and Abigail curtsies after shutting it behind her. Her gaze is fixed on the floor, probably assuming I'm in some state of compromising position and attempting to be polite. When I don't address her immediately, Abigail raises her face to mine and little creases of concern and confusion carve the space between her eyes. Her gaze moves from me to take in the entire room before her, and her eyes widen as large as saucers.

"My Lady, what is going on? What happened?"

"Get the king and queen. Please."

• • • ☽ • ◯ • ☾ • • •

"Did you touch anything?" Father shakes me roughly, his hands gripping my arms too tightly. "Nora, this is important, did you eat anything!?"

"Just the food on the plate."

My voice is high-pitched and warbly in a bad way. Abigail didn't just bring back Mother and Father, but also Mother's lady's maid Lady Wimple, Marshall, King Hemi, and Queen Ululani. The rooms that were supposed to be my honeymoon suite are now overcrowded. Too many people and smells and sounds. Too much.

"Nothing else?"

I shake my head. Alon is still on the couch. The wine is still soaking into the carpet. He's still dead.

"Jasper, let her go. You're hurting her."

Father releases me. His eyebrows knit together as he studies Alon. "What did he eat?"

"All he had was the wine."

"You're sure?"

"Yes." My voice is strangled, and I clear my throat awkwardly.

Queen Ululani scoops up the carafe of Koralan wine and smells it deeply. Pouring herself a glass, she holds it to the light of the fire and inspects it carefully, but she does not drink it. Dipping an abandoned napkin into it, she spreads it out and watches the blotchy stain as it dries.

"Hemi," she says, "it's poison."

"You're sure, My Dove?"

"Without a doubt."

"Marshall, alert the guard." Father is back in control again. "We need to lock down the exits immediately. It's probably too late to figure out who planted the poison, but it is imperative that we –"

"King Jasper," King Hemi interrupts. He bows his head respectfully, but soldiers on. "I understand your first instinct, but I ask that you do nothing at this time. Please help me move my son into the bedroom."

"You cannot be serious." Father's anger has been replaced by shock.

"I am serious. Please help me move my son into the bedroom where he will be more comfortable."

"Comfortable!?" Father gapes at King Hemi. "Why should it matter if the bed is more comfortable?"

"Please, Jasper."

With muttered instructions, Father and King Hemi take Alon's shoulders and Marshal lifts his feet. They awkwardly carry his bulk into the adjoining bedroom where Queen Ululani arranges the blankets over him just so. She follows the rest out of the bedroom and closes the door delicately behind her.

"Will you please explain what is going on?"

Father is trying to be diplomatic, but his patience is wearing thin. A brief shiver runs through me at the thought of what he will do if he loses control. It doesn't happen often, but it's scary when it does.

"This is something better discussed privately." King Hemi makes a pointed look at Lady Wimple, Abigail, and Marshall now hovering unsure by the door. Abigail stares at the couch like it's going to bite her. I know how she feels.

Mother turns to the small group and steps in front of them, blocking their view into the rest of the room. "Clear the table and return to your posts as normal. Tell no one of this on pain of death."

Three sets of wide eyes meet hers and then fall, fixing on our shoes as they nod. They load their arms with the abandoned platters of food and flee out to the rest of the palace. I have never wanted to run from this room more than now.

"Do you know what kind of poison, Ululani?" King Hemi asks. His voice seems small, or maybe the room feels larger now that the servants have left. "Was there any chance for him?"

"It was cubozoa venom. Even if we knew it was in there it would have been impossible to stop it."

"Would someone please tell us what is going on?" Mother is getting impatient now. Her voice has taken on the warbly shaking it gets when she is trying hard to maintain control.

"Please, dear Clarice, trust us." Ululani steps towards Mother and reaches out her hands. "I promise we will explain everything we can, but we must wait for Alon."

"What is cubozoa venom?" It's hard to believe my voice is as steady as it is. "Why did you say there was nothing we could have done?"

Silence blankets us, disturbed only by the crackling of the fire. Queen Ululani takes my hands and leads me gently to the empty table, settling across from me in one of the hardback chairs.

"In Korala we have creatures called sea jellies. They are mostly harmless, but there are a few that contain poison. One of these is the cubozoa."

I latch onto every word Queen Ululani says. Her soothing tone is like a balm, quieting my erratic heartbeat and shooing away the fear that is still so close to the surface. Father and Mother watch her with inscrutable expressions. Another glance towards the couch and I find King Hemi carefully piling folded napkins on the wine stain. Any number of servants in this palace and yet he chooses to clean up the mess himself.

"We warn our children and our visitors to be wary of all sea jellies, but especially the cubozoa. They have long spiraling tentacles that trail beneath them and one sting can render a person paralyzed. Two can cause permanent damage and three can cause death. It's hard to know just how much Alon ingested."

"How can you be sure?" Mother hovers behind me now, her hands resting on the back of my chair. "How do you know it was poison?"

"Before I became queen I was set on a path of discovery. My home island, Lorvhelm, is a place of scientific experimentation. I have many fond memories of growing up with my grandfather exploring the world around me and cultivating my interest in flora and fauna. When I married Hemi and moved to Korala it became a chance to learn more about the world outside my own kingdom."

Ululani lifts the glass of wine back to the firelight so we can see. Small dark spots mar the sparkling burgundy liquid.

"Cubozoa venom does not mix well with any liquid, but especially not with the alcohol in wine. It is a unique property only to them. The wine can break the venom into smaller parts, but the two will never truly combine. You can see it here –" she spreads out the napkin in front of her again "– in the winestain. See the dark spots throughout? That is the venom's tell."

"How would someone have gotten it?" Mother's voice is steadier, but it's still deep with fear. "We don't have sea jellies this far north."

"It would have had to come from warmer waters. The only place I have ever seen them has been around Korala. Some have tried to harvest their venom before, but most attempts lead to death."

"Is there a black market in Sephiroth? Or some place where illegal items can be purchased or traded?" King Hemi now stands behind Queen Ululani's chair. He watches me owlishly even though he's asking Father the question.

"Yes, but we have never been able to pin it down. It changes location weekly and the only way to know where it will be next is through word of mouth." Father rubs his temples. "I will try to plant some individuals to learn where the next market will be. If they're selling this poison freely then none of us are safe."

He goes to walk towards the door again, but King Hemi stops him with a hand on his shoulder. "Please, my friend, just wait."

"Your son is lying dead in the other room!" Father roars, "and you would rather we sit here twiddling our thumbs than go through the proper steps to try to –"

"Jasper!" Mother snaps. "Control yourself. Hemi and Ululani clearly need us to trust them as they have trusted us in coming here. They say they will give us answers and we should just wait as they have asked us to."

"Fine!" Father throws up his hands in defeat. "Fine, we can sit here and wait while the murderer gets away. But I'm getting a drink and I'm getting this damn carpet removed."

Chapter 12

In Which Life Returns

Alon

Consciousness returns in fits and spurts. It takes far too long for me to regain enough control to open my eyes and even longer for me to figure out where I am. I'm in the bed of the honeymoon suite, the canopy floating above me like a rain cloud. Pain lashes through my head and threatens to split my skull in two. Moaning, I sink deeper into the pillows to try and ignore it so I can go back to sleep. No such luck, unfortunately. The insistent hammering paired with the urgent voices filtering in from beyond the door make it impossible to sleep.

I rise slowly. My mouth is patchy like I had tried to swallow sawdust. Scooching to the edge of the bed, I carefully place one foot and then the other on the floor. Hauling myself to my feet practically makes me wretch from the shock of pain it sends through my head and my knuckles turn white as I grip the bed frame. It's been a while since this happened.

With careful movements, I wrap myself in a dressing gown abandoned at the bottom of the bed and slowly pick my way to the door. The heaviness in my hands makes it almost impossible to turn the door handle. Gritting my teeth, I force my fingers to close around the knob, my wrist to turn. The door swings open with barely a sound, and I am bathed in sunshine. I cringe away from the sudden onslaught of light and almost fall back into the cool darkness of the bedroom.

My eyes open slowly, trying to adjust to so much light. Mama and Baba are sitting at the table that held dinner last night. It's now laden with breakfast items – pastries, carafes of tea and coffee, coddled eggs, and more. My stomach turns slightly at the smell.

A muffled shriek from across the room pulls my attention and there they are – Queen Clarice, King Jasper, and Nora standing next to the sofa looking like they've seen a ghost. Well, Queen Clarice and Nora look like they've seen a ghost. King Jasper looks like he's ready to murder me with his bare hands.

"What is going on?" Nora bites off the words like she doesn't like the taste of them. "You died last night. I saw it. We all saw you. What the hell are you doing here?!"

Queen Clarice flinches at the profanity but doesn't correct her daughter. Her fear is palpable. King Jasper looks like he can't decide whether to try and kill me again himself or if he should let Nora do it. *There's a tempting idea...*

My breath whooshes from my lungs in wheezes. I think I cracked a rib when I fell. "It was poison. The wine. Tasted like it had spoiled somehow."

Baba nods. "We found it last night. Mama says it was cubozoa venom."

"We are looking into what happened." King Jasper's voice is vibrating with barely contained anger. Each word is bit off and enunciated clearly to ensure each one is heard and understood. "Per the request of your parents, however, we are keeping the details of last night quiet even though they refuse to tell us why. We should be alerting the High Counsel and our staff to root out who is responsible for this heinous act, not trying to sweep it all back under the rug! While you appear to stand before us as healthy as yesterday, not all would have suffered the same fate."

King Jasper looks pointedly at Nora, and I nod listlessly when I understand his implications. Nora's stubbornness to do the exact opposite of what I suggested saved her life last night. If she had actually taken my advice and had the wine with me then I would still be here, but she would not.

Mama sets a plate piled high with fresh fruit and pastries in front of me, the china clinking against the cutlery as her hands shake. Nothing like some sugar to jumpstart the system. Strawberries burst on my tongue, releasing juices so ripe and flavorful tears start welling in my still stinging eyes. Damn poison. I'm always more wishy washy after something like this happens.

"Please," I say to Nora. My voice is so weak I'm not sure if she can hear it. "Let us explain."

The atmosphere is tense. Our two families face off from opposite sides of the room, the floor stretching between us like a canyon so wide it's almost impossible to cross. Wait, wasn't there a carpet in here last night?

"Will you sit with us?" Mother's hand shakes ever so slightly as she gestures to the remaining seats at the table. "Please."

Nora is the only one to accept the offer. She carefully picks her way across the unofficial center line and perches reluctantly on one of the high-backed chairs. I shift awkwardly in my own seat. These things are so unforgiving and uncomfortable. Honestly, it seems fitting to have to have such an uncomfortable conversation while sitting in them.

"This is not something we expected to have come up." Mama looks nervous now, almost ashamed. It's clear she's struggling to find the words she wants, and I curse my own weakness. I should be the one telling this story. "This all started when Alon was six months old. He fell ill and no one knew what was wrong or how to help him. It was Hemi's mother, Alon's *Tutu*, who saved him."

Chapter 13

In Which a Blessing is Given

After three weeks of vigils and prayers for the return of the prince's health, it was clear that the "normal" rights of healing were not having an effect on Alon's illness. Every day that passed saw his breathing grow fainter and his strength lessen. There were whispers that the prince would be mourned, and the royal family would suffer another loss so soon after their beloved King had just passed. King Hemi was still so new to his role as leader. It would be devastating to lose the young prince as well.

Queen Ululani did not leave Alon's side. She prayed over him, sang to him, and hovered anxiously as all manner of physicians examined him. Even a well-practiced Sephiroth physician found his way to the Manor House and prescribed several tinctures for the fading child. But no amount of herbs, lotions, or poultices could bring back his waning strength. Almost a month after the prince fell ill, the Dowager queen came to visit Ululani and, with her, she brought a little glimmer of hope.

"Ululani," the Dowager whispered as she sat beside the grieving mother, "I may have found a solution."

Hope rushed through Ululani like a tidal wave. She raised tear-stained eyes to meet the lined face looking back at her and the Dowager felt an answering ache in her own heart.

"We need to take him to the Falls."

"The Falls?" Confusion clouded Ululani's eyes. "What do you mean take him to the Falls? There's nothing there. He can barely breathe; he won't be able to make the journey!"

"Please." The Dowager clasped her hands around Ululani's and pulled her closer. "This is the only choice we have. When I was a child, my own *Tutu* knew of a servant in the manor whose baby suffered a similar illness. The family took the child to the Falls and spoke with the Elders there. When they returned the child thrived and lived a long and happy life."

"This is madness." Ululani's hope left her just as quickly as it came.

"What other choice do we have?"

In desperation, Ululani agreed to the journey, but Hemi would not hear of it. He forbade them from removing Alon from the house or attempting the trip. The only problem with something being forbidden is that it makes it even more important to try. Under the light of the stars, the Dowager and Ululani stole away in a commandeered carriage with Prince Alon wrapped in blankets to try and keep him warm and comfortable.

The two women barely slept over the course of their journey across the mountain pass. They were set upon by thieves twice and almost lost their lives several times more from unexpected roadside obstacles. It was only by the grace of the gods that they found their way through the mountains and to the other side with their safety.

The carriage was abandoned at the end of the road and the women hiked the rest of the way through the dense forest. Weaving through the trees, their footsteps disappeared into the murky air and the only sound following them was the occasional shallow cry of the baby from his basket. Ululani did her best to keep the basket steady, but after so many days of hard travel her arms drooped, and her feet stumbled.

The sounds of rushing water were soon heard filtering through the trees. They turned in its direction and followed the sound down a deer path, arriving out of breath and exhausted on the shores of a small lake.

The lakeside closest to them tapered off into a river, winding back through the darkening forest to parts unknown. On the far side, a never-ending rush of water dropped from the highest cliffs in a beautiful thundering arch. The last rays of the sun bounced and glittered off the water, catching the spray and sending rainbows dancing in the corners of their eyes. They had made it to the Falls.

The one footman that had accompanied the women started a fire and, once all was settled, left them there alone under much duress and several threats. The Dowager claimed it could be only them and the baby who met the Elders. No one else. It was on that unknown shore that Ululani's fears grew as long as the shadows cast by the firelight.

"Have you ever met the Elders before?" Her voice quavered. "Are the stories true?"

The Dowager studied her daughter-in-law in the low light. The prince's illness and their journey through the mountains had aged her significantly in recent days. Ululani's thick hair had the faintest streaks of gray beginning to show at the temples and the canyon between her eyes had deepened dramatically. Sighing gently, the Dowager placed a comforting hand on her shoulder.

"I have never met them. As for the stories, it's hard to tell what's real and what's not. The Elders are a part of our kingdom's history, but not a part of our lives as we know it."

"Can you tell me what happened to them?"

"I'm sorry, my dear." The Dowager smiled kindly at Ululani, her eyes crinkling at the corners. "You are so much at home on our island I forget that you were not born here."

She readjusts briefly and settles her skirts against the blanket they had laid down to keep the damp earth from their clothes. After a few minutes of contemplation, the Dowager continues.

"It's thought that many years ago, when our kingdom was still just a fledgling in its early days, they were the original inhabitants of the island. The first settlers to Korala were respectful of their ways and kept themselves to the coasts while the Elders remained further inland. Neither group bothered the other and each lived peacefully."

Alon stirred and cried faintly from his swaddle of blankets. Both women leaned over him nervously. The prince coughed once, twice, three times. He wrestled with the blankets before settling down to a fitful sleep, his chest rising and falling in quick succession. Once assured he was unrestricted, the Dowager continued.

"As the kingdom of Korala slowly started to grow, it began to spread outwards. Land disputes between the Koralans and the Elders grew in numbers. The reigning family did what they could to mitigate the intrusions and to ensure there was peace between the two peoples, but on such a small island it was difficult to maintain.

"An uprising by the prominent families led to the king being overthrown and locked in his own home as a hostage. They banded together and used fear and violence to keep people in check. War was declared against the Elders and many men and women on both sides lost their lives and their loved ones as fighting broke out throughout the island."

"Who restored peace?" Queen Ululani had taken Alon into her arms and was gently rocking him back and forth as he slept.

The Dowager watched the mother and son with unguarded feeling. "The first queen, Queen Lily, managed to convince a guard to free her from her rooms. Once released from her prison, she made her way to the battlefield. Do you know the field just over the hill before the orchards? She walked through the middle of that field with her head held high as death reached out from all sides to greet her. At the very center, the last of the patriarchs were fighting with the leaders of the Elders.

"With a voice like thunder she commanded them to stop and instead struck a bargain. As a gesture of goodwill, she would return with the Elders into the wild spaces on the far side of the island and remain with them until the end of her days. Her husband would be reinstated as king, and he and their sons would ensure their family line kept the kingdom in check and off their lands. After so much loss and bloodshed, the Elders agreed to her bargain, and she went with them willingly. That was the start of the treaty between their people and ours."

"What happened to the people who overthrew the king and queen? Why would they have been allowed to resume their rule? And what happened to the Elders?" Ululani's questions are quiet in the darkness.

The Dowager tilted her head up to survey the stars above them. "There were not many remaining from the uprising. The ones that were left were put on trial and banished from Koralan lands. Their lineages are still barred from ever returning to the island.

"As for the Elders, it is said they took up residence here, at the Falls. After that it's even more unreliable legends and stories, but since that day we have respected the treaty she made on our behalf. We do not expand beyond our means, and they keep the wild spaces for themselves."

The loud calling of an owl echoed over the rushing water. The two women startled, exchanging worried looks.

"What will they do when they find us?"

The Dowager opened her mouth to speak, but snapped it shut when a large figure stepped out of the gloom next to them. Ululani stifled her scream, but the Dowager rose and looked him in the eye. Her back was ramrod straight and her chin held in a graceful arch.

"I respectfully ask that you bring us to a healer. This child is sick."

The figure studied them. He towered above the two women, all long limbs and strong shoulders. Clad only in dark pants, the light from their fire sparkled in his eyes and danced off the tattoos along his bare chest. After a few moments of deliberation, he nodded silently and gestured for them to follow.

The Dowager helped Ululani to her feet, and together the two women followed this strange man. As they made their way around the pool closer to the Falls, three more figures stepped out of the woods and surrounded the women in shadowy silence. They carried no visible weapons, but it was clear from their build and athleticism that they didn't need them.

The figure at the front led the group to a narrow passage cut into the rock at the base of the water. The Falls were so loud that the noise crashed and ricocheted around the space like thunder. The rocks were slick, and Ululani paused only briefly to tie the blankets around Alon into a sling to allow her to have more freedom with her hands.

Struggling to see in the darkness, Ululani focused on the back of their guide and followed it through the gloom. The farther they went, the noisier it got. The rushing water fell in a curtain behind them, the sound echoing across the pockmarked walls. They slipped down a side passage and began to climb. Up and up and up they went. The noise from the water receded behind them and was replaced with the heavy breathing of Ululani and the Dowager as they climbed.

After what felt like an eternity, the group left the hewn rock passageway and entered into a clearing ringed with trees. Ululani gasped as she surveyed the village below her. In the moonlight, she could see a mix of wood and mud huts and various tents decorated with cheery flowers in pinks, blues, lavenders, and whites. From all corners wafted the rich smells of spices that assaulted the senses. It was clear the Elders thrived in the moonlight. The sounds of songs, laughter, and music wove between the houses even though the hour was well beyond sunset.

Their guide grunted once and then led them in a winding path through the settlement to an inconspicuous hut marked only by a crescent moon above the door. The man stood to one side, unlatched it quietly, and motioned for them to go in. Exchanging worried glances, Ululani and the Dowager stepped inside.

The hut was small, with a clean swept floor and a fire happily chattering in the hearth across the room. A woman sat in a rocking chair in front of the flames humming quietly to herself as she knitted absentmindedly. At the sound of their footsteps, she turned and greeted them with a smile.

The knot of fear in Ululani's chest slowly loosened as she took in the wizened motherly figure before her. Deep lines crested her face and crinkled at the corners of her eyes and mouth. She clearly spent much of her days laughing.

Her hair was beginning to gray at the temples and was twisted delicately into a braided crown upon her head. Tucked into the braids were small white and pink flowers that gave her the appearance of a halo. Her clothing was a simple dress, but expertly sewn. The color plain and the garment well taken care of. It was clear to see this woman's life was full of love.

"Welcome," she said, gesturing to an empty bench across from her. "I was expecting you sooner."

"You...were expecting us?" Ululani's questions stutter out of her in awkward fits and starts. "How? Why?"

The woman smiled at them kindly and offered some tea from a steaming pot on the fire before her. Ululani and the Dowager accepted cups of the warm liquid and sipped it as they awkwardly settled on the too small bench. Even with the cramped quarters it was a relief for them to rest their weary legs. Ululani settled Alon on her lap and he fussed briefly, small protestations before he succumbed again to his fevered sleep.

"May I hold him?" The woman reached gently towards Ululani. "He is sick, correct? That is why you are here?"

The Dowager carefully removed Alon from Ululani's lap and handed him to the woman. "How did you know?"

"Every few generations there is one. Not all come to us, but I have seen six in my lifetime. He is the seventh."

Ululani studied the woman with new interest. While she appeared ordinary, in the flickering light of the flames Ululani now saw traces of otherworldliness to her. The shape of her ears was just slightly too curved at the top, her eyes a shade of blue that's too purple. Along her hairline small swirling markings framed her face and faded back beneath her braids.

"What is wrong with him?" Ululani couldn't keep the fear from her voice, but the woman seemed unconcerned.

"In our culture we celebrate the moon. While you and your people thrive in the sunlight, we thrive in the moonlight. There are four points in the year when the moon is at its closest. We call it

Perigean. It's an auspicious day for us; one we hold in the highest esteem. Weddings on Perigean are blessed, deals have a weight and bond that are unbreakable, and any child brought into this world during Perigean is honored. Many become prominent and respected members and leaders of our people.

"For your people, however, a child born during Perigean can contract what we refer to as Moon Sickness." She paused to coo gently at Alon as he stirred. "Not all children contract it. The babe struggles to thrive in the sunlight and the only way to cure Moon Sickness is to bring him here to my people."

"Does that mean you can help him?" The small bud of hope that had been growing in Ululani's chest began to slowly unfurl its petals. "Please. I can't lose him."

The woman smiled at her kindly. "Yes. I can help him. All I ask is that you do not interfere with our ceremony. Once we begin, we must see it through to completion or your son may pass on."

Ululani nodded her consent. She and the Dowager followed the woman out of her hut and to a large reflecting pool in the center of the clearing. All around them, members of the Elder tribe moved forward and fell back, an undulating sea of bodies. As one, their voices rang out in beautiful unbroken melodies as they began to sing in time with their movements.

The woman carefully unwrapped Alon from his swaddle and gracefully stepped into the pool. Wading to the center, she lifted her voice with the others, and it rose above and wove throughout in its own haunting melody. Ululani and the Dowager watched as the moon above them seemed to grow brighter and brighter until it pulsed once and then went out. A woman made of the purest light stood in the center of the reflecting pool, surveying the little prince.

The Elders knelt and bowed their heads to the muddy earth in deference to the women standing in the pool, but they continued to sing. The woman of light gently took Alon in her arms and spoke to him in quiet, soothing tones. She scooped up some of the water from the pool and made a symbol on Alon's forehead that glowed brightly before fading again. Ululani felt the hope in her chest come to full bloom as Alon cried briefly, the strong cry of a healthy child and not the strangled gasping from before.

The woman smiled down at the prince and brushed his hair from his forehead. He opened his eyes briefly and gently reached out to touch her face. His hand was a dark shadow against her cheek, the faintest glow of pink outlining his fingers. Smiling, the woman of moonlight reached down for more water. She drew another symbol on Alon's chest, blew on it briefly to make it glow like the one before, and then tickled him gently before kissing his forehead. Speaking quietly to the Elder woman, the glowing woman disappeared in a flash of light and once again the moon shone through the night skies.

Slowly, the song around Ululani and the Dowager changed. It took on tones of thanks and adoration. One by one the voices slowly tapered out as the Elders rose and returned to their homes. The Elder woman waded to the edge of the pool and handed Prince Alon back to Ululani. He was alert and watched the world around him. When he saw his mother's face he broke into a toothless smile that brought tears of relief to Ululani's eyes.

"The Moon Goddess has healed his Moon Sickness. She has also blessed him with a gift, although She did not share what that gift was. I'm sure in time it will become known." She bowed to Ululani and the Dowager and gestured to a square jawed man waiting off to the side. "Evander will guide you back to your camp. There are reports of a royal party nearing the Falls. It will be more peaceful for you to join them and share the good news."

The Dowager clasped her hands around the woman's and bowed deeply. "Thank you for your help. We will not forget it."

A smile as bright as a crescent moon spread over the woman's face. She bowed in turn and slipped away into the village. Ululani and the Dowager followed their guide back the way they came, the journey seemingly shorter than before.

Once they were safely returned to the smoldering remains of their campfire, Evander bowed to the women and disappeared into the trees without a trace. Ululani and the Dowager held each other close, Alon between them, as they cried freely together.

With the dawn ushering in the first of the birdsong, so did it bring King Hemi and a party of royal guards. He was overjoyed to find his family safe and shed tears of his own when he saw the improvement to his son. Prince Alon woke again as the sun crested the hills, and he smiled as he saw the people he loved crowded around him. Their journey home was thankfully uneventful, punctuated only by the growing demands of a hungry baby and his relieved family.

Chapter 14

In Which a Truth is Revealed

Nora

I can't take my eyes off Queen Ululani. The whole time she's telling her story I practically have to remind myself to breathe. My body is heavy and unresponsive. Almost like I'm stuck in mud and I'm struggling to float.

Father has migrated from the sofa to the window, his temper seemingly to have calmed since first seeing Alon. He stands with his hands clasped behind his back, appearing to survey the gardens, but I can tell from his profile his eyes are closed. Mother is drawn and worried. Her brows knit together, and she remains unnaturally still. Queen Ululani and King Hemi seem mildly awkward, but overall unperturbed. Alon just pushes fruit around his plate. I can barely stand to look at him.

"When did you learn the...gift...he was given was that he could not die?" Mother's voice is barely above a whisper. The room is so quiet that it doesn't even matter.

"When he was three," King Hemi says calmly. "Alon slipped away from his nurse before a hurricane hit the coast. He wandered too close to the edge of the cliffs and fell. We found his body later that night after the storm passed. We held a silent vigil throughout the night, as is our custom, but when the sun rose in the morning...he awoke with seemingly no memory of what happened. A small blessing."

"The next time I was nine." Alon's voice is thin and reedy. "A traveler infected with an unknown disease came to our shores. He caused a great sickness to sweep through the kingdom. It brought many deaths. Including mine."

"Maybe it would be faster to tell us about the last time you...died." The strain in Mother's voice is getting worse. She is bothered by more than just Alon coming back to life, but I don't know exactly what.

"I was nineteen. I had been ab–"

"We do not speak of it," King Hemi interrupts curtly. "It was a terrible accident and not one we like to dwell on."

"So, he cannot die? Ever?" Father breaks his silence as he faces the rest of the room. The sunlight pouring through the window rings him in a golden halo.

"We don't know for sure." Queen Ululani says gently, soothingly. "Alon continues to age the same as his brothers. It could be that once he reaches a certain age he will be in danger of passing on by an accident. Or he may have to die from old age. The only way to know would be to make a pilgrimage back to the Elders."

"It was a journey I was supposed to make for my twenty-first birthday." Alon glances at me briefly. I meet his gaze with a stony look. "I'm sure I don't need to point out how those plans were interrupted."

Mother and Father exchange a look, and Mother joins him at the window. They bow their heads together and whisper frantically, almost like they're having an argument. How odd. Mother and Father rarely argue and, when they do, they are always careful to make sure that no one sees. My jaw clenches and unclenches, my own tell-tale sign of frustration, and I actively fight to stop.

I survey the table. King Hemi and Queen Ululani continue to focus on their plates, blocking out the obvious argument happening across the room. Queen Ululani clucks occasionally at Alon as he shuffles his food around and tries to get him to eat more. Alon himself looks a bit green around the edges. So far, he's only managed a bit of fruit despite his mother's imploring.

This is madness. Complete and utter madness. I need to talk to Teddy. Almost in a trance, I rise from the table, ignoring the surprised looks from those still seated, and slip out the door.

• • • ☽ • ◯ • ☾ • • •

"He can't die!?" Teddy's incredulity oozes over me like honey, validating my own feelings of shock. "That's impossible!"

I had found Teddy in his favorite chair in the library poring over a dusty leather-bound edition of short stories. He had protested slightly when I grabbed his hand and led him to the old nursery through a roundabout path to make sure no one saw us. Once the door was safely shut and we collapsed onto the sheet covered sofa, I told Teddy what had happened since retiring to the honeymoon suite last night. At first, he had objected, claiming he didn't want to hash out the details of my love life with another man. But once he actually listened to what I was saying he quickly fell quiet.

"They claim he was given a gift by the Moon Goddess, and he can't die. So far, he's died at least three times and has always come back. I guess, at least four now…"

Teddy blows out an incredulous breath and slumps backwards. "What happens now?"

"I don't know."

"Do you think they'll annul the marriage?"

"And risk angering our people and the High Counsel? Unlikely. Father is so concerned about these rumors that keep popping up about revolution coming. He and Hayden already have so much on their plate already...I doubt Mother and Father will even consider annulling the marriage."

"You could ask."

"And if they say no?"

"Then you could always...make the journey with him." Teddy's voice is quiet. Careful. "To figure out if it's possible to remove it ourselves."

Hold on. There's no way he actually just said that. Did I hear what I think I just heard? "Do you mean we would kill him?"

"No!" The answer is quick. Firm. Teddy grabs my hands and pulls them to his chest. "It's just to figure out if it *can* be removed. If it can be...and if something were to happen to him...and maybe he *didn't* come back well...then we could be together."

"Teddy, this is insane. I can't kill him!"

"Nora, you're being ridiculous. I'm not asking you to!" Anger colors the edges of Teddy's words and he bites it back down. "All we want are answers. That's it."

From beyond the door are the sounds of the palace truly waking. Members of the court slowly begin to leave their nests, and the servants are taking full advantage of their absences. As much as the courtiers choose to ignore them, it's clear to me that without a large staff of highly trained workers making their beds, cleaning their rooms, and ensuring that all their little specificities are met, the highborn would flounder. More people out in the halls puts us at a much higher risk of getting caught, even in the far-removed nursery. Teddy gently brushes a few stray hairs from my face and cups my cheek.

"I will do anything to be with you, Nora," he says gently. "Anything."

Leaning in, he kisses me softly before rising and slipping out the door. I lay back on the sheet covered couch and try to become one of the old cushions. Light dances off the cheerful blue walls and the soothing familiarity of the room helps calm the confusion and fear brewing in my stomach. There's no question about it. I need to talk to Mother and Father.

"I would like the marriage annulled."

Mother and Father look up from the map they were considering together, blinking at my sudden appearance. I had broken one of the cardinal rules and entered Father's study without invitation. Decorum be damned at a time like this.

"I want the marriage annulled," I repeat, cursing the slight waver to my voice.

Mother regains her composure first; her words crisp as a winter morning. "Don't be absurd. There's no reason for an annulment."

"There is every reason for it," I fire back. "You would rather shackle me to this stranger who claims to have been blessed by the moon instead of elevating one of our own who deserves the position."

"Nora." Father's voice has taken on the soothing tones he uses to try and head off an argument, "it's not as simple as—"

"It is that simple." I hold my hand up to stop him. "I have seen the old records, Father. You've made me study them. There have been several members of the royal family that have married one of the common people in our kingdom and elevated their rank and status. There is no reason the High Counsel would not agree to do the same with Teddy. He is well deserving of the honor and —"

"It will not happen." Mother has found her voice again, icy and cold. "Stop behaving like a child."

I rear back, my head held high. How typical. I express an opinion different from my parents, and I'm accused of behaving like a child.

"I am no child, Mother. Do I need to remind you that I am now a married woman?" Mother flinches at my words and I take more pleasure in that than I should. "I have gone along with your little scheme to marry me off to appease the High Counsel. Even they would see reason for the annulment and agree to it. I would persuade them. Once this farce is annulled then I will approach them with the possibility of Teddy and I —"

"You cannot marry him!"

Mother's shriek rings through the room like thunder and leaves me silent. Father places a hand on her shoulder and she shrugs it off, watching me. It doesn't take long before I find my own voice again.

"Why not?"

"He will die."

Father says it so quietly I can't even be sure I heard him correctly. "What do you mean?"

"I speak the truth, child. If you marry Theodore, then he will die."

"Jasper! No!"

"We must tell her." Father's voice resonates with quiet authority. My heart skips an agitated beat. "Nora, the reason we cannot allow you to marry Theodore is because he will die. Do you know why magic is prohibited in the kingdom?"

"What?" I was struggling to keep up with the sudden change in conversation. "Someone did something they weren't supposed to right? That's why it was outlawed?"

"That is what we teach, but it is not the full story."

Father's eyebrows draw together, creasing his forehead and making him look worn beyond his years. He gestures to the chairs in front of his desk, and I carefully lower myself into one. Mother collapses into the other and Father settles himself behind his desk.

"When you were a child, a curse was placed on you."

I inhale sharply. *A curse? What does that mean?*

"I don't understand." My words are unsure of themselves. Like if I ask the questions, I'm going to find answers I don't really want. "How can I be cursed? What does this have to do with anything?"

"It happened when you were still very small." Mother's voice is choked with tears. She carefully wipes her eyes and repeats the words I already heard once this morning. "Please, Nora, let us explain.

Chapter 15

In Which a Curse is Bestowed

The queen was expecting again. King Jasper and Queen Clarice were overjoyed at the possibility of another to add to their brood, but they were not without fear at the prospect. After Clarice had lost the last baby during her pregnancy, the royal physicians had discouraged them at the time from continuing to have any more children. There were concerns that, even if Clarice was able to carry a child to term, she would not live long enough to see it grow. When Clarice fell pregnant again, she and Jasper tried to hide their fears and ignore the unhappy whispers from those around them.

Each day that passed without issue was one they celebrated together. The young princes were excited at the idea of another playmate and naturally hoped for another brother to join their group. Jasper and Clarice, however, secretly hoped it would be a little girl instead. She loved her boys to pieces, but Clarice had always wanted a little girl.

The weeks passed. Little by little the physicians became cautiously optimistic that they had been wrong. Each uneventful day that passed was marked and scrutinized. No one dared speak their hopes aloud for fear of them being yanked away. As Clarice's time drew closer, the palace buzzed with the hope that comes with welcoming new life into the world.

Almost three months before the child was due, Clarice experienced sharp pains and began to bleed. The physicians rushed to stop her labor, and, after many hours of intense work, she and the baby were stabilized. The bleeding ebbed and, on the surface, all seemed well. Renewed concerns were brought forth to Jasper and he was encouraged to begin making peace with the idea that Clarice or the baby may not survive childbirth. He refused.

Physicians from across the kingdom were brought in to examine Clarice. Jasper hoped to find one that knew how to ensure the survival of both his wife and his child. One by one the parade of specialists and midwives made their examinations and one by one they all shook their heads and told Jasper the same thing: Clarice was very weak. Her chances of survival were low. Even highly skilled specialists at the forefront of developing new techniques for childbirth could promise nothing more than to make her as comfortable as possible.

Not knowing what else to do, Jasper turned to spiritual healers and advisors. He summoned countless shamans and medicine women to try and find someone who could help. Each offered many ways to help mitigate Clarice's pain and ease her passage, but not one could ensure that both she and the baby would survive.

A rumor from the palace staff brought forth the possibility of a woman on the outskirts of the city that sold talismans and protective spells for anyone willing to pay. King Jasper had initially rejected the idea – a witch's magic was unpredictable and dangerous. However, as Clarice's strength faded and she began to waste away, he became more desperate for the answer he wanted. Jasper sent out runners into the city and surrounding wood to try and find the rumored witch.

A tense week passed. Clarice grew weaker each day; a shell of the vibrant woman Jasper knew and loved. The morning of the seventh day, Jasper received word that the woman had been found and was being escorted to the palace. He instructed his staff to notify him the moment she arrived and to show the women directly into his study. He did not want Clarice to know what he was doing for fear nothing came of it.

The woman that arrived late that night was not what Jasper was expecting. A halo of tawny frizz glowed in the flickering firelight, framing a heart shaped face and turned up nose. She was slight, but carried herself with the air of a station far beyond the roughspun pauper clothing that adorned her frame. Upon entering Jasper's study, she knelt.

"Your Majesty."

"Are you the one they call the witch?"

"Yes." her voice was as rough as a felled tree.

"I need to know if you are able to help my queen. She is sick."

"Surely Your Majesty has access to the best physicians in this land and the next. Why call upon me?"

Jasper bristled at the faint mock ringing through her words. "They do not give me the answers I want."

"And what answers are you looking for?"

"I want the queen and my child to survive."

The woman nodded briefly. "If you are willing to pay, I am willing to help."

"Anything."

The word hangs between them, hovering above the polished wood of his desk. The witch lifted her head and assessed Jasper with unflinching eyes. She could see he would trade his soul if that was what she wanted. A slow smile spread across her face, transforming her features into a sinister mask in the firelight. Jasper felt a niggling voice of fear struggling to be heard but squashed its protests.

"That is a dangerous promise to make, Your Majesty. It is quite easy for someone less honorable than I to take advantage of."

Jasper swallowed nervously. "We will do anything. Name your price. Please. Just help them."

The woman considered him for a moment; head tilted like a horse contemplating its rider. "I will help. I will wait to collect payment until after the child is born."

"I agree to the terms."

Her grin was sly as a fox and sharp as a tack. "Then we have a deal."

Jasper escorted the witch through the back corridors of the palace and into the kitchens. Once there, she pulled various herbs and spices out of the pockets in her patchy cloak and ground them together with mortar and pestle. Jasper did not recognize the plants she used and looked on with fearful skepticism. With a final flourish, the woman handed him a small bowl full of the ground mixture. Its pungent smell wafted up and hung in his nose, unwelcome and bitter.

"Use this to make tea three times a day for your queen. She must drink the entire cup each time." She pulled a small talisman from another hidden pocket and presented it to Jasper. "Place this above the bed where Her Majesty sleeps. It will fend off evil spirits and protect her and the babe. When the child is born, I will return for my payment."

King Jasper accepted the proffered bowl. "How do you know this will work?"

Silence surrounded him. He looked around the room, but the woman was gone. The only creature in the kitchen beside him was the cat lazing in front of the banked fire.

Summoning the guards from the door, he questioned where the witch went, but they claimed to have not seen anyone leave. Jasper ordered a full sweep of the palace, but no one could find the woman that claimed to provide the cure he had so desperately wanted. His options spent, Jasper gave the bowl and its contents to the newly rousted cook and instructed her to ensure a cup was provided for Clarice with every meal. He himself tucked the talisman into the ruffled fabric at the top of her four-poster bed.

Within a week, Clarice's color was restored. She was still weak, but her strength began to return in leaps and bounds. The baby's kicks became stronger and there were times it felt like she was dancing within the confines of the queen's body. The physicians pronounced it a miracle, but King Jasper knew better. Clarice continued to drink a cup of tea with every meal up until it came time for her to give birth.

Word came in the middle of Jasper's daily meetings with the High Counsel that Clarice was in labor. He rushed from the Counsel chambers to her side, ignoring the proper etiquette that dictated he remain outside the room. Clarice wanted him there so there he would be.

The labor was long and painful. Several times the physicians threw up their hands and pronounced nothing could be done only to turn around and continue working. Against all odds, after thirty-six hours of labor, a healthy baby girl came kicking and screaming into the world. The kingdom celebrated the birth of the new princess, and she was given the name of Eleanor.

Jasper waited for the witch to return for her payment. When the princess was born, he sent another party of guards out to the witch's house to pay her, however the hut was abandoned, and no one knew of the woman they inquired about. The days bled into weeks, the weeks into months, and eventually the months into years. With each sunset that passed, Jasper stopped watching for her return.

• • • ☽ • ◯ • ☾ • • •

The morning after Eleanor's fourth birthday dawned clear and crisp, but it did not take long for a bank of clouds to descend and leave the sky a pale milky gray. After much contemplation on whether he should wake Clarice or not, Jasper kissed her on the cheek and descended alone to the drawing room to break his fast. The palace was still abuzz with the energy from the princess' birthday party the night before and while the staff looked weary, they were in fine spirits.

Halfway through his coddled eggs, Marshall, the butler, arrived and announced himself with a stately bow.

"My apologies for interrupting, Your Majesty," he intoned drolly. "There is a woman refusing to leave until she has an audience with Your Majesty or Her Majesty."

"What are you on about Marshall? What woman?"

"She gave no name, Your Majesty, just that she needed to speak with You and has refused to remove herself from the premises until that happens. Would You like me to show her in here?"

"No." Jasper pondered for a moment. "Give me ten minutes and then show her to the receiving room. If she begs an audience with her king, then I cannot refuse."

"Very good, Your Majesty." Marshall bowed and closed the door softly behind him.

Scarfing down a few more bites of egg, Jasper pushed back from the table and hurried to the receiving room. On his way he bid a maid servant to alert Lady Wimple and have her wake Clarice. If this woman was adamant that she needed an audience, it was only right that the queen was present as well.

A few minutes after Jasper settled in the stately hard backed throne on the dais in the receiving room, Marshall escorted the woman in. Recognition came slowly, but it did not take long for Jasper to realize it was the same witch from years before. Her hair was now streaked with gray and the heart-shaped face he remembered from before was leaner, sharper. She still carried herself with the same grace and poise of a woman assured of her place in the world. It was only when she got closer and Jasper was able to look her in the eye in broad daylight that he felt the first pang of unrest through his body. Her eyes were mismatched. One was as pale as winter ice and the other dark as the mud at the bottom of the lake.

"Your Majesty." Reaching the steps to the throne, the woman bowed low in greeting. "I pray you forgive my intrusion. I was delayed in returning for my payment all those years ago, however I have now come to collect."

Clarice quietly entered the chamber. Pausing in the doorway, she took in the odd woman at the foot of the dais. She felt something was wrong. A shadow of fear crossed her face, and she carefully composed herself before crossing the room and taking her place in the throne beside Jasper's. She nodded her greeting, and he gave her a strained smile in return.

"Jasper, who is this woman?"

"My name is Belladonna, Your Majesty." Her voice was sticky sweet. "I have come to remind your family of a debt that needs to be paid."

"What is she talking about, My Love?" Clarice's confusion bled through her careful mask. Outside one of the many windows in the hall a single crow could be heard calling through the cloudy morning.

"I was the one that helped ensure Your Majesty and the princess survived the night," Belladonna said as she turned her off-balance gaze towards Clarice. "I informed His Majesty that I would return for payment once the baby was born."

"And what payment do you require?" Jasper studied her, suddenly wary.

"My payment will be the child."

Clarice gasped in horror. "Never!"

"His Majesty agreed to pay me whatever I asked without listening to the terms of the agreement. Payment for my services is the child. She is what, four now? Old enough to learn and young enough to mold."

"You shall never have her!" Clarice's outburst was enough to silence Belladonna's musings. "You cannot come into my home and demand my child for a bargain I was not made aware of."

Jasper visibly flinches. "There must be something else you can accept as payment."

Belladonna bared her teeth in a threatening smile. "There is only one payment. The child. I warn you not to refuse the terms."

"You will not have the princess. That is final."

A moment of silence passed as the three studied each other. Clarice was visibly distraught, her brows furrowed and her hands shaking. Jasper gripped her hand tightly in his, trying to calm her nerves. Worry was etched through every line on his face.

"Fine." The word was sharp as glass. "Your bargain has been broken."

Belladonna clapped her hands together and began mumbling in a harsh tongue. As she pulled her palms apart and swirled her hands through the air, a howling vortex of indigo and purple wind burst through the windows into the hall. It circled the room in eddies and tides, scouring the dais and whipping Jasper and Clarice's hair into a frenzy. One by one the windows along the walls slammed shut again, the light outside dimming as the air turned muddy and charged with electricity.

"As you have broken your word then so shall you suffer the consequences." The witch's eyes glowed purple and gold, her voice deep and timbered. "From this day forth let it be known that if the princess has not wed by her twenty-first birthday, then her life is forfeit and I will collect her soul."

The winds sweeping through the room deepened to a bruised purple so dark it was practically black.

"In exchange for her soul, I will take that of her wedded partner. A life for a life. So, I have spoken."

Golden threads of light snaked between Jasper, Clarice, and Belladonna. The sparkling chain flashed once and faded. With it, the winds dropped and all was quiet again.

Clarice and Jasper blinked the dust and remaining fog from their eyes and surveyed the room before them. The windows were open again, the light filtering through unencumbered. Belladonna was gone. They stared at the empty hall and then at each other, eyes wide with fear.

"What are we going to do?"

Chapter 16

In Which Words Cannot be Unsaid

Nora

"Are you alright, Your Highness?"

Teddy's voice cuts through the haze and I blink at him slowly. After talking with Mother and Father, I had stumbled my way out of Father's study into the gardens in a trance. I collapsed on the first bench I had found, ugly and wooden and next to the azaleas that always make me sneeze when they're in bloom.

Teddy hovers on the path nearby, a couple of his friends, other young men of the court, awkwardly behind him watching me. The weight of their stares pulls me further down and I can do nothing but stare back stupidly. Teddy murmurs a few quiet words to his companions, and they bow quickly before retreating behind the shrubs. Teddy plunks down on the bench making sure to leave a respectable distance between us. In the busier parts of the gardens, we need to be careful.

"Nora," he says softly, "what's wrong?"

"It was because of me. All of this is because of me."

"What do you mean?"

"I'm the reason magic was outlawed. I'm the reason my kingdom went through years of witch hunts and banishments. I'm the reason I was forced to marry." I bury my face in my hands, my voice barely more than a whisper. "I'm the reason we can never be together."

"Slow down," Teddy murmurs soothingly. He carefully reaches a hand across the space between us and pats my shoulder gently. "Start at the beginning. Tell me what happened."

With halting, hiccuping breaths I tell him everything. He's silent as I share how Mother and Father finally told me the truth – that I was cursed as a child because they went back on their bargain with a witch. How magic was banned and that caused the mass fear and witch hunts for so many years afterwards. How they saw Alon being unable to die as a gift and that they would not annul the marriage.

"A gift," Teddy snorts derisively. "They got lucky. He was a lamb to be slaughtered."

"Teddy!" I admonish. The gardens are too open, too easy to be heard in. He needs to be careful. "They won't change their minds."

Teddy looks around us. Assured no one is watching, he slides closer and clasps my hands in his.

"We need to know how his curse works," he whispers fervently. "We need to know if it can be removed."

"Teddy, I already told you we can't —"

"We're not going to kill him." Teddy admonishes, earnestly.

He falls silent, dropping my hands and scooting quickly back to the other end of the bench. Voices announce the parade of Lords and Ladies as they pass us in their finery, tittering behind hands and fans at Teddy and I sitting on the same bench. Thankfully, they know better than to voice their thoughts aloud where it matters. The last of the bright skirts and heeled shoes had barely made it around the shrubbery before Teddy was next to me again.

"Nora, I don't think you understand the implications of your situation. Alon himself may not seem dangerous, but the truth of the matter is that, until he can be taken by the witch, you are at risk." Seeing my widening eyes, Teddy continues quickly. "But that doesn't mean we have to be helpless. What if the witch returns because she hasn't been able to claim him? She'll come after you again and do you really think he'll protect you? We need to make sure we can keep you safe. We need to know how to remove his gift. I can't lose you."

Teddy's voice breaks and he takes a moment to steady it. "You've always wanted to see more than just Sephiroth. Try and convince him to let you go with him to figure out how to remove it. It's the only way we can keep you safe."

My stomach lurches like it's trying to turn itself inside out. He's right. Just because magic was outlawed doesn't mean the witch can't come back and try to claim me again. Father himself admitted they had never been able to find Belladonna. What if she comes back and tries to claim my life or Teddy's because she can't have Alon? What if she does something worse because she feels like Mother and Father cheated her out of the life owed? If it comes down to saving myself or saving Alon the equation is simple. I just can't tell him that.

• • • ☽ • ◯ • ☾ • • •

Alon is in the stables with several of his brothers. I still can't tell them apart. He is all too happy to follow me into one of the many tack rooms and shut the door behind us. I settle on the small wooden stool near the door and Alon makes a move to come closer, but my glare scares him off and he slouches lazily against the far wall instead.

"What did you want to talk about?" His eyes are hooded, sultry. As if he *actually* thinks I had invited him in here to do more than just talk.

"We need to know more about your gift. Can it be undone? Can it be exploited?"

"I already told you, I don't know." Alon's eyes narrow, watching me carefully. "I had been planning to make a pilgrimage to the Elders for my twenty-first birthday to learn about my gift. I just ended up here instead."

"Do you still want to make that journey?"

"Yes. Why do you ask?"

"Because I want to go with you."

Alon tries to keep his thoughts off his face, but I can read them all – intrigue, suspicion, and hope. To distract myself, I rise from the stool and go stand at the small window on the far wall. Grass sways in the late afternoon sun and grooms wash their charges, currying coats and polishing hooves until they shine. Everything is the same and everything is inexplicably different.

"I would love for you to join me. Does this mean you have accepted our union?"

"No." I spit the word with such venom I can taste it. Taking a breath, I continue. "We will never work."

"Why?"

The question seems so simple, but it's not one easily answered. How do I tell him about my curse? *Can* I even tell him about my curse? How do I make him understand that the love I have for Teddy is not one that can just be released on a whim? Instead, I just shrug helplessly.

"That's not an answer, Nora. Why are you so convinced that we cannot work? You feel like a part of me, and I've only known you a short while. Like two halves of a coin – without one there cannot be the other."

I sense Alon moving behind me. He gently puts his hands on my waist and turns me away from the window to face him. I lose my balance halfway through and almost land on the sawdusty floor. Alon catches me with a steady arm and pulls me close. Too close. We stand – chest to chest, toe to toe – breathing in the familiar smell of leather and horses.

I study his face for the first time since our meeting. This close, I can see the humor in the corners of his mouth, the kindness around his eyes, the slight point to his chin. The bump in his nose seems even more pronounced up close and a soft stubble grows like moss across his jawline.

It's his eyes, though, that demand the most attention. Ringed with eyelashes several shades darker than his hair, his eyes crinkle at the corners and are filled with an unexplainable intensity as he watches me. They're kind eyes. Trusting.

We stand together, the rise and fall of our chests punctuated only by the echo of our heartbeats. A small voice of doubt in the back of my head asks if I could really lie to him and try to take his gift away without him knowing. *I'm not doing anything wrong*, I chide her angrily, *I just want to know how it works*. To keep me and Teddy safe if Belladonna comes back.

Despite knowing that, however, I can't shake the desire to reach out and run my fingers along his jaw. To trace that bump on his nose and sink my hands deep within his hair. *I wonder if it feels as soft as it looks*. Hold on, where did *that* come from?

Alon watches me as intently as I study him. Keeping an arm around my waist, he reaches up and gently brushes some curls out of my face, tucking them carefully behind my ear. A small smile crosses his lips as he brings his hand down to cup my cheek with his palm.

"You are the most captivating woman I have ever had the privilege of meeting." The husky sound of his voice raises goosebumps along my arms and the back of my neck. Alon leans in slowly, his mouth millimeters from mine, his breath on my lips. "I just wish that you could see how happy we could be together."

And just like that, the moment is gone. Regaining my footing, I push him away from me. He releases his hold on my waist and stumbles backwards a few steps before straightening again; hands shoved into his pockets.

"Remember yourself." My voice squeaks and I take a deep breath to steady it. "I still stand with my earlier claims. I will never love you."

"We can still be happy companions even if you didn't love me."

The heat starts from deep within my body, spreading outwards as quickly as my heart beats in my chest. My blood turns to fire within my veins. This man is infuriating.

"No, we can't. You are unbelievably arrogant for one and we won't last more than five minutes together without me wanting to run you through with a sword."

Alon grins at me. That lazy, pompous grin. My resolve hardens like the cornerstone to the barn – strong and dependable.

"You're really going to stand there and tell me you're not even a little curious to try? See if it's worth the risk? You seem like the kind of woman that likes a little danger in her life."

My arms cross against my chest, and I force them to drop to my sides. The last thing I want is to be called defensive. Or to look like a sulking child.

"It's clear to me we don't work, and we never will." With each word the storm in his eyes gets deeper, his face hardening ever so slightly. "I do not love you nor do I wish to. I don't want you or whatever life you claim to be able to give me. I simply want to join you on a journey to the Elders because I want to travel. To learn about the world outside Sephiroth."

"So, you'd rather throw away the opportunity of an equal match with someone that could never leave you for a boy you've known longer." Alon's anger is a thick undercurrent weighing his words down like stones.

"Teddy is not a boy. He knows me better than anyone."

"And does dear old Teddy seriously think that the two of you will one day be together? He must be an idiot if he thinks it's ever going to be possible."

"Don't insult him. Especially not to me. He is twice the man you could ever hope to be!"

"Seeing as how I have yet to have a conversation with him I'll have to take your word for it, Princess."

I cringe at the use of my title. It's a twisted mockery in his mouth.

"Don't call me that."

"What? Princess?" Alon laughs coldly. "That's what you are after all. I just never realized you were truly so entitled to hope you could have him."

"That's what love does."

In our anger, we had returned to standing toe to toe. Now Alon pulls back. "What did you say?"

"You heard me. You said we are two sides of the same coin, but you're wrong. Teddy and I are. We are the balance for each other. We belong together. You may think I'm ridiculous for holding onto him, but the fact remains that I love him. Not you, *him*. And holding onto each other in spite of hardship is what love does."

"Is this what you want?" Alon's question comes so softly I almost miss it.

I answer without hesitation, "yes."

Alon nods once and then steps back. Where once was anger I can see only acceptance and resolution.

"Okay." His voice is devoid of all emotion. "We will go to the Elders. Together."

For the first time in months hope starts to take root. This is happening. I will be able to get the answers I need to make sure Teddy and I are safe and we can be together without Mother and Father needing to worry. I turn back to the window and inhale deeply. I don't even notice Alon slipping out behind me.

Chapter 17

In Which Life is Celebrated

Alan

I wander aimlessly through the grounds, Nora's words echoing in my head: *you are unbelievably arrogant.... I love Teddy.... Holding onto each other is what love does.... I love Teddy...*

I hear her words, and they hurt. There is an unmistakable pull that draws me to this infuriating woman. An ache behind my heart that loosens when she is near, when I can hear her voice and watch her smile. I want to know her. To learn about her. To share her secrets so she doesn't have to carry them alone. And no matter how I try to explain that I can't seem to find the right words to make her understand.

Around me swirl the whispers of various courtiers and nobility as I wander aimlessly by. I'm sure tongues will be wagging nonstop as they have been since my family and I arrived, though no one is brave enough to tell me what they're actually thinking to my face.

Rounding a corner, I see Mama and Queen Clarice settled in an alcove cut into the shrubbery. Their matched chairs are pulled close together, the arms almost touching as they lean across them talking quietly over their teacups. A teapot steams gently on the table before them, and I can just make out the servants waiting discreetly on the veranda above should they need anything. I clear my throat to announce my presence and approach.

"Alon!" Mama jumps briefly. Concern washes over her as she sees my face. "Is everything alright, Starfish?"

"Yes Mama." I lean down to kiss her cheek. "Just taking a walk."

Relief relaxes her tensed forehead as Mama settles back into her chair. I swallow a tang of guilt. Mama doesn't need to know what Nora and I talked about. She doesn't need to hear how our marriage is less of a marriage and more of a rocky valley full of sand traps.

"Nora and I would like to visit Korala and journey to see the Elders. Like I had planned to do before...all this." Neither of them looks particularly convinced and I attempt to smile encouragingly. "We were thinking of setting sail within the next few days. Maybe you and Baba can sail back with us?"

"Oh, you must stay at least through the end of the week!" Queen Clarice fixes me with a gaze that makes it perfectly clear I cannot refuse. "Your birthdays are almost here, and I have been planning to throw a party to celebrate. Your Mama has been helping with some last-minute planning."

"Oh, yes and that reminds me, Clarice, we really should —"

And I am already forgotten, the draw of planning a party overshadowing any lingering concerns they have about me. Mama always loved to celebrate with family. Now that the family has grown, she is excited to learn the traditions and customs of Sephiroth up close.

"May I make one request?" I ask. Mama and Queen Clarice look at me encouragingly. "Can we hold it in the gardens?"

"That sounds lovely, Alon. We can hold it on the southern patio. The dahlias and sunflowers will be in full bloom, and it will be absolutely perfect. They're Nora's favorites, you know, and —"

They were off and chattering again. I hover for a few more minutes as they plan away, ideas flying so fast I can barely keep up with them all. I smile as I watch. It's nice Mama has found a friend.

Nodding to the servant who came to replenish their pot of tea, I back away quietly from the alcove and amble up onto the veranda and into the palace. Slipping down a hall, through an oversized arch, and dodging into the first room with an open door, I find myself in an understated drawing room decorated in lavender and white. The gloriously stuffed armchair near the large window practically swallows me whole as I survey the view of the stables. *I wonder if Nora's still in there...*

I've never cared before whether I was particularly well-spoken or not, but right now I really wish I was able to be honest with Nora and really tell her how I feel. Explain about this damn aching in my chest that doesn't go away unless I'm with her. How even though we've only known each other for a short time, I think I am falling helplessly in love with her. How do I tell her all of that without scaring her off?

Words have never been my strong suit and I've never had to rely on them so much before. It would be so much easier if Nora could just see inside my head, see all my thoughts and feelings laid bare to her. But she can't. And I can't seem to find a way to tell her.

Despite myself, a slow grin spreads across my face as a small thought takes root and begins to grow. Just because I can't *tell* her doesn't mean I can't do my best to *show* her. Nora may be convinced there's only one path forward, but I'm can do whatever I can to show her that she has another choice. And I've got some planning of my own to do.

$$\bullet \bullet \bullet \,) \bullet \bigcirc \bullet (\, \bullet \bullet \bullet$$

The next week passes quickly. I pack and repack in preparation for our journey back to Korala. I even do a little here and there helping Mama and Queen Clarice plan the joint birthday, but that's mostly to learn more about Nora. And I set my own plans in motion. After all, what's life for if not falling in love and wooing my wife?

The first part of my plan is unsurprisingly very easy. On the recommendation of King Jasper, I consult with a team of skilled jewelers he claims are the best. They seem fairly incredulous at my request and try valiantly to convince me to change my mind countless times, but I hold firm and eventually they concede. I know what I want and there's nothing that will convince me otherwise.

The second part of my plan proves much harder than expected. I spend several afternoons ambling through the gardens trying to find the hidden clearing where I had first seen Nora. Unfortunately, my ability to retrace a path chosen by pure chance is not very good.

With no hint of finding it myself, I track down Nora's maidservant Abigail and convince her to show me how to get there. Abigail was understandably hesitant at first, but, after assuring her I wouldn't tell a soul of her involvement, she led me down a twisting set of paths that seemed to turn back on each other so often I practically got lost again while following her. Thankfully, I had the self preservation to draw a map as we went and that made navigation much easier.

Thrice more I make my way back to the clearing where I first saw Nora. Each visit makes it easier for me to find, and I rely on my hand drawn map less and less. After my final test run in the dark, I'm fairly confident I can find my way without issue. On my last visit, I stash a basket with candles and blankets under the bench. It's almost time.

The day of our birthday dawns with a clear blue sky. Birds sing to each other from the trees, and the palace is humming with energy. You would have thought there was another wedding taking place with all the excitement. Our two families come together for a large breakfast in honor of me and Nora. All our collective brothers jostle and joke with each other like old friends, but Nora remains distant with me despite my attempts at conversation. I smile to myself, hopefully my surprise later will help change that.

After breakfast, I meet with the jewelers and collect my gift for Nora. The little box seems so tiny and unassuming. It's perfect. Several of the jewelers express concern that anyone in the royal family could possibly like what I had designed, but I just smile politely and promise to look at their wares at a different time. An easy promise to make since I am setting sail on the morrow and who knows when I will be back.

I make one last trip out to the garden to test my memory and check on my basket to make sure everything is still there. My previous practices were not in vain because I managed to find my way there without looking at my map once. The scene I find when I arrive, however, leaves me wishing I had taken longer to get there.

Nora and Teddy stand under the archway in the center of the clearing. Lost in each other, they are unaware of my approach. I briefly consider interrupting them but ultimately decide it's better to leave quietly. Let them have their moment. Interrupting will not help me change Nora's opinion about me.

The afternoon thankfully passes quickly and it's not long before we are readying ourselves for the party. Mama had insisted on us all wearing traditional Sephiroth clothing again and I send up a quiet prayer of thanks as I take my place with Nora at the end of the line. My Koralan clothing definitely does not fit in here.

Similar to what our wedding procession must have looked like from the back, our families stretch ahead of us waiting to make their grand entrances. One by one they are announced and proceed through the large double doors out onto the southern patio. We shuffle forward little by little until it's just the two of us standing together.

"Did you have a nice day?" I ask pleasantly.

Nora looks at me with a hint of suspicion. "I did, thank you. And you?"

"I did."

The doors open in front of us, and our names ring out in the night like the bells of a church. I smile at Nora and offer my arm. She grudgingly takes it and together we make our entrance to the cheers and well wishes of the court. If Mama and Queen Clarice had outdone themselves for the wedding, then this party is something else entirely.

The southern patio is the size of a ballroom, paved with smooth sand and pink colored stones. Three sides are ringed with flowerbeds where coneflowers, lavenders, pink dahlias the size of dinner plates, and golden sunflowers sway together in time to the music from the string quartet. Various gravel walkways branch off from the main patio and lead to other smaller patios hidden among the gardens. Benches nestle among the flowers to create a world almost entirely isolated in itself.

Tables are scattered almost haphazardly around the edges of the patio and visibly groan under the weight of their wares. Fresh fruits, pastries, small cakes, sparkling glasses of punch and champagne, and various trays of vegetables, cheeses, and even chocolates call enticingly to anyone wandering close enough. More than a few have succumbed to their siren song if the plates gripped in white gloved hands is any indication.

Standing candelabras had been brought out and placed anywhere the stone was believed stable, making the whole place sparkle and flicker like a pleasant dream. The light shines off the jewelry of the courtiers and they make constellations as they move around the dance floor. The quartet paused briefly when we were announced, but now they seamlessly transitioned to a familiar song from Korala.

I bow to Nora and extend my hand in invitation. Her annoyance is barely concealed. Clearly, she was hoping I wasn't going to ask to dance. Reluctantly, she takes my hand, and I sweep her out onto the dance floor into the familiar waltz. It doesn't take more than one turn around the floor before other guests pair up and join in. Halfway through our third turn, Nora steps on my foot. Hard.

"Must you? Really? This is a party after all," I murmur quietly.

"I didn't mean to."

Nora steps on my foot again and I flinch. I glance down at her and see a pink flush growing across her neck. A few steps later and she bungles the footwork again, the flush spreading to her ears. Her smile remains on her face the whole time. Unless you were watching closely you would never know.

"Are you alright?" I ask cautiously.

"Fine," she snaps. After a beat she continues, "I'm not a very good dancer."

I throw back my head and laugh. "And here I thought you could do anything," I tease.

Nora bares her teeth just for me and attempts to continue with the dance. With a final flourish, I spin her out and bring her back in for a dip as the song ends. All around us the court applauds, but it's only Nora I care about.

"Later tonight," I say quietly, "I'd like to show you something."

There's a moment of hesitation and then Nora nods. I sweep her back into an upright position, not letting go until her feet are firmly level on the pavers. She bobs a shallow curtsy and bustles off the dance floor, gown swishing behind her.

Abandoned by my partner, I wander off the dance floor as well to find some company. A night of dancing, drinking, eating, and enjoying myself is exactly what I need. Nora may spend it mostly ignoring me, but I won't take it personally. I've got time.

• • • ☽ • ◯ • ☾ • • •

Around one in the morning, the party begins to wind down and people head back inside to their warm beds. I can only imagine the number of hangovers that will be plaguing the halls of the palace in the morning. It makes my head hurt just thinking about them. I kiss Mama and Baba good night, duck various swings from assorted brothers, and make my way to the bench where Nora waits for me.

Surrounded by flowers, she looks like a garden spirit in her leaf green dress. The corseted top hugs her figure and the splayed skirts swirl around her in a never-ending current. My sore feet and aching back protest as I bow, extending my hand to Nora. She hesitantly accepts my offer, and together we wander out into the moonlight with our arms linked.

We don't speak as we walk. I'm sure Nora knows exactly where we're going, but she doesn't say anything. She seems perfectly content to be pulled along, letting me take the lead and direct where we're going.

A quiet gasp from beside me is the only sound as we step onto the slate pavers in the clearing. Small candles line the stepping-stones and illuminate a flickering path to the center patio and archway. The greenery and late summer flowers are lit from below with more candles, casting dancing shadows across Nora's skirts.

I hang back, letting Nora take the lead as she cautiously moves between the candles and settles herself on one of the waiting blankets. I track her progress, enjoying her wonder at each new discovery as I slowly follow. Claiming my own patch of blanket, I open a basket I don't recognize and find it filled with mulled wine and some of the canapes from the party. *Abigail, you are a saint!* I'll need to get her something to say thank you.

Sliding out one of the plates, I carefully place a few canapes on it and hand it to Nora. She takes it automatically and nibbles at some of the cheese. I help myself to a chocolate eclair and settle in beside her. We listen to the sounds of the night all around us and watch fireflies dance through the flowers. After a while, Nora turns to look at me.

"What's all this for? Did you do this?"

I watch Nora carefully. "A party is always fun, but I thought you might like something a little quieter to ring in another year older. Here –" I shift slightly closer to her and pull out the jewelry box from my pocket "– this is for you. Happy birthday, Nora."

Nora eyes the box like it's going to bite her, but she accepts it nonetheless. She carefully unsnaps the latch and opens the lid.

"It's beautiful," she breathes. "Thank you."

While my design had been questioned, it was clear to see that Nora loved the necklace. A perfect circle of brown blown glass is etched with swirling designs like a snail's shell. It is safely wrapped in alternating petals of amber and honey yellow tourmaline. The sunflower pendant rests gently on a blue velvet pillow and, in the candlelight, the yellow gems and gold edgings flicker invitingly.

"Your mother mentioned sunflowers are your favorite." I carefully remove the necklace from the box and hold it up. "May I?'

Nora turns slightly away from me. Careful not to get the necklace tangled in her hair, I place it around her neck and latch the clasp. Nora turns back to me expectantly. The gold chain rests lightly on her collarbone and the sunflower settles an inch or two lower. Nora raises a hand to touch it gently as I move back, giving her more space.

A cloud shifts in front of the moon briefly and then moves on, letting the moonlight cascade down around us again. Nora scoots to the edge of the little patio and turns her face up, breathing in the crisp air and surveying the moon and stars above. A few moments pass in easy silence.

"This doesn't change anything."

Her words are soft. Hesitating. Like she's not sure if she needs to say them aloud or not.

"I know."

"Thank you for the present, Alon. Happy birthday."

Nora rises and disappears back down the path like the breeze through the trees – one minute there, the next gone. I sit for a while longer thinking back on all that happened tonight. Seeing Nora soak in the moonlight makes it even more obvious to me that I am completely and utterly in love with her. Honestly, there's no point even pretending I'm not at this point.

But it's somehow even more than that. Every cell in my body calls out for her, craves her. Wants to be near her and to be consumed by her. Just thinking those words makes the place behind my heart prickle uncomfortably. I love her. And seeing as how I can't actually find the words to tell her how much I love her, I am going to have to do what I can to show her that love instead.

Humming to myself, I collect the candles and blankets and remaining food, carefully repacking them in their baskets and slinging everything over my arms. It's weird not being able to see my feet that well, but even so I practically dance my way back to the palace and to my own bed. Tomorrow we leave for Korala, and I get to show Nora my home.

Chapter 18

In Which Chaos is Planned

Boar

The damp itches at my eyes and seeps into my clothes with unsettling fingers. *Why on earth did we choose to make this dingy forgotten basement cave our headquarters?* Of all the unused parts of the city we could have taken advantage of, why did we decide to go with this one? Our presence may have been more noticeable in a tavern basement, but at least we'd be comfortable for gods' sake.

My compatriots are more subdued than the last time we met, their eyes hard and mouths downturned. They're all a bit drunk from the birthday celebration, but there's not a tankard of ale in sight on our table tonight. A smile creeps across my face. It's about time they started taking things seriously.

"Everything was in place. Everything. I confirmed with my maid, and she told me she saw the princess's lady's maid herself getting rid of the wine and burying the wineskin in the kitchen gardens." Wolf absently rubs his head, sending his prematurely greying hair in all directions. "What no one seems to know is how he managed to survive."

"Or why the royals aren't raiding the henhouse to figure out what's going on." Lion's tawny mane is bent low; his forehead furrowed in concentration. "You would have thought that an attempt on the princeling's life would have started an investigation of some kind."

"They're closing ranks and pulling inward. Making it harder for us to figure out what went wrong." This from Hawk at the far side of the table. His beady black eyes peek furtively out from beneath his mousey brown hair.

Nervous mutterings from the rest remind me of the crows mumbling together in the gardens. We had attempted a much more ambitious disruption of the fishing trade several days ago and it had failed spectacularly. Wolf and Lion almost got caught and it was only because Hawk shot the guard down where he stood that they managed to make it out undetected.

Even with our failure to eliminate the foreigner we are still making traction with the commoners. Our seeds of distrust and doubt run rampant through the slums and brothels, an assignment Spaniel took immense pleasure in seeing out. Thankfully, Bull went with him and kept them on task. If he hadn't, I have no doubt that Spaniel would still be out there whoring his way through the few pleasure houses that remain on the outskirts of the city. That man will whip it out for anything so long as it buys him a stiff drink first. Hell, he probably doesn't even need the drink first.

"Gentlemen," I say, casting my voice out over their sullen frames. "This week has been rife with disappointments, but we cannot lose hope now."

"You'd know a thing or two about disappointment, eh Boar?" Spaniel's pointed chin pulls taut under his glazed smile. "I imagine it's not easy seeing – oof!"

Wolf's elbow drives deep into Spaniel's stomach, leaving him gasping. "I'd suggest you watch your tongue, Lord Spaniel, or you risk losing it. And won't that be difficult to explain to your dear father."

Spaniel only wheezes feebly. All eyes turn back to me, watching expectantly. Father was right. Arranging to have them almost caught has pulled them closer in. Their loyalty to our cause and, by association, to me grows stronger by the day.

"We should not let our failure with the prince distract us from our next steps." Thank the gods my voice is more confident than I feel. They don't need to see my doubts too. "Now that the rumors have spread it's time to move again. We just need to wait a few days before we start our next phase."

"Aw, why?" Spaniel whines.

"Because the royals will be on high alert with the princess sailing out tomorrow you half-wit," Wolf snaps peevishly. "We have to wait until they're lulled back into their false sense of security and then strike again. The real question is whether we'll lose our hold on the princess while she's gone and what we should do if she doesn't come back."

Eleven pairs of guarded eyes bore into me. Their gaze crawls across me like spiders and sets me on edge.

"The princess sailing off with the foreigner is a small hiccup in our plans, but not something to worry about at the moment." I take a small swig from a water flask at my hip to stall for time. My own doubts about the princess returning have been nagging at me like ticks on a bitch. "If the time comes, we will discuss plans to carry out in the event she absconds and abandons her people to their fate. Right now, we need to focus on the task at hand."

"I will gladly take another assignment, Boar." Spaniel grins enticingly at me. Like somehow that's going to be what convinces me to send him back out. "There are a few lovely ladies out there I didn't have the pleasure of – would you stop that!?"

Wolf bares his teeth menacingly. "When you stop acting like a prick and take this seriously I will."

"I think Bull is better suited to the job at hand." Good gods just let them stop bickering. I want to go to bed.

"What d'you want me to do, boss?" Bull asks disinterestedly, scraping dirt out from under his nails with a small knife.

"We need to start leaving bodies."

It goes so quiet you could hear an ant sneeze. I have Bull's full attention now. His thin lips distort over blocky teeth as he smiles and leans expectantly forward.

"How do you want it done? Poison? Enemy daggers carving ancient runic texts into their bodies? Dropping dead from natural causes? Oh, I know! Keep your wives and daughters inside because a raging lunatic will have his way with them and then split them open neck to navel for the dogs to finish off."

My stomach drops out in unease. Bull doesn't often say much, but when he does it's always unpleasant. How he's the son of one of the high priestesses and a nobleman will always be a mystery to me.

"Damn, Bull, you know ancient runic texts? I didn't even know you could read!"

Spaniel's tittering is cut short this time by a dagger nicking his ear and slicing neatly through a curl before embedding itself in the back of his chair. He clamps his hand to his ear with a squeak, pulling a monogrammed handkerchief from his pocket to staunch the bleeding. Serves the asshole right.

I pinch the bridge of my nose. The damn headache I always get from these meetings is slowly latching on with a vengeance.

"We're going to do the best of both worlds. Spaniel you and Bull will go out together. Stick your prick in whoever you want regardless of their interest. When he's done, Bull, you can have your fun and cut them open and leave runes on their dead flesh. People will panic more if they think magic is coming back."

"Where do you want us to start?" Bull is completely focused on the task at hand, fingering the daggers on the table in front of him.

I gesture dismissively. "Wherever. Commoners are all the same really. Just make sure you don't stay in one place too long and get around the city. More bodies mean more panic and more panic means more mistakes by the incompetents in charge."

A sharp whistle from the door signals the end to our meeting and the lordlings pull their cloaks around themselves, disappearing off into the gloom in twos and threes. Only Wolf stays behind, watching me warily as he pulls his own cloak tight around him.

"Are you truly not worried about the princess abandoning Sephiroth and staying in Korala with the foreigner?"

I contemplate the man before me. How much should I tell him? How much *can* I tell him? The last thing I want, or need, is for him to turn around and sow his own seeds of distrust among the group. If I don't have their loyalty, then there is no way for this to work. I suppose a little honesty may not be the worst idea given the circumstances. It will at least give me an idea of where his loyalties lie.

"Of course I'm worried. Our bond is still strong, but it's not what it used to be. There's doubt there now."

"You sure she will join our cause when it's time to bring her in?"

"She'll join. No matter what."

Wolf studies me for a few moments and then heads off. I slump back in my chair. Things have gotten complicated and the chances of us needing an alternate plan are growing more likely every day. Propping my elbows on the table, I lean forward and massage my aching temples. Gods above I need a drink!

Chapter 19

In Which Goodbyes are Exchanged

Nora

The morning dawns overcast with a slight chill to the air, a reminder of the cooler weather lurking just out of sight hanging ever present. I'm restless and unsettled. Awake far earlier than I really want or need to be, I wander aimlessly around my rooms waiting for Abigail to arrive.

Since the disaster that was our wedding night, Alon remains in the honeymoon suite while I use a set of rooms across the hall. I had wanted to just take up residence in my old rooms, but Mother forbade it. She claimed the servants would talk too much and we couldn't have the world thinking we had a rift between us already. Honestly, I was just glad she had given in and allowed me to have my own rooms, although I bet it's because she was worried I would try and smother Alon in his sleep. Not that that would have done any good anyway...

Flopping down in the chair in front of the mirrored dressing table, the morning light flashes off the sunflower necklace. How did I forget I was still wearing it? Reaching back, I gently unclasp my birthday present and hold it out to study it closer. It was clear Alon had talked with the palace jewelers — I would recognize their skilled handiwork anywhere and Thomas' signature swirls were etched among the gold — but I had never seen them create anything quite like this. It's dainty and sturdy at the same time. Mother favors silver to gold so most of their designs heavily feature the icy metal.

I wonder if Alon designed this himself...a strange thing to do given the circumstances, but I guess stranger things could happen. I ponder it for a few more moments. The necklace truly is beautiful. If I'm being honest with myself, it's something that I would cherish under possibly different circumstances. Although I can't deny that it already means more to me than I care to admit.

Abigail sweeps in and visibly jumps when she sees that I am already up. "Beg pardon, Your Highness." She bobs a quick, although slightly awkward, curtsy. "If I'd known you were awake I would have come sooner."

"Don't worry, Abigail. I just needed some time with my thoughts."

Abigail's eyes drop to the sunflower pendant swaying gently in front of me and a knowing look crosses her face. "Of course, Your Highness. I have instructed water to be brought up for a bath and breakfast to be brought in shortly. We shall have you ready for travel in no time."

I grimace briefly at the thought. While I have always wanted to travel outside of Sephiroth, I am not the biggest fan of traveling over water. Mother and Father took us all for a short visit to the shore when I was sixteen and Ren insisted we try sailing. It was one of the most unpleasant afternoons of my life and that includes my wedding day. Hopefully being on a larger ship instead of a small sailboat will make the journey more tolerable.

Father has commissioned a small group of ships to go with us on our journey. I believe they will be remaining in Korala as part of the new navy that were part of the negotiations for our marriage. Father and Mother decided to remain in Sephiroth, but Alon and I will be traveling with King Hemi and Queen Ululani as well as one of his brothers on the ship they sailed over for the wedding on.

The rest of the brothers plan to remain at court here in Sephiroth although I can't figure out why. Being at court is stuffy and too many rules dictate what you can and can't do, but I suppose them being men means there are more exceptions made for them.

I bathe quickly and devour the breakfast of warm rolls and cream that had been sent up. Cook even managed to find some strawberries from the hot houses and smoked sausages to round out the meal. The heady scents bring back memories of childhood mornings spent fighting with my brothers over who got to eat the last roll with cream. Father usually settled the arguments by eating it himself and declaring it tax for having to listen to us.

Maids bustle in and out under the watchful eye of Abigail. They finish their minor packing and begin to carry my various trunks and parcels out of the room. Without knowing what kind of weather to expect on our journey and in Korala, Abigail decided it was better to bring everything and anything deemed even remotely important.

The last thing to be packed, so to speak, is me. Abigail helps me into the traveling suit she had prepared and fusses around making last minute adjustments while I study myself in the mirror. She had really outdone herself this time. A soft tunic of deep purple parted elegantly around my thighs to reveal cream-colored breeches made of silk and wool spun together. My feet are clad in lightweight boots that hug my calves, somehow being both incredibly sturdy and flexible at the same time. A delicate summer wool shawl of pale gray wraps around my shoulders like a hug. Warm and sturdy, it's clear my outfit can withstand riding or sailing.

"It needs a little something," Abigail murmurs absently, rifling through the jewelry that was not packed. "Aha!"

Reaching around, she fastens Alon's sunflower pendant around my neck. The delicate flower settles against the tunic and looks like I am carrying my own personal sunbeam.

"Perfect!" Abigail brushes a few wrinkles out of the shawl. "Now we must be going, Your Highness. We don't want to be late."

I step out into the hallway at the same time Alon is leaving his own rooms. He looks good. In a completely annoying and always has to have the last word kind of way. The kind of good that's going to make the next however many weeks of my life a living hell. Oh boy.

His gaze rakes over me from the simple chignon on my head to the very tips of my boots. His eyes light up like fireflies when he sees I'm wearing his gift and he winks. Fighting not to roll my eyes, I politely nod good morning and stalk down the hallway. I need to find Teddy. We promised to see each other before I leave and I don't have much time left.

Teddy is in the stables inspecting a horse his father is considering purchasing. He bows briefly to me as I pass, as is appropriate, and I can feel his eyes lingering on me. I wink and slip up the stairs to the haylofts.

Settling amongst the bales in the back corner, I watch the light from the cathedral windows flicker through the rafters. Many thought Father was ridiculous for installing such large windows on either end of the barn, but they have been crucial in helping ventilate the lofts and stables during the warmer months and ensure the hay stays dry. The last thing we need is another fire.

It's not long before I can hear Teddy's familiar steps echoing up the stairs. His boots rustle softly as he climbs through the bales and pulls me into his arms to embrace me. We fall together and I try to sink into his depths, to lose myself in the feeling of being near him, but I can't get my mind to settle. It keeps wandering to the journey ahead, to the answers I need to find, and to the annoying prickling that has taken up residence in the space behind my heart.

Teddy can sense my distraction and does what he can to pull my attention back to him. To us. To now. Unfortunately, his lips are not enough to pull me away and I absently shrug off his touch.

He gives up, stretching out next to me in the hay and watches the sunlight and haymotes floating through the air. I know I need to go, but even now I don't want to leave. Teddy is my home. He's safe. He is the consistency I crave in my life. Especially right now.

"I have something for you."

I lift my head off Teddy's shoulder and eye the small leather pouch resting in his outstretched palm.

"You didn't have to get me anything."

"I know, but it was your birthday." He kisses my forehead gently. "Turning twenty-one is a big deal. If you want, think of this as a way to remember me while you're off visiting unknown island nations and falling in love with the locals."

The words are flippant. Loose. He's trying to hide how he really feels about this journey, but we both know what local he's talking about.

"No local could ever tempt me away from you." I peck him on the cheek.

Teddy's ears redden slightly, and he grins. "Here. Open it."

Sitting upright, I accept the pouch and carefully pour the contents out into my palm. A bracelet and ring clink gently together before coming to rest on my outstretched hand. The light glints off the silver bands and they feel cold to my touch.

They are clearly meant to be a matched set. Delicate silver bands are woven into a simple swirling pattern. Small inset purple tourmaline and tanzanite give the appearance of tiny lavender and lilac flowers growing amongst the silver. They are works of art, but I can't help feeling like they pale in comparison to the sunflower resting against my chest.

"They're your favorite, right? You always stop to smell the lilacs in the spring when we go out walking."

I'm not sure what to say so I just nod and try to smile. He's just distracted. He knows they're not my favorite flowers...right? Teddy must have read something in my face, his own expression becoming cloudy and guarded.

"Look I know it's not as fancy as that —" he gestures dismissively to the sunflower "— but I hope you like them. If not, I can get something else."

I give myself a mental shake and clasp my hands to his cheeks, forcing him to look me in the eye.

"Teddy, they're beautiful." The words feel strange in my mouth. Like someone else is saying them. "Thank you."

"Come back to me."

Teddy's eyes are soft pools of liquid stars. I fall into them, feeling their warmth surround me like a hug.

"Always," I promise.

He smiles and slips the jewelry onto my right hand. They look cold and out of place next to my clothing. Like something my mother would wear. I hide my discomfort as best I can. They are wonderful presents, and he worked hard to design them with me in mind. That must count for something right?

Kissing him softly one last time, I murmur goodbye and slip out of the lofts to the front of the palace. I can't avoid my fate any longer. It's time to truly start my journey, to find the answers I need. To ensure Teddy and I will be safe.

Chapter 20

In Which a Storm Arises

Alon

While life at sea isn't quite home, not anymore anyway, it is the closest thing I have to a home away from home. I rise each morning with the sun and spend my days on deck or in the rigging. Our crew are happy to be heading back towards the warmer shores of Korala. The men sing as they work and I join in most days, lifting my voice with theirs as we go about daily tasks.

Mama and Baba spend much of their time on the upper deck on the specialty platform they had constructed. It allows them to be part of the hustle and bustle of ship life without being in the way of the crew. They spend most days reading, planning with the captain, and discussing various topics from astronomy to which cousin Mama last heard from before leaving Sephiroth. The balance of life slowly starts to shift back towards something I recognize, something I am comfortable with.

The first several weeks of our journey, Nora remained below. She had tried to pretend that she was unaffected by the sea, but after showing up for dinner the first night looking positively green around the gills, she had admitted her sailing experience was minimal and not something she remembered fondly. Mama had sent her to bed and made sure to check on her every day.

Thankfully, our ship is built with comfortable lodgings for nine. Nora and I have adjoining, although separate, rooms and no one seems to bat an eye. Every morning, I bring Nora warm biscuits, jam, and tea and sit with her for as long as she tolerates me. Some days she's too sick to do anything other than stare out the windows and ignore me, but on other days she feels strong enough to curse my presence and demand me gone. Those days are always the most fun. Eventually, her stomach settles. She slowly starts to venture out to the rest of the ship but rarely allows me to accompany her.

Nora does grant me the privilege of acting as her attendant once – the first day she felt well enough to leave her cabin for a grand tour of the ship. I could tell during our walk that she had opinions about various aspects of life at sea, but she decided to keep them to herself. Whether that's for her benefit or mine it's hard to say. Now that Nora is more comfortable moving topside, she often joins Mama and Baba on their platform and spends most of her time reading or needlepointing something.

Cove and I spar together to stay in practice. Sparring on land is one thing but sparring while on the water is another beast entirely. You must be in tune with the sea and her movements, to be able to predict where she and the ship will go next. If you can't, then you're more likely to get in your own way and give your enemy the advantage.

After a few days of watching, Nora asks to join in with us, but she still refuses to spar with me directly. She prefers working with Cove or one of the crew as they teach her the basics of how to fight while at sea. I don't take it personally. Nora will come around when she's ready. Spirits are high, the sea is calm, and life moves steadily onwards just like always.

••• ☽ • ◯ • ☾ •••

Barely after the halfway mark of our journey, the weather takes a dramatic turn. Clouds roll in thick banks across the sky, blocking out the sun and threatening rain. Fear begins to slink its way from my stomach up my spine, and I spend most days with a murky feeling I can't seem to shake. It's storm season in Korala. We always knew there was a chance that we would run into inclement weather on our return journey, but the fear of actually meeting a storm hangs over us all. There are few things as dangerous as a storm cell on the open ocean.

The bank of clouds refuses to lift as the days pass. I watch them carefully, trying to convince myself that everything is fine. Mama says I get as prickly as a sea urchin when I'm scared, and it takes all my self-control to not give in to the bristly feeling in my bones. Instead, I try to immerse myself more in ship life. I redouble my efforts to engage with Nora and talk to her, but even with the restrictions of the ship she somehow manages to find new and inventive ways to avoid me.

The further along we go, the darker and thicker the clouds. The air becomes heavy. Charged. I can't shake the tendrils of fear that stroke the back of my neck and whisper in my ears. It leaves me off balance and distracted, consuming my focus.

Baba spends his time on deck now watching the weather, conferring with the captain, and issuing commands to be relayed back to the rest of the ships in our convoy. The Sephiroth sailors have never seen a Koralan storm and Baba wants to make sure they are as well prepared as possible. We can't afford to lose any of them.

My discomfort reaches such a peak that I retire to my cabin early in the afternoon and remain there through the evening meal. Fear constricts my stomach as the winds grow and the sea tosses and churns like water about to boil in a kettle. I don't trust myself to keep my agitation in check around others, so avoidance is the safest choice.

Thunder rumbles overhead and lightning calls back in response, the hot white light illuminating the familiar cabin around me. With each crash my fear surges, with each flash it claws up my throat and into my mouth until I can taste nothing but the sharp metallic bite of desperation. Below, the ship rocks and creaks with the violence that only an angry sea can bring.

My back is pressed against the wall, knees clutched to my chest, as I gasp my way through some breathing exercises. I have to try and get my breathing steady. My gasping breaths drive the erratic pounding in my chest in a flood throughout my body. No, no, no I need to calm it down. *Calm down!* The longer the storm wracks our ship the tighter my fear closes its fist around me.

The waves grow more violent, the pitch of the ship harder to manage. I slide back and forth across the smoothed planks of the floor as they move beneath me. The thunder grows deeper, the lightning brighter, the fear stronger.

My heart refuses to calm its rhythm. The beats echo in my head like a scattering drum, pushing me further into a panicked shell of myself. My lungs can't expand completely. There's no air. *I'm drowning.*

Sweat beads across my face and I desperately try to move, but my body is heavy. Weighed down. Hopeless.

Gasping, I pull myself to the bed and drag the blanket off, trying to wrap it around myself with useless fumbling hands. My fingers won't bend. The movement of the ship sends me careening towards the wall and I let myself be carried. I wedge further into the space between my bunk and a small table bolted to the floor. *Breathe dammit!*

I can't breathe. Air in. Air out. Legs are numb. Water everywhere. I'm alone. Lost. Drowning.

$\cdots\;\supset\;\cdot\;\bigcirc\;\cdot\;\subset\;\cdots$

The voice is soft. Gentle. It meticulously wades through the fog in my head, dusting the cobwebs and tidying the floor. Gradually, I return to myself.

My heart is slower, my breathing more even. Warm hands are wrapped around mine and the rhythm of the ship has quieted. The sea is still angry, but she is no longer threatening to pull us down to her depths.

My eyelids are inflexible and stubborn. Forcing them open, I find Nora sitting in front of me. It's *her* hands around mine, *her* warmth bringing me back to myself. Her eyes are closed, deep purple crescent moons beneath, and she's absently singing a funny little song about a chicken.

I inhale deeply, relishing in the unrestricted feeling of bringing air into my lungs. Nora must have heard me inhale because her eyes flash open and snap to mine. There's no denying the concern and fear ringing the irises. She stops singing and the low rumblings of the thunder flood back in like unwelcome guests. Nora just sits there, watching me. Studying me the same way I have seen her evaluate a painting or listen to her father explain something.

"Why are you here?" My voice is throaty, cracked. I swallow hard. "And why are you singing about a chicken?"

"It was the only thing I could think of."

A small smile turns up the corners of her mouth. She is entirely too enticing. *If only she'd lean in a little closer, I could –*

Hold on now we're not going there. Now is not the time and it is definitely not the place to be thinking things like that. I need to get out of here first.

"Can you…?"

Thankfully, Nora doesn't require more of an explanation. She scootches back, creating distance between us. I squirm and wriggle, but nothing allows me to extract my body from the space it now occupies. I had somehow managed to wedge my almost six-foot frame into the not quite three-foot space between my bunk and table.

"Maybe a shoehorn?" Nora suggests drollfully.

Her mouth quirks again, eyes glinting with humor. She's trying to hide it, but I know her well enough now to know where to look for it. She giggles, pressing a hand to her mouth to stifle it. I fix her with a look, but I'm sure it's ruined by my own grin splitting my face in two.

"Can you help me please?"

Nora contemplates me for a few moments before taking my hands again and bracing her feet against the wooden planks of the floor. She pulls gently at first, and then much harder when she realizes it's going to take some oomph to get me out. My prison doesn't want to let me go.

Little by little, I am dragged forward until I pop out faster than a cork from a bottle. We slam together and sprawl across the floor in a heap to the opposite wall, somehow getting wrapped in the blanket I had abandoned earlier. Stunned silence lasts for only a moment before we dissolve into peals of laughter. Nora's ribs shake alongside mine as we lay tangled together, her hair in my face and my arms around her waist.

We settle into an affable quiet. Untangling my legs first from the blanket and then from around Nora, I help her to her feet and we both sway briefly as we readjust to the motion of the ship. Nora folds the blanket and tosses it on my bunk before she unceremoniously plops down on top of it.

I opt for the chair next to the table. It's only then that I catch sight of the covered tray in the little hollowed out groove in the tabletop. The faint aroma of Cook's brown gravy permeates the space. An embarrassingly loud grumble from my stomach practically drowns out the lingering thunder.

"Did you bring me dinner?"

"Yes."

"Thank you." I lift the lid and breathe deeply. Potatoes, chicken, and carrots swim together in a veritable ocean of brown gravy. My favorite. "And thank you for...you know."

A faint crimson colors Nora's cheeks, and she looks away quickly. Her curiosity gets the better of her, though, because I catch her watching me again as I tuck into the food. Even lukewarm it's still delicious.

"Does that happen often?"

"Reliably three times a day, but I do love a good snack in between meals."

Nora eyes me unamused. "You know what I mean."

I take a few moments to consider my answer. "Only when I'm on the water during a storm."

"Why?"

The question sits between us, an uninvited third guest to our small party of two. Should I tell her? *Can* I tell her? No. Not yet. Not like this.

"I'm sorry, Nora." I smile hesitantly, trying to soften the blow of refusal." I can't tell you that. Not yet anyway. Someday I will. I promise."

Her brows raise. Understandably, she's skeptical and I can't say I blame her. If I had seen the same thing she did, I'd want answers too. And quickly.

I watch the internal war waging behind her eyes. What am I going to do if she demands an answer? *Please don't make me tell you right now.* I can see the moment she decides not to push further. Her eyes quiet and her eyebrows unkink. Nodding, she stands.

"I should head to bed. It's late."

I catch her hand as she moves past me. She pauses, hovering at my shoulder.

"Thank you, Nora."

She squeezes my hand once and then moves to the connecting door to our cabins, slipping through without a sound. As if she is nothing more than a phantom, disappearing as quickly as she seemed to have appeared in the first place.

I finish my dinner in silence. Even the thunder has decided it's time to move on to better waters. There's a nagging feeling that I'm missing something, but I can't figure out what. It's not until later, tucked safely in bed with the lights doused, that I realize what it is. That was the first time since we met that Nora has willingly initiated contact with me.

Chapter 21

In Which Home is Found

Nora

"Land ho!"

The call echoes throughout the decks like a breath of fresh air. Alon and I lock eyes over our breakfast dishes and make a mad dash for the stairs. I want to see Korala just as much as he does. Unfortunately, Alon's longer legs and better balance means he's able to get on deck faster than my own clumsy self.

I catch up to him at the railing, out of breath and still slightly unsteady. Even after so much time at sea you'd think I'd be more comfortable with the rocking motion of the ship, but the natural balance with which Alon and Cove navigate the decks continues to elude me. It's clear that if I want to improve my sea-legs I need to spend more time at sea and that's honestly one of the last things I want to do.

All around us, fishing boats full of Koralans yell greetings and marvel at the accompanying warships Father sent for the new navy. I can't help but notice their clothes are well made, if very plain. The people themselves look tired in their good spirits. Most are adults, but there are some older children that are all elbows and knees and shoulders poking out of their thin frames. Alon calls out to his people, greeting some by name, and waves as we join their group.

Korala itself rises before us like a stately gentleman at an important luncheon. Dignified mountains line the far horizon before giving way to gently rolling hills. Tall cliffs sweep around the sides of the island like a stiff collar, gradually sloping down to the bustling seaport. Sanded beaches ring the base of the cliffs and, in the distance, I see children and dogs running along them.

Set back from the port, an elegant and simple palace nestles between the hills to keep watch over its subjects with care and attention. Its slightly squat stature makes it look like a mother hen surveying its brood from her nest. Everywhere, bright roof tiles glint in the sunlight and hint at what's to come.

"Can you swim?"

The question startles me. "What?"

"Can you swim?"

There's a mischievous look in Alon's eyes that I've never seen before. It lights up his whole face and I can see what he looked like as a fresh-faced young boy many years before.

"Ye-es...why?"

"Do you trust me?"

The hand offered to me is paired with a smile so genuine it almost hurts. The funny thing is that I do. Trust him, that is. Despite not ever really spending time with him or knowing much about him, even after Alon's best attempts, I do trust him. Maybe it's because I saw how vulnerable he was through the storm. Or maybe it's simply because he listens to what I tell him and isn't pushing for anything more than I'm willing to give. Regardless, I do trust him.

I take Alon's hand, his smile glinting mischievously, and in one smooth motion he pulls me up and over the railing on the side of the deck. A shriek tears from my throat and my free hand desperately claws the air to try and slow my fall as we plunge downwards. My scream is cut short as water surrounds me in a swirling confusion of blue and green bubbles. Alon squeezes my hand, and half drags me back to the surface. He laughs as I come up, sputtering and indignant.

"A warning would have been appreciated!"

I huff seawater from my nose and mouth and shake it from my ears. Not for the first time, I mumble a quiet prayer of thanks that Abigail was waiting until we touched down in Korala before breaking out the court clothing and unpacking all the dresses we had brought. My breeches and tunic may be completely soaked through and probably ruined by the saltwater, but there's no denying that pants make everything easier. Especially while at sea. Not to mention, I'm pretty sure the excess fabric of the skirts and petticoats would have made me too heavy to stay afloat.

"And ruin the surprise? Never!" Alon lets out a triumphant crow that echoes among the boats above us. Cove calls in return while he stands on the stern and waves alongside King Hemi and Queen Ululani. "Come on!"

Alon strikes out in smooth strokes while I awkwardly try to follow. While I do know how to swim, it's one of the few pastimes Mother had put her foot down about and restricted. She had deemed it unlady-like and too dangerous for long periods of time. I was taught the basics, as were my brothers, but I wasn't allowed to spend much time conditioning and don't consider myself a particularly strong swimmer. Samael was by far the best swimmer out of all of us. He's a natural, spending many afternoons out in the ponds or the fishing lake even now.

I do my best to keep up, but without the strength and practice I lag behind. Thankfully, Alon notices I'm having trouble before I drown. He doubles back, slowing his own pace to keep up with me. He even tows me around several of the boats to make sure I don't get too close. All around us the fishermen and sailors laugh and whistle, pressing the heels of their right hand to their foreheads and then gesturing at us.

"Why do they do that?" I awkwardly brush my wet hair out of my eyes and clumsily follow Alon around another boat. "The gesturing, I mean."

"It's a way of greeting each other. Our way of saying we were thinking of you on your journey, and we welcome you home."

With Alon's help, we reach the wave break quickly and ride the tides the rest of the way to the sand. The children that had been playing on the beach race towards us and surround Alon, clambering for his attention. He shoots me an apologetic look but allows himself to be enveloped in their noise and chaos.

Honestly, I'm just glad to have solid ground beneath me again. At least, I *think* it's solid ground. The sand slips and heaves beneath my feet the same way the deck of the boat moves on the sea. *Gods damn it all.*

I stand for a few minutes, hands on my hips, and let everything settle so it's no longer moving. The air is salty and vibrant, the feeling of it moving in and out of my lungs absolutely delicious. I'd forgotten how it feels to really breathe after swimming.

Carefully untangling myself from the outskirts of the crowd, I climb further up the beach where the hard packed sand turns softer. Large rocks pepper the shores, creating a maze that stretches to the base of the cliffs. They've been worn smooth by the high tides and soak in the heat from the sun above until they're warm to the touch.

I find a large one that has just the faintest dip in the center and settle down, basking in the warmth radiating from the stone. With the sunshine above me and the heat from the rock beneath, my eyelids begin to droop lower and lower...

• • •) • ◯ • (• • •

A wet, slobbery, *something* rubs across my cheek and startles me from my nap. I open my eyes and then snap them shut against the blinding sun that sends stars flashing behind my eyelids. A funny chorus of giggles and shushes wash over me.

Rubbing my hand across my face, I sit up and carefully open my eyes, shading them from the worst of the light. I'm surrounded by the gaggle of children from before and one noticeably happy looking mutt that had presumably just had his nose wiped across my face. How charming. Alon stands at the back of the throng, a sheepish look on his face.

" 'S not safe to sleep in the sun," a small girl missing her two front teeth pronounces. "You can get dee-hi-dray-ted."

She says the last word carefully. Like it's a brand new sweet she's rolling around on her tongue and savoring the flavor.

"You'll have to pardon my ignorance." I smile at her reassuringly. "I was waiting for you all to finish and this rock is just so warm and cozy."

They dissolve into giggles again as I dramatically collapse back onto the rock and pretend to fall asleep again. Like the idea of a rock being cozy is the silliest thing they've ever heard.

"Come on, everyone," Alon says as he pushes through the gathered crowd and offers me a hand. "Let's show Princess Nora our home."

I brush past his proffered hand, opting instead to scoot myself to the edge and carefully make my own way back to the sand. The soft grains at the base of the rock make the dismount a touch hard, but I manage to not to make too big a fool of myself. I should probably have just accepted his help, but that stubborn streak has kicked back in again, and I don't want to make him think anything will happen because of his good manners.

As soon as I am upright, it's like the calm spell shatters with the wind. Children and dogs run every which way and the little girl with the gap-toothed smile grins and flees with the rest. I can't help smiling at the chaos and follow the herd, running and yelling with them as we scare gulls and chase the waves from the sand.

The closer we get to the port, the more activity surrounds us. It doesn't take long before we are lost in the confusion of the quay with sailors, merchants, and pickpockets just the same as back home in Sephiroth. I inhale deeply. The smells of salt, spices, sweat, and oils are undercut with a richness I've never experienced before. It fills my nose and my chest and something loosens within me. Like my soul has finally found what it has been yearning for all this time.

Alon begins playing tour guide but gives up as I keep wandering away. There's so much to see and do and taste and smell and I keep getting distracted, my focus not able to remain on something for too long before being caught by the next shiny thing. He trails along behind, greeting people and making sure I don't find myself somewhere I shouldn't be.

At first glance, Korala seems like an unassuming old town. You have to look closer to get it to reveal its secrets to you like a new lover. And look closer I do. From the brightly patterned roof tiles that gently curve upwards on the ends ("the better to shed water during storm season and keep evil spirits from landing on your roof."), to the masterful architecture ("these were created by Isolde Amaranth. She even designed buildings in Sephiroth!"), to the eclectic collection of houses and businesses all crammed together, Korala burns with a spark and life I have never experienced back home. In all my travels throughout Sephiroth I have never felt this type of energy, this passion, that moves through everything. Korala feels *alive*. Its rhythm mimicking the ocean, creating a heartbeat easily detected just below the surface.

The church bells jauntily announce the two o'clock hour as we duck into Alon's favorite bakery, the Crusty Loaf. The woman working the counter is overcome when she sees Alon. They jabber away for several minutes while she prepares a wicker basket for us to take along with us when we leave. I half listen to their conversation, more interested in surveying the crammed cases in front of us. With each new pastry or savory pasty I see, my stomach lets out a grumbling cry of want. Breakfast was way too long ago.

With many thanks and promises to return soon, Alon peaks inside the basket and loudly declares it fit for a king. A beautiful pink tinges the woman's cheeks as she waves us back out into the afternoon sun.

Alon leads the way through a few twisting streets until we reach an open plaza. Merchants line the outside ring of businesses and spread their wares on blankets and in baskets in front of their stores, calling loudly to the crowds to try and get them to stop and purchase something. We thread our way through the throngs to the very heart of the space.

I barely stifle my gasp when I see it. Made of white stone that glows in the afternoon sun, the fountain is oval at its base instead of the traditional round shape I am most familiar with. While most fountains in Sephiroth have cherubs or warriors as their central figure, this one has a woman. She is exquisitely carved of the same white stone as the base, but I have never seen a sculptor able to create such emotion and life from a lifeless being.

She balances perfectly on one leg, the other stretching behind her in a gentle arabesque. Her arms are flung above her head with abandon, hair swirling around her face and falling down her back. Joy and fearlessness are carved in her expression with masterful strokes. Water bubbles up from her palms and makes her look as if she is dancing in a rainshower. The afternoon sunlight catches the fine mist surrounding the statue and rainbows dance alongside her, wavering and ethereal. I would be content to sit here and watch the fountain all afternoon.

My grumbling stomach demands another course of fate, however. Alon settles along the side of the fountain, popping open the basket. He places several bottles of a slightly murky liquid directly in the water and then spreads out a feast of braided bread, dried meats, and some sort of fried dough ball.

I plop down on the opposite side of our impromptu picnic, and we eat in companionable silence. The bread and meats are delicious, but it's the dough balls that are the true star of the show. Deliciously soft and buttery, they're rolled in a cinnamon sugar mixture that's sweet and spicy. It takes way too much self control not to shove the entire plate in my mouth.

"What are these?" I ask around a mouthful.

"They're called *malasadas*. Here, this one's filled with coconut cream."

I thought the plain *malasada* was everything I'd hoped for, but the filled coconut cream makes a compelling argument for top spot. It bursts on my tongue, a lazy river of cool sweetness flooding my mouth. I polish off two more before Alon has a chance to steal them away.

The one thing I definitely don't care for is the drink Alon brought. The slightly murky liquid is sour and tastes strongly of lemons and citrus. Alon dissolves into barely contained mirth at my puckered mouth. I thrust the bottle back at him, trying to keep from coughing.

Thankfully, he doesn't push me to finish it. Instead, he swaps it with a flask of chilled water that had been cooling in the fountain as well. I accept the water gratefully, downing another *malasada* to get the taste out of my mouth.

We sit and eat and talk and eat and watch the merchants sell their wares and eat some more. When our lunch is no more than crumbs and wishful dreams, Alon disappears and comes back with two bowls of shaved ice. I can't decide which one I want so we split them, swapping the bowls back and forth as we go. The syrups render my fingers so sticky they're practically useless. The delicious and mellow flavors of mango, strawberry, and coconut dance across my tongue in a spirited jig.

My empty stomach finally satiated, my limbs stretch lazily along the side of the fountain. Merchants have begun to pack up their wares in the lengthening shadows, calling to each other as they close down their shops for the day. Alon gathers up the few remnants from lunch, returning them to the basket, and extends a hand in invitation. Pulling me back to my feet, we set off for the palace on the hill.

To call it a palace, though, is generous. It really is more of an elevated manor house, grand and stately with just the right amount of auspiciousness to hint at its importance. It's something Mother and Father would have deemed worthy only for a summer house.

My thoughts flit briefly to Teddy and a pang of guilt climbs up my spine. I haven't thought of him once in several days. I should write him a letter. I *will* write him a letter. Just as soon as I'm shown to my rooms. He'll want to know everything about this place. Maybe one day I can even bring him. I just know he would love it here as much as I do.

The cobblestone road leading from the port is well kept and tidy. Alon greets people as we make our way along it like they're old friends. For all I know maybe they are.

The climb to the palace is steeper than I expected. By the time we reach the top, I'm mildly winded, my breath huffing out of me in noticeable bursts. Not enough to be completely embarrassing, but enough to put me on edge. Nothing is worse than feeling weak and out of control. Those weeks of sea sickness have definitely taken their toll on me. I'll need to spend some extra time conditioning to start building my strength back. Now that I'm here, and Mother is not, it would also be a good idea for me to practice my swimming.

So lost in my own thoughts, I don't even notice when we crest the front steps, Alon waiting for me to take the lead. I pause just outside the door and take a few steadying breaths. I'm about to see Alon's home for the first time. It's intimidating and overwhelming. It's almost like Alon can read my mind because he looks at me reassuringly.

"Ready?"

We step through the doors together.

Chapter 22

In Which Futures are Read

Alan

Watching Nora take in my childhood home is infectious. She inspects every little detail of the front hall with such intense curiosity that I can't help but try and see the world through her eyes. With fresh sight, I revel in the understated grandeur of my home.

While not nearly as fancy as the palace in Sephiroth, the Manor House has many elegant and understated touches woven throughout in subtle ways. From the seashell patterns in the tiles on the floor to the echoing shape in the carved plaster above our heads, each piece was lovingly found, designed, created, and placed just so to maximize the natural beauty and balance of the space. After all, the sea herself is balance. I used to think she was true beauty as well, but it's clear to me now that another contender has joined the race.

I give Nora the grand tour and make sure to show her all the things I think she will love the most – the rainbow seashells in the library, the koi pond and fountain in the back, my favorite painting of disheveled chickens by the kitchens. She takes in each new discovery with the excitement and inquisitiveness of a child.

With each utterance of joy, my heart grows that much larger, the space behind it continuing to expand to make room for her. There is no doubt in my mind that I utterly in love with this woman. She is the only one I want to spend the rest of my life with. If only I could get her to feel the same way about me....

Mama finds us in an upper alcove studying the ships in bottles Baba and *Tutu Kane* used to build together. Well, Nora is inspecting the ships. I'm inspecting Nora.

"There you two are! Nice trip through the port?"

"It was absolutely lovely." Nora turns from the ships to face Mama. With her rosy cheeks and bright eyes, she radiates happiness and the faintest hint of a sunburn. "Alon showed me this beautiful fountain that looked like a woman dancing."

"That's one of my favorites too. Said to have been brought to Korala many years ago as a gift for the reigning queen to try and win her heart and her hand." Mama's eyes gleam. "Follow me. I want to show you to your rooms."

Nora glances briefly over her shoulder to make sure I'm following, and we both trail after Mama back through the house. She leads us to the family quarters, chattering the whole time about different rooms and paintings we pass, before stopping in front of the Sunset Rooms. Throwing open the door, she steps back and lets Nora walk in first. Nora audibly gasps and freezes for a moment just inside the doorway as she takes it all in.

The early evening sun streams through high arched windows that overlook the port and the ocean. Someone had been in before us and opened all the windows in preparation. The sea breeze capers around the room like an old friend, teasing Nora's hair into whirlwinds. The air is heavy with the briny smell of the water and the pearlescent pink walls almost make it feel like you're stepping into a clamshell.

Nora stands in the center of the room, turning slowly as she inspects the space. Her shoes sink into the soft throw carpets scattered on the floor, her footsteps muffled as she explores the dried corals and sea glass decorating the windowsills and bedside tables. She eventually comes to roost in front of the windows, hands clasped under her chin, and surveys the fishing boats slowly beginning to make their way back to port.

I settle on the side of the armchair in the corner nearest the door and just watch as Nora explores. I crave her wonder. She is able to experience my home with the freshness of new eyes, to see it as a child would see something new and exciting. I'm jealous.

Mama follows us inside and gently closes the door behind her. "I know you two are working through some things," she says diplomatically. Nora turns to face her, her features guarded. "For appearances sake we needed to put you two together in the same room. However, this room has a secret."

Mama skirts around the large four poster canopy bed to the far side and gently nudges the bedside table out of the way. Lifting a tiny latch, she swings open a hidden door that leads to another room. Nora and I crowd behind her, both too curious to keep a respectable distance. While not as grand as the bedroom we stand in, the room beyond the door is decorated in a matching style with a bed, dresser, table, and washbasin tucked inside.

"This set of rooms is one we have not used since I came to Korala." Mama walks wistfully into the room and settles onto the end of the bed, lost in her memories. "I slept in the larger room there and the chaperone my mother had sent to accompany me slept in here. It seemed prudent for Alon to sleep in here and Nora you will remain in the larger room." Mama levels me with a look. "You will be responsible for maintaining your own rooms, however, because the maids will not be cleaning up after you."

"Yes, Mama." I kiss her cheek. "Thank you."

Her face breaks out into a smile. "Good. You two settle in. Dinner will be in an hour on the southern veranda. Oh! Before I forget, Nora, dearest, this came for you."

Mama passes over a carefully folded letter and Nora's face lights up like the sunrise. I can tell by the crooked handwriting on the front it's from Teddy. *Ugh.* Jealousy surges within me again, although this one is much uglier than my feelings of envy from before. I am not let it win today, though. After all, Nora is here in Korala. With me.

Mama bustles back into the hallway and carefully swings the door closed behind her again. Nora retreats into the larger bedroom to read her letter, leaning close to the windows to catch the sunlight. Surveying the little room, I flop down on the bed and sprawl out across the blankets. Not quite as comfortable as my cot in the loft, but it will have to do. Add in that Nora is significantly less than icy towards me and I can't help but smile. This might just work.

With so many of my brothers staying in Sephiroth, dinner is a much quieter affair than usual. Mama and Baba always encouraged us to take meals together as a family and it set a comfortable air of familiarity and competitiveness. With just Cove to compete with, though, the banter is fairly minimal. We try hard to make sure Nora is included in our rapid-fire conversation. She sits across from me instead of beside me, so I do my best to engage with her as much as possible. It doesn't take long for her to begin debating something with Cove and the two argue good-naturedly.

The only interruption comes in the form of *Tutu* arriving. She sweeps dramatically onto the veranda in a cloud of purple silks and jasmine incense, proclaiming loud welcomes and compliments. *Tutu* greets Mama and Baba first with hugs and loud kisses on cheeks. Cove and I are inspected and signed off on with nods of approval and a firm shoulder pat. Then *Tutu* sees Nora hovering awkwardly in her chair and bustles over to her, all business.

"You, my dear, must be Nora. Welcome." *Tutu*'s face widens into an impossibly warm smile, and she pulls Nora up from the table to kiss her on both cheeks. "I'm so glad to finally meet you."

"I apologize." Nora's voice is small. "I don't know who you are."

Tutu throws back her head and laughs, the sound bouncing off the high ceiling and echoing around us. Nora smiles, clearly unsure of what to do, and continues to lurk awkwardly next to her chair.

"Nora, this is my *Tutu*," I say, leaning across the table. "My grandmother."

The flush of color to Nora's cheeks is swift and strong. "Of course! I'm so sorry, it's an honor to meet you."

She bobs a slightly clumsy curtsy and *Tutu* laughs again. "No need for that, my child. I am well beyond the age of social graces, and I am fortunate enough to be in a position where my rudeness is tolerated. If it's not overlooked altogether that is." Her eyes twinkle as she looks between me and Nora. "If you will let me, I would like to read your flames later."

"Mama." Baba's voice is heavy with warning. "We have only just arrived. Let them settle before you start badgering."

"Nonsense, Hemi! The decision is up to them. I am simply asking for permission."

"I don't know what reading my flame means, but you can read mine." Nora's voice is collected and steady, but the slight flush on her neck gives away her earlier embarrassment. "I am curious to know more about the ceremony."

"And you, Alon?" *Tutu* levels me with a stern eye. Clearly there is only one right answer.

"Of course, *Tutu*."

She smiles again and declares we finish our meal before meeting later in the library. *Tutu* insists on sitting next to Nora for the remainder of supper. The two converse together quietly like old friends sharing secrets. Even sitting across the table I can't hear their words over the sounds of the distant waves and Mama and Cove talking. Before the last plate has been cleared away, *Tutu* looks at me across the table with a knowing grin and winks.

• • • ☽ • ◯ • ☾ • • •

"Is this a normal practice for your people to do?"

Nora sits drowsily in one of the overstuffed armchairs scattered throughout the library. They are the best places to disappear into with a good book when stormy weather makes the sea too dangerous to be out on. Nora isn't impervious to their charms and has sunk so low in hers that I'm concerned she won't be able to get out of it without help. Just the thought of helping her out of the chair sends a shiver through my body.

Down boy. Don't need anything embarrassing happening after all.

"Sitting?" I tease good-naturedly. "Yes, that is a fairly normal thing for us to do here."

Nora sticks her tongue out at me and scoffs. "No. Flame reading. What is it anyway?"

"I really think it might be better if *Tutu* ex—"

"Flame reading is what it sounds like, my dear." *Tutu* strolls in from behind me and gently places two ornately carved incense holders on the low tea table in front of us. "You light the incense, and I read the smoke."

Nora looks at me and my shoulders rise to my ears in a shrug. This is something *Tutu* has been interested in since I was a young child. She spent many years since Baba became king, after *Tutu Kane* passed on, learning more about flame reading. She even visited Heyanth to train with their skilled readers.

Tutu places two unused pieces of incense in the holders and fetches a long piece of kindling that she lights from one of the wall sconces. Nora straightens in the chair next to me, placing both feet flat on the floor. *Tutu* folds herself into a chair across the table from us and hands me the kindling.

"Light the incense."

I carefully hold the lit kindling to the stick of incense closest to me until it bursts into flame and then blow it out to release a steady stream of perfumed smoke. Nora takes the kindling from me and dutifully lights her own stick of incense, sending the rich smell of vanilla mingling with the jasmine from mine. *Tutu* carefully reclaims the kindling from Nora, throwing it in the empty fireplace to smolder. She returns to her seat, hands clasped together in her lap, and closes her eyes.

"What happens now?" Nora whispers out of the corner of her mouth.

"I don't know," I murmur back, careful to not take my eyes off *Tutu*. "She's never done a reading for me before."

The smell of vanilla and jasmine wrap around us like a cloak. I settle back in my chair, relaxing as the familiar smells that follow *Tutu* around calm me. We sit in silence as the incense burns in their holders before us.

My eyelids droop the longer we wait, and I start to doze. *Tutu* clapping her hands together demands my attention and I startle awake. Our sticks of incense are half burned away, the charred remains falling into the little ashtray built into the holder.

"It is time." *Tutu* studies the smoke rising from the incense closely. After a few moments, her face creases into a small smile. "What do you see?"

"Smoke?" I ask, puzzled. What else would she be expecting?

"They move together," Nora says quietly.

Tutu's smile widens. My focus shifts from her back onto the incense and now I can see what Nora means. Normally, the smoke from incense is erratic and travels wherever the breeze takes it. Ours is drawn to each other.

The pale gray rising from the jasmine incense in front of me twists and curls around the white rising from the vanilla incense in front of Nora. It's a gentle and loving dance, the way the sea cradles the shores at high tides. We watch them rise together until they dissipate near the ceiling and leave only their sweet fragrances behind.

"What does it mean?" Nora's question is quiet, wonder in her voice as she watches the impossible.

"Flame reading is an old tradition in the kingdom of Heyanth," *Tutu* says, absently fiddling with the small box she keeps her incense in. "We had a visiting delegation many years ago that introduced me to it. They use it as a matchmaking tool.

"After Alon's *Tutu Kane* passed and his Baba and Mama stepped in as the rulers of Korala, I had too much time on my hands. I traveled often and spent much time in Heyanth. They taught me the art of flame reading and I enjoy it greatly. It can reveal a great many things about a couple."

"But what does it mean?" I echo Nora's question. "That our smoke moves like that."

Tutu hesitates. "The smoke reveals many things. The truly gifted Readers can see the smallest details of a person's life in how it moves. I once saw a Reader be able to accurately predict that a woman would have two husbands in her lifetime. Of course, what is seen and how that information is used depends on how much the people being read believe."

"*Tutu*," I steady her with a gaze, "what does it mean?"

"I have seen this pattern only once before, with your Mama and Baba when I read their flames some time ago. It is the pattern the ancient texts call *Anima Mate*. The closest interpretation for us is soulmate."

My heart swells as *Tutu* speaks and I gulp down deep breaths of jasmine and vanilla like a drowning man. The words hang heavy in the air like the early morning fog. *Anima Mate*. Soulmates.

That's why I am drawn to Nora. Why I can't resolve myself to be second place consolation prize and let her pretend to play happy family with Teddy. Why I feel this pulling behind my heart to be near her. To listen to her. To love her. Because we are one. Kindred. Two halves of the same whole. Soulmates.

Chapter 23

In Which a Heart Begins to Soften

Nora

My body snaps back from the table, sending the incense holders juddering. Alon sits there staring at his grandmother with stars in his eyes. *This is not good.* How can she sit there and calmly proclaim we're soulmates? This doesn't make any sense! Calm down. Remember to breathe. This only has as much weight as we allow it. *Tutu* said so herself. She's probably just seeing what she wants to see.

Yeah. That definitely has to be it. Everyone has been so focused on forcing me to accept Alon as a husband so we can play happy family and be together forever. *Ew.*

Alon turns that star filled gaze to me and a gentle pull behind my heart reaches out for him. The same feeling I had when I first saw him in the gardens back home. I really need to figure out what is going on with me. I mean I guess Alon's good looking or whatever, but I'm not attracted to him like I am Teddy. Right?

I give myself a mental shake and stand. "Thank you, *Tutu*." I curtsy carefully and try to keep my voice as level as possible. "You have given us a lot to think about."

She bows her head in return, and I stalk out of the library. My legs are practically vibrating with the effort to not run until I hit the shoreline. Alon continues to just sit there, unmoving and unspeaking. With that look on his face I can only imagine the amount of misguided hope he's now feeling. My stomach churns almost as badly as it did those first few weeks at sea. Oh gods, I'm going to be sick. Everything just got so much more complicated.

Once I'm through the library doors and out of sight, I run. Thankfully, the palace is not nearly so grand as back home. It takes me very little time to find my way back to the set of rooms Queen Ululani showed me and Alon to earlier. One of the servants had closed the windows against the chill of night, but I throw them open again and drink in the salty air deeply. It doesn't take long for the briny smell of the water to wash away all traces of the jasmine and vanilla incense.

My letter from Teddy sits on the little reading desk in the corner. My jaw works furiously, clenching and unclenching as I contemplate the offending piece of paper. Whether I'm on edge because of what Alon's grandmother had said or because of that damn letter is hard to say. I was so happy to have already had news from home waiting for me when I got here, but that happiness had waned considerably once I actually read the missive. It's so obvious Teddy's much more interested in learning about Alon's perceived faults than in my own wellbeing and journey here.

I snort, making a mildly rude gesture towards the writing desk. This would be so much easier if I could just *talk* to Teddy. I'm sure he was just short on time, or something, before the mailboats left and just wanted to try and keep things as short as possible. If he had time and space in the letter he would have definitely asked after me. Yeah, that's got to be it.

If nothing else, I might as well just get changed for bed at this point. I'm sure Abigail has her hands full with other things. I'll write a reply to Teddy later. Definitely. Probably...

Nestling into the bed, the soft cotton sheets wrap me in a calming cocoon. Unsurprisingly, it doesn't take too long for the exhaustion from our journey to overtake me. I crash into sleep like a drunkard looking for his next pint and sleep just as unsteadily.

$$\bullet \bullet \bullet \;)\; \bullet \;\bigcirc\; \bullet \;(\; \bullet \bullet \bullet$$

I'm back home in my rooms in Sephiroth. A fire crackles in the hearth and rain beats down on the windowpanes. It sends a scattering pulse through the room that's echoed with my own heartbeat. Or maybe that's because Teddy is rubbing my back. Yeah, it's probably because of that.

His deft hands work in perfect unison, smoothing out the kinked muscles in my lower back. A groan slips past my lips as he eases a particularly tight spot into submission. His hands leave a sparking trail of fire across my bare skin as they move up and down my body.

The urge to see him, to have him, consumes me. I roll over to face him, settling beneath him with ease. The blanket is soft along my skin and Teddy assesses me with a greedy smile on his lips.

I pull Teddy against me, our nakedness colliding in a slippery tangle of limbs and need and desperation. He nips at my lip as he slides his hands across every inch of my flesh. Every touch sets flames flickering beneath my skin.

But something feels off. I pull back from Teddy and watch as a crack of lightning illuminates the dark window. A shuddering crash of thunder follows soon after, setting goosebumps prickling across my body and unease coursing through my veins.

I turn to Teddy again. But it's not Teddy. It's Alon. What is he doing here? Another booming crash of thunder rings out and then a third.

"Nora," Alon says and reaches out a hand to gently cup –

Another thud and muttered curse disturbs my nightmare, wrenching me back to wakefulness. My eyes fly open, but I force myself to remain still. I don't want to risk whoever is in the room knowing I'm awake. In the faint light coming in from the window I can just make out Alon walking across the room. He must have bumped into almost every piece of furniture possible trying to get to his room.

He comes closer to the bed and my body goes rigid. Forcing myself to relax my tense muscles, I close my eyes again and feign sleep. I can hear him pause next to me, a gentle hand brushing the hair from my shoulder.

"Goodnight, *Ku'u Lei*," he murmurs gently.

He shuffles forward and the soft snick of the door to the adjoining room closing announces his retreat to his quarters. I roll over, sweeping my hair out from under me so it doesn't get wrenched as I move.

Goosebumps rise all along my body and It's hard to know if it's because of the slight chill in the air or because of my dream. Gods, that dream. Alon must have made so much noise trying to be quiet that it interrupted my dream. It's really such a shame because it was shaping up to be quite a nice one with Teddy. Guess I'll just have to see if I get a repeat performance or not.

Far out in the night, the waves croon their lullabies. The soothing sound helps ground me, steadying my uneven pulse and rapid breathing. I sink further back into the pillows and fall into an easy sleep.

A soft knock echoes through the morning light.

"Nora? Is it alright if I come in?" Alon calls from the other side of our shared door.

Shaking the last remnants of sleep from my eyes, I force myself out of the warm nest of blankets and shrug on my slightly ratty robe. I had insisted we bring it from Sephiroth and the familiar smell of peony from back home lingers on it even now. I settle onto the small couch at the end of the bed and try to make it seem like Alon didn't just wake me up.

"Come in," I call primly.

Alon enters and seems unsurprised that I am upright and mostly presentable. "About last night—"

"I don't want to talk about last night."

"Are you sure?" He eyes me warily. "You seemed pretty upset after *Tutu* —"

"Of course I was upset, Alon. Everyone seems to believe we're destined to be together. We both know better."

"We do?"

His lips quirk into an amused smile. Gods the arrogance of this man.

"We do. Your *Tutu* said herself that the reading only holds weight for those who believe in it. Same way every superstition needs someone to believe it to be true."

"You're telling me you don't believe she could be right? That we could be *Anima Mate*? You saw the smoke just like I did."

"I did see the smoke," I acknowledge with a nod. "The difference between you and me is that I believe it's just smoke."
Alon watches me for a long moment, his face unreadable. I hold perfectly still. He won't see me squirm. Not this time.

"Okay."

"Okay?"

"Okay." Alon shrugs. "If that's what you believe then that's what you believe. I can't tell you any differently."

"Exactly." I eye him suspiciously. He's taking this all too well.

"I did want to ask you —" *uh huh here it comes* "— if you would give me the honor of allowing me to escort you to our Remembrance Ceremony later tonight."

The change in topic is baffling. Did he really just accept what I was telling him without an argument? "What?"

"The Remembrance Ceremony. Tonight. It marks the end of storm season. We all come together to show our thanks to the gods that we were spared and to mourn those we lost. Would you do me the honor of accompanying me tonight?"

He seems so sincere, so well-intended. It honestly makes me wonder if he's got ulterior motives. "Sure, Alon. I'll go with you."

"Wonderful!" Alon's smile is so large it threatens to split his face in two. "I need to help Baba and Cove with some things today, so I won't be able to show you around again. I'll meet you at the front steps right before sunset. Don't worry about dinner. Mama and Baba give the servants the night off to celebrate so we eat at the festival. I'll see you tonight. Oh! And don't wear shoes!"

The last part is called absently over his shoulder as he leaves my room. I stare at the door as it swings shut behind him and hope I didn't just make a big mistake. What did I just get myself into?

• • • ☽ • ◯ • ☾ • • •

Sunset can't come fast enough. The day itself passes unbearably slowly. I spend most of it aimlessly floating between various menial tasks unable to really focus on anything for very long. Even my attempts at training are cut short when I find myself, more often than not, staring out windows instead of focusing on the activity at hand.

Our conversation with Alon's *Tutu* keeps running over and over through my mind on repeat. It makes me restless, off balance. I actually do manage to write a letter to Teddy and purposefully ignore his multitude of questions about Koralan defenses. Instead, I tell him about our crossing, the storm we encountered, and my favorite things I discovered yesterday upon arrival.

It's shameful to admit, but there's a prickling unease at the thought of Teddy knowing that Alon showed me around. I do my best to frame it as a solo exploration instead. The last thing I want, or need, is for Teddy to get jealous and do something we'll both regret. This trip is for a reason, and he needs to make sure he doesn't do something that could make things worse. Or maybe it's because I know Teddy will be able to see that I'm actually starting to like Alon in spite of everything going on around us.

I sit on the front steps of the palace fidgeting with the sunflower pendant Alon gave me. I know it gives him the wrong impression, but I just can't seem to take it off. I've worn it almost every day on our journey from Sephiroth and even Abigail has stopped suggesting other jewelry to me. It's truly a beautiful work of art. Something I would have chosen for myself if I had ever been granted that much freedom to make the decision.

Out of defiance, I also wear the ring Teddy gave me tonight. It's impossible to deny how much the two pieces clash horribly with each other and I can't help comparing them. While one is delicate and feminine, the other is clunky and too hard. The sunflower is warm and welcoming, the ring stiff and cold.

How is it that the man who had not spent more than three hours with me over several weeks knew me well enough that he could design jewelry for me that would make my heart sing? *Because you're* Anima Mate. *That's why*. And then I banish the thought with my next breath. *No, we're not*.

Footsteps echo behind me and I turn to see Alon. He's dressed simply in loose pants and a pale blue shirt that's open at the collar. His hair had lightened on our trip from Sephiroth and in the fading light it looks almost bronze. The faint aroma of salt and jasmine cling to him like a second skin.

It's his eyes, though, that captivate me. I had thought they were both brown, but I couldn't be more wrong. His right eye *is* actually a brown so dark it would be easy to lose myself in it, the sunlight falling into its depths like a bottomless pool. His left eye, however, is a green as dark as the moss back home and shines like the sea glass on the windowsill in my room in the evening sun. Deep patches of brown intertwine with the green and sparkle like stars when they catch the light.

With a skitter, my heart skips a beat or two and warmth flushes my body. Uh oh. This is not good. This is a weird feeling and I don't think it's a feeling I should be feeling for anyone but Teddy. I'm not even sure if I've ever had this feeling while being around Teddy. At least not for a while.

I clear my throat nervously, oh gods I'm staring, and tear my gaze from his. My hands fidget with the navy-blue dress Abigail had chosen for me to wear. I focus on not wrinkling the fabric beyond repair while trying to discreetly dry off my suddenly sweaty palms. Next to Alon's simplistic outfit, I am hopelessly overdressed and obviously out of my element.

"Are you okay, Nora?"

"I'm fine." The words stick in my throat and come out muted and strained. "Where are we going?"

Alon appraises me with a smile and holds out his arm. "May I escort you to the ceremony, Your Highness?"

My arm links with his and I try to keep my sweaty palms to myself. If I leave smears on his shirt then everyone will know how I'm feeling. Hell, I don't even quite know how I'm feeling right now. Seriously, what's up with that?

We descend the steps together and head off down to the port. The nearer to the town we get the more people join us on the roads dressed in their festival best. Shades of grays, greens, and blues converge to create an ocean on land. Instead of water, however, this one is made of solemnity, remembrance, and sorrow.

We follow the current through the port and down onto the beaches. Women stand next to the pathways and hewn stone steps with huge woven baskets filled to the brim with folded lotus flowers in various shades of pinks, purples, blues, and oranges. Alon bows deeply to one of the women and selects two flowers from her basket.

She smiles and bows in return and then we're swept out onto the sand with the rest of the crowds.

Trailing in Alon's wake, he leads me to a small stall set up on the hard packed sand full of various writing utensils. We each pull a stick of charcoal from a well-loved cup before retreating down towards some flat rocks to sit cross legged facing each other. Alon holds out the flowers to me and I pick the pearl pink one, leaving him with one the color of butter.

"Are these paper?" I ask, studying the flower. Delicate petals had been creased and folded around the center in an intricate spiral.

"Rice paper, yes. It's a place of honor to be chosen to fold and distribute the flowers every year. The people chosen are usually nominated by their peers and voted in every year. Before Mama and Baba changed things it was the same group of older women who folded them every year and they did not handle outsiders very well."

"But why paper?"

Alon grins at me and carefully hands me one of the sticks of charcoal. "Here. Write the name of someone you lost in the center of the flower. Can be anyone you want it to be."

I ponder the waves for a few moments and watch other people walking in and out of the surf. I'd always considered it a blessing to not have many family I knew that had passed on, but now that I needed one to write down, I was coming up empty. There must have been someone in my extended family I was close to. Right?

Huffing in defeat, I write down the name of my childhood cat, Lucy. Pets have to count too, right? Lucy had adopted me when I was four and slept on my bed every night for thirteen years, leaving fluffy tawny hair everywhere. Mother hated her because Lucy always violently hissed every time Mother or Father got close to her, but she was always gentle with me. I cried for days when she disappeared, and no one knew where she had gone or what had happened to her. Besides Teddy, she was the closest thing I had for a friend growing up.

Once we have written names on our paper flowers, Alon returns our charcoal to the man at the booth and then leads me to the water's edge.

"Ready?"

"It's hard to know if I'm ready for something if I don't actually know what's happening."

Alon's laugh bubbles up like a stream before spilling over. He crosses the hard sand, wading out a few feet into the surf, and then waits as I hurriedly collect my skirts to join him. We slosh out side by side until the water is almost knee height, the waves lapping at our legs.

"We use paper so it doesn't hurt the ocean." Alon leans down and places his paper lotus in the water. He murmurs quietly, "go in spirit and in peace."

I watch as his yellow flower floats briefly in front of him, the petals darkening as the water seeps in. It slowly bobs out towards the open ocean as the waves carry it away. Making sure not to drop my skirts, I set my pink flower into the water and give it a gentle nudge so it follows.

"Go in spirit and in peace," Alon murmurs beside me. I echo him softly.

As the last rays of sunlight fade, Alon and I stand together in the water and watch as hundreds of paper lotuses float peacefully out to sea. Each one carries the name of someone lost but not forgotten. All around us people wade out to send their flowers out on the waves, wishing their loved ones peace and eternal rest. The sight makes me shiver and Alon gestures for us to go back to shore.

Abigail appears, seemingly out of nowhere, as we climb back onto the hard packed sand. She helps me with a thick pair of socks and warm shoes. I wiggle my toes, grateful for the sudden warmth after the chill from the water. Wrapping a light wool cloak around my shoulders, Abigail gives my hand a comforting squeeze and then disappears back into the anonymity of the crowd. I don't know how she does it, but she is a godsend.

Alon and I sit together on the same flat rock as before and sip steaming mugs of warm cider he retrieved from a different booth. Now that the sun has truly set, a slight chill hangs in the air. Not nearly as bad as Sephiroth, but enough to make you shiver. From above us on the cliffs a whoop rings out over the crowd.

"What's going on?" I ask. Alon grins at me and sets off across the beach with long strides. I scrabble after. "Hey, wait for me!"

My feet struggle to find purchase in the soft sand and by the time I catch up I am breathless and panting. Trailing Alon back through the port, it's obvious the once morose crowd has changed. All around us people begin to play music, dance, and sing. They carry lanterns with colorful paper pasted to the glass to give off blue, green, pink, yellow, and purple light. Stalls decorated with streamers and selling delicious smelling food and drink are every few feet with merchants loudly calling to the crowds. Long strings of wooden beads hang from every available surface and from round the necks of adults and children alike.

Alon looks back every now and again to make sure I'm still following as he cuts through the throng and heads to the courtyard that holds the fountain of the woman. He ducks inside what looks like an old church and I follow on his heels. We trek through the slightly dusty sanctuary and begin to climb an endless set of stairs, surfacing at the top inside a little belfry covered in dirt and bird poo. A gray blanket lays on the side closest to the square and a basket is perched precariously on top.

"After you," Alon says and gives me a slight bow.

My heart stutters and I close my eyes briefly, forcing myself to use the breathing exercises Hayden taught me. After the Incident I don't care much for heights. *You're okay. There's nothing to worry about.*

My arms barely go halfway around the massive bell as I hug it, inching my way around it to carefully settle onto the blanket. My feet hang in open space over the side of the tower. A small ledge runs alongside the outside of the belfry a few feet below the soles of my shoes. If I fall, I will *probably* be okay, but the thought is still unnerving and I fight to keep my fears in check.

Alon settles down next to me, shoes also dangling over the edge. He opens the basket and hands me bread, smoked meats, cheeses, and more *malasadas*. Together we feast, watching the people in the square beneath us.

"Why are we up here? I thought we were going to the festival?"

Alon's lips stretch into that all too familiar crooked smile. "We're at the festival."

"Ha, ha. I thought when you said you wanted to escort me to the festival that we'd be down there. You know, with the rest of the people."

"Trust me, okay? My favorite part is going to start soon and it's so much better to watch it up here."

I huff and eat a few more *malasadas*. It was all for show, though. Other than the lightheadedness that comes with being in the belfry, there is no way I can actually be in a bad mood right now.

From below, I hear calls and cheering and a gaggle of brightly dressed people push into the square from all sides. As one, they form an undulating mass around the plaza, stepping in time to the band of musicians that climb onto the curved edges of the fountain at the very center. The crowds begin to dance and sing, whirling around the fountain and each other with the grace and elegance of birds in flight. These were just birds I had never seen before.

In the colored lights from the lanterns and with their swirling skirts, the dancers become a veritable kaleidoscope far below me. From our vantage point in the tower, I can see the rippling designs of color and movement in a way that would have been lost if I had been on the ground with them. I look at Alon and he is watching the dance with pure unadulterated joy on his face. I feel that same tug against my heart again. *This isn't so bad.* What if Alon's *Tutu* is right?

With my next breath I give myself a shake. No. Stop looking. Teddy is real and he loves you and you love him. Stick to the plan.

The dance ends below us in a flurry of bows and clash of cymbals. Alon turns to me grinning. He must see something on my face because he falters briefly.

"Ready for more?"

I smile and together we descend back down the stairs to the plaza.

Chapter 24

In Which a Path is Charted

Alon

Something is clearly wrong with Nora. She's been so open and honest with me tonight, unafraid to let me see her thoughts and emotions as they play out across her face. Now she's closed off again. Guarded. She laughs politely and smiles calmly and it's obvious there's so much more that she's thinking and feeling that I'm not allowed to see. What happened in the belfry? I thought we had connected....

Nevertheless, I do my best to make the most of the rest of the night. After we watch the dancers from our vantage point in the tower, I take Nora on a small tour of the puppet shows around the various squares and marketplaces. Each one depicts the storm of a different year, the favorites drawing larger crowds. People boo and cheer as the stories are shared. Nora's heart isn't in it anymore, though, and I suggest we head back home. She quickly agrees and together we wander back the way we came.

My attempts to strike up conversation with her on the walk home fall helplessly flay. Nora is refusing to engage with me. Again.

She's buried in her own thoughts and clearly there is no space for me to join her. The lighthearted mood we had at the beginning of the evening has been replaced with a melancholy heaviness I am just not entirely sure how to interpret.

Together, we drift through the manor to our connecting rooms. Nora settles herself at the little desk that she was using as a vanity and Abigail hurries in to help prepare her for bed. I pause briefly behind Nora so she can see me in the mirror, but words are just too hard right now. My chin drops as I turn and head to my own room. Gods, I wish she would just talk to me.

"Good night, Nora," I say, my hand on the latch.

Nora turns to look at me, a small, sad smile crossing her lips. "Good night, Alon. Thank you for escorting me tonight. I really did enjoy the ceremony."

My tongue is thick and heavy. I am a storm on the open sea, wild and unchecked and uncontrolled. I can't find the words. *Why* can't I find the words!? Forget words. I should just do what I have been wanting to do since I met her and take Nora into my arms and—

The door closes behind me, the click of the latch ringing throughout the space with finality. Want and frustration wrestle deep in my body and render me confusedly frozen in place.

Someone was in my room earlier to turn down the bed and light the lanterns. I assume Abigail has taken it upon herself to see to my needs as well as Nora's. I'm not sure what she's paid as compensation, but that woman deserves so much more.

With deliberate movements, I strip off my shirt and boots. My jittering hands slowly calm as I go through the familiar movements of preparing for bed. After dousing all the lanterns flickering around the room, I finally give in to the emotional exhaustion and collapse onto the bed. The open window lets in the faintest sounds of the festival still going on down below at the port. The pungent scent of saltwater drowns out any lingering smells from the food stalls. It permeates the room and is both comforting and unsettling. I fall into a fitful sleep and dream of waves crashing far above me.

•••)•○•(•••

It's too early to be awake yet here I am. My mind is both annoyingly alert and incredibly groggy, like I didn't actually sleep at all last night and just drank copious amounts of the imported black tea Baba likes to drink in the mornings. My eyelashes are almost too heavy to lift, and my limbs move slowly as I stretch in the predawn light. With too many objections and several concerning pops from various joints, I manage to dress myself and creep quietly through Nora's room and out to the hall. She's nestled in amongst the blankets, breathing heavily. Her face is so calm and peaceful when she sleeps.

Everyone in the manor is asleep, the servants just starting to rustle around making ready for the day. I steal down to one of my favorite places to hide out – the kitchens. Cook is just getting the fire stoked as I perch on a well-worn stool in the corner. She takes one look at me and starts tsking.

"Now tha' won't do, now, will it? Sit down, Highness, I have jus' the things."

The familiar flurry of activities in the kitchen is comforting. I settle in and watch as Cook blusters around giving orders to various servants as the day's preparations get truly underway. It isn't long before she hands me a steaming mug of thick chocolate topped with sweet cream. Her hands and apron are covered in flour and jam, some brushing off onto the plate of warm pastries she thrusts into my hands.

While I eat, she tells me the old familiar stories of her homeland. Cook grew up in a northern kingdom far from the sunny shores she now calls home, but she's never confirmed just where exactly she's from. Says she likes to keep the mystery alive and claims to enjoy people believing her to be a nomadic wanderer. She came to Korala when I was very young and has spent the past eighteen years working in the kitchens. No one has ever pressed for more information about her past. With the type of food she makes no one wants to risk angering her and having her pack up and move on again.

It doesn't take nearly as long as I hoped it would for breakfast to be prepared and ready to be delivered to the rest of the family. I wander upstairs carrying a tea tray laden with warmed cups and a pot of fresh tea steeping softly. One of the servants had tried to take the tray from me, bless her, but Cook loudly proclaimed I may be a prince, but I was more than capable of carrying a pot of tea. Thankfully, everyone took it well and the poor girl only flushed a deep shade of crimson before handing it back to me.

Mama, Baba, and *Tutu* all sit on the veranda talking quietly and sipping from already steaming mugs. The weather in Korala never gets truly cold, but there is starting to be a bit of a bite in the early morning air. Just enough to remind us that the days are getting just a little bit shorter and just a little bit cooler than we like.

There's no sign of Cove yet, but I doubt we'll be seeing much of him until later. Last year he didn't show up until after we had finished dinner with a flask in each hand and a concerned woman making sure he didn't swallow his tongue as he tried, and failed I might add, to walk in a straight line.

Setting the fresh pot of tea on the waiting cozy, I plop down next to *Tutu* and help myself to some of the breakfast offerings. Piling my plate high with eggs, bacon, danish, and fried potatoes, I sit watching the various ships coming in and out of the port. I can just make out the cluster of warships that comprise our new navy. Baba wasn't sure where to dock them, so they've been awkwardly patrolling the immediate shores to try and scare off any potential pirates.

"Good morning, my dear! Did you enjoy the festival last night?"

Mama's cheery voice interrupts my melancholy musing. I lazily look over to see Nora hovering just inside the doorway. Just the sight of her is like a jolt to my system. Every cell of my body is on high alert, hoping and praying that she comes closer. I automatically straighten in my chair as a smile slinks across my face. Nora glances at me briefly, but refuses to meet my eye. I guess we really are back to this after all. Damn.

"Yes, I did. Thank you. I don't want to intrude if you are having a private conversation."

"Not at all. Please, come sit." Baba offers her the remaining seat at the table, waving away one of the man servants to pull it out for Nora himself.

Nora's legs are jittering under the table, I can hear the sound of her feet tapping an absent pattern on the wood floor beneath us. I don't know how she manages to not bite her cheek with the way her jaw is clenching and unclenching. Nora perches on the very edge of the high-backed seat like it's going to bite her. Is it because of last night? Or something I did?

Nora takes an orange from the bowl on the table, carefully peeling it into a tidy mess in front of her. Mama and Baba return to their quiet conversation, but *Tutu* studies Nora intently. I can practically feel Nora squirming in her seat.

"Did you —"

"I wanted to —"

My words trail off at the same time Nora's mouth snaps shut. The tension lays thick around us like fog.

"You first."

Nora finally looks at me, giving me a small smile. "I wanted to talk to you about the next leg of our journey. You said we would need to go around Korala to the Falls on the other side to find the Elders, right?"

"Yes. We could go through the mountain pass which would be several days if we really pushed the horses. Otherwise, we would need to sail around the island and that takes longer. My guess is it would take us about a week to get to the other side provided we had favorable winds."

"Why does it take so long by sea?"

"The shape of the island. Korala is almost twice as long as it is wide. We'd have to sail around at the widest point and then double back."

"Then we should go by horse. To be honest I'm much more comfortable on horseback than I am on a ship. We wouldn't even need a carriage. It'll save us more time than —"

"You can't go by horse."

Tutu sits cradling her cup, blowing on her tea gently to cool it. She is completely unperturbed by the rest of the table gawking at her. Even Mama and Baba are paying attention to our conversation now.

"Why?"

"Bandits."

"What do you mean bandits?" Nora's face pales under her faint sunburn.

"Bandits roam the mountain paths during the fall and winter months. It's not safe to travel that far up the roads during this time of year. You'll go by ship."

"Mama, really," Baba says, "we haven't seen bandits in —"

Tutu waves her hand dismissively, cutting Baba off. "It's been decided. You'll go by ship and have a lovely and safe journey around the island. I will alert Captain Skye to begin making preparations. Leave it to me."

With her proclamation made, *Tutu* stands and wanders back inside. Her abandoned teacup remains where she left it, steam slowly rising as the liquid inside cools. Nora cuts her eyes to me, her face creasing with fear.

"Are there really bandits?"

"Sometimes," Baba says bluntly, "but there really is nothing to worry about. We haven't seen bandits in many years, and the pass is quite safe. Especially with an armed escort."

"Then shouldn't we go by horse?"

"No, darling," Mama says gently. "Once *Tutu* gets something into her head it's best to let it happen. Trust me, a trip around the island will be wonderful. You will have the chance to explore more of the beauty of Korala on your way. I will help *Tutu* make the preparations so you don't need to worry about it."

"Wait for me, My Love. I'll come and make sure she doesn't do anything completely outrageous."

Mama and Baba rise together and hurry after *Tutu*. They must be really concerned she's going to plan something crazy if they're moving that fast. Or they just don't want to spend any more time with me and Nora and this damnable silence.

Nora refuses to look at me even now, preferring instead to continue organizing and reorganizing the pile of orange segments and peelings on her plate. My brain is at war with itself. I don't want to push for a conversation Nora doesn't want nor isn't ready to have, but this silence is going to drive me insane.

After a few more moments of unbearable tension, Nora clears her throat. "Thank you for escorting me last night. I had a nice time."

"You're welcome. I hope you understand why it's one of my favorite celebrations. Maybe next year we can see the follies that…"

I trail off. Nora isn't looking at me again. The silence is unbearable. What did I do wrong?

"Please, excuse me." Nora rises from her chair and bobs a stiff curtsy. She hasn't curtsied to me since we met before our wedding. "I must go see Abigail. She will want to begin packing for our trip."

There's nothing I can do right now. My chin dips in a nod and I watch mutely as Nora flees the veranda. It's just all so, so wrong. Like all the progress I made the last few weeks is gone and we're back to being complete strangers.

But we're not strangers. Not anymore. And honestly, I'm not sure if we ever truly were strangers. There's a piece of me that knows her, craves her, like we met before in a past life. That ever-present space behind my heart calls out for Nora again, aching to be made whole when she somehow feels even further away than ever.

Breakfast sits heavy in my stomach, weighing me down even further. I shove back from the table, pacing up and down the veranda. The pale stones ring slightly as I stomp back and forth, but they remain as unperturbed as ever. The ships on the distant water catch my attention again and I pause to watch them.

Baba was right. The mountain pass is plenty safe with or without an armed guard. It doesn't make sense for *Tutu* to insist so heavily on going by ship...though if nothing else I should probably thank her. She just bought me more time to win Nora over before we reach the Elders and our time together ends.

Swallowing the uncomfortable lump in my throat, I flex and stretch each muscle across my shoulders and down my arms to try and center myself. Everything is going to be okay. I've got more time to make things right.

Chapter 25

In Which Faith is Tested

Boar

"By the gods we need to do something or –"

"It's been a week, Boar, and there hasn't been any word from the princess –"

"Do you know if she's returning or not?!"

Their words fly at me like arrows, each one finding its mark and leaving me full of holes. I gaze around the table into the angry and distrustful faces of my companions. For the first time, real fear grips me. If they turn on me now this will all be for nothing. I can't lose their loyalty.

"Don't be naive, brothers. Do you truly expect us to receive any sort of news while the princess is at sea?" The distrust in their faces is cowed, but only just. "Even you should understand that it's hard to find a mail barge to deliver letters when you're on the water."

"But we should have –"

"We should have nothing, Hawk." I pin him to his chair with malice. He flinches beneath my gaze. Good. "Until the princess reaches Koralan shores it is ridiculous to assume that we will hear any news from her."

"And you assume we'll go along with whatever you say." Spaniel is out of his seat now; hands pressed to the table as he challenges me. "You claim your hold over the princess is unbreakable, but she's off to parts unknown and we're still here fighting to put her on the throne!"

"Fine!" I snap. "You want to go on without me then by all means, go ahead. I'm sure you'll make a fine leader Spaniel."

The boy flinches back and sits again. The conniving bastard really thinks he can challenge me?

"No? You're not interested?" My anger has its roots sunk deep now. "How about you, Wolf? You want to hold a coup and roust me out? Or how about you, Bull? Ready to take on the mantle of leader?"

One by one their gazes drop, and they bow their heads in deference. Self-important pricks every single one of them. They want to play at resistance, but we're too far into this for games. There's a trail of bodies behind us now and the only way out is forward.

"If there are no takers, can we please get back to the task at hand? There is still much to discuss before we can overthrow the king."

"All we want is some assurance, Boar." Wolf eyes me uneasily. "The princess is the lynch pin. If she doesn't return and we can't eliminate the princeling then we are dead men walking. Everything rests on her coming back."

"The princess is collecting vital information for our cause and investigating how to remove the foreigner as a problem." I stare into their eyes one by one. The distrust is still there, but it's tempered now. Quieter. A heavy sigh rushes through me, and I sit again, settling back against the hardwood. "Until the princess truly commits to the cause there will be doubts. But have faith, brothers. She will answer the call."

"What is our next step?"

For once, Spaniel looks appropriately serious for the subject at hand. He's alert in his chair, leaning forward with hands clasped in front of him on the dinged tabletop. He's been more subdued since he and Bull went out on their last rampage. Forcing himself on terrified women has apparently lost its novelty.

"We should target the Council members not involved," Wolf says from beside me. The last few meetings he's taken to standing like a guard dog next to me instead of sitting with the rest. "If they are not neutralized by the time we need to move we risk them being too strong."

"You are correct, Wolf," I say approvingly. He flushes slightly. How odd. "Kentworth, Brewster, Fitzroy, and Halstead are all liabilities. We need to begin removing them from favor."

"I'm friends with Brewster's nephew," Bull pipes up from where he has sat silently. "He visits his uncle's estate during Harvest Tide."

"But Lord Brewster oversees the Harvest Tide celebration here."

"It's not his uncle he goes to share fellowship with." Bull's lewd grin contorts his face into a thin smear. "I hear Lady Brewster gets lonely during the winter while his Lordship resides at court."

"Then you will also go to visit Lady Brewster," I announce dismissively. As always, I'm filled with disgust and pure loathing for the violent man sitting at the table. "See what you can do to cast suspicion on Lord Brewster among his people, but don't let the lady of the house figure out what you're doing."

"Fitzeroy and Halstead have estates close to here and their families travel in for Harvest Tide every year," Lion pipes up from the far end of the table. "They have several daughters between them and they've both approached my father in the hopes of forging an alliance through me."

"Good. You and Spaniel get closer to the girls and figure out what you can learn about the Lords."

"What do we do if they decide to get, ahem, familiar with us?"

Oh, great we're back to this already. Disgusting prick.

"You will do nothing, Lord Spaniel, or you risk losing your head and your tongue." Lion glares at Spaniel with an unreadable look on his face. "These are noblewomen, and your familiarity will begin and end with nothing more than a kiss if the lady so chooses to give it."

"Oh, come on, Lion, after all we've done you're still on this?" Spaniel teases back. "After the last round of attacks I would have thought –"

"Enough." My voice is like ice on a winter's day. "Lion is right. The girls are innocents in this and not worth disgracing. A court scandal risks our exposure."

Lion shoots me a grateful smile. He's the youngest of the group by several years and does his best to keep up, but he's been taking things the hardest when it comes to our...activities. He wants change, but not the way we have to go about creating it.

"You guys are no fun," Spaniel pouts and slumps back in his seat. Thankfully, he doesn't push the issue anymore.

"That leaves Kentworth."

The name hangs over us like a cloud. Kentworth is the newest member to the High Counsel and replaced his uncle last year. He's young, ambitious, and wholly supports the monarchy. I wish we could have recruited him to our cause, but we were not ready to begin pushing back when he was sworn in. He would have been a formidable ally, but that makes him just as dangerous as an enemy.

"I'm friends with Kentworth." Hawk eyes us all from under his fringe and shrugs. "We run the palace grounds almost every morning."

"Really, Hawk? You run?"

"Oh, shut up, Spaniel!" I snap. This arrogant asshole needs to learn when to keep his mouth shut. "Hawk, do you have access to Kentworth's rooms?"

He nods slowly. Clearly the thought of taking advantage of his friend isn't sitting well with him. I should have cut him and Lion loose months ago while this was still just a game. The only problem is now they know too much. I don't particularly want even more blood on my hands, so I'm stuck with them for the foreseeable future. At least they'll be easy canon fodder if it comes down to it.

"I want you to get us a key."

"I can do that." The relief in Hawk's voice is potent. Did he honestly think I'd have him murder Kentworth or something? "I'll see him tomorrow for a run and try to get him to take me back to his rooms. I'll nick the key and make a copy."

"Good." I rub my temples as they throb in time with my heartbeat. I should really see a physician about these headaches. "Then if there is nothing else to discuss, brothers, I will take my leave."

Everyone watches as I rise from my place at the table and wrap my cloak around me. Wolf steps back as I turn from the group and head up and out of our hidden cave. The Autumn air is sharp as a whip and stings my nose. I breathe deeply, watching the stars as I clear the musty air from my lungs. The sharp snap of twigs underfoot announces Wolf's presence.

"You really think this is going to work?"

"I don't know." I shrug helplessly. "When the princess was still here, I would have said yes without hesitation. But now....Until she returns we just have to keep going."

"And what if she doesn't come back?"

I find him in the night, watching me with heavy eyes. The scant moonlight illuminates the gray at his temples and sets it glowing.

"Then you should make peace with the gods because we're all damned."

Chapter 26

In Which Danger is Outrun

Nora

Water flows by us at a lazily slow pace. My annoyance creeps back in and I try to keep it tamped down. With each passing day it gets harder and harder to keep it in check. We've been sailing for almost a week and thankfully we're finally getting close to our destination. I know *Tutu* insisted on us sailing for our protection, but this has been one of the most boring journeys of my life and I'm ready for it to end.

True to her words, *Tutu* oversaw all the preparations for me and Alon to sail to the Falls to find the Elders. She arranged the captain, crew, ship, and all supplies. When Cove surfaced from gods know where he had wanted to join us, but *Tutu* had crushed that plan with such a look it made me want to stand up straighter and smooth my dress for inspection. If he'd have come, I would at least have had someone to talk to.

There's Alon, of course, but after the Remembrance Festival I have been trying to be more mindful of limiting our interactions and keeping my distance. It's painfully clear that he grows more comfortable with me by the day and it's even more concerning, to me at least, that that comfort is mirrored in my own actions. Alon cares for me very deeply, but I cannot reciprocate that feeling. He feels about me the same way I felt about Teddy. I mean, the same way I *feel* about Teddy. Present tense. Right?

That all too familiar prickling feeling in my chest is back and I absently rub the space above my heart. I really need to have a physician look at it once I return to Sephiroth. Knowing my luck I'm probably allergic to salt water or something and it's making my chest ache.

A sharp low whistle disturbs me from my thoughts. All around me, crew members check lines and stow supplies, their shoulders taut and muscles coiled to spring. Alon and Captain Skye stand on the bridge deck together, talking in rapidly rising voices. A nervous energy surrounds them and it's clearly now affecting everyone on board. There's general unrest moving among the crew like a thick fog. I carefully weave through the deck crew and pick my way aft to join them.

"We should add as much sail as possible to outrun them. The wind is favorable in our direction."

"With respect, Your Highness, if the wind is favorable to us then it is also favorable to them. We can try to outrun them, but we should prepare for —"

"I said no!"

Captain Skye jerks back a step, letting her composure slip for a moment before clawing it back into place. I was surprised when I first met the genteel woman that introduced herself as Captain Georgiana Skye. She met my gaze without flinching and swept into a low bow that could have graced the courts back home. Mother would have had a fit if she saw the captain dressed in her well tailored coat and breeches arrive to be presented at court. A thought that gave me immense pleasure and sorely tempted me to try it myself.

"You forget yourself, Your Highness." Captain Skye's face is hard. Controlled. Her voice rings out with an iron strength. "The Dowager Queen placed me in charge of the welfare of all souls on board and it is my duty to ensure we reach our destination unscathed."

"I am the prince. If I command that we raise full sails and outrun the other ship, then that is what we will do."

"You may be the son of our king, but I am captain of this ship. I will not move forward with a plan that puts myself and my crew at risk. My men deserve better."

"Alon," I say carefully as I approach. He and Captain Skye turn to face me. "She's right."

Thankfully Alon is looking at me and not the captain, so he doesn't see the satisfied smile of victory that crosses her face.

"No, she's not. We're going to outrun them."

"Captain Skye said we can try, but we still need a plan in case we can't."

"Look, Nora, I know you're not as familiar with sailing as I am but let me clear that up for you. We *will* outrun them and you and Cap —"

"Oh, we are absolutely not doing this!" I square my shoulders, my spine stiffening to bring me to my full height. Alon is still taller, but Mother always says good posture and the right attitude can make the most stubborn man yield. "You are not allowed to be con-descending and tell me I'm wrong. That may work for others, but not me. I am not your subject, and you are not allowed to treat me like a child. If I wanted that I would go talk to my mother."

Alon flinches. Good. He eyes me warily; his mouth set in a hard line that refuses to give.

"Captain Skye is right, and you know it. We need to plan for the worst and if you're not willing to listen to her then you are no longer welcome in this conversation."

Alon rears back like I had slapped him. "Who do you think you are? You can't just dismiss me I'm —"

"Yes, I'm well aware of who you are, *husband*." I spit the word with malice, like that can somehow get the bad taste from it off my tongue. "Now don't you forget who *I* am. If you will not listen to reason, then we no longer need you here. Go below."

The only sounds are the waves below and the snapping of canvas from the sails above us. The crew watch with bated breath, fear and curiosity keeping them rooted to the spot as this spectacle unfolds before them. Captain Skye had backed several paces away when Alon and I squared off. Clearly her sense of self-preservation is strong. Good. We're going to need all of it if we're going to get out of this mess.

Alon straightens up to his full height, looming over me by several inches. His eyes flash with a steel I've never seen before. "I am well aware of who you are, *wife*, and in case you have forgotten it is my job to protect you and the crew of this ship."

"I believe Captain Skye has already claimed the responsibility for our souls while at sea. Your *protection*, as you put it, is neither needed nor wanted, seeing as how you insist on standing in the way of reason and logic." I look him in the eye, issuing my own challenge. "I am more than capable of assisting the captain with this myself. Go below and get out of our way before I drag you there myself."

Alon looks like he wants to keep arguing, but instead he surprises me. Snorting in disgust, he stalks off the bridge. He pauses at the stairs and turns back to us, face contorting as he hisses, "when the two of you realize you're in over your heads and need my help I'll be in our cabin."

Every ounce of courage remaining in my body goes towards holding myself steady, arms at my sides and my hands relaxed and unclenched. I refuse to cow to his anger. *Don't let him see he gets to you.*

Alon disappears down the stairs and a few moments later we hear the door to the cabin slam shut. The resounding echo breaks the hold on the crew, and they move again, this time with more urgency than before. Furtive glances and rapid whispers sweep across the decks, and I pretend not to notice they're mostly directed at me. Being at court, you get used to the whispers.

I turn to Captain Skye. "Please tell me you have a plan."

"Not yet, no."

"Shit." The start of a tension headache grips the base of my skull, and I pinch the bridge of my nose. "Wait, do we know who the other ship is?"

"They're not close enough yet. We pulled our colors as soon as we suspected another ship was near us to try and limit the possibility of an ambush. With how they're gaining, I would not be surprised if we could see their colors within the hour."

The spark of an idea takes root. A grin slides across my face as it grows larger into a crackling flame.

"I have an idea."

• • • ☽ • ◯ • ☾ • • •

Several hours later, I carefully make my way to the cabin Alon and I are forced to share to keep up appearances. It's a cramped little thing with barely enough room for a table, chair, and a bunk and clever trundle bed hidden beneath. I tap lightly on the door with the toe of my boot, shifting the tray in my arms.

"Alon? Are you awake? I brought food."

Cookie had insisted on preparing a shipwide meal after the almost fiasco that was running into the other ship. Thankfully, we got out lucky. The only casualties were some minor bruises among the more spirited crew members and a broken toe from an improperly lashed barrel getting loose. I tap again.

"Alon? You in there?"

I wait a few more beats and then let out a huff. This is ridiculous. It's my cabin too, after all, and I can enter as I please.

Shifting the tray to one hip, I use my newly freed hand to turn the weathered knob. The unlocked door swings open and I step into the hazy dusk of the cabin. My eyes blink rapidly as they work to adjust to the darkness.

The heavy tray threatens to become familiar with the shifting deck beneath me and I adjust my grip to try and keep from dropping it. Setting it in the curved hollow of the table, my gaze flicks quickly around the slightly musty room. Alon isn't here. The bed is unmade, the trundle tucked away in its hiding space, and the chair empty. With rising panic, I search the cabin once more to see if he had managed to wedge himself somewhere again. But Alon isn't here.

Swallowing the lump of fear in my throat, I hurry back out onto the deck and ask some of the crew if they've seen him. Captain Skye is back on the bridge surveying her queendom and nods briefly towards the crow's nest. In the early evening light I can see a richly clad foot hanging over the edge of the platform between the slatted railing.

Oh, come on. There's only one way to reach the crow's nest and it's not one I ever want to use. I lean over the deck railing to watch the waves crash against the ship far below. We're making good time with the wind behind us, but it also means that if you fall off it's easier to be hurt or left behind.

The rope ladder of rigging that grants access to the crow's nest sways in the breeze next to me. If it wasn't an inanimate object, I'd almost think it was taunting me. The only thing worse than heights is having to climb unsteady rope ladders *into* the heights. *It's okay. You'll be okay. There's no one here to push you.*

Taking a deep breath, I step up onto the slick railing at the side of the ship. My hands grip the scratchy ropes for balance as everything moves in tandem. Before I can think better of it, I twist on the ball of my right foot to allow my left leg to swing out over nothingness. My left foot comes to rest on the sorry excuse for a ladder beside me. I'm now half on and half off the rigging, my back pressed against the open air above the waves. Every fiber of my being is screaming at me that this is a terrible idea.

The ropes tremble beneath me, and panic starts to rise already. My lungs refuse to expand properly. I force several shallow breaths into the stubborn organs and count to ten in Latin. Then, I deliberately remove my right foot from the fleeting solidity of the railing and bring it over onto the shifting ropes. The only thing left to do now is climb.

My heart drops with every bounce and sway of the rigging. Thankfully, the sails don't need to be adjusted, so it's only me and the wind among the large pillows of canvas. With embarrassing slowness, I pull myself closer and closer to the crow's nest. It seems to tower above me, taunting my fear.

My luck from earlier hasn't worn out yet, thought, because I manage to reach the base of the crow's nest without incident. Just as I reach my hand out to grab the side of the wooden slats to pull myself up, a sharp crack of wind tears through the sails and sets everything jittering. Including me. A shriek bursts from me as my clammy hands slip, and my body falls sideways into –

A warm hand clamps around my wrist, pulling me upwards. A second hand closes around my arm. My face whips up and there he is above me. Holding me. *Saving* me. Clasping my free hand around his, Alon pulls me upwards and through the access gap for the crow's nest.

Chapter 27

In Which an Honest Conversation is Had

Alon

Nora sits, shaking, against the wooden slats of the crow's nest. Her hands are gripped around my arm like a vice, palms sweaty and jittering so much she can barely hang on. I carefully remove a hand from hers and gently wipe the tears from her cheeks.

"Are you okay? Are you hurt?"

It's hard to keep the panic from my voice. The last thing I want is for her to see just how worried I really am. I don't want to scare her but seeing her falling from the rigging has my teeth on edge. I almost lost her.

Nora shakes her head and gasps through her sobs, "don't like heights....Was – was – was pushed as – as a kid."

"Why didn't you ask me to come down then?"

"Did – didn't want to – to make a – a – a scene."

I shake my head in disbelief. This stubborn woman would rather climb to the heavens than admit she needed help. How very Nora.

We sit together with our hands clasped as the shadows grow longer and the sun slowly begins to sink towards the horizon. Little by little, Nora's sobs grow quieter until they stop altogether. Letting me go, she rubs her face and arms and wraps them around herself. It's hard not to stare as the sunlight glints off her hair and draws out the honey blonde strands amidst all the reds.

"Captain Skye told me what you did earlier. It was very clever. Well done."

"Thank you." Nora blinks at me owlishly. "You're...not mad then?"

"I can't say I'm particularly thrilled with how you chose to go about removing me from the bridge, but I am also not so prideful that I can't admit it was the right decision. You and Captain Skye were both right."

A warm swell of pride envelopes me for the woman sitting before me. Nora kept her head and stayed rational in a situation that I had found too stressful. I let my own fears and emotions get the better of me. If Nora hadn't ordered me off the bridge there is a very good chance things would not gone as well as they did.

Captain Skye spoke very highly of Nora in her report and did not hide her obvious admiration. They had gone ahead with attempting to outrun the other ship as I had been pushing for, the need to escape becoming even more tangible when it was confirmed the origins of said ship were undeniably questionable. It didn't take long for it to become clear that running was impossible for exactly the reason Captain Skye had pointed out – the winds really were just as favorable to them as they were to us.

Instead of waiting for the inevitable, Captain Skye had altered course into one of the many coves around Korala. This one had two entrances hidden from each other by a long curving rock formation. The channel that connected them narrowed in the center so only one ship can pass through at a time. As soon as we were in the cove and out of immediate sight, several sailors were dispatched to string up a thick rope soaked in cooking oil and wrapped in rags drenched with deck stain just above the water. How they came up with that ingenious combination remains to be seen.

It wasn't long after the crew had returned that the enemy vessel entered the cove as they pursued us. Once they had come far enough in to make it impossible to turn around, Nora herself shot several well-placed flaming arrows to set the rope ablaze. With no chance of moving forward and no possible way to reverse, the other ship was forced to drop all canvas in the hopes of avoiding the fire. Captain Skye expertly maneuvered us back into open waters and we fled under full sails. There has been no sign of the other ship since then and, provided we make it through the night without any sightings, it's fair to say we made a fast escape with no casualties.

My pride feeds that ever present longing behind my heart. It's plagued me since I first laid eyes on Nora so long ago in the gardens in Sephiroth. Even with her sitting a few scant feet away, our legs practically intertwined in the cramped quarters of the crow's nest, she still feels a million miles away somehow. It hurts knowing that, no matter what I do, Nora will still probably be in love another man at the end of our journey together and will choose him over me. Whether she believes in the flame reading or not, I do think *Tutu* was onto something.

Nora is quiet across from me, contemplating the clouds lazily wending through the skies above us. We sit in restful silence. There's an ease between us that hasn't been present since the night of the Remembrance Festival. If only it could always be like this.

"I think you owe me an answer."

Nora's eyes sparkle in the sunlight and watch me with an intensity I wish I could hide from. If we weren't stuck in a teeny tiny, slatted basket at the very top of the ship, I probably would have found a way to escape already.

"Only if you answer a question for me in return."

Nora cocks her head and studies me. I can see her weighing the options before her and deciding which is the lesser of the two evils.

"Fine. Ask away."

I choose my words carefully. "Why are you so insistent that you could never love me? Has nothing in our time together so far made you reconsider, even for a moment, that being married to me wouldn't actually be that horrible? We could be happy together, Nora."

As the words leave my mouth, I immediately know it's the wrong thing to ask. Nora shrinks inwards and closes herself off to me again.

"That's more than one question."

"Humor me."

"It's not as simple as just the possibility of being happy." She chews on her words, tasting them carefully before sharing them with me. "Teddy and I had always planned on getting married ever since we were about fourteen. Everyone thought we would too. It was only until this last year that my parents forbade it, and I didn't even understand why.

"He's more than just some boy to me. He's my oldest and dearest friend. My companion. In many ways he's my home. That kind of love is not one that can just be thrown away on a whim and the possibility that you could be happy with someone else."

"Is being happy not enough?"

Nora gives me a withering look. "There is more to life than just being happy. Why should I settle for just being happy when I have someone who celebrates me for who I am and knows me almost better than I know myself? Teddy has never asked me to change who I am or to apologize for it."

"Does he challenge you?"

"What do you mean?"

"Does he challenge you? You say he loves you and he doesn't ask you to change, but does he challenge you to keep growing? Keep learning? Keep working towards becoming the person you want to be?"

"Y-yes."

Nora is not convinced of her answer. It hangs between us like a cobweb – seemingly strong but will crumble at the slightest outside push by something larger. I'm not going to push any further. Nora is clearly working through some things and there's no reason for me to try and insert myself any more than I already have.

"I'm sorry if I have ever made you feel like you needed to apologize for who you are around me." I incline my head sincerely. "That was never my intention. Please, ask your questions. It's only fair."

I sit quietly, watching as Nora recenters herself. She finds the question she had wanted to ask me all along and I can tell she's fighting with herself about it before she even opens her mouth. If I was a betting man, I would put money on already knowing *exactly* what she is going to ask about.

"On our journey from Sephiroth you had some kind of an...episode...during the storm. And today you argued with Captain Skye without giving her a chance to speak. You refused to listen, and you snapped at me. I want to know why."

"Why what?"

I try to keep my voice innocent. I definitely know what Nora is asking, but I want her to spell it out for me anyway.

"Why did you react the way you did?" Nora chews lightly on her bottom lip.

That small gesture is unbelievably distracting. Gods if she keeps doing that then I'm –

"It's obvious the two events are connected to each other and whatever happened to you when you were sixteen. Your Baba just wouldn't talk about it, so I don't know what actually happened. I want to know. You owe me that."

I take a deep breath and slowly blow it out through my nose. "You're right, Nora, they're all connected." My heart is already starting to race at the idea of telling the story, having to relive the events. "I'll tell you, but I need to ask you for something in return."

She turns a skeptical eye towards me.

"I need you to just sit and not interrupt. This is not an easy thing for me to talk about and constantly having to stop and start to answer questions will make it so much worse. Can you do this for me?"

Nora nods, the skepticism replaced by bald faced curiosity. I can't say I blame her. Everyone wants to know this story. Well, they *think* they want to know it. But when they *actually* know it, they realize they preferred to stay in the dark.

Taking a deep breath, I slowly begin. "It all started during a normal game of capture the flag..."

Chapter 28

In Which a Story is Shared

"C'mon Alon it's got to be down here!"

Alon trails along behind Kalani down the coast, dodging between rocks, tide pools, and the slowly rising waters. Alon isn't convinced Caspian and Ryo would have come anywhere near here, but Kalani had insisted on looking just in case. They all knew the dangers of getting caught in the tide and usually avoided the caves as a rule. Too many people each year disappeared to the cave system that runs below parts of the island. It's all too easy to misjudge the waters and get swept so deep into the caves with the rising tides they never found their way out again.

Water and condensation dripped down from the heavy rocks overhead. Everything was slick and cold, the water already almost knee deep. A shiver climbs Alon's back as he surveys the looming darkness in front of him. It takes all his focus not to trip and slide beneath the surface.

"There's nothing here, Kalani. Mama and Baba would have our heads if they knew we were down here."

"Alright you big baby. Let's go then. There's no way those two are smart enough to really hide their flag. We must have missed it."

Alon huffed quietly as he waded back through the water. The chill soaked through his boots, chilling his feet even though they remained dry. The brothers picked their way back across the sand and rocks, racing the ever-rising ocean tide as it came closer and closer to the cliffs.

"What about the old granary?" Alon fidgeted with his hands as he watched his older brother survey the beach. "Caspian uses the storage loft as a hideout sometimes when he doesn't want Mama to know he's stolen food from the kitchen."

A sly smile crossed Kalani's face. "How do you know that?"

"Because I've caught him," said Alon with a matching grin. "C'mon it can't hurt to look. We've already checked everywhere else."

Korala's original settlers had tried to create their own town much further inland and away from the sea. The granary, meeting house, church, and the bones of a few houses still stood as monuments to their efforts. Long abandoned, they were pitfalls of rotted wood and mossy ivy hiding holes that could break legs just as easily as twist ankles.

A lopsided shrug of agreement from Kalani and the two break out in a mad dash back across the beach, through the port city, and towards the cliff sides where the old settlement perched precariously against the weather. With matched strides, the two brothers careened up the pathways and around sharp corners, jumping rocks and ruts and calling out insults as the other faltered. Neither wanted the other to win and neither wanted to face his own downfall. Warring beliefs on whether the eldest should yield to the youngest or the youngest yield to the eldest crossed through their minds just as quickly as their feet raced across the uneven ground. With heaving sides and a final burst of speed, Alon hurdled a fallen tree and slapped his hand on the corner of one of the decrepit buildings before bending over double.

"I win!" He crowed, lungs burning and eyes watering.

"Yeah, yeah. I let you win."

Alon's only response is to flip his middle finger at Kalani while he focuses on filling his lungs. The two bump and jostle each other as they clambered around the granary together. One by one they checked and re-checked every nook and cranny that could feasibly hide a flag. After their third search through all the remaining buildings revealed no hidden secrets, it was decided the flag really wasn't at the old settlement and they needed to look elsewhere.

"You go on ahead," Alon said to Kalani as he perched on a rock amidst the grass edging the cliffs. "I'm going to sit for a few minutes and see if I can figure out where Caspian would have hidden this thing."

"Alright, but if I figure it out and get the flag without your help then you owe me dessert for a week." Kalani's eyes twinkled at the familiar barter the brothers had used ever since they were small children.

Alon tipped back his head and laughed. "Deal. And if I do it without you then you have to be *Tutu*'s escort the next time Mama and Baba host visiting nobility."

Kalani winced, dancing was not one of his strong suits, but eventually he agreed to the terms. They shook hands to seal their bargain and planned to meet up within the hour to put their heads back together to keep looking for the flag. As Kalani loped off down the road, Alon settled back onto his rock and turned his gaze to the sea.

The waves had been unsettled all day, and it was clear a storm was coming in. The gray water mirrored the heavy bank of clouds that had been haunting Korala for the past week. Storm seasons were always difficult to get through. This year was no different.

Footsteps approached from behind, but Alon didn't turn around.

"Have an idea already?" He called absently over his shoulder.

"No' exactly," came an unfamiliar bark.

A sharp blow to the side of Alon's head knocked him sideways off his perch. He slammed into the ground; the air knocked from his lungs. Stars danced across his eyelids before going dark.

• • • ☽ • ◯ • ☾ • • •

Alon blinked hazily in the murky light. Blood pounded through his head and threatened to open his skull with the force of the pressure. After several groggy moments he realized, that he was not swaying on his feet as he had initially thought, but that he was tied by his feet to a rafter. His hands were bound tightly behind his back, rope cutting into his wrists.

He swung gently back and forth, the light from the round porthole just strong enough for him to see the trail of dried blood on the floor beneath him. Outside the light was dim, but the familiar salty brine of the ocean permeated everything. Alon was on a ship.

Raised voices from the hallway staggered closer and closer until the door to the room swung open and two burly men tumbled through. They continued yelling and swearing good naturedly at each other while setting up a small table and two chairs in the center of the space. Alon was helpless to do anything other than hang there like a fish caught in a net.

The pressure in Alon's head continued to build the longer he swung. He could feel where he had been hit, it pulsed with a depth of pain previously unknown to him. The rocking of the boat threatened to turn Alon's stomach, and it was an experience he had never known before. Alon had spent arguably more time on the sea growing up than on land. His body was more familiar with the ebbs and flows of the tides than he sometimes was walking in a straight line down the hallways of the Manor House. If he was seasick, it was a sure sign that things were not well.

The larger of the two men – more accurately described as a Small Mountain while his companion was really a Large Boulder – released a previously unnoticed lever on the far wall nearest the door and the rope holding Alon went slack. Without hands to break his fall, it was a miracle that hitting the crusty deck beneath him did not knock him out again.

Adrenaline surged white hot through Alon's body when he felt the rope give way. He managed to tuck his head just enough that his shoulders took the brunt of the fall, rolling gracelessly onto his back with the wind knocked from his body. Gasping like a beached fish, Alon lay on the floor desperately trying to refill his bruised lungs with the stale air.

The Large Boulder hauled him up into one of the chairs and secured his hands roughly behind him. Alon didn't know for sure, but he wouldn't have been surprised if they had tied his hands to the chair itself. With heaving sides, he decided it was best to be docile. He sat limply and focused instead on his breathing. He blinked through the pouding in his head and tried not to flinch as he could feel his body begin to regulate back to normal after being hung upside down for so long.

The two men clumped off through the door just as quickly as they had arrived and Alon was left with nothing but the familiar sounds of a ship. It was oddly comforting. The waves on the other side of the wall, the sounds of orders being called from above, the familiar clicking and creaking as things shifted with the back-and-forth motion of the sea. It helped quiet his mind and calm his racing heart.

As Alon slowly returned to himself and began to contemplate possible escape, he heard another set of footsteps approaching the door. The two men from before had footsteps that reflected their personality – loud, brash, and unencumbered. This new set was reserved, almost collected. Controlled. They strode with purpose and intention towards the room. Pausing only briefly outside the door, the footsteps, and subsequently the man attached to them, clipped through the door and settled beneath the same table that Alon himself sat at.

The man these footsteps belonged to was of a slight frame and average height. His cleft chin looked out of place on his heart shaped face, accentuated by long dark hair pulled back into a low tail at the nape of his neck. A widow's peak dipped ever so slightly down the middle of his forehead and disappeared into his permanently wrinkled brow. Though he seemed innocent enough, Alon knew the most dangerous men were those that did not outwardly appear to be so.

The two sat in silence. Alon was determined to not break it first. He wanted this newcomer to concede the upper hand, to give a voice to who he was and what he had done. The minutes ticked by in slow increments as the two watched each other warily. Eventually the man winked and bared his teeth in what Alon assumed was supposed to be a smile.

"Come now, Your Royal Highness, how long shall we sit in silence?" The man's voice was soft and condescending, hard-edged beneath the surface of politeness. "Sulking does you no good, Kalani. May I call you Kalani? Seems only appropriate given the cir-cumstances."

Alon's head began to spin again, but this time not from being hung upside down. *They were after Kalani*, he thought frantically.

Why were they trying to get Kalani? Knowledge is power, so until Alon knew more he chose to remain silent.

"Did you really think you could break the engagement with my sister and suffer no consequences? Omorose is distraught, Father is furious, and I believe we are owed some compensation. I think some trade secrets are in order, don't you? Seems only fair."

"I'm not–" Alon paused to clear some of the blood and phlegm from his throat. His voice came out in a rasp "–I'm not Kalani."

The man crossed his arms and chortled. "No, of course you're not. And I'm the queen of Ailona." A sharp glint in the man's eye chilled Alon to the bone. "You have wronged my family, and I will have what is owed to us. We will have our pound of flesh repaid."

"I'm not Kalani. I was with him at the old settlement where you took me. He went on ahead and I stayed behind. I'm Alon. The seventh. You have the wrong brother. I don't know who you or Omorose are."

Alon watched as surprise, anger, disgust, and hatred flashed across the man's features. He slammed back from the table and began to pace back and forth in the small space muttering to himself. Every third or fourth pass he speared Alon with a look of such malice that, if looks could kill, Alon would have never made it out of that conversation alive.

Finally, having reached some sort of conclusion, the man returned to his seat and pulled a small case out from his pocket. He set it deliberately in the center of the table and fixed Alon with a menacing stare.

You are not the brother I intended to get," he sniffed disdainfully, "but you'll do. Now tell me...Alon, how well would you say you handle pain?"

What followed can only be described as some of the worst moments of Alon's life. This unknown man refused to accept that Alon knew nothing of his father's plans for Korala's future or the extent of its trade routes. With each demanded question going unanswered, the man became more erratic and violent. He slid needles beneath Alon's fingernails, clamped rough wooden pegs around soft parts of his body, and even pulled one of his molars from his mouth. Still, Alon could do nothing more than repeat he knew nothing of the information the man sought and plead for his mercy.

It was to no avail, however. On and on they went in the same never-ending loop. The same questions asked, the same answers given. Nothing ever changed.

The torture eventually came to a close only because the Small Mountain from before entered the room and whispered something into the man's ear. He let out a cry of rage and backhanded Alon across the table. The force of the blow knocked his chair off balance and Alon plummeted to the floor, mercifully going unconscious again as his head struck the rough-hewn planks.

Alon woke later to complete darkness. From the odd heavy feeling in his head and weightlessness in his body he could tell they had strung him back up again. He helplessly swung from the rafters as the floor pitched and rolled beneath him. Frantic yelling and thunderous pounding from above his feet told him he was in even more danger than before. The storm had finally arrived.

Storm season was not something the Koralans ever joked about. Hurricanes whipped up so fast you couldn't see them until they were practically right on top of you. The sea took what she believed she was owed, and it was clear that she believed this ship needed to pay its debts.

Alon continued to sway back and forth as the water became rougher, the waves getting higher. Thunder roared from above and below. With every flash of lightning, Alon could see the room thrown into sharp relief for only a moment before plunging back into darkness. An ear-splitting crack echoed through the storm as the main mast snapped in two. All around came the screams of men as they plunged through the confusion, trying to get out of the path of the falling wood and canvas. Those unlucky enough to be in the rigging trying to wrestle the sails were plunged into the icy water below and lost to the depths.

Fear coursed through Alon with a sharp bitterness beneath his tongue. He desperately tried to free himself from his bonds, but the ropes holding his hands behind his back cut through his wrists and drew slick blood to the surface. He tried to cry out, to let someone know he was still there, but with the storm outside no one could hear his calls.

Another sharp snap cut through the night followed by more screams. The ship juddered sharply one way and then the other before settling with a sigh and a moan. From far below, Alon heard the tell-tale rush of water entering the hull. The bitterness of fear in his mouth settled into an icy terror in his stomach as he realized that the ship must have struck rock and was starting to break apart. If it sank, he would go down with it.

With every crash of thunder from above and groan of seawater from below, Alon struggled against his bindings. Every time he felt like they were loosening, a sudden jolt and rock from the ship sent him swaying and tightened the knots again.

A deafening crack as the ship split in two chilled him to the bone. Goosebumps tore across his body as fear turned his blood to ice. Seawater flooded the interior decks and crashed through them with such severity that those caught in the flow barely had time to draw breath for a scream.

Alon tipped as the ship sank beneath the waves. The water he'd grown up on rose up to meet him like an old friend. It cradled him in a swirl of coldness that knocked what little air had settled into his bruised lungs back out. Every bruise and cut across his body sang out in pain as salt licked his wounds and caressed his cheeks. The tears falling from Alon's eyes mixed with the brine until you couldn't tell where one ended and the other began. No matter how much Alon fought to free himself from his bonds and rise to the surface, the sea only whispered to him gently as she claimed him for herself.

In Which Doubts Begin to Form

Nora

Alon is withdrawn and contemplative. His usual cocky and confident demeanor has given way to the shell of the man before me. The more he shares with me about what happened the more he retreats into himself. His knees are pulled tight to his chest, his shoulders curling over them. It's almost like he's trying to be as small and unnoticeable as possible. There's a hollowness in his eyes as he watches me. Like he's trying to figure out if he told me too much and if I'm going to run away from him screaming.

"It took them over a week to find me. At least, I think it was that long."

"A – a week?"

He nods. I gape at him. Dammit I need to close my mouth. My chin jerks up, teeth clicking together with the effort. Alon is a caged animal trapped between hunters. My heart goes out to him, and my arms reach out on their volition to try and wrap him in my embrace. Words dance across my tongue, but they're all the wrong ones to say.

"How did you...survive...for a week?"

"I didn't"

"I don't understand."

Alon's eyes harden considerably while he watches me. "They didn't find me for over a week."

"Yeah, I heard you the first time. What I don't understand is how you survived."

"I told you. I didn't."

I throw my hands up, exasperated. "I don't know what that means!"

"It means every day for over a week I died!"

Alon's voice cracks. He buries his face in his hands and his shoulders hitch as he tries to breathe. A creeping chill catches on my ankles and slowly climbs up my legs to spread across my body.

"You died every day for over a week?"

Alon nods, choosing to speak quietly into his knees than to address me directly. "I revive every morning with the sun. I drowned five times. At least, I think it was only five. My memory is a little patchy, but every morning I awoke and drowned all over again."

The chill sinks into my chest and icy tendrils stroke my heart as I fully understand everything he had endured. "How did they find you?"

"The ship broke into pieces as it sank. The room I was being held in had the most pressure and split down the middle. I ended up floating tied to the floor once I reached the seabed. For four days the movement of the water around me caused the rope holding me to rub against other pieces of broken wood and rocks. It frayed enough that on the fifth day, in my struggle while I drowned again, I managed to break the remaining bit of rope and get to the surface. But I went too fast, I got diver's disease. I managed to surface and climb onto a part of the ship that had not sunk beneath the water, but with the diver's disease and the seawater still in my lungs I was dead by nightfall.

"When I woke the next morning, every breath felt like fire and my body could barely move. I was able to find a broken blade sunk into the wood of the ship and cut off the remaining ropes, but I was still stranded with no idea where I was. Without food and water my body was spent, and my mind began to fracture. I stayed on the shipwreck until Mama and Baba were able to rescue me."

"How many –" I fought to get my question out around the acid taste on my tongue "– how many more times did you die? Before they found you, I mean."

Alon levels me with a stare, my heart rapidly rising as his eyes bore into mine. All that pain and suffering is etched clearly across his gaze.

"Three more times. When I die and return my body needs excess food to restore itself. Without it, my hold on reality is...tenuous at best. Twice more I died from lack of food and water. The third time I slipped and hit my head when I tried to climb into what remained of the rigging to see if I could find my own way out. In my weakened state, it did not take much to send me over the edge again."

"Did you ever figure out where you were?"

"Funnily enough, I was on the other side of a beach my brothers and I loved to play on as children." Alon snorts disdainfully. "The beach is tucked away in a cove that borders the line between our kingdom and the Elders' territory. Many avoid the place for fear of accidentally crossing the line and breaking the treaty, but for a band of boys intent on playing rebellion it called to us. The other side of the cove is a maze of rocks and underwater currents. That's where they wrecked. I was so close to home and didn't even realize it....Couldn't even save myself..."

I hesitantly reach out and rest a hand on his knee. "No one blames you for that. What you experienced was...it was horrifying. I would not wish that on my worst enemy and yet you came through it and you still sail. You don't let your fear control you."

"It took longer than you think before I went back on the water again," Alon says wryly. His thumb absently rubs the back of my hand in lazy circular patterns. "It's taken many years for me to feel comfortable sailing again. But that experience? It still haunts me. You saw it on our journey from Sephiroth when we were caught in that storm. And again when that ship threatened us. All I could think about earlier was that everything was happening all over again and that I —" he looks up at me suddenly "— that I couldn't protect you."

The words hang between us, heavy with meaning. There's that same tugging behind my heart. Why does it always start at the most inopportune times? Ignoring it is impossible. The longer we talk the louder it gets. Squeezing Alon's hand gently, I remove mine from his knee and settle it in my own lap. It tingles slightly like a ghostly caress, reminding me of him.

"You don't need to protect me." I say quietly. "I never asked you to."

"Your journey to the crow's nest says otherwise."

Alon's mouth lifts into a half smile. That stupid familiar cocky gesture that leaves my heart fluttering. *Gods, I love that smile.* That's a weird thought, but we are not going to try and unpack it right now. Instead, I stick my tongue out at him, crossing my eyes for good measure.

I turn my face upwards. The last of the sunset streaks across the sky above us in pale pinks and fiery oranges. A few low hanging clouds muddle through the colors like pigs in a sty, but otherwise all is calm. The first of the stars have begun to peep out and show their faces.

"I know —" Alon clears his throat awkwardly "— I know you don't love me. I accept that. I just wish you would not close yourself off to the idea of being my friend. We could be happy together."

"Alon, I love —"

"Teddy. Yes, I know." He smiles at me sadly. "I do not fault you for that love. All I'm asking for right now is the chance to live our lives in companionship as friends. Nothing more. Just think about it, *Ku'u Lei*. For me. If your decision is still the same when we reach the end of our journey, then I will gladly step aside for you to create the life you want. We will remain married in name and nothing more."

We sit in silence for a few more minutes, the light really starting to fade around us. Alon's gaze is heavy as he watches me, but I ignore it and survey the waves breaking far below. *How am I ever going to get down from here?*

"You staying up here any longer?" Alon sits with his legs dangling off the edge of the crow's nest. He looks at me expectantly. "I was going to head down."

"No, I'll come down. You go ahead and I'll follow."

Alon nimbly slides off the platform and twists to catch the ropes beneath. I peer over the edge and can already feel my heart starting to race. And not even in the good way. Coming up here was such a bad idea.

Alon hangs on the ropes several feet down and just waits for me to follow. Turning onto my belly, I carefully slide my legs over the edge and flail for a second before finding purchase on the rungs. Another few breaths and then I slide the rest of the way off, clutching the rope with shaking hands.

"Did I ever tell you about my dog Hector?"

Alon's voice floats up from below me. I slowly begin to climb down and then freeze as the rope jostles under his movements.

"No," I call down. My voice shakes. Traitor.

"He was a funny little dog. A mutt I found on my ramblings that I brought home ."

Another breath, another step. Keep going. You can do this.

"Mama said I could keep him as long as I took care of him. He followed me around everywhere and loved being included in everything. Had a thing for socks, though. I suppose we all have our vices."

Alon's voice is like a balm to my fear. With every word my shoulders slowly drop from my ears, my muscles shaking slightly from exertion rather than fear. Move your foot. Now your hand. And your foot again. Keep going.

"What happened to him?" I ask distractedly. The ropes are becoming slacker as we descend closer to the deck, and it takes more concentration to remain upright.

"He passed on a while back. We gave him traditional funeral rights and buried him at sea."

Strong hands wrap around my waist as my shoes touch the railing. They lift me gently, carefully guide me the last few feet down to the deck. Once Alon is sure I'm steady again, he drops his hands but continues to linger. He distractedly smoothes my collar and brushes a stray piece of hair out of my face. He gives me a small smile, his eyes soft.

"Thank you for listening, Nora." Alon takes my hand, kissing it softly, and then ambles away across the deck, calling out to some of the crew as he goes.

It's like he's stolen all the air from my body with his show of chivalry and I slump back against the railing. It's so nice to be back on mostly solid ground. The gentle rocking of the deck is a vast improvement over the jostling of the ropes and something I am at least comfortable with.

There's no question that Alon made my own descent far easier than it would have been had I tried alone. Above me, a few more stars finish dressing their hair and now shine down blithely on my upturned face as I fill my lungs with the salt-crusted air.

My mind wanders back to Alon's story and can't help but compare the vulnerable and honest man I just saw with the cocky self assured one that irritates me to no end. If I had seen this side of Alon sooner, would I have changed my mind? Would I have pushed back harder against Teddy when he insisted we needed to know how to remove his gift in case Belladonna ever came back? The answer eludes me, and my hands twist against the railing in annoyance.

Teddy is what I've always known. The person I have always loved. His promises to me are all or nothing and I guess I thought I had to promise him the same in return. A niggling in the back of my mind grows stronger, pushing to the forefront. Teddy seems to accept that we can't be truly married, but then he turns around and says he wants more for us. For me. Is it truly more for me? Or is it more for him?

My breath huffs out in frustration. Things have gotten so perplexing lately. It seemed so obvious at the start. It was me and Teddy against the world. Nothing could stand in our way and keep us from the life we had planned out.

And then Alon happened. He came crashing into my life with his self-assurance and challenging questions. He somehow sets my heart beating faster in my chest with every cocky grin he sends my way. He is infuriating and confusing and someone I think I could be more than a friend with if I just allowed myself to give in to the feeling.

Teddy said we need to know how to remove Alon's gift in case Belladonna comes back so we can protect ourselves. At the time I really did think he was right. It seemed like a logical choice to ensure my survival. But now I don't know. I can't seem to shake the feeling that if it comes down to it, Alon would sacrifice himself to protect me without me even having to ask. And that thought is both scary and thrilling, filling me with a cacophony of emotions I struggle to put a name to.

I rub absently at the prickling in my chest, trying to soothe my seemingly ever-present agitation. I'm not going to find any answers tonight and the person I want to talk to is waiting for me back in Sephiroth.

What if, that traitorous little voice whispers quietly, *you're making the wrong choice?*

Chapter 30

In Which Company is Found

Alon

Seagulls dance above us as we sail calmly through the last leg of our journey. The railing presses against my hips as I watch the slightly unfamiliar cliffs and crags of this side of Korala amble past us at a leisurely pace.

The last few days have been kind of lonely. After our conversation in the crow's nest, it seemed like it would be prudent to give Nora some space and time as well. I don't know why I felt like I could tell her about what happened to me. It felt right. *She* feels right. And safe. The first person I've ever really felt like that with before.

So, while I'm not technically avoiding Nora, per se, I also haven't been going out of my way to cross paths with her like I had been before. I *have* been avoiding our cramped cabin though. It was always too small for two people to cohabitate comfortably in anyway. The few times I saw Nora during the day she was clearly chewing on things of her own. She needs time to move towards a decision of some kind, and I can only pray whatever path she chooses to walk will be favorable for me.

That damn incessant tug pulling behind my heart keeps growing stronger though. It definitely grew more noticeable as I watched her learn about my home and navigate her way through its unfamiliar territory with grace. But it's reached a new fevered pitch because I haven't seen her as much lately. If it's this annoyingly insistent after several days of not talking to Nora, I hate to know what it'll feel like when she inevitably goes back to Teddy.

Each new day brings a new fissure in my resolve to let her make her own decision on who she wants to be with. With each new crack there is still just the tiniest bit of hope that maybe, just maybe, she'll choose me after all. She still wears her sunflower pendant nearly every day. If she didn't care for me even a little, then why would she do that? Do women continue to wear jewelry gifted to them by men they claim not to like? I've told Nora I would be more than happy to be her friend and companion with no expectations for anything more and that's completely true. But gods I crave something more.

Captain Skye's purposeful appearance interrupts my musing.

"Good morning, Your Highness." She bows her head briefly. "We will be dropping sail within the hour. I have arranged a rowboat to take you and Nor – Her Highness to shore."

A flush creeps up Captain Skye's neck at the slip with Nora's title and I catch myself grinning. I didn't realize she and Nora were on first name terms with each other. Captain Skye is always so careful around me to address me with the proper titles even after I insisted she call me Alon. It's just like Nora to convince the captain it's not a big deal to use their given names with each other.

"Thank you, Captain. I will let Nora know."

"No need, Your Highness." The blush deepens another shade and spreads to the captain's cheeks. "Her Highness joined me for a light luncheon and I informed her already. Her maid is assisting her in preparing to go ashore as we speak. We shall remain anchored here until you are ready to return."

With a slight bow, Captain Skye steps away and strides back towards the bridge of the ship. Turning my face to the afternoon sun, I revel in the familiar smells of salt, tar, and earth. Our journey is so close to its end. I'd been hoping to have made more progress in getting closer with Nora, but I'm still being held at arm's length.

Sighing, I push off from the railing and make my way down below decks to the borrowed bunk I've been using the past several nights. No time like the present to gather my things and prepare to go ashore.

$$\bullet \bullet \bullet \;) \bullet \bigcirc \bullet (\; \bullet \bullet \bullet$$

"You and Captain Skye seem friendly."

After being ferried to the beach, Nora and I had struck out towards the Falls in silence. The only conversation so far had been a few minor course corrections as we trekked. The quietness that had once been peaceful is heavy again, weighed down with unspoken things and unasked questions.

For some reason, I picked one of the dumbest topics to try and break that silence. Why did I ask about her relationship with the captain? There are so many other questions I want to ask instead. Nora just looks at me like a diver coming up after spending too long underwater – disoriented and grasping for a handhold.

"What did you say?"

"You and Captain Skye. You seem friendly. She mentioned you took your lunch together today."

"Oh. Yes." Nora stumbles over her words. "Georgie has been very helpful in teaching me more about sailing and has offered me some guidance on some personal matters. I guess you could say that we have grown friendly with one another."

She peters out and we are back to silence. Taking a breath, I steel myself for the possible reaction to what I am going to say next.

"I'm sorry."

Now Nora does look at me directly, eyes boring into me with an intensity that sends a prickling sensation across my body. She studies me like I've suddenly grown six more arms and I'm pretending to be an octopus.

"You're sorry? For what?"

"I should have been more careful in sharing what happened to me. Only one person knows the full story of what really happened and –"

"You've been avoiding me because you think I'm upset by what happened to you?"

There's fire in Nora's voice and a small zing jolts through me. She did notice my absence the last several days!

"No, I —"

"Because that's just ridiculous! I'm not some fragile flower to keep hidden in a hot house!"

"I know."

"Do you? Because you've been walking on glass around me, Alon, and treating me like I'll break if you look at me too hard."

"That was not my intention. I wanted to give you space."

"Space."

"Yes."

"Why?"

"Most people need space after learning what you did. The only person that I've told what happened to me in its entirety was Baba and I even left out some of the worst of it. I didn't with you, though. After I told him he could barely speak or look at me for a week without getting emotional."

Nora snorts derisively. "It takes more than that to scare me."

"Then what does scare you?"

"Losing the people I love."

The answer is said so simply and without a care in the world. Like it was right in front of me the whole time. I suppose it was. Gods how I hope I'm on that list of people she loves.

"Is that why you've been so...pensive... lately?"

"Well, that's a nice way to put it. Mother always called me melancholy. It's part of it yes, but not all."

"Would you tell me the rest?"

"No."

"Why?"

"Because I don't want to."

My annoyance fights against my self-control. "Please, Nora. Let me in."

"Alon," Nora sighs wearily. "Please. I have so much I have to think about lately and the least troubling is why someone who I thought was becoming my frie—" she catches herself and starts again "– a person who told me about a horrible thing that happened to him is avoiding me. I don't mean to dismiss your experience or the pain you carry from it, but there are decisions I have to make approaching very quickly and I have a lot on my mind."

The stamping and blowing of horses filters through the trees, muffled somewhat by the underbrush. The faintest whiff of woodsmoke floats gently on the breeze and welcomes me like an old friend.

"Nora, I think —"

"Please, Alon, just respect this and don't push."

"No, Nora, be quiet. I don't think we're alone."

With wide eyes, Nora stops to listen with me. Above the faint sound of running water, we can hear voices calling to each other and to their horses. There's no doubt about it now. There are several people up ahead, but are they the people we're looking for? There's woodsmoke among the trees and the distinct smell of cooking meat. An encampment maybe?

I gesture to Nora, and she takes up position behind me and slightly to the side. Slipping a dagger from her sleeve, she rocks forward to the balls of her feet and slowly follows me as we creep through the trees. We move like shadows, careful to avoid snapping twigs and sticking to the soft earth and dead pine needles to keep our approach as silent as possible. After a few moments, we arrive at the edge of a small clearing and take shelter behind some blackberry bushes.

A simple wagon is parked on the far side of the small clearing. Beside it, three horses whicker back and forth from their patch of grass. Three cloth tents, two small and one large, are pitched under the trees while four men perch on logs around a crackling fire, warming their hands and stirring various pots and pans. They all wear the matching grey livery of *Tutu*'s personal guard.

"It's okay," I whisper to Nora, "I think *Tutu* sent them. That's her crest."

"As long as you're sure." She looks less than convinced.

Still keeping her dagger pressed to her side, Nora straightens and follows me into the clearing. One of the men catches sight of us as we emerge from the bushes and leaps up to bow deeply. The other men also stand and bow as we approach.

"I beg pardon, Your Highnesses, for our relaxed states." The man's voice is a deep baritone, comforting and commanding. "We were not expecting you for another hour at least."

"No need to apologize. We walked fast."

Nora's wry comment is lost on the men, but I chuckle appreciatively. "Don't worry, Commander, I won't tell *Tutu*. We were not expecting to find company."

"The Dowager Queen sent us over the mountain pass. We were to set up camp and meet you on your journey to the Falls. She wanted to make sure you were protected and, in her words, were well fed before meeting the Elders."

Rich smells of cooking game waft over us again and my stomach gives a demanding groan. I had been too wrapped up in my own thoughts to remember to eat before leaving the ship earlier. My stomach was trying to tie itself in knots after so much uphill walking.

"A warm meal is definitely inviting." I hold my arm out to Nora. "Shall we?"

"After so long eating ship's rations I could go for some game."

Nora links her arm through mine, neatly slipping her dagger back into her sleeve, and together we take seats on one of the logs. The meal is loud and raucous, *Tutu*'s guards regaling us with stories of dinner parties gone wrong, escapades watching *Tutu*'s old lapdog, and different legends about Korala.

"Oh, Commander Fletchling, I just have to ask. Did you see any bandits on your journey here?"

"No, Your Highness," Fletchling's brow furrows in confusion. "The mountain pass is safe for quite a while longer. There haven't been any confirmed bandit sightings in several years. Honestly, the goats are more of a problem than bandits. Why do you ask?"

"Oh no reason." Nora's mouth twitches as she tries to hide a smirk and fixes me with a knowing look. "Just a rumor I heard."

My laugh bubbles up from deep within me and overflows, my shoulders bumping into my companions as they shake. Nora joins me and, after a few minutes, the rest of the men chortle hesitantly. Together we sit, side by side. Our elbows brush and our shoulders knock into each other as we eat, drink, and share stories in the fading evening light.

Chapter 31

In Which a Destination is Reached

Nora

"So...what do we do now?"

"Mama and *Tutu* said they just waited at the bottom of the Falls and the Elders found them so.... Wait? I guess?"

My chin dips as I nod, stretching out on the blanket spread out on the hard packed earth near the water. The Falls roar on the far side, sending bits of spray in all directions. It pounds into the small basin at the bottom before careening into the rest of the lake and eventually funneling into a river. Beside us, the river narrows and flows lazily down the hillside back towards the warm sea. All around, crickets and frogs sing in the evening air and trees sway together in the breeze.

After finishing our meal with *Tutu*'s guards, Alon and I hiked the rest of the way to the Falls together. The path was faint and more of a deer trail than an actual walking path, but we found our way through the trees in the last of the evening light. Thankfully, we were only a twenty-minute walk or so from the Falls and we spent the time in a companionable silence. Much different from the one earlier in the afternoon.

What I had told Alon earlier was true – I do have a lot to think about. Choices he doesn't even know I have to make loom in front of me. Their approach is hurtling towards me faster than I care to think about and it's terrifying.

While I still love Teddy and know that he holds a piece of my heart, it's very easy for me to see that he no longer holds the entire thing. Alon snuck up from somewhere and laid claim to his own piece, becoming just as important to me as Teddy is in the process. He's even someone I would consider more than just a friend.

Growing up I had been fairly isolated. As the only princess in a royal family with very few aunties and female cousins my own age to confide in, it's impossible *not* to be isolated to some degree. Mother was always extremely strict with ensuring no one would be able to take advantage of me, but in doing so she also made it very difficult for me to get close to people and make friends. I'd be lying if I said that, because of that, I didn't cling to every friendship I possibly could. Sometimes to my detriment.

What Alon said has been weighing on my heart for a while. The short answer is that he was right. I could be incredibly happy as his wife, living out our time together as companions and friends. As much as I hate to admit it, there is definitely physical attraction between us if that dream is any indication. Heat rushes to my cheeks at the thought of that dream. Thank the gods it's dark enough Alon can't see it.

I honestly believe Alan and I could, hopefully, have a fulfilling life together. Provided he doesn't try to control me and stop me from welcoming Teddy into my bed. If I want Teddy in my bed, that is.

The problem I keep coming back to is that it's obvious Teddy wants more. He wants to be more to me than just a consort even though he says differently. He wants to be a partner. An equal. A husband. And I wanted to be able to give him that, but I don't know if that's something I want anymore. Is giving Teddy what he wants worth destroying a person that truly has become a dear friend? The answer to that question is still annoyingly elusive.

We lay on our backs, watching the stars as the moon rises over the treetops. I've never had a head for astronomy, but Alon points out the constellations with ease and tells me stories about them. How the great bear was harnessed by the old gods and immortalized in the stars. Why Orion wears his belt with pride as he hunts beasts across the night skies. Being with Alon is peaceful. Easy. And yet I'm still clinging to the idea of staying with Teddy. Why?

Alon is in the middle of telling me about the constellation Leo when he falls silent and sits up.

"Is everything okay?"

"Someone's out there."

I jerk upright, squinting through the darkness. The only shapes outside the faint ring of light from our smoldering campfire is the dark silhouettes of the trees. Every muscle in my body goes rigid. My senses click into high alert, my eyes scanning the forest edge for any sign of danger. My dagger slips easily from my sleeve, the weight comforting in my hand.

"There is no need for that."

The voice from behind us is a growly lilt that sends a shiver running down my spine. Turning together, Alon and I find ourselves being watched by three figures standing at the edge of the water. They are definitely human, but it's hard not to think of them as otherworldly after all the stories and legends I've heard.

Their tall bodies have the grace and ease of a cat. Long dark hair cascades down over their shoulders in intricate twists and braids. As they step into the firelight, I catch sight of delicate tattoos weaving around their bodies. They're clad in simple woven clothing and leather, bows slung across their backs and long spears with wickedly glinting tips at their sides.

The three study us intently. Alon and I stare back. Their direct gaze is unsettling, and I reach out for Alon. He laces his fingers through mine, his palm slightly sweaty. The leader, marked only by colorful beads weighing down the ends of his braids, bows his head to Alon.

"It is not often children of the moon return to us. Come."

Without waiting to see if we would follow, he and his companions set off towards the Falls. I glance at Alon, and we both frantically scramble to follow. At the base of the cliffs to the left of the waterfall, two of the men take up sentry while the one with the beads slips behind the water.

I hesitate. The water crashing down is deafening. If I fall, I'll be too disoriented to try and swim. Alon places a hand on the small of my back and gives me a gentle push.

"I'll be right behind you."

Taking a breath, I slink around the backside of the water and Alon trails along behind. The rocks are slick and craggy, threatening to turn ankles and nip elbows. Above us, the faint blue glow of phosphorescence offers just enough light to pick our way through the gloom.

The farther we go, the more the temperature of the air around us drops and small patches of ice crouch among the rocks. Alon's feet slide out from underneath him and it's only by pure luck that a rock outcropping catches him around the middle and keeps him upright.

Our guide turns off into a rough-hewn tunnel and the ground becomes hard packed earth, the ice replaced with the occasional muddy patch. Up and up we climb. My calves threaten collapse, and my breathing becomes heavy and labored. Thankfully, I'm at least wearing breeches because this would have been nearly impossible to do in a gown and corset. It feels like I can barely get enough air into my lungs as it is.

We duck through an opening and emerge into the moonlight at the top of a meadow. It's just like Queen Ululani had described, but almost entirely different at the same time. She had made it seem like the Elders were poor villagers squatting in mud huts and eating acorns. What spreads before us is clearly a developed and civilized culture thriving in their homes.

Trees ring the meadow to create a natural protective barrier to hide the village, but do nothing to block out the skies above. The meadow itself is so large that I can barely make out the trees on the far side. Wildflowers carpet the ground and seem to parade around with their last blooms before the autumn and winter chill sets in. Well, before whatever counts as a chill in Korala sets in anyway.

The village before us is alive with noise and color. The Elders cook, sing, dance, and braid their hair with bright ribbons and beads. There are even a few people getting tattoos done. The same swirling patterns I recognize from our guide seem to be the most popular motif, but I can also spot several constellations, moths, and even an owl.

Glowing campfires illuminate houses made of a mix of rough-hewn wood and sunbaked clay bricks. Moss and wildflowers grow on the roofs and some even have mushrooms sprouting from them. In the very center of the village rests a reflecting pool that twinkles in the moonlight. An air of joy and frivolity sinks into our bellies and strokes our hearts with soothing words.

Our guide leads us through the village in a winding path. Many call out greetings, but he continues without stopping. We come to rest at the door of a hut with carvings of the moon's phases above the lintel. The Elder gestures for Alon and I to enter. We exchange a wary look before Alon pushes the door open and steps through.

The interior is dusky and lit primarily by the fire cheerfully chattering away in the hearth on the far side. The walls are lined with drying bark while herbs hang from the ceiling in bunches. Small windows on both the east and west walls are filled with frosted panes of glass similar to those found on a carriage. I wonder where they got them.

In front of the hearth, a woman in a well-loved rocking chair is silhouetted by the flames. She hums as she gently rocks back and forth, her knitting needles flashing in the firelight. When she hears the door latch shut, she stands and turns to face us. Smiling, she bows and beckons us forward.

"I was wondering when you would return, Prince Alon. Please. Sit."

Chapter 32

In Which Wishes are Made

Alon

"You remember me?"

The question slips out before I can stop it and I wince. Nothing like immediately demanding answers to make a good first impression. The woman only smiles and beckons us closer to sit on a rickety wooden bench near the fire. It's a bit tight, but Nora and I manage to perch on either end of it without it collapsing beneath us.

"Yes, I remember you," the woman says quietly. "I remember all who come to visit and all who still need to make their journey."

She returns to her knitting, seemingly oblivious to the eyes watching her. Silver gray hair is twisted into a braided crown around her head and a simple woven circlet of leather adorns her brow. Her nose is straight and proud, her brows heavy.

She gently hums a folk song to herself. Wait, I know that song. *Tutu* used to sing it to me when I was a child. The woman's hands move deftly as her needles flash in the light, keeping time with her song. Nora is as tense as a ship under full canvas beside me and I try to ignore the nervous energy radiating off her.

After a few minutes, the woman finishes her row and sets aside her knitting in a basket tucked near her chair. A kettle on the fire begins to sing and she deftly maneuvers it off the flames. She makes a move to collect several mugs off one of the shelves on the wall and I stop her.

"Please. Let me."

The lessons Tutu gave me as a child flood in as I go through the motions of preparing the tea. The woman nods her approval and accepts the steaming mug. She settles back in her rocking chair, taking up the same rhythm as before. I pass Nora a mug and maneuver myself back onto my end of the bench. Nora glares at me as I jostle her briefly, but I ignore it. Nothing I can really do about the cramped quarters anyway.

"What may we call you?"

Nora's words are respectful, but very direct. I elbow her and give her a look. The woman only laughs. It's a deep, motherly laugh that resonates in my chest.

"You may call me Aurelia, child."

My voice is sticky in my throat. "Aurelia, we were hoping you could give us some answers. Give *me*...some answers."

Aurelia turns her attention to me. Her gaze is unsettling. The blue of her eyes is just the slightest bit too violet to be normal. Faint swirling tattoos line the edges of her face and fade back beneath her hair.

"What answers do you seek?"

"I would like to know more about my gift. Why was it given to me? And –" I pause briefly to clear my throat again "– can it be removed?"

Aurelia watches me with a bemused stare. It's almost like I'm a riddle she's trying to solve. I shift nervously under her gaze. Nora rests a hand briefly on my knee and I manage to still myself before my wiggling causes the whole bench to topple over and send us sprawling.

"You will get the answers you seek, child." Aurelia's voice is gentle. Reassuring. "Once our Wishing Ceremony is complete, we will come together to talk about your gift."

"Wishing Ceremony?" Nora just can't seem to keep quiet. "What's that?"

Aurelia's smile is so joyful that it's infectious. "Our Wishing Ceremony is what my people do every Autumn to prepare for the year ahead. We dance, sing, share food, and release our wishes to the Moon Goddess. The two of you are more than welcome to join us for the ceremony. All are welcome."

"Yes please!"

Nora's excitement is just as infectious as always. I can feel my own enthusiasm at war with my nerves. I'm not sure which one will win at the moment.

"I must spend some time in self reflection tonight to find the answers that you seek. Evander will act as your guide. I will see you two later at the reflecting pool."

With her promise made, Aurelia takes up her knitting again and turns back to face the fire. She begins humming the folk song absently to herself again. Nora and I leave our empty mugs on the table and slip back out the front door to find the same man who led us to the village waiting outside. He's kicking a ball with some children, but once he sees us he straightens and is all business again.

"Are you Evander?" I ask cautiously. He nods once in reply. "Aurelia said she needed to self-reflect, but invited us to join the Wishing Ceremony. She said you would escort us?"

Evander gives nothing away, but a small smile crosses his face as he gestures for us to follow. He leads the way through the village towards the reflecting pool that we had been able to see from the tunnel entrance.

All around us, the Elders call to each other amongst the smell of fresh cooking food and pungent spices. Children and dogs run alongside us singing songs and chattering together in a language I don't recognize. It sounds so like the common tongue we use in Korala, but it's been transformed enough that I can't make out more than a few words here and there.

Evander shows me and Nora to the far side of the reflecting pool where a long wooden table has been placed. On one side is a basket with scraps of parchment, cups with bits of half burned sticks, and strips of fabric in bright colors. Villagers approach the table, write something on their selected parchment with the burnt charcoal ends of the wood, and then choose a strip of fabric before wandering off to the trees.

"Write your wish on the paper."

Nora and I just look at each other. I can see my own questions reflected in her eyes and I can only shrug in return. Evander doesn't seem like the type to give any more information than what is believed to be strictly necessary.

We select our own slips of parchment and half burned sticks to write with. What should I wish for? There are so many thoughts running around my head in a cat's cradle jumble of tangled strings I struggle to follow them to a complete thought. How can I pick just one?

Nora makes a small humming noise as she contemplates her own parchment, and I feel that same unmistakeable tug behind my heart. There's really only one thing I could wish for. *I wish she would choose me.*

The letters are shaky. Awkward. The truth behind them bleeds through the crumbling charcoal, smearing ever so slightly. I quickly roll my paper up so Nora can't see and pull a strip of yellow cloth from the basket. Nora picks out a scrap of dark gray.

Now that we have our wishes, Evander motions for us to follow him again. We trek through the village to the ring of trees at the edge. Villagers approach the trees and tie their wishes to the branches, touching their hearts with their left hands and gesturing to the sky after the cloth is secured. Nora and I approach a tree so decorated with ribboned parchments it's hard to tell what kind it actually is underneath. We tie our wishes to a low hanging branch that has just enough space to nestle them in together.

Touching our hearts with our left hands and gesturing to the sky, Nora and I return to Evander. He leads us back to the same table we started at, although now the opposite end is crowded with a feast. Roast mutton, vegetables, soups, ales, and some fruits I have never seen before vying for attention on the groaning tabletop. We fill our plates and sit near the edge of the reflecting pool in silence, watching the villagers as they move around us.

It's easy to see the reflecting pool truly is the center of everything. It ties the village together and is both a revered space and a meeting place. The pool mirrors the lady in the rain statue from the square back home in size, but that's about where the similarities end. While the statue on the far side of the island is made of white stone, the edges of this pool were crafted of a silvery gray stone that glows in the moonlight. All around the edges are endless carvings of the lunar phases interspersed with runes I can't read. It's beautiful and enchanting and invites you into its warmth and comfort.

A hush falls over the crowd when Aurelia separates herself from the throng and wades into the center of the pool. All around us the Elders join together and form concentric circles radiating outwards. Nora and I are swept up into the innermost circle, arms linked with villagers on either side. I watch Aurelia intently.

"My family." She raises her arms to address the crowd as it falls silent. "With another Autumn comes another Wishing Ceremony. Let us sing together so that the Moon Goddess may hear our good intentions and grant our wishes for the year to come."

All around us, voices rise to sing a hauntingly happy tune. I hum wordlessly along with them, trying to mimic the rise and fall of their voices. Nora is infinitely more successful than me and is even able to pick up some of their words. Her voice rises and falls with the rest, becoming one and splitting apart as she muddles her way through the unfamiliar song. Aurelia's voice rings out from the center of the pool. Her face is turned upwards as she basks in the light from the moon hanging low in the sky.

"Look!" Nora whispers to me, "her tattoos!"

My gaze snaps back to Aurelia. The swirling tattoos along her hairline have begun to glow with a silvery light. Faint glowing across her neck and shoulders and wrists where her clothing leaves her skin bare suggests that the tattoos are across her whole body and not just framing her face.

As we sing, her tattoos glow brighter and brighter until they wreathe Aurelia in a silken cocoon. A strong wind swirls through the meadow, caressing us and whistling through all the parchment tied to the trees. The papers chatter and whisper together like they're telling our secrets. Aurelia lets out a high, undulating cry and the moon above us pulses once with a beautiful surge of light before fading again.

"It is done," Aurelia announces. Her tattoos have faded to their faint purplish color again. "The Moon Goddess has heard our wishes. Let Her be the one to decide which of us are worthy to have them granted."

The cheers from the crowd around us are infectious. I let out a crow of my own and am swept into a hug by the man standing to my left. I turn to do the same with Nora, but she fends me off with a stern look and shake of her head. Shrugging, I gladly accept hugs from the other villagers near me.

With the ceremony over, I can't ignore the similarities to our own Remembrance Ceremony. They're so similar, but at the same time so totally foreign that it leaves me wondering which came first. Which was inspired by the other? Were the Elders and Koralans once one people that cohabitated peacefully despite the widely accepted folklore? If we were once whole, why did we break apart? Is it possible to become one again?

Aurelia wades through the pool towards me and Nora. I offer my hand to help her out and she gratefully takes it, leaning on me heavily for support. While clearly a powerful woman, the ceremony has taken much of Aurelia's strength to perform. She wobbles unsteadily as she climbs over the lip of the reflecting pool and carefully climbs down to rest on solid ground again. She looks frailer and much older than when we had first met only hours before.

"Come," she says, "it is time to find your answers."

Chapter 33

In Which Answers are Given

Nora

Alon and I are back on the small bench in Aurelia's hut. I swallow a groan. It was uncomfortable the first time around and somehow feels even more uncomfortable now.

Instead of tea, we now hold warm mugs of cider thick with spices and small cookies that drop crumbs absolutely everywhere. My attempts to discreetly brush crumbs off me while I eat are futile. Alon keeps worrying his cookie into crumbs and leaves bits absolutely everywhere. Aurelia settles back into her rocking chair, just rocking herself absently while watching the fire sleepily hum to itself.

From outside come the sounds of the deep night as the last of the ceremony is cleared away and the villagers return to their homes. Children are sung to sleep, fires banked for the night, and dogs quietly admonished for their barking. It's impossible to tell what time of night it actually is, but my body is heavy and my eyelids droop as the warmth from the fire cradles me. The long day of travel and the excitement from the Wishing Ceremony have left me mentally and physically exhausted.

"Are you ready to find your answers, child?"

I snap back to attention and straighten on the bench as much as I can. Alon slumps next to me, drawing himself closer to Aurelia.

"I would like to know more about my gift. Why was it given to me?"

Aurelia's words are calm. Measured. "The Moon Goddess grants gifts to those She believes worthy. Those who She believes will do great things with their lives. How She decides those gifts or who those people are is not something shared with me as Her humble servant. What I *can* tell you is that She must have seen something in you. Something special that could not be ignored."

The vibrating energy off Alon is palpable as he fights to keep control. I can only imagine how he feels. As the fourth child and only daughter of my family, there were definitely times I had felt like I was less than. Less important. Less memorable. Less wanted. It's why I had tried so hard to be involved with Sephiroth and its people. For them to see me and to know me. I suppose it was a way for me to try and find my own place in the world.

As the youngest of seven, I can only imagine how much harder it was for Alon to have people see him. There was always someone louder demanding more attention, another brother for him to be measured next to. For him to have an immortal goddess see him as someone worthy of bestowing a gift upon would fill a hole I wasn't even sure he was aware was there.

"And –" the question claws at his throat and doesn't want him to give a voice to it "– can it be removed?"

"Yes." Aurelia takes a pouch from a hidden pocket in her skirt and removes a small piece of white fabric from inside. Pulling back the folds, she presents us with a delicate white bloom. "This is *Ipomoea Alba*. You would call it moonflower. They bloom only in the moonlight and close again during the day. It is custom that when an offer of marriage is made that whoever does the asking will present a moonflower to whom they would like to become a lifelong partner with."

Alon takes the fabric wrapped flower and studies it intently. "This is what removes the gift?"

"Yes. If you wish to remove the gift given to you then you will need the seeds of the moonflower and a silver basin filled with water. Place the blooming flower into the water and recite *with the moon this blessing was given. With the moon it shall be returned.*"

A soft knock echoes from the door before it swings open, clunking against the wall behind. A young woman about my age stands framed in the entrance carrying an armful of logs.

"I'm so sorry, grandmama. I didn't know you had a consultation."

Aurelia waves her apology away. "Do not worry, Diara. I believe we are just finishing."

Diara crosses the hut and crouches awkwardly in the small space to place the logs she's carrying onto the fire. They crackle and spit as the flames eagerly lick their way along the dry bark.

"I'm sorry it's taken me so long to bring you firewood. Mama needed help with Elio."

"Well, he is a handful," Aurelia chuckles, her eyes twinkling. "Alon would you be so kind as to assist my granddaughter in fetching more wood for the fire?"

"Of course. I would be honored."

Alon carefully hands me the moonflower bundle and trails Diara out of the hut. The door closes softly behind them. I gaze longingly at it for a few moments, wishing I wasn't left alone with Aurelia.

"He cares for you deeply."

I turn back to the older women, careful to keep my face neutral the way Mother taught me for court. "That is what he has said to me, yes."

"And you don't believe him?"

"It's not that I don't believe him." I hesitate, trying to find the right words. "I know he cares for me. I care for him as well."

"But you also care for another."

The flat statement hangs between us like a rash. I flinch involuntarily.

"Yes."

"Only you can decide who your heart truly belongs to."

Aurelia watches me. I try to meet her gaze, but the intensity is too much, and I end up looking just above her shoulder.

"Are you aware he looks at you like you are the moon?"

My mouth drops open and my once tired limbs go rigid. "What did you say?"

"He looks at you with such wonder and adoration I can see the love and respect he carries for you in his gaze," Aurelia says as she smoothes her skirts. "It's the same look he has when he speaks of the seas or studies the moon in the sky. He looks at you like you are the moon."

Aurelia rises with stiff joints, gently pats my shoulder, and makes her way outside. *What the hell just happened?* I think back to the words I had scrawled on that piece of parchment earlier:

If Alon is truly the right choice for me, let him love me like the moon.

How did she know? My thoughts are disjointed and stuttered. *Did she read my wish?* No, that's silly. Aurelia was nowhere to be seen when we wrote our wishes. With so many already on the tree when we tied ours on there's no way she'd have been able to single mine out and read it. That's just ridiculous. *Then how did she know!?*

Teddy always called me his sun, the center of his universe. Like I'm to be worshipped while present and lamented when I disappear behind a cloud. The love we had together was fast burning and too much could render those around us barren and burnt. There were times I had experienced that burning myself, leaving our meetings with my skin feeling tight and uncomfortable. I was always unsure if the residual burns were worth the pain.

Since becoming friends with Alon, I've finally realized that I don't want to be loved like the sun. I don't want to be cursed at for things I can't control and dangerous to those who spend time in my presence. I don't want to risk burning so hot that I damage those around me as I fade in a brilliant burst of light and heat.

I want to be celebrated and respected. To be allowed to change and evolve. To have sway in the world and my own place in the skies, but to not be tied down to the same thing day after day after day. I want to be loved in a quieter way. I want to be loved like the moon.

I grip the sunflower pendant around my neck. The pendant Alon gave me. *My* pendant. Teddy's silver ring clinks sharply against it, that cold silver band weighing down my finger. All those small moments that I had dismissed now seem more important than ever. Why had I managed Teddy's bad moods for him? Why had I placated him when he lashed out and let him treat me like I was the problem when I had done nothing to provoke it?

This whole trip had started because Teddy convinced me there wasn't another choice and pushed me into doing it. He was wrong then and he's wrong now. There was *always* another choice. He just didn't want to accept it, and I was too blind to realize it was what I wanted.

I had written my wish carelessly because I thought it was impossible, like there was absolutely no way for it to happen. No one would ever actually love me the way I wanted to be loved. I didn't think I deserved that. I had thought I was destined to be loved like the sun and that if I just loved Teddy hard enough back it would make up for all the uncomfortableness that came along with it.

But I was wrong. Aurelia's words prove that. I've been foolish and blind this whole time, closing myself off from the love and friendship I had so desperately craved because I was holding on too tightly to what I already had. Something that was too bright and hot to see beyond.

Now I know better. I know that I've been holding on too tight to something bad for me out of fear of never finding anyone else who could love me for me. And it's time for me to let go. It's time for me to accept that I deserve to be loved the way I want to be loved and not the way someone else *chooses* to love me.

The prickling ache behind my heart swells and bursts. An electric warmth floods throughout my body, sending my fingers and toes tingling. The answer has been right in front of me this whole time and I have just been too blind to see it for what it is. But no more. I know what my choice is.

Chapter 34

In Which Everything Changes

Alon

I round the corner of Aurelia's hut and almost crash into her as she swings the door shut behind her. She steps deftly out of the way and reaches out a steadying hand on my elbow to keep me from falling. Once my balance is regained, she releases me and smooths her embroidered skirts with careful hands.

"Nora is inside by the fire. The two of you are welcome to stay the night in my hut."

"We couldn't possibly do that." My arm is getting sore from the weight of the wood, and I shift the bundle awkwardly to my other side. "We don't want to put you out and be an inconvenience."

"It is no inconvenience, my child." Aurelia's smile sparkles like the first stars at dusk. "My daughter is watching all my grandchildren in addition to her own tonight, and they can be quite the handful when all together. I will be lending her an extra pair of hands to tame the animals. I will see you in the morning."

She bows her head slightly and disappears off into the maze of the village. My gaze lingers on her for a moment and then turns back to the door. Thankfully, it's a simple pull latch so I am able to open the door and maneuver my way through without needing more help. Dodging the table, I settle my armful of wood next to the hearth.

"Aurelia invited us to stay here tonight. She said she'll be helping her daughter with her kids. I'll see what I can find for us to use as blan — are you alright?"

Nora sits on the bench where I left her only minutes earlier. She stares unblinking into the fire like she's not even seeing the flames. Her hand clutches her sunflower pendant, neck flushed and shoulders heaving.

"Nora? Are you okay?" No answer. I reach out and touch her shoulder gently. "Nora?"

She visibly startles and recoils, the bench thumping into the wall behind her. In my panic to move away from her I collide with Aurelia's rocking chair. Falling awkwardly into the well-worn seat, the entire chair practically falls over backwards with my momentum. Nora looks at me with an odd mixture of fear and wonder in her eyes. Almost like a caged animal that doesn't know who to trust or what to do next.

"Are you okay?" I repeat. I reach out as if to touch her again, but then think better of it and pull back.

"Yes." She clears her throat. "I'm okay."

"Okay. Good."

We sit and stare at each other. The fire snickers between us, making fun of our indecisiveness.

"What were you saying? When you came in?"

"Oh. Um. Aurelia invited us to stay here tonight."

"That was nice of her."

"Yes."

I rock absently just to have something to do. The only sounds in the room are the fire in the hearth, the chair's rockers on the hard floor, and my heartbeat pounding in my ears. Nora just keeps sitting there and looking at me. I take a chance.

"I assume we should talk about what happens next?"

"What happens next?"

"Ye-es," I say slowly. It's like Nora's not even listening to me. "With us."

"Oh."

Another unbearable silence falls between us. I hate this so much.

"Now that we found our answers I figure we need to talk about what this means moving forward. I know you want to be with Teddy, but we need to decide what us being married looks like. What are the time obligations you expect to have between Sephiroth and Korala?"

"What if —" Nora hesitates "— what if we didn't?"

"I'm not sure I understand."

"What if we didn't talk about it? Didn't make any plans."

"I'm confused. Wasn't the whole point of this trip to find the answers about my gift so that we could both go back to our regular lives and pretend we aren't married? We have the answers. Don't we now need to talk about what comes next?"

"I guess," Nora answers absently. She stares into the fire again.

"Well, we have the answers so..."

"I know."

"Nora, you have to help me out here. We came all this way to talk to the Elders. We did what we set out to do and have everything we need. You can now get what you want – me out of your way of your happily ever after. Kind of. Why the hesitation?"

"What if I changed my mind?"

The question threatens to knock me over with the force of the blow. "What do you mean you changed your mind?"

Nora looks at me like I'm stupid. "I mean it literally. I changed my mind."

A hot flash of anger bubbles deep within my stomach. We came all this way together and Nora always made it perfectly clear how she felt and where she stood. Now that we're looking at leaving the Elders and going home, she says she changed her mind and is expecting me to go along with her whims? And with no explanation as to why either. Did she decide it's better to keep me around as a pet or a cover for her and Teddy? To make it easier for them to sneak around? Or is there something more she's refusing to share?

"So, what now? Am I just supposed to take you at your word and hope you don't change your mind again? How am I supposed to silence that voice that says you don't actually want me for me, but you want me as a means to an end? Being a consolation prize is no way to live."

"Do you think so little of me? That I would decide one day to be done with you and have that be the end of it?"

"Considering how adamant you've been that you will never love nor accept me as a partner, what am I supposed to think, Nora? I will gladly be your friend and your lover and your husband, but I refuse to do it based on a whim. If you want to be with me then it needs to be because you actually want to be with *me*."

Nora flinches at the bitterness in my voice and it fills me with a sick sort of pleasure. She's finally experiencing some of the hurt and pain she caused me without a second thought. I should be angry at her for what she put me through, for what she put us through. Her behavior since we met is not easy to just brush past.

The sight of Nora's tears, though, causes my anger to disappear as quickly as it came on. This is Nora. No matter how much easier it would be if I didn't care for her, we are still bound together as *Anima Mate*. Nothing will ever change that.

An uncomfortable silence descends. We sit in front of the fire on our opposite sides of the hearth. Neither of us speaks or looks at the other.

"I have said some horrible things and required things of you I should never have asked for." Nora's voice is thick with unshed tears she's trying to hold back. "I was so wrapped up in what I thought I wanted that I failed to see what was right in front of me. I should never have asked you to make this trip. To risk sacrificing everything for me. It was not fair. I'm sorry."

Nora's shoulders are hunched like she's trying to make herself as small as possible, her hand still clutching her sunflower. Beside her, the moonflower rests undisturbed on its scrap of fabric. I don't really know what to say so I say nothing.

After a few minutes, Nora nods resolutely to herself and stands. She gently touches my shoulder and turns to leave. I catch her hand, and she pauses next to me, but refuses to meet my gaze.

"What changed?" I'm almost too scared to learn the answer.

"I finally realized there is more than one way to be loved. And that as much as I tried to believe otherwise, your *Tutu* was right all along. I love you, Alon. And I'm sorry. For everything."

Nora pushes past me and out the door, lost to the stars and the night. Gone. All the breath whooshes from lungs, collapsing me even further back into the rocker. *She loves me. I can't believe she loves me.* Should I go after her? No. Not tonight. Aurelia is letting us stay here. She'll be back and we can talk tomorrow.

The fire croons love songs as I rock lazily in its warmth. The space behind my heart that has ached so much on our journey here relaxes with a lazy pur. It finally settles down for a comfortable nap, secure in the knowledge that Nora loves me. *Nora loves me.* The heat from the fire comforts my worn body and eases my soul into a restful slumber. With my chin nodding to my chest, I surrender to my fatigue.

I startle briefly to the sound of dishes clinking together and children giggling. My eyelids protest at my attempts to move them, but eventually relent and open slowly, blinking in the daylight filtering in through the windows. Aurelia hushes several small children as they settle various trenchers onto the table.

I stick my tongue out at them, careful not to let Aurelia see me. As soon as they start giggling again, I pretend to be asleep, and Aurelia shushes them once more.

"Grandmama, he's awake," the youngest, a girl of maybe six, says as she ducks under the table and approaches me. "Hi."

"Hi, yourself." Sleeping in the rocking chair has made my bones ache and my muscles stiff. My body needs a good stretch and a good swim. "Good morning, Aurelia."

"Good morning, my child." Aurelia finishes arranging the dishes and waves the children out the door to a chorus of laughter. Her brow wrinkles in concern as she surveys the hut. "Is Nora not here with you?"

"I haven't seen her, but I just woke up. I would have assumed she would be with you?"

"No one in the village has seen her yet this morning. I thought she was still asleep."

"No, she...." My mouth goes dry as the puzzle pieces of what happened last night click together. "Aurelia last night we spoke. Argued. Nora left the hut. I thought she would be back because we had not planned to leave until this morning, so I didn't go after her or try to stop her. Is she alright?"

Aurelia's frown deepens, the furrows in her skin taking on their own creases. Fear and panic climb up my spine with unsettling ease. Nora is probably somewhere in the village playing with the kids. Or maybe she's at the reflecting pool. Everything's fine. She has to be fine.

Evander ducks through the open doorway and Aurelia moves with a speed I did not know she possessed. She whirls to face him, and the movement takes the large man by surprise. He stumbles slightly in the tense atmosphere and regards us with practiced wariness. It's probably the same expression he has when judging who is safe to bring back to their encampment or not.

"Please forgive the intrusion. Prince Alon, this is for you."

He holds out a small piece of parchment folded into a swan. My breath catches for a moment. It's one of the leftover pieces of parchment from the Wishing Ceremony last night. I thought they picked them all up last night so where did Nora get one?

I cross the floor in quick strides and snatch the paper bird from his outstretched hand. The parchment unfolds easily, the swan disassembling into nothing more than creased paper covered in charcoal. The frosted windows let in just enough light to read by and I huddle beside it, desperate to take advantage of any and all light available to me. Her writing is a little smudged. The charcoal bleeds a bit around the folds.

Alon,

In case you have not realized it yet, I have left. Much happened last night and everything has changed. If I'm being honest, things have been changing between us for a while now and I just didn't want to see it. Everything has somehow gotten even more confusing than before, which I didn't think was possible. I meant every word that I said last night: I do love you and I am sorry for every hardship you have gone through because of me.

Though I am loath to admit it, this trip was an end to my own selfish means, and I took advantage of your trust. I'm sorry. You deserve so much more than that.

There is no easy way to say this, but I am returning to Sephiroth. The journey ahead will provide me with some time to find much needed clarity on some matters. I need to resolve some things I should have handled before leaving with you in the first place. I will write when I can.

Yours,
Nora

My knees have turned to water and it's unclear how long they'll hold me. I lean heavily on the wall for support, the wind knocked out of me. She's gone.

"When did she give this to you?" My voice is barely more than a whisper. I clear my throat and try again. "Evander, when did Nora give this to you?"

"Last night. She said the two of you were not speaking and asked me to deliver it today." The big man looks uncomfortable. "Is everything okay?"

"She's gone."

"Surely you don't mean —"

"She left. Last night." I hold the letter up as proof even though neither Aurelia nor Evander are close enough to read the words. "Aurelia, I beg your forgiveness, but I must leave. Now."

Grim determination settles across Aurelia's face, and she nods. She carefully moves next to me and places her hands on my shoulders, forehead resting gently against mine.

"Of course, my child. Go with courage and the strength of the Moon Goddess. May She guide you and keep your path straight. Evander, escort him back to the Falls. And quickly."

I draw Aurelia in for the briefest of hugs. She stiffens slightly in surprise and then hugs me back with the fierceness of a protective mother. Her unfamiliar floral scent surrounds me for the briefest moment before we separate.

I take off after Evander, struggling to keep up with the taller man's longer strides as we weave through the unfamiliar landscape. The village looks so different in the sunlight, and I struggle to gain my bearings. One thought courses through my body, pushing me forward: *I need to find Nora.*

"Commander Fletchling!" My voice echoes through the clearing, too loud in the morning air. The four soldiers around the campfire topple off their seats and scramble to make themselves presentable. "Commander!"

"Yes, Your Highness." The broad-shouldered man is the first to right himself and bow. The rest follow suit. "How can we help?"

"Have you seen Nora? Is she here?"

"No, Your Highness. We haven't seen Her Highness since you left yesterday for the Falls. Is she not with you?"

"I need a horse."

"Of course, Your Highness, only…"

"What is it?"

"My horse went missing in the night along with some of our supplies. We only have two horses remaining and we will not be able to pull the wagon with just one. If we stay here for another night we are in breach of the treaty and, with respect Your Highness, I do not wish to be responsible for the start of a civil war."

I mutter a few choice curses under my breath. Nora must have taken the horse and headed for the mountain path. The Commander showed her their maps yesterday after we had eaten. It would be easy for her to find it again by herself. She's had over half a day's head start. With the wagon, provisions, and five men to carry it will take upwards of five days to get across the pass. As a single rider Nora can do it in three.

I curse again and kick the underbrush. "Break camp at once. We leave immediately."

Chapter 35

In Which an Identity is Revealed

Boar

The letters swim before my eyes, words and sentences blurring and breaking apart before coming back into focus. I stare out the window at the frosted trees and slump back in my chair. My letter has gone widely ignored, the questions easily sidestepped. Instead of learning more about the weaknesses of the princeling and his family, I get to hear about the architecture and a damned fountain. If I'd cared about that at all I would have just gone to Korala myself.

But no. Here I am stuck in Sephiroth feeling like everything is starting to spin out of control and losing the faith of everyone around me. If she doesn't come back or I can't get her to join our cause, then we are well and truly dead men walking. Without her there's no way to make this work.

I shove back from my desk in disgust. Sitting here isn't going to solve anything. Pulling on my jacket and hat, I wander out into the rest of the palace. It's still too early for the the court to be awake and there's only a handful of servants in the halls stoking fires and opening curtains. They pause in their chores to bow while I pass, but they're insignificant and beneath my attention. They're not worth my time.

The morning air is sharp as broken glass and just as dangerous. It sticks to my lungs, permeating everything with a chill that can leave you shivering for hours if you're not careful. My boots follow the familiar path around the front of the palace, frosted gravel crunching beneath my soles. It's so cold this morning the birds haven't even begun to sing yet. Everything is perfectly still.

I wander absently through the grounds, reveling in the relative quiet. Nothing like some fresh air to clear the senses and get you thinking again. Now what am I going to do about our problem princess?

Rapid footsteps on the path behind me announce Hawk's arrival. He doubles over briefly, blowing out huffs of white in the frigid air, before straightening again.

"She's back!"

"Where?"

"Front entrance. Cabby just dropped her off. She's walking down the drive."

I'm already moving before he's finished speaking, limbs awkward in all my layers. Hawk falls in easily beside me as we run and our footsteps pound in time across the mostly frozen ground. A slick patch causes my foot to slide out and my ankle to almost roll, but thankfully there's no damage done. We slow as we reach the front drive to the palace, ducking behind the trees lining the avenue.

There she is. Clad in a jacket too light for the cold with a small traveling case in her hands, she meanders down the drive focused on everything except the palace in front of her. A trail of footprints mark her slightly wobbly procession.

"Alert Wolf she's back," I whisper to Hawk. "Have him get Bull and Spaniel and meet me in the gardens. It's time for plan B."

Hawk nods and slips silently away. I turn back to the drive and track her progress a few more minutes as she stops to examine the trees overhead. With how early she arrived there's a good chance no one knows she's here. I'd rather keep it that way. Taking a deep breath, I step out from behind the tree and approach her.

"Nora? Is that really you?"

Chapter 36

In Which a Homecoming Occurs

Nora

The late Autumn wind outside the carriage is stiff and crisp with the impending winter. The warmth of Korala, no matter how brief, seems to have made me forget what true cold really feels like. I had to stop in the marketplace near the port and purchase a woolen jacket, cap, and mittens from some of the other merchants unloading their goods. They help against my involuntary shivering, but I long for thick boots and my winter wool stockings. In all our plans to sail for Korala, neither Abigail nor I had thought to pack winter clothing for the return trip home.

A sharp pang echoes through my chest. Abigail. She'll never forgive me for sneaking in and out and sailing off without her. She must have been beside herself with worry when Alon returned without me.

It had been surprisingly easy to make my way back from the Elder's village by myself. While lovable, *Tutu*'s guards had made the foolish mistake of not posting a watch while they slept. It was almost comical how easy it had been to saddle the Commander's horse and steal away. The mountain path was a bit harder to find in the dark, but the Elders had maintained the trail on their side of the island. Once I found that it really was a straight shot up and over. Sleeping on the ground without a tent and wearing the same clothes for so many days in a row was less than ideal, but it couldn't be helped.

Sneaking back into my rooms at the palace and pulling together some funds and clothing for my journey had also been shockingly easy. I made a mental note to talk to King Hemi about his security measures. They are lacking at best and a mere joke at worst. If I, someone still fairly unfamiliar with Korala and the palace itself, could sneak in and out that easily then I shudder to think what someone intimately familiar with the place could do.

With the alliance made between our kingdoms, it was child's play to spot the Sephiroth merchants docked in the Koralan port. There was a most accommodating sir that was thrilled to take me on as a passenger for his journey home. He was so pleased to have royalty on his ship he even skipped several of his stops at the smaller trading ports to deliver me back in a timely manner. Goes to show what a crown, a good disposition, and a well-endowed coin purse can accomplish.

It was a bit difficult to find a carriage to take me the rest of the way to the palace, but a very nice gentlemen at the post rousted his best pair of drivers from bed to ensure I made it to my destination safely. And now I'm here, bouncing and swaying over the frozen ruts in the road while trying hard not to bite my lips with my chattering teeth. Snow probably won't be an issue for several more weeks, but constant overnight freezings and warmer days wreak havoc on the roads and fields. Repairs are always one of Father's first projects after the spring thaws to mend the damage in preparation for the first plantings.

"Nearly there, Your Highness," the driver calls through the small window at the front. "Just another few minutes and you should be able to see the palace momentarily."

We round a corner, and the grand palace of my ancestors rises seemingly out of nowhere. The marbled glass of the carriage windows distorts the imposing towers into wiggly outlines that grow clearer and straighter the closer we get. Another few moments and I'm standing at the front gates of the palace with only my small travelling bag to keep me company. The driver tries to insist on escorting me all the way to the door, but I wave him off with a reassuring smile and double his payment. I want to walk in on my own.

I slip through the side door next to the locked guard house and tramp down the tree lined drive. Gravel crunches underfoot, wispy footprints leaving a trail in the frost behind me. The trees have already shed their bright leaves and now sport the frosted tips they favor for the winter season. They arch high above me with branches only just touching, as if to share secrets and a dance when the wind rattles through their arms.

The familiar noises of palace life grow louder ahead of me with each step. A little knot of dread that has been sitting in my stomach since meeting the Elders unfurls and lazily stretches its spindly vines up my spine. I desperately want to turn and run, but I need to stay strong. I need to –

"Nora?" A familiar dubious voice cleaves through the chilly fog in my brain. "Is that really you?"

Strong arms sweep around me, and I revel in the familiar scent of cinnamon and spice. Teddy. *My* Teddy. I really am home. Tears well up and over, freely falling down my cheeks as he hugs me even tighter.

"What are you doing here? Why didn't you write that you were coming back?"

"It was a bit unplanned," I snuffle back. "Teddy, you're squishing me."

"Oh, sorry." He lets me go and already I miss his warmth. "I just can't believe you're back. Have you told the king and queen?"

I shake my head. "No, I didn't have a chance to tell Mother and Father I was coming either. I should go and see them. Let them know I'm home."

"Wait." Teddy stops me with a hand on my shoulder and tries to look at me, but I can't meet his eyes. "Are you okay? Nora? Did something happen? Did...*he*...do something to you?"

"No!" My voice is sharper than I intended, and I take a moment to soften it. "No nothing like that, Teddy. I'm just tired. It's been a long journey, and I need to talk to you about something, but I really should go see —"

"Their Royal Majesties can wait another hour." A wolfish grin creeps across Teddy's face. "Let me take your bag. I'll sneak it in so you don't have to lug it around. Meet me in our spot. I'll be there soon."

Grudgingly, I allow my traveling case to be pulled from my hands and primly accept the kiss Teddy gives me. My heart's not in it though and I'm sure he can tell. My feet remain rooted to the frosty drive as I watch Teddy's strong back getting farther and farther away. If only I could skip this part.

A sigh hums out of me and creates a thick white cloud that dissipates almost as quickly as it was created. Might as well head to the gardens. Stay strong. You can do this. You *need* to do this.

Thankfully, I it's easy to skirt around the palace and find my way through the gardens without running into any of the guards, stable boys, or servants moving about their daily tasks. Apparently, I haven't lost my edge for sneaking around yet. A small comfort for sure.

As much as I don't want to do this, it'll be easier to just talk to Teddy now and get it over with. Then I can collapse in bed and hide from the world for a few hours. Or days. Or maybe weeks. Once I officially return to court life it will be easy to avoid Teddy and keep space between us until Alon arrives or I head back to Korala.

A pinprick of pain behind my heart knocks me breathless. Alon. There's no way he wouldn't have followed me once he found out I had left. He'll probably arrive in the next few days or so depending on how favorable the winds are for him. It'll give me just enough time to talk to Teddy, kind of reacclimate to the weather, and figure out how I'm going to explain my disappearing act. Alon must be furious with me.

Frost clings to the gardens like thick icing on a cake. Here and there late blooming flowers are preserved in icy coatings that make the petals seem even more fragile than usual. I'd always loved when my governesses allowed me to play in the gardens after a frost. It was the best time to look for fairy footprints after all.

My feet follow the familiar path to the back garden without any conscious thought. I've walked these same steps so many times I can probably get here blindfolded and half asleep. The gardens are peaceful with only the creaking of trees, chittering squirrels, and an occasional icy crack to disrupt the quiet.

Wrapping my coat even tighter around me, I settle onto the familiar curved bench. I should have at least insisted on getting something warmer to wear first. The stone is freezing to the touch and saps as much warmth from my body as it can get. Even through all my layers it greedily steals what little heat I've managed to create.

Shivering, I watch aimlessly as the sunlight tries to burn through the early morning frost. Shards of ice climb into my nose and down my throat. My breath turns white with every exhale and the tip of my nose tingles painfully. If Teddy doesn't get here soon, I'm going to park myself in front of a fireplace and try to talk to him later.

A sharp snap of half frozen twigs from the trees behind me sends my heart panging into my throat. Turning on the bench, I scan the treeline for anomalies. The trees stand at the edge of the clearing just as stately and undisturbed as ever. There's no sound now, no footprints marring the frost.

It must have just been one of the deer Father keeps stocked in the forest to hunt with the other nobles. They usually wander closer to the palace during the colder months. It's not uncommon for the kitchen staff to leave food for them during the coldests parts of winter. Even still, the uneasy feeling of being watched is hard to shake off.

Footsteps crunch from the pathway and I turn back to see Teddy hop-scotching his way through the brittle and dying plants. My hand lifts in greeting. His eyes snap to mine, fear darkening his face. Jolting to my feet, I take an uncertain step towards him.

"Teddy?" I call. "Is everything —"

Sharp pain threatens to split my world in half. A shriek tears itself from my lips and my hands clutch my head, knees cracking against the frigid stones beneath me. Frost melts through my skirts, leaving my legs damp and cold. Through the ringing in my head are the disjointed sounds of fighting. It's coming from somewhere. But where? Teddy's yelling. What is he yelling?

Heartbeats pound through my body. Or is that the rhythm of the footsteps on all sides of me? My face is wet and warm and tingling and cold. Gritting my teeth, I try to push off from the ground. I need to get away. A heavy boot sinks into my back, another into my abdomen. All the air rushes from my lungs as I gasp and I convulse.

Bile and blood swirl together in my mouth and threaten to choke me. I must have bitten my tongue somehow. I need to clear my mouth. How do I clear my mouth? The ground beneath me is flecked with blood and spit as I gurgle and cough. *Breathe dammit!*

A sharp blow to my ankle stresses the bone to the point of breaking and lights a fire inside my already aching head. Another shriek of pain tears through me, but with my half empty lungs it comes out a raspy groan.

Another blow to my stomach curls me inwards, knees to my chest and my arms wrapped tightly around my head. This isn't right. I can't breathe. I can't breathe. I can't—

It's too much. Pain overwhelms me, the world mercifully falling black.

Chapter 37

In Which Alon Arrives

Alon

Impatience jitters through me like a drumbeat. The carriage wheels have barely rolled to a stop in front of the palace before I'm opening the door and jumping down. The gravel underfoot chafes against the soles of my boots much the same way my frustrations have chafed against my restrictions on my journey. Ever since Nora left without telling me I have been irritable and tightly strung. I need to see her. To talk to her. To figure out why she bloody well ran off without talking to me first!

Mama and Baba were horrified when I returned home in the company of *Tutu*'s guards instead of with Nora. That blasted wagon slowed us down so much that it took almost a full week to get over the mountain pass and back to the manor. I had half a mind to commandeer one of the horses once we were officially back on Koralan lands, but I couldn't bring myself to leave Commander Fletchling and his men stuck in the mountains until someone could bring them a fresh horse.

I had also considered commandeering Captain Skye's ship and pushing it to its limits, but it was a cruising ship and not one built for speed. It may have almost six days to get across the path by wagon, but it took us more than double that to get around Korala to the Falls by ship. Neither choice was good, but the wagon was the lesser of the two evils. Thankfully with good winds, and a very fast ship, I was able to make better time on the crossing from Korala to Sephiroth. Now I just need to find Nora.

A bitter wind chases me up the front steps and through the doors. The growing cold on my journey back to Sephiroth made it painfully obvious that I am out of my element. Cold in Korala is short lived and punctuated only by the temperatures dropping enough to make the tips of our noses and ears mildly uncomfortable. Cold in Sephiroth chills your lungs, chips away at your bones, and crushes your spirit. I hate it.

All around me the sounds of evening life in the palace echo off the high ceilings and polished floors. Servants pull huge velvet drapes closed against the dark skies. Candles and chandeliers are being lit. Fireplaces are stoked to try and stave off the frost creeping across the windowpanes. The resounding chime of a clock from deep within the palace reverberates through the halls announcing the six o'clock hour.

Ignoring calls and beckens from several people, I strike off towards the drawing room the family takes their meals in. Thankfully, I'm unchallenged as I make my way through the maze of corridors. Staff are scurrying about their respective tasks and I only illicit a few odd looks as we pass by.

The decorative doors to the drawing room loom in front of me as I pause slightly to catch my breath. Before I can push through them, however, the guards on either side stop me.

"Beg pardon," the one on the left says. "Their Royal Majesties have instructed that no one be allowed to enter the room while the family sups."

"Family? I *am* family."

The two guards eye me and exchange a familiar look. It's the same look my family and I saw everywhere when we first arrived in Sephiroth: one of mild disgust and disbelief that we were the ones welcomed into the palace and the courts. Like we're inherently worth less than the rest of the nobility because we are not native to Sephiroth.

"With respect," the one on the right says, "we were told only family. Those are our orders. We can't let you in."

The anger I've kept at bay for so long burns within me and I nurture the flame. I let it grow into a crackling blaze, hot and fiery. Raising myself up to my full height, I let the haughty and condescending look I've seen Baba and Kalani use on people that overstepped their boundaries cloud my face. Staring hard at each of the guards in turn, they visibly start to squirm when I don't back down.

"As I said earlier." My voice slowly becomes more undone the longer I speak, anger coursing beneath it in a thick undercurrent. "I *am* family. Now let me in before I —"

"Alon?" King Jasper stands in the open doorway looking curiously at the scene before him. "What is going on out here? Why are you shouting?"

"These two —" the venom in my voice causes the two guards to flinch "— have refused me access. Claim only family is allowed inside."

A thunderstorm crosses King Jasper's face and threatens to spill out. Thank the gods I'm not the target of his rage this time. "Let him through," he spits.

The two guards slink back to their posts and King Jasper ushers me through the door, muttering about needing to speak with the captain of his guard.

"Darling, is everything al — why Alon we didn't know you'd be coming!" Queen Clarice rises from her seat at the table to pull me into a hug. "How lovely to see you. Will Nora be joining us for dinner as well or is she too tired from your journey?"

The small feeling of victory from getting past the guards evaporates when Queen Clarice's question sinks in.

"What do you mean is Nora joining us? Isn't she here?"

"No. Why would she be here?" Queen Clarice's smile drops as fear clouds her eyes. "Alon, is something wrong?"

"What the devil is going on?" King Jasper grunts. He swings the door shut and locks it. Sitting at the table, he gestures for us to do the same. "Tell us what happened."

"Nora left me in Korala." Horrified gasps from Queen Clarice interrupt me briefly, but I push forwards. "We had made it to the Elders and found the answers we were looking for. Nora and I – we argued. She left the hut we were staying in for the night and I-I thought —" my voice cracks "– I thought she'd come back so I didn't go after her.

"The next morning, we couldn't find her. I found our encampment with the guards from my *Tutu*. The commander's horse was stolen during the night. We tracked Nora back to my family's home and then to the port. I don't know when she would have set sail, but she had several days head start on me. I would have thought she'd have been back now for a week at least. You're sure you haven't seen her?"

"Are you certain she was coming back here?" King Jasper's voice is cool, level. He watches me with unnerving intensity.

"She left me a note. She said she was going back to Sephiroth to take care of a few things she hadn't done before she left."

"Jasper." Queen Clarice's voice is thin. "Do you think –"

"No. We'd have heard something by now. I'm going to speak with the guards, get my most trusted men on it. We *will* find her."

He flees from the room, pausing only briefly to unlock the door again and throw it open with abandon before barking commands. His supper lays abandoned on the table, half eaten and quickly cooling despite the warm fire singing happily in the hearth. Queen Clarice stares into the flames in silence. Her hands idly play with one of her earrings as she contemplates.

"I am going to contact my network through the churches and hospitals." Resolve settles into the creases around Queen Clarice's eyes and mouth. "If Nora was hurt or seeking sanctuary she'll be in one of those places. I'll also reach out to the libraries to see if she has sought refuge among the books. Please excuse me, Alon. I will have the servants prepare you a room and bring you a plate. I imagine you're hungry and tired after your journey."

The only sound is my stomach gurgling loudly in agreement. Queen Clarice sweeps gracefully from the room, shutting the door quietly behind her. The click of the latch shutting seems to break any resolve left in my body. My knees give out and I collapse into one of the chairs. The overwhelming fear that has clung to me since realizing Nora left me in Korala can't be held back anymore. Tears stream silently down my face.

When the maid arrives to show me to my room, she politely ignores my red eyes and dripping nose. By some miracle I manage to compose myself enough to pass discreetly through the halls as she leads me to the same suite of rooms Nora and I shared briefly after our wedding. They look almost exactly the same as before but they're even gloomier. Empty.

The maid places the dinner tray on the table and thankfully bows out quietly. For the first time in weeks, I am alone. I don't actually want to be alone right now, but I also don't want more prying eyes watching my every move. I wish I was with Nora.

My stomach cries out for food, but it's tied into so many knots it has trouble keeping anything down. I kick off my boots and yank my shirt over my head, collapsing onto the bed and burrowing under the mound of blankets.

$$\cdots \cdot \,) \cdot \bigcirc \cdot (\, \cdot \cdots$$

Quiet chattering of maids in the adjoining sitting room startle me awake. Groaning, I listen to their idle prattle. It's mostly just admonishing each other, but whoever Sarai is better be careful because she is not on this group's good side.

Their gossip fades as they leave, and I lay in the darkness alone for a few more moments. My eyes are swollen, and my tongue is dry from crying the night before. *I need to find Nora.* That thought alone is enough to get me up and out of bed, wrenching off the covers and stumbling out into the next room.

My traveling case had been brought up some time during the night and left next to the couch. Sitting next to it is a pile of clothing with a note on top. Unfolding the paper, my eyes skim across the elegant looping script:

Alon,

I am sure you are not used to the cold, and I wanted to try and make you as comfortable as possible. I hope these fit. If you need a different size, please let me know and I will make the proper arrangements. Despite your welcome last night, we are very glad you are here.

Clarice

My heart swells at the selflessness that is my mother-in-law. Several pairs of lined breeches, thick socks, heavy woolen sweaters, and even a new coat and lined mittens are among the pile of clothing. I pull them on, grateful for their warmth. Already the day seems that much more manageable. Now I need to find breakfast.

The halls are busy, but subdued. There's a distinct feeling that the servants are doing their best to avoid me and blend into the background even more than usual. Even the friendly Lady Wimple averts her eyes and hurries off to parts unknown with nothing more than a brief curtsy.

I thread my way back through the palace towards the green drawing room. It'll be the best place to find King Jasper, Queen Clarice, and breakfast all at the same time. Just down the hall from my destination, I quite literally run into Teddy as he rounds a corner from a different hallway. He bounces off me with a groan and falls with a wheezing slump to the polished flooring.

"I'm sorry. I didn't see you," I say as I help him to his feet. "Are you alright?"

Teddy looks awful. His right eye is ringed with a yellow and green bruise that stretches halfway down his cheekbone. He lists slightly to the side as if he's favoring his left leg and his breathing is in small, controlled bursts.

"I'm fine. Just worried about Nora being missing."

"Did you get into a fight with someone?"

A small smirk slides across his face. "Yeah. Something like that. The last letter I received from Nora said that the two of you had reached Korala and you'd be heading out to some place called the Falls next. She didn't really give any details beyond that though. What happened?"

"We argued. She came back alone."

Teddy nods absently and winces imperceptibly. I don't know who would dare fight the son of one of the nobility, even a lesser Lord like his father, but they definitely did a number on him.

"His Majesty King Jasper is forming search parties to look for Nora. There were several dispatched last night and more are going out today. I want to join as well, but they won't let me ride in my condition."

"I was going to ask to ride out with them today."

"Will you ride with me instead?"

"You want to ride together?" I struggle to keep the incredulity from my voice. The man that hates me for marrying the love of his life and getting in the way of his happy ending wants to work together? "Why?"

"Because I know you and I feel the same way about Nora. We'll be able to cover more ground than the larger search parties and people will be more willing to talk to us alone than with the guards. Please. For Nora."

The logic is sound.

"Okay. I will tell the king and queen. Let's meet in the stables after breakfast."

"I can't go out today," Teddy shrugs awkwardly. "My father wants me to oversee the servants finishing the winterization of our ancestral home. I'll be leaving shortly."

My annoyance chafes against me. "How long will you be gone?"

"Not long. It's a half day's ride from here. I'll be leaving early tomorrow in the hopes of being back by noon. We can begin then."

"Fine. I will ask King Jasper about joining the search party today. Tomorrow, we set out together as soon as you return and get a fresh mount. Safe journey."

Teddy nods and sets off down the hallway. My gaze lingers on him for a few moments. He's definitely favoring his left leg. Gods above, whoever did that to him was definitely quite the fighter. I really wonder what the other guy looks like.

Chapter 38

In Which a Mask is Removed

Nora

Sleep stubbornly holds onto me, but the briefest prick of panic puts me on high alert. Where am I? I blink against the light filtering in from the window. The mostly familiar surroundings slowly settle back into place and the tension in my chest eases somewhat. It's okay. *You're safe.*

There's that same clattering noise again and I rouse myself from the armchair I had been napping in. The library in Teddy's ancestral home, Moore Hall, is cozy and inviting. Matching worn armchairs are everywhere, a fire always crackles in the hearth, and books teeter on every flat surface. I've spent most of the last week holed up in here reading.

Well, the time I wasn't spending on my injuries was spent in the library. While the Moore family physician could confirm that my ribs were not broken, at best they were badly bruised and at worst cracked. His best advice was to rest and let my body heal. Teddy and Lord Moore were more than happy to let me stay with them while they figured out who attacked us.

It's a miracle that we got out of the gardens in as good a shape as we did. I'm still not sure how Teddy managed to fight off the other attackers and get me safely to his home. Poor Teddy. He's been going back and forth from here to the palace almost every day to try and root out who was behind the attack. So far there has been very little news.

My reflection in the gilt framed mirror catches my eye and I make a face. Bruises cover my cheeks and body in muted shades of yellow and green. I'm just glad they've faded from their bright reds and purples when we first arrived. Mother's voice echoes in my head: *ugly and unseemly!* Teddy wanders through the door with a mug of warm tea and smiles widely.

"Glad to see you're up and about!"

I try to match his enthusiasm, but I can see in the mirror it falls flat. The guilt of knowing I haven't told him what I need to has been gnawing at me more and more with each passing day. I need to tell him. But I don't want to. Especially not like this.

"How has your afternoon been? I apologize if we woke you. Father insisted on having the last of the eaves cleaned today and I was helping Jeremy and Lonnie."

"No, you didn't wake me." *Liar* echoes through my head. It seems all I do lately is lie to Teddy. "I didn't realize you were coming back today. Is there any news?"

Teddy's eyes cloud over. "No. Nothing yet."

We stand in awkward silence, just watching each other. Before, our moments of quiet were peaceful and comforting. Now they're heavy with unspoken words. The clock on the mantelpiece chimes and a maid steps in behind Teddy and bobs a quick curtsy.

"Dinner is ready."

She scuttles off quickly. Teddy offers me his arm and escorts me to the formal dining room. Its understated beauty seems to mock me as Teddy deposits me in a chair and then plunks down in the one across from me. Lord Moore sits between us at the head of the table.

Teddy and Lord Moore argue good-naturedly together about different improvements they want to make to the property and what still needs to be done before the snow falls. I mostly sit and pick at the food. Lord Moore has an excellent cook, but my appetite is just not what it should be. Probably because of the guilt I've been carrying around since we got here.

With the last of the dinner dishes taken away, I clear my throat awkwardly. Teddy and Lord Moore turn to me with just a touch of surprise.

"I would like to go home. Back to the palace."

The two men exchange a glance. It's scarily similar to the looks Mother and Father sometimes exchange. An entire conversation was just had with that look, and I am not privy to its details.

"You can't. It's not safe." Teddy says it so matter of factly that I almost believe him. I *want* to believe him.

"Teddy, it's been a week. There has been no news about what happened to us. You're getting nowhere in your investigation. It might be time to ask —"

"Ask who? The king? Hah!" Teddy snorts derisively. "Their Royal Majesties have done nothing but keep us apart and cause hardship. They should be ashamed of their behavior."

I'm stunned by the malice in his voice. "Teddy, you don't mean that."

"Trust me, Nora." He levels me with a gaze. "I really do."

Lord Moore clamps a hand on Teddy's shoulder. "This is not the time for this conversation. Let's all retire to the music room and we can —"

"No, this is exactly the time for this conversation." Teddy shrugs off the hand. "I know you're keeping something from me, Nora. What is it?"

The blood drains from my face and my stomach drops to my knees. I apparently haven't been hiding it as well as I thought.

"What do you mean?"

"You can't lie to me, Nora, I can read you like a book. You've been avoiding me and clearly have something to tell me. You just don't want to."

"Teddy, I don't think this is how we should do this."

"Do what? Talk?"

From the edges of my vision, I see Lord Moore push back from the table and slip through the adjoining door to his study. The heavy door swings mostly shut behind him but doesn't latch. He's apparently above witnessing our argument in person, but not so far above to not blatantly eavesdrop. A sharp pang of annoyance severs my last shred of patience.

"Fine. You want to talk? Let's talk."

Teddy throws up his hands. "It's about time!"

I inhale deeply and try to keep my voice calm. The words I need to speak will not come out correctly if they're full of anger. "I came back because I needed to take care of some things. I needed to talk to you."

The fire in Teddy seems to settle just as quickly as it flamed. "You needed to talk to me?"

"Yes."

"Why?"

"Because I needed to talk about us."

"Us." It's hard to look past the contempt in his face. "I think it's fairly clear there is no us. Not anymore. Not since *him.*"

"I know you don't like Alon, but that doesn't change the fact that I have a duty to my family and my people to do the right thing. It's expected of me to marry someone approved by the High Counsel and you know I can't risk upsetting them."

"Oh, don't try that with me Nora," Teddy sneers. "The 'doing my duty' argument doesn't work on me. I've listened to you rage against your mother for hours about her lectures on honor and duty and —"

"And regardless of what I thought at the time, she was right. There are certain expectations that need to be met when you are a woman and part of a monarchy. One of those is marriage. The High Counsel was threatening my father if I didn't marry by my twenty-first birthday. I told you this!"

"Then why couldn't you have married me?"

"You know why."

"Do I, Nora? Because all we know is what your parents told us. Do we have any tangible proof that you're cursed? For all we know, that could have just been a story they told you to get their way. Don't be so naive."

I gape at Teddy. "You believed it too!"

Teddy waves a hand dismissively. "Of course I believed you! You were acting crazy and babbling about witches and curses. I'd tell you anything to get you to shut up and stop drawing attention to yourself. I was trying to help you!"

This can't be happening. Please tell me this isn't happening. Teddy *believed* me. Right?

"You had a chance to stand up to your parents, to stand up for me. And you did nothing. You went along and married him and sailed off to some magical country looking for answers to a problem I couldn't possibly understand." Teddy slumps back into his chair and his words come out with such sadness it digs its claws into my heart and pulls the cracks that much deeper. "I'm just waiting for you to tell me that you're done with me. That you love him and you're moving on."

Something in my expression must give me away. Teddy sinks lower into his seat, shock painfully obvious on his face. "So that's it. You love him."

"I do."

"What about me? You said you loved me too."

"I do love you. I think there will always be a piece of me that loves you."

"There's something seriously wrong with you. This –" he between us "– isn't love. If you loved me, you wouldn't be saying these things."

Teddy's words cut deeper and deeper into my resolve. I should just do what I always do and apologize and stop pushing. I can try to have this conversation again later when he's less upset. The words are on the tip of my tongue, fighting to come out. No, don't say them. I swallow them down and readjust in my chair.

My sunflower brushes back and forth against my chest as I settle, it's weight a reassurance. *I can do this*. Teddy is rightfully upset, but that doesn't change what I need to say. It's not my responsibility to appease him.

"We're no longer the two kids that fell in love all those years ago, Teddy. We've grown up and, as much as it pains me to say, we've grown apart. We're different people now. We want different things in our lives, and they are not things that we can have together. It's taken me a while to accept that." I grasp at my words. "Love is more than just the heady rush we experienced in our youth. Love is sacrifice and companionship and, sometimes, hard work."

"And it's not something you feel for me anymore."

I inhale deeply. "I do, and probably always will, love you. But the love I feel for you now is no longer the same love that you feel for me. I don't want to lead you on, to keep you hoping that somehow, we'll defy all odds and get married one day. It's not fair to either of us and especially not to you. It's better that I step away now to give you the best chance to heal and move on. To find someone who loves you the way that you want to be loved. You deserve that."

Teddy buries his face into his hands and his shoulders shake. A low guttural sound reverberates in the room. Should I comfort him? No, probably not. It'll probably just make things worse.

"I think it's time for me to leave," I say gently, rising from my chair. "Father and Hayden can continue looking into what happened. They will make sure I'm safe."

Teddy raises his head to look at me and, for the first time, fear surges through my body when I see him. His mouth is twisted into a goading, inhuman smile and it's clear to see that he wasn't crying. He was laughing.

I instinctively take a step back and immediately can tell it's the wrong thing to do. Teddy slinks from his chair and stalks around the table towards me. Like he's hunting me.

"Oh Nora." His voice is cruelty personified, every word mocking me. "Poor little Princess Nora. How hard your life has been having everything handed to you. How easy you made this for me. You see, my dear, I —" he's right next to me now, leaning down to whisper intimately in my ear "– am the one inciting the rebellion to overthrow your family."

Anger wrestles with my fear and leaves me panicked. My heart races as adrenaline burns through my veins. I shove against Teddy and stumble backwards, my foot catching on a chair as I fall to the thick carpet in a heap. Teddy grabs my wrists tightly and hauls me roughly to my feet, his face inches from mine. Too tight. Too close. The remnants of dinner are on his breath.

"Why are you doing this?" The question comes out as a whisper. I struggle not to close my eyes and turn away from him. "I thought you loved me."

Teddy shoves me down into a chair and laughs. "Well, isn't this rich? I suppose at one point I did love you. As the years went on, I realized that you were much more useful as a means to an end. Your family has ruled Sephiroth unquestioned for generations. It's time for a change. My father and I have devised a plan to make those changes happen. It just so happens that you are the lock that opens the door, and I am the key.

"And it was so easy." His face becomes a simpering imitation of the Teddy I know. "It was so easy to convince you that I loved you because you were so desperate to be loved by someone that you didn't care who actually loved you. The further and further you deluded yourself into believing I loved you, the easier it was to maintain because you didn't see it. You didn't *want* to see it. And now it's too late. For you. For them. For that sad excuse you call a husband. Your times are all coming and I can't wait to see them run out."

Teddy strides to the door and barks down the hallway, "Guards!" It doesn't take long for several of Lord Moore's private guards and manservants dressed in matching livery to appear in the doorway. From the other side of the table Lord Moore appears from his study, watching everything, but not interfering.

"I had hoped to do things the easy way with your cooperation, but we can do this the hard way instead if you're so intent on painting me as the villain. I do love a good challenge."

"Remember, Theodore," Lord Moore intones dolefully, "we need her alive and unharmed."

"Don't worry, Father, she'll be fine. Take her to her room and keep her there."

The guards grab my arms and pull me roughly from the chair. My bruised ribs and sore ankle scream in revolt, and I bite my tongue until it almost bleeds to stifle my cry of pain. Once upright, I shake off their hands. Steeling my nerves and straightening my back, I glare at them.

"I can walk by myself." I turn to Teddy and try to look as regal and menacing as possible. There's no doubt that in my bruised state it's a poor attempt at looking like my mother. "You won't get away with this."

"You're mistaken, Princess. I already have."

I stalk out of the room. The guards hurry to keep up and surround me, two in front and two behind. We clump through the dim hallways and upstairs to the round room I had called my own for the past week. The guards deposit me inside, slamming the door behind me, before turning the key in the lock. As the final tumbler clicks into place and the key is removed, I let out a sob and sink to the floor. The thick carpet underneath absorbs my tears as I mourn Teddy's betrayal, my bad luck, and the loss of my first love.

Chapter 39

In Which Trust is Betrayed

Alon

After so much time in the saddle my body is strained and sore. Pain radiates through my hips and tailbone, and I can barely walk once dismounted. The first day I rode out with one of the search parties King Jasper had put together. We only ventured into the city and traced Nora's path from the merchant ship to the hired carriage to the gates of the palace. After that, the trail went cold. It's like she disappeared without a trace.

Teddy and I rode out together after he returned. Much to my chagrin, he seems nonplussed by the long days in the saddle. A small twinge of hatred at his ease on horseback sets my lower back on fire, but it's quickly overpowered by another wave of exhaustion.

In all honesty, I can understand why Nora loves him. He is kind to all he meets and has helped indiscriminately when we come across people on our travels that need assistance. Just this morning, I watched him rock an infant and help the mother prepare breakfast while I entertained the rest of her brood. He really is a good person. Unsurprisingly, Nora was right.

We had widened our search to Longwhenth, the next town over. No one there had seen Nora, and, despite our best efforts, we seemed to cause a bit of a stir when people realized she's missing. All our efforts ended with the same disappointment and fear that we would never find her.

We had started back from Longwhenth late in the afternoon and I regret not pushing to stay another night in one of the inns. The air is blustery cold and makes it very clear Sephiroth is heading into winter. And soon. There's a peculiar smell in the air that mixes with the piney scent of the forest around us. I've never smelled it before and, honestly, it's probably better to keep it to myself. The last thing I need is Teddy thinking I've completely lost it.

"My family home isn't far from here." Teddy's teeth are chattering. Guess I'm not the only one feeling the cold. "We can spend the night there and continue back to the palace tomorrow."

"What about our search?"

"Our search is pointless if we die from frostbite and exposure to the elements. Something tells me Nora will not begrudge us one night's rest out of the cold."

A warm meal and a bed sound unbelievably inviting so I just nod stiffly. Teddy turns off the main road and leads me down a winding trail through the trees. A brook burbles cheerfully next to us, only somewhat muted by the ice hugging its banks. *Nora, I swear if we get out of this, we are spending every winter in Korala.*

Rounding a copse of trees, Teddy's family home jumps into view. While it's not the largest I've seen, it's clear the house is well made and well cared for. Standing three stories high, the gray stones are covered in a thin layer of frost that makes the house almost disappear in the waning light. Warm firelight beckons from the windows and woodsmoke wafts from multiple chimneys. Through the haze of woodsmoke, I can just make out the smell of something warm and delicious being prepared inside. I swallow repeatedly as my mouth waters and my stomach threatens to revolt if I don't feed it immediately.

Teddy guides me up the packed earthen drive and across a pocked yard to a large barn. We leave our horses with the stable hands and trek through a tunnel connecting the barn to the house. Without the wind beating around us, the air is already warmer. I offer up a silent prayer of thanks for the brief respite.

"My father had this constructed several years ago," Teddy says. He absently rubs his hands together to get some warmth back into them. "He hated having to walk through the yard during the winter, so he hired some carpenters and stone masons. They constructed this for him, and it's been a larger blessing than I thought."

I grunt in agreement. The wooden door at the end of the tunnel opens to the kitchens and we step through into the delicious warmth. The cold knot in my chest slowly loosens itself as the cook clucks and fusses over us, ordering us upstairs for hot baths. Teddy insists on seeing his father first, but I gladly follow the serving girl to one of the spare rooms on the second floor. Time slips by too quickly as I spend a luxurious hour soaking in the combined heat of the fireplace and warm water.

Just as I finish redressing, a soft knock comes from the door. The same serving girl as before waits for me on the other side. She bows her head and motions for me to follow before setting off wordlessly. I meander along behind, never letting her get too far ahead, but allowing myself time to take in the manor.

The inside of the house has been lightly whitewashed to reflect the light flickering from the wall sconces. All along the hallways are portraits of various people I assume are previous generations of the Moore family. There's even one of a very fat basset hound complete with hat, war medal on a sash around its chest, and a large string of drool hanging from its mouth. I've *got* to ask Teddy about that one later.

The wooden banister on the front stairs is smooth oak and polished to a shine. It's easy to see that Teddy and Lord Moore take excellent care of their home and are proud of its history. I poke my head through a doorway and find a cozy, well stocked library. A sharp pang resonates through me. I bet Nora would love this place. *I wonder if she's ever been here...*

The serving girl stops next to a short hallway and waits for me to walk beyond her. The smell of food beckons to me like a lover. I eagerly step into a well-lit dining room complete with high ceilings and rounded windows. Fires are lit in hearths on both ends of the room to ensure the vast space is warm and inviting. Teddy waits at the table with another man that can only be his father.

"Your Highness," Teddy says, standing respectfully. The other man does the same and they bow briefly. "May I present my father, Lord Moore. Father, this is His Highness Prince Alon from Korala."

"An honor," I say as I take my seat. Teddy and Lord Moore return to their chairs. "Thank you for allowing us to spend the night."

"The honor is all mine, Your Highness," Lord Moore says delicately. "Theodore has said you have had no leads on finding Her Highness."

"No. Not yet."

"Does His Royal Majesty know where she could have gone? Theodore said you rode with the royal search parties a few days ago."

"I did, yes. The most we learned was that Nora took a merchant ship from Korala to Sephiroth and then hired a public driver to take her to the palace. The merchant swears she got in the carriage and the driver swears he left her at the front gate. Is that warm cider?"

"Hmm? Oh, yes. Please, help yourself."

The steaming mug in front of me is thick with the smell of cinnamon and ginger. The cider slides down my throat with ease and warms my belly in a way I haven't felt since returning to Sephiroth. I down half of it, letting out a contented sigh, before turning my attention to the heaping plate of food in front of me. Lord Moore's cook has outdone herself. Slow roasted venison smothered in gravy, boiled potatoes, some sort of roasted orange vegetable I don't recognize, mashed turnips, and fresh soft bread flirt shamelessly for my attention.

"I can't understand why Her Highness didn't insist on the driver escorting her to the front doors of the palace. He should not have just driven off and left her there to fend for herself."

Teddy and I exchange a look across the table.

"Father, if there is one thing I know about Nora it's that she is altogether too opinionated. If she decided she should be let out at the gate, then the driver would let her out at the gate and to hell with the consequences."

"Yes. Well. The consequences are that she's missing so I hope that fool understands just what he's done."

"I'm sure —" my tongue has started to feel a bit heavy. How odd. I try to clear my throat "— I'm sure he didn't mean any harm. No one could —" I drink some more cider and try to swallow the quickly forming lump in my throat "— no one could have known this would happen."

"I say, are you alright?"

Teddy's voice sounds like it's coming from farther away than just across the table. I look at him, but my eyes seem to be having trouble focusing. He wavers back and forth. Or am I the one moving?

"Yesh." My voice is weak and slurred. This doesn't make any sense. What's happening? "Yesh, I fink so. I fink – I fink I'm jusht tired. May – maybe a –a schleep..."

The world falls dark around me.

• • • ☽ • ◯ • ☾ • • •

Consciousness returns with fits and starts. The first to return is my hearing, flooded with the distant sounds of whickering horses and footsteps on wood. My head is as heavy as a stone, my body tight and swollen. There's a swaying feeling like I'm back on a ship, but that doesn't make any sense. There's no way I can be on the sea.

Wrenching my eyes open, a forge sits in front of me. But it's backwards, upside down. Looking up, I see a mix of straw and sawdust covering wooden boards. I'm upside down. No, no, no this definitely can't be happening again!

Fear takes complete control of me. I thrash and struggle against the ropes binding me. Fireworks explode behind my eyes with each new rope burn. My struggle sends me swinging back and forth, twisting me in circles. *Not again.* Please don't make me do this again!

Tears pool in my eyes before snaking across my forehead and falling to the dusty floor. The ache of riding for the past three days roars through my body, exacerbated by being hung from the roof like a pig for slaughter. *This is how I'm going to die.*

Soft footsteps echo around me and a pair of well-oiled riding boots come into view. I know those boots. They're the same ones that have spent the last several days riding beside me. Teddy. With a few disappointed sounds, he turns me around and sits in a chair I didn't notice before.

"Well, well, well. Just look at what we have here. Do you like our little game?"

I stare at him, willing my fear and panic to not overwhelm me. "Where's Nora?"

My voice is creaky and full of sawdust. Teddy chuckles, folding his hands across his stomach and leaning back in his chair.

"Oh, don't worry, Your Highness." He spits my title at me, malice oozing over me with every word. "She's safe. For now. But if you don't cooperate, I can't promise she'll stay that way."

"What do you want?"

"Isn't it obvious? I want Nora. And I want answers." Teddy examines his fingernails disinterestedly. "Specifically, I want to know how to remove your – what is that you call it? Your gift?"

"Why?"

"Well, I'd have thought the answer to that question as obvious as my dislike for you. I want to kill you."

If I die, then Nora's on her own. But if I don't tell him what he wants then I condemn us both. Only one of us can survive that.

"Why should I tell you anything?"

"Well like I said, you give me the answers I want, and Nora stays safe. You don't and...well let's just say things will get messy."

"You wouldn't dare hurt her."

"Wouldn't I?" Teddy's grin is animalistic, all bared teeth and menace lurking in his eyes. "Look at what I've done to you after all. Nora mentioned in passing that you had once been hung upside down from your toes. It was such a wonderful idea I thought it would be fun to recreate it. Don't you think so?"

All the anger and fear flooding through me leaves me with a bad taste in my mouth and I spit at him. Gods damn my lack of impulse control. With how Teddy's sitting, I strike him square in the face.

Cursing, Teddy wipes his face and lashes out, his fist assaulting the side of my head. Hard. I swing wildly side to side from the impact, coughing and snorting as I try to clear my nose and mouth of welling blood.

"Fine," he growls. "I guess we'll do this the hard way then."

Chapter 40

In Which She Escapes

Nora

The energy of the house is different. I could have sworn I heard horses return earlier, but with no windows overlooking the front or back of the house it's impossible for me to know for sure. The small murmurings of the servants and guards from beyond my door confirm my suspicions though. Teddy is back and he has someone with him. Now's my chance.

I wolf down the scant potatoes and bread that had been delivered for my supper and knock on the door to let the guard know I'm finished. No matter what time of day it is, they always refuse to meet my eye. I hope the guilt of holding me here eats at them from the inside out. Sitting on the side of the bed, I wait for the guard to enter and retrieve the dishes left just outside the path of the door's swing.

"I do not wish to be disturbed tonight," I announce in a haughty voice once he steps into the room. The boy set as my guard tonight trembles briefly, and I squash a small pang of pity for him. He's not personally responsible for my imprisonment and I'm sure he is well aware what would happen to him if he's found guilty of holding me against my will. "Please ensure no one comes down the hall or into my room. I wish to sleep."

"Yes, Your Highness," he squeaks out. It's clear he's still very green and guarding me is considered a job only worthy of the new grunts. "As you wish."

He retreats in a hurry, the door snapping shut behind him and the familiar clink of the key turning in the lock heralding his departure. A grin quirks my lips, mirroring the feeling of elation coursing through my body. *I can do this.*

From underneath the bed I retrieve the strips of fabric I tore earlier from the random assortment of ball gowns, sheets, and spare blankets I had found in the wardrobe upon first inspecting my prison. The gowns were all made to my size, and I took great satisfaction in tearing them to pieces. It was easier than imagining what Teddy had intended for me to wear them for.

Padding quietly to the wardrobe, I pull out the length of knotted rope I had created so far. It was tedious and time consuming, but over the last two days I had managed to tear, knot, and braid almost ten feet of fabric rope. I probably could have tried tying the bedclothes together, but they ripped too easily when I tested their strength, and I don't particularly want to risk falling from the third story. With the fabric I have left, I estimate I can get another six or eight feet done easily. I just need to work quickly and quietly before anyone figures out what I'm doing.

Keeping a close ear on the door, I tie, twist, knot, and braid the fabric together. My rope grows foot by foot and every so often I test its strength the best I can. Knowing my luck, I'll probably get halfway down and it'll snap in two.

The clock on the mantle chimes six-thirty. Then seven. Then seven-thirty. When it cheerfully announces the eight o'clock hour it's clear I'm running out of time. I've managed to securely braid only another four feet. Hopefully, that's enough.

On bare feet, I pull a plain cotton chemise and a simple wool dress over my nightgown. I wish I had pants or breeches to wear, but the ones I was wearing upon my arrival in Sephiroth mysteriously disappeared once we arrived at Moore Hall. I'm not too surprised, unfortunately. Teddy always hated it when I wore pants or breeches and claimed they made me look too masculine. I roll my eyes at the memory. Could I have really been that blind to who he really was this entire time?

Three pairs of stockings and a pair of heavy wool socks go on under my dresses. My feet are so thick I can barely lace up the boots I found in the wardrobe. The sturdy leather is unforgiving and groans under the pressure of the added bulk. The one saving grace is that they are several sizes too large which means there's just enough room to cram my swollen feet inside. The extra bulk helps protect my still tender ankle and make it more stable for the journey ahead. Good.

Teddy must be very secure in my inability to escape because he left me my wool coat, hat, and mittens in the room within easy reach. They're still not enough for the cold that's waiting for me, but they're better than nothing. Wrapping some of the heavier leftover fabric pieces around my neck as a makeshift scarf, I tiptoe to the door and listen. The only sounds from the other side are heavy breathing from the guard and the very far off sounds of the kitchens. *It's time.* Now or never.

I carefully tie one end of my fabric rope to the bottom of the four-poster bed and drag the rest to the window. It's a good thing Lord Moore takes so much pride in his home. The double windows swing open effortlessly on well-oiled hinges. The blast of frigid air they let in kisses my nose and inspects the room in fits and spurts. It smells of trees, rot, and snow. A shiver courses through me, raising goosebumps along the back of my neck. Definitely don't want to get caught in the snow.

I toss the rest of my rope through the window. It doesn't touch the ground like I'd hoped. From what I can see, there's probably a five-foot gap between the end and the ground. My stomach drops as I lean out over the sill, and I start doing my breathing exercises. If I had any other way to get out of here, I would take it. But it's going to be okay. I can do this. I *have* to do this.

Pulling my hat low and making sure my mittens are tucked securely in my pocket; I swing a leg out the window and begin to shimmy down. It's a miracle I don't immediately fall off and plunge to the ground. My arms scream bloody murder as I cling to the fabric and my aching ribs squeeze the breath out of me in wheezes. The cold pries at my fingertips and threatens to loosen their grip so I fall. I've always thought I was a fairly in shape person, but after being seasick, at sail, and then attacked, it's pretty clear I am lacking much of my strength. *If I get out of here, I swear —*

My oath is cut short as a strong wind forces me sideways and I cling on for dear life. Through sheer will, I manage to shimmy down to the end of the rope. Staring down at the dark ground beneath me, it's painfully obvious I drastically miscalculated the length of my rope. I forgot to account for the distance between the bed and the window and what's left is not the manageable five feet I had first thought it was. Instead, an intimidating twelve-foot gap stretches out between me and the frozen ground below. Even swinging precariously on the very end of the rope means there's still more than six feet of space until I touch down again. But I don't have a choice. I'm out of options and quickly running out of time.

Steeling myself for what's coming next, I let go and plummet to the frozen ground below. Ren always told me to roll on the landing when jumping from something to try and make sure you don't injure yourself. Praying he was right; I let my momentum carry me backwards and end up on my back. My lungs gasp at the frigid air, my ribs and ankles tingling from impact. I can still wiggle my toes in their cramped condition, so I *think* I've managed to avoid doing more damage to my barely healed ankle. Luck seems to be on my side so far. Here's hoping it holds out.

Rolling to the side of the house, my body automatically makes itself as small as possible while I crouch in the shadows. My hands are so cold I can barely get my mittens on and pull my hat down further. Clamping my hands under my arms to try to warm them up faster, I strain my senses to figure out what's going on out in the dark. Voices echo from behind the house, but I can't figure out what they're saying. No alarm has been raised at my disappearance yet.

Staying in the shadows as best I can, I creep around to the front of the house and make a mad dash for the edge of the forest lining the drive. My back presses into the rough bark of an evergreen as I slump down, trying to calm the beating in my chest. With so much fear and adrenaline coursing through my body I need to be careful not to start jumping at shadows and give myself away. I haven't come all this way for nothing.

Once the rush of blood in my ears has died down, I listen again. There's still no shouts of alarm or sounds of pursuit echoing through the dark. Sending up a silent prayer for protection, I pick my way through the trees parallel to the drive as quietly as I can. The pine needles help obscure my path and the little brook is more than happy to help cover any sounds I make. I need to move quickly before they discover I'm gone.

By the time I reach the road I'm both overheating and almost chilled to the bone. I had been hoping my layers would have offered protection and ventilation, but so far all they're doing is working against me. I can't risk taking anything off for fear of freezing to death. The one positive thing is that I can feel all my fingers and toes, so I don't need to worry about that for the moment.

After a brief deliberation, I set off in the direction of the palace. It would probably be faster to walk directly on the road itself, but I walk just off the side on the frozen embankment. It'll be easier to duck into the trees to avoid being seen if needed.

The first snowflakes begin to fall in whispery clumps around me and mute the natural sounds of the night. Bracing myself, I push through at a brisk pace and blink the flakes out of my eyes. It's going to be a long night.

My breath blows out in front of me in thick white clouds. The snow that had kept me company overnight kisses my face and sticks to my eyelashes in frozen clumps. Drifts formed overnight along the sides of the road. Up ahead are guards clearing out the front gate to the palace, their shovels and brooms flashing in the cloudy light.

Hope and relief surge through me with a fire. It fills my sore and aching limbs with renewed energy, promising an end to my journey. I break out into a run, awkwardly wading through the snow on clumsy legs.

"Here! I'm here!" I yell as I run, waving leaden arms over my head. "Help me! Please!"

The guards flood towards me, swarming from their posts. I'm caught up in the current as they practically carry me through the front gates, down the snow-covered drive, and up into the palace itself. I'm so, so tired it's a blessing to have them take me the rest of the way home. Several higher-ranking officers pepper me with questions, but they're yelling over each other, and the shuffling of the group leaves me muddled and confused.

"Mo–Mother. Father. Please." There's more wetness on my cheeks that's probably melting snow, but I'm surprised to find that I'm crying. "Please. I need to speak with them."

The guards sweep me back up and move together, up the stairs and around corners. The shuffling of their feet is partially drowned out by orders being yelled, fueling a frenetic energy I can't seem to understand. One of the captains at the front of the swarm flings open the doors to the Counsel chambers and escorts me inside, leaving the rest to stand at attention in the hallway. I stare mutely at the faces of Mother, Father, and the High Counsel peering back at me.

"Please forgive my intrusion, Your Majesties and My Lords. Her Highness Princess Eleanor has been found."

"Nora!" Mother's shrill voice strips away the fog in my brain like a balm. Warm hands yank me into my mother's embrace. "What happened to you? Are you alright? Are you hurt?"

"Clarive, give her a chance." Father gently wraps his arms around the two of us and buries his face in my half-melted hat. "I'm so glad you're safe."

All the fear I wouldn't let myself feel during my stay at Moore Hall spills over and fresh tears course down my face. I'm finally safe. I'm finally home. And I'm being held by the people that love me. We stand together, the three of us, arms wrapped around one another crying freely.

A throat clearing from somewhere in the room prompts Father to give me one last squeeze and then step away, rubbing his hands discreetly across his face to clear the lingering tears. I turn to the table of men and, I can't lie, I'm surprised to see watery eyes and relieved looks among them. There are a few empty seats, but only one I care about in this moment – Lord Moore's. A hard knot of anger ties itself tighter in my stomach. He and Teddy will pay for what they did. One way or another.

"I'm so glad you're safe," Mother says as she brushes a few strands of hair from my face. "Did Alon find you?"

"Alon's here?" There's that hope again. It slinks through my words, holding them close. "Where is he?"

"He went looking for you. He and Theodore have been searching together for the past several days. They must have gotten caught in the snow."

I can't feel my face. Everything goes numb as my stomach drops to my feet. The visitor at Moore Hall. The distraction that had allowed me to get away. It was *Alon.*

"No," I gasp, "you're wrong. Where is he? He has to be here!"

"Are you alright, Nora?" Father asks carefully. He's using the same voice he uses when he's unsure if I'm experiencing a 'womanly ailment' or not. "They can still travel in the snow. They'll be back today, I'm sure."

"No, he won't. You don't understand. I need to go back. I *have* to go back."

"You're not going anywhere until you tell us exactly what is going on." Mother's voice is sharp. She pushes me into one of the empty seats closest to the fire and dispatches a maid to bring blankets, food, and something warm to drink. "Where have you been?"

The exhaustion of walking through the night finally settles into my bones and it's impossible to fight any longer. I gratefully collapse back into the chair, peering at all the expectant faces around me. If there is anyone here that I can trust, that I *need* to trust, to find a way to fix things, it's them.

"I took a merchant ship from Korala," I begin shakily. "I had a driver drop me at the front gates. It was stupid, I know, but I wanted to walk the rest of the way."

"I walked through the night and arrived at the gates this morning. I just know Teddy has done something horrible to Alon. I know it. I have to go back for him."

The grim faces of the High Counsel watch in silence. I had paused only briefly in my retelling of the events of my arrival in Sephiroth to shrug off my coat, accept a blanket, and occasionally drink from the mug of mulled wine that had been brought for me. The more I said, the more I could see the Counsel becoming angrier and angrier. If their feeling of betrayal at Lord Moore's behavior is anything like the feelings I have towards Teddy's, then I pity anyone who crosses them. For the first time, I truly understand how much power these men hold and why it was entrusted to them in the first place.

Their fury shines just that little bit brighter in Father's face. Its echoing call resonates in my own body as well, but it's a tired fury. Worn thin. Like the sunlight in winter as it struggles to heat the world. I'm happy to let someone else take control and be angry on my behalf.

"We will go back," Father promises, "but we need to have a plan."

From all around the room, the Lords of the High Counsel echo assent and begin offering possible solutions. The chamber fills with voices and noise as plans are made, reflected on, and different guards and members of staff summoned and then dismissed. The exhaustion settling through me licks at my sore muscles and soothes my weariness. Under the blankets, I descend into a fugue state, not really awake, but not completely asleep either.

"Jasper," Mother says quietly, "can you carry her to bed?"

Strong arms cradle me gently and I'm vaguely aware of the rocking motion of footsteps down a hall.

"I want to go back," I murmur sleepily. "I need to go."

"You will," Father soothes.

"Promise?"

"I promise."

Then the arms are replaced with soft sheets and pillows. My many layers of woolen clothing with soft cottons and downy blankets. My body exhales with relief and slumbers.

Chapter 41

In Which Hell is Repeated

Alan

My head lolls back as Teddy hits me again. And again. And again. Time has no meaning anymore. I don't know how long it's been since I left the palace or how long I've been trapped here in this place. The days and nights bleed together in trails of blood, pain, and fear.

My ribs creak from the beating Teddy gave me when he discovered Nora had escaped. It's the small shred of hope I still cling to, the one thing that helps me withstand the long hours. And the pain. Nora escaped and he can't find her. She's safe. I hope.

Another fist connects with the side of my face. Blood and tears run together in rivulets down my cheeks and drip onto the stains of coagulating blood across the front of my shirt. It's hard to tell which one is worse, the blatant anger and violence that comes with the outright beatings or the more sophisticated torture methods Teddy seems to prefer.

He almost broke me. Almost convinced me that dying and never coming back was better than this. But then I would hear Nora saying that she loved me, feeling that longing behind my heart as it called out to her. I need to see her again. To talk to her. To tell her that I love her too and I will do anything for her. Even if it means I have to sacrifice myself to keep her safe.

With each new torture method, it becomes clearer and clearer that not only is Teddy good at this, but he enjoys it too. He knows exactly which buttons to push, which wounds to allow to fester. He always stops just before he goes too far and pushes me over the edge of no return. I'm sure if I actually died and returned the next morning it would send him into a fit and lead to more cruelty than I dared to imagine. Instead, he keeps me right at the brink, backing off just before he goes too far.

"Look at me!"

The demand comes hard and fast. Teddy and Lord Moore have been taking turns trying to get the information they want from me. When I fail to answer, they escalate until they need to rest. Or they run the risk of killing me. At this point, I'm not even sure if I'm more man than bloodied tissue, but I still hold on. I *have* to hold on.

When I don't look at Teddy fast enough, rough hands grab my hair and drag my head up and around. My eyes blink in and out of focus. Pain and blood make the world hazy and hard to make sense of. Teddy's face swims before me, leering as he tries to find answers in the bloodied mess.

"Tell me what I want to know." Teddy's voice is guttural. The hours of yelling have reduced it to a hoarse grating scratch. "How do we remove it?"

I turn inwards, focusing on the space behind my heart. I can feel Nora there. It pulses, but whether that's from pain, my heartbeat, or delusion I really can't tell. My lungs groan with every breath, all attempts to calm my racing heart failing miserably. The pain recedes slightly as I draw inwards, but my body is so bruised and broken it's impossible to ignore it completely.

"Theodore, I think we need a different tact."

"We've tried your way, Father, and it did nothing."

"And if we keep going like this then you will reduce him to a bloody pulp, and we'll never get our answers! Especially because you let our leverage escape. If we can't make him talk, then I think we should try making him sing."

A pregnant pause hovers over me as Teddy considers his father's words. "What do you have in mind?"

"Take off his boots and prop his legs up on something."

Another chair clunks in front of me and those same rough hands yank my limp legs up onto the seat. My knees are bent at odd angles and scream in protest, but it's quickly lost among the rest of the pain. The soft leather of my boots are torn from resisting calves and cast aside, lost to the dark corners of my filthy prison. My eyes slip closed again. It takes too much effort to keep them open.

"What are you going to do with that?"

"An old trick, my boy. He may be able to resist once or twice, but they never hold out for long."

Searing pain shudders up through my leg and a scream rips itself from my lips, the sound a gurgling wail. The acrid smell of burning flesh fills the air and stars blink and flash behind my eyelids. I force my swollen eyes apart and see Lord Moore standing in front of me with a branding iron.

"How do we remove it?"

He pauses, and when I don't answer he presses the branding iron to my other foot. My scream is louder this time and echoes hollowly in my ears. My body vibrates with energy, writhing against the ropes binding me to my chair to no avail. All other pain falls to the wayside. The scorching heat commands front and center attention.

Every part of me cries out, begging for release. For sleep. For an end to all this pain and suffering. Another wail slips through clenched teeth as Lord Moore presses the branding iron to my feet once, twice, three times more. Tears slink out and mix with the blood already running down my nose.

"Please," I beg weakly, my voice barely more than whisper. "Please don't do this. Please stop. Let me – let me go."

"Again, Father."

"You're making good progress I see."

This new voice parts the pain like lemonade quenches thirst on a hot summer's day. I must be hallucinating. There's no way I'm hearing —

"Nora?" Teddy's disbelief is clear. "You came back."

"I did."

"Why?"

"Call it a change of heart." Rustling fabric fills the space as she moves closer. "I decided you were right, Teddy. It's time for a change. If this is the way to make that change happen then so be it."

"No. Nora." My voice is strained and raspy. "Don't. Run."

"Well, it's about time you came to your senses." A clunk rings out as Lord Moore tosses the brand back to its resting place near the bellows. "It still doesn't solve the problem of how to rid him of that infernal curse and be done with him."

"It also doesn't solve the problem of your own curse, Nora." Teddy's suspicious now. Back on guard. "Or did you forget you told me about that when you shared all your secrets with me?"

What are they talking about? Nora never told me she was cursed.

"I didn't forget."

"Then you know there is no way we can marry until he dies and *stays* dead."

"I know. That's why I tracked down the witch that put the curse on me myself," Nora says dismissively. "I'd had my suspicions that my own little problem was solved when Alon and I were married. He drank poisoned wine on our wedding night and he died. The only stipulation to my curse was that my partner had to die. Nothing was said against them returning the next morning."

"So, it's done? You're sure?"

"Yes."

"Perfect." Teddy's triumph radiates through the room, stinging my skin with thousands of tiny pinpricks. "Then our next steps should be easy."

"Hold on." Lord Moore's deep baritone sweeps through the room like a gale force wind. "Theodore, you are altogether too trusting of her. How are we to know she is being truthful and not playing a part?"

"Do you think so little of me, Lord Moore?"

"I think you, like all women, can be clever if they so choose to be. That cleverness is used to take advantage of us men when it best suits you."

"Then how would you recommend I prove my loyalty to the cause?"

Nora's voice is careless, disinterested. Though her words carry a challenge, it's easy for me to hear she doesn't actually want to know the answer. She should never have come back.

"Brand him," says Teddy triumphantly. Clearly, he thinks he's won. "If you want to prove your loyalty to me and to our cause then use the branding iron on him yourself."

"Fine. Give it here."

Fear drips down my back and pools in my stomach. My legs pulse with a throbbing heat, the skin on my feet tight and blistered. Nora stands before me; the branding iron clutched tightly in her hand. There's no way she can seriously be considering this. She'd never –

Fresh heat licks up my legs as the burning hot iron is pressed to my ruined feet once more. There's not as much force behind the pain as when Lord Moore did it, but it's enough to make me scream again. I quiet to pitiful mewling and snuffling while Nora throws the iron into a bucket of water, making it sizzle and spit its disapproval.

"Happy now?"

"Quite. Why don't we go back to the house for something warm," Lord Moore suggests. The approval in his voice is undeniable. What a disgusting man. "We can plan out our next steps and I'll have the servants clean up this mess."

There's no question about what mess he's referring to.

"Nora," I cough again weakly, "don't. Please."

My eyes have fallen shut again, tears leaking out of the corners as I sit in my pain. Nora's skirts rustle as she approaches and I'm bathed in her familiar smell of peonies and vanilla. Nora kneels next to me in the smeared sawdust and dried blood. Her hands are gentle as she pats my shoulder, giving my hand a careful squeeze.

"Don't worry, Alon," she reassures me. "This will all be over soon. I promise."

Receding footsteps and the sharp snap of a door closing mark their exit from the barn. It's just me and the horses left among the hay and sawdust littering the floor. They left me. *She* left me. I can't believe she left me. Again.

There is nothing but my own misery and the ever-present pain coursing through my body to keep me company. Blood, sweat, salt, and peonies fill the air around me and burn my nose. This isn't right. I can't just sit here; I need to do something. To stop them. But I'm so, so tired. I fight to stay awake for as long as possible, but it's too much pain and I succumb to the darkness.

Chapter 42

In Which Justice is Found

Nora

My hands shake as I follow Lord Moore and Teddy to the house, but whether it's from the cold or what I just had to do I can't tell. *I can't believe I did that.*

Alon will never forgive me for using the branding iron on him like that. He'll probably be so angry with everything I've put him through since our wedding that he'll decide I'm just not worth it and leave me. Please, gods, I don't want him to leave me. Hopefully, once we get him out, he'll see I had no other choice. I need them to believe me, to trust me. I need this to work.

The cold is tempered by the confines of the tunnel leading from the barn to the house, but it's not perfect. Even my racing heart can't keep my body from shivering violently as I follow Teddy and Lord Moore. I'm wearing the same coat and dress I escaped in four days ago. While they're perfectly adequate for a fall day, they are horribly unprepared to handle the bitter winter cold that seems to have settled over Sephiroth earlier than usual. I can only imagine how

Alon feels. He's never experienced a true winter. Depending on how the night goes, he may not ever.

"Shall we retire to the sitting room for a cup of something warm?" Lord Moore offers as he generously holds open the door for me.

"No." I strip off my coat and hand it to a waiting maid absently. "I think the study is more fitting for our needs. Seems more practical for planning."

Lord Moore nods approvingly and barks at the cook to have a tray of warm cider and biscuits brought to the study. I catch him leering briefly at the maidservant that took my coat. What an odiously unpleasant man. I guess I now know where Teddy gets it from. He leads the way as Teddy and I follow through the house, delicious warmth sinking its teeth further into me with every step.

I've never been in Lord Moore's study before. It's an unspoken rule that you never enter the private study of a nobleman without an explicit invitation to do so. A barely stifled gasp slips through my lips as I step through the heavy door. Taking up the entire end of one side of the first floor, the room itself is a rectangle with just the right amount of difference between the length and width to make it feel spacious and open.

The far-left wall boasts a stately fireplace that clucks and cackles like a nervous mama hen watching over the two lumbering chairs settled before it. Windows peer out from between built in bookshelves running along the opposite wall from where I now stand just inside the doorway. The first rays of moonlight illuminate the fresh snow stretching out unbroken to the tree line.

Wooden planks stained a deep mahogany have been fixed to all sides of the room over the stonework. Portraits of family, pets, and a beautiful landscape of the manor house in autumn hang from the walls.

Farther down, the wall to my right houses a door that stands slightly ajar. It's the same door that joins the study to the dining room. Behind me is the door to the hallway and several feet down the same wall is a matching polished door that leads into the library.

It had always seemed odd to me to have one's study attached to the dining room, but Lord Moore had always insisted it was the perfect place. He boasted often about its easy access to the archives stored in the library and how quick it was to make a trip to the dining room for a meal with minimal distraction. Now that I'm actually here in the room, I completely understand his reasoning. I wouldn't want to leave here unless absolutely necessary either.

Thick carpeting absorbs all sound as we walk further into the room. My knees seem to have turned into jelly, and I collapse as gracefully as I can manage into one of the heavy hardbacked chairs in front of the desk. Teddy and Lord Moore chat amiably about their fall harvests as another log is thrown onto the fire and the wall sconces are lit. They are very nonchalant for two men that have a member of the royal family tied up and beaten bloody in their barn.

A soft tap from the door announces the entrance of a maid bearing a heavy tray. She carefully places it on the side of the desk closest to me, catching my eye and bowing her head apologetically before she leaves as quickly as she arrived. Steaming mugs and a plate of biscuits beckon to me from their place on the polished silver tray. I choose one of the mugs, sipping gratefully at the warmed cider.

Once the room has reached the exact unknown specifications of light requirements, Teddy seats himself in the armchair next to me and Lord Moore settles behind his desk. His chair must be slightly taller than mine because there's no way he can tower over us like that without his chair purposefully being raised higher. He watches Teddy and I with an odd mixture of pride, judgement, and just the barest hint of suspicion. *Don't squirm*, I remind myself.

"Now then," he says, steepling his fingers under his chin. "Where should we begin?"

"How about telling me what the two of you have already figured out?" My voice is significantly more confident sounding than I feel. Good. "Then I can tell you if I know of a better way to do it."

"And what makes you think you know more than we do?"

Damm. Now he's defensive. *Do I pull back or keep pushing?*

"Father!"

"It's alright, Teddy." I level Lord Moore with a stony gaze. "I think I can find a better way to do it because without me this doesn't work. Now tell me what your plan is."

A look of contempt crosses Lord Moore's face briefly before he pulls it back under control. "Fine. To begin with, I would like to speak with this witch you claim to have found and confirm she's actually telling the truth. Assuming you are being honest with us –" a stony glare washes across me, but I keep my head high. *Don't let them see you squirm.* "– then the general next steps are fairly simple. You will annul the marriage to the whelp in the barn and marry Theodore. We will need you to sire a son immediately to continue the bloodline and establish your place as a viable contender for the throne.

"Once married, we will work on strengthening support for the two of you amongst the nobility and genteel families. When the time is right, you will be crowned, and you will step in to rule. Your first act as regents will be to remove the High Counsel from power and claim the long standing right of a monarchy to not be beholden to others. From there we can do what we need to right the wrongs that have infected our society so wholly."

I snort in disbelief. "So that's your entire plan? Get me married and with child? Is there no one backing you and promising their strength? Lord Moore you've been on the High Counsel for many years. You should know that unless you have support from the majority there is no way to stage your little coup and ensure its success. You will need the other Lord's military connections."

"We don't need the Lords," Teddy says carelessly. "We have their sons."

"Theodore!" Lord Moore barks. Clearly Teddy has said too much.

Suppressing a shudder, I reach out and gently cover his hand with my own. I gaze imploringly at Teddy and fix him with a pleading, saccharine smile. "What do you mean you have their sons?"

Teddy shifts importantly in his seat. "Almost every Lord that sits at the High Counsel has a son eager to make his mark on the world and do better than his father. I am friends with a great many of them. We share the same ideals and beliefs on what needs to happen to help Sephiroth advance to a better future."

"And why would they help? What did you promise them in return?"

"They will take over their father's seats on the High Counsel," Lord Moore says boredly. I guess Teddy really has let the cat out of the bag. "They just don't realize that title will be worthless once all is said and done."

"And how do you plan to subdue the rioting young Lords once you betray them? They just helped you stage a coup to overthrow the current monarchs. Who's to say they won't do the same to you?"

"Father and I can be very...persuasive when we need to be." Teddy's voice is vinegar coated in sugar. The threat is perfectly clear – if I don't cooperate then I will be *persuaded* as well.

"And do you expect your prowess at persuasion to yield the same results achieved with Alon? Because from what I can see you still don't have the information you want."

Teddy's face hardens and the valley in his forehead deepens. His hand twitches beneath mine, but he doesn't pull away. "They won't be nearly as resistant."

"What do you plan to do with my family after the revolution? With my mother and father? My brothers?" I fight to keep my voice steady. "With Alon?"

"The King and Queen will be executed —" I stifle a gasp and fight to keep my face as neutral as possible. I need to look like I don't care "— and your brothers will be offered the option of execution or banishment. What happens to Alon is up to Theodore."

My heart drops to my stomach. The malice on Teddy's face is enough to make a grown man cower in fear. If Teddy is allowed to do whatever he wants with Alon it will be excruciatingly long and unbelievably painful.

"I have a few ideas already." Teddy cracks his knuckles for emphasis. "And I will enjoy it immensely. Although I'd still like confirmation that he can actually die. Did you figure out how to get his curse removed?"

"Yes." I wave a hand dismissively. "I can take care of that don't worry. It sounds like the two of you truly have thought of everything."

"Then let us have a toast," says Lord Moore, raising his mug. "To the future of Sephiroth."

Teddy and I both mumble "to the future!" and clink mugs before drinking. A knock from behind us echoes through the sudden stillness. We barely have enough time to turn and look at the door before Father throws it open. Always one for the dramatic, he's flanked on either side with guards dressed to the nines in their full battle armor.

"Father!" I gasp, dropping my mug into a puddle on the floor and vaulting out of my seat. I retreat towards the fireplace and half step behind one of the chairs crouching before it. "What are you doing here?"

"Your Majesty." Lord Moore and Teddy bow awkwardly, exchanging furtive glances. "Welcome to our home. It is such an honor –"

"How dare you pretend like you did not just plan my murder mere minutes ago," Father thunders. His anger makes him as dangerous as a predator, striding into the room with such presence that my knees threaten to buckle again even though his wrath is not directed towards me. "Oh yes, Moore, I heard everything."

A malignant smile leisurely slinks across Lord Moore's face as he studies the room. "And you decided it was best to intervene with just two guards? I can't say that was the wisest choice, Your Majesty, but I don't think you'll have to worry about making those for too much longer."

The room erupts into total chaos. Lord Moore flings his mug at Father and skirts his desk with more grace than I expected from the large man. He gives me a conspiratorial wink as he slips through the library door into the darkness beyond. How truly stupid does he have to be to think Father is here with just two guards?

Teddy hefts one of the heavy chairs and tries to throw it at father, but he lacks the brute strength to make it go further than a couple of feet before it crashes to the floor with a resounding thump. Despite his failure, it creates enough of a distraction to allow him to flee out the other door to the dining room.

Father had ducked when the mug of cider came towards him and now straightens, smiling questioningly at me. My chin dips in return, hands clutching the back of the chair in front of me. The polished wood slides along my sweaty palms even as my nails bite into the plush fabric covering.

Yelling and the sounds of fighting break out in the rooms on either side of us. I manage to smile weakly at Father. It's almost over.

It doesn't take long for the noise to die down. Both doors swing open simultaneously and Lord Moore and Teddy are frog-marched back into the study by several imposing guards. With encouraging shoves, they sink to the floor in front of the desk. Lord Moore ends up in the puddle of cider from my dropped mug. Serves the bastard right.

"You know, you were right, Lord Moore." Father's voice is humorous, but the anger beneath threatens to drown us all. "I did need more than two guards."

Lord Moore spits at Father and one of the guards backhands him smartly across the face. Teddy stares at me with pleading eyes, but I draw myself up and let an icy frost cloud my gaze. This man has tried to take so much from me. I won't let him see me cry. Not now, not ever again. Teddy flinches and his eyes harden with malevolence, but he still drops his gaze in submission.

"Lord Elthius Moore and Sir Theodore Moore," the Captain of the Guard intones as he oversees the manacles being attached to their wrists and ankles. "You are hereby charged with abduction of Their Highnesses Princess Eleanor of Sephiroth and Prince Alon of Korala. You are hereby charged with high treason including, but not limited to, torture, plotting to incite rebellion and overthrow the monarchy, and the planning of the murder of Their Royal Majesties King Jasper and Queen Clarice of Sephiroth and His Highness Prince

Alon of Korala. You will be brought before a court for your crimes to be read and have judgment cast upon you. May the gods have mercy on your souls."

With a unit of guards surrounding them, Lord Moore and Teddy are half carried, half marched, out of the study. I circle the chair I had hid behind and sink gratefully into the soft cushions. My body is still not fully recovered from my escape from this very house and each minute saps even more strength from me. Better to sit down now than risk collapsing from the struggle to remain upright. The fire sings soothingly from the hearth, its heat gently caressing my sore limbs.

"We will need to interview the sons of the High Counsel." Father's voice carries throughout the room, commanding as always. "Unfortunately, if we are unable to find anything linking them directly to this mess, then the most we can do is alert their fathers to their suspected misdeeds and keep a watchful eye on them."

"Your Majesty." A guard enters the study and bows low. "We were able to extract His Highness from the barn. He is being transported to the medical infirmary near the training university in the city as we speak."

Hot prickling tears of relief drip down my cheeks and the knotted tension in my chest slowly begins to release. *He's okay.* Alon is okay. We did it.

Chapter 43

In Which a Reunion is Had

Alon

Frigid air swirls around me like a blanket. Beneath the wind there's a constant creaking of wood and leather, blustering from horses. My lungs ache in the cold and I gasp, struggling to draw breath.

In. Out. In. Out. Keep Breathing. A heavy jostle throws me sideways into the edge of something hard and unforgiving. My cheek scrapes against roughly hewn wood.

• • • ☽ • ◯ • ☾ • • •

"Doctor, this is the worst I've ever seen. What if he —"

"None of that Nurse Lider. Hold pressure steady on that wound. We'll move him in three, two, one, pull!"

Fire crackles from my feet and heat races up my spine in an inferno. Bright dots of energy course through my body and my jaw clenches in a silent scream. My limbs convulse and thrash, desperately looking for release from the pain.

"We need to sedate him before he makes it worse. Get the opium! Hold him down!"

A sharp pinprick stings through the chaos. From its point flows a steady cooling that lazily seeps through my body. I drift along, sinking beneath its current.

Soft hands push my hair from my face.

"Shhh," a soothing voice says tenderly. I know that voice, but why? "It's going to be alright."

My body is slick with sweat. The fabric beneath me sticks to my back, my legs. Heat pounds through me and my limbs shake with effort.

"Stay with me, Alon." The voice is encouraging, but it hurts too much. I don't want to. "Stay with me."

Dappled light dances across my eyelids. For the first time in – actually I'm not sure how long it's been, but the pain is gone. Well, the pain is *mostly* gone. It still rings through my ribs, knocks at the nape of my neck, and sizzles across my feet. My lungs are swollen and bruised, my eyes cry out in protest as I try to open them.

Bracing myself, I pry my eyelids apart and squint at the room beyond. White walls surround me on all sides. The window to my right lets in sunlight as it falls through the hazy branches of a tree outside. Beyond the end of the bed, a door holds its own silent counsel next to a depressing painting of a landscape in winter. The soft patter of footsteps and the murmuring of voices filter in from somewhere. Someone is moaning.

My neck protests loudly as I shift on the bed and try to turn my head. A small table is to the left of the bed, a burnt-out candle and book resting on top. Pressing against the wall is a high-backed cane chair and a figure slumped over the side, breathing deeply. Her clothes are plain, her posture relaxed in sleep, a red mane falling half over her shoulders and into her face. My heart leaps when I realize it's –

"Nora," I call. My voice is hoarse and barely more than a harsh whisper. "Nora!"

She rustles briefly, eyes opening sleepily. Those beautiful eyes. When she sees me, she startles and lunges towards the side of the bed. Her knees make a hollow clunking when they hit the floor and I wince.

"Alon! You're awake!"

"Water," I croak.

"Of course. Wait right here."

Nora heaves up from the side of the bed and disappears out the door. It doesn't latch completely behind her, and I can hear more of the world beyond the room. There are children crying, people being chastised, coughing, sneezing, and the hushed voices of people discussing things they don't wish others to overhear. The sounds crowd towards me in a cacophony of confusion.

I close my eyes, hoping it will help block out some of the noise. Unfortunately, it does nothing. The rustling of fabric announces Nora's return, and I watch as a soft faced man in a neat tunic and a white apron follows her in. Thankfully, he closes the door behind him, shutting out the rest of the world.

With one on either side of the bed, they raise my stiff body into a sitting position and prop me up with pillows. Nora gingerly lifts a glass to my lips. The water trickles into my mouth and sets me coughing as it hits the clenched tissue in my throat. Spasms wrack my already ruined body as I cough, and it takes both Nora and the man to hold me steady.

The second attempt goes smoother, but I still swallow around the pain as I drink. Once I'm done, they settle me back down among the pillows and Nora sets the glass of water onto the table. They watch me expectantly, but I don't know what they're waiting for me to do.

"Your Highness, it's a pleasure to see you awake," the man says. His voice is calm and reassuring. Almost like he's talking to a scared child. "I am Doctor Plains and have been overseeing your care. You gave us all quite a scare when you came in. How are you feeling now?"

"Hurts." It's the only word I can manage.

"Yes, I imagine it does. I am going to give you some more opium to help with the pain." His hands are too fast for me to track his movements, pulling a syringe out from somewhere and drawing a draft from a clear bottle. "Now hold still please. You will most likely feel sleepy, and I urge you to give into it. Your body needs rest to heal."

I watch with gross fascination as he carefully inserts the needle into the vein in my arm, depressing the plunger with measured practice. The same cooling feeling from before spreads through my body in a lazy current. My aching muscles relax, and the pain is practically gone. My lungs allow me to take deep, measured breaths without fear.

Doctor Plains has a short, whispered conference with Nora at the end of the bed and then ducks back out of the room. She returns to her chair and pulls it closer to my bedside. I awkwardly slide a hand across my blankets towards her. My limbs feel like they're moving underwater. I feel her warmth as she takes my hand in both of hers.

My eyelids are heavy again. So, so heavy. I can't keep them open. A gentle weightlessness dances with the exhaustion stored in my muscles and I slip effortlessly into a heavy drowse. *She's here. She's really here.*

$$\cdots) \cdot \bigcirc \cdot (\cdots$$

Someone is reading aloud. A funny story about something called a hippopotamus wanting to dance. Wait. I know that voice.

With a strength and ease I haven't possessed in days, I open my eyes to the same white room from before. Afternoon light puddles lazily on the floor and the shadow of the tree outside dances across the walls.

Nora sits in the same chair as before, a picture in midnight blue and gold. Her sunflower pendant nestles in the cozy hollow just beneath her collarbones, the sunlight illuminating the gems and making them glow. A familiar tugging behind my heart calls out to her, yearning to be close to her. A book of children's stories sits open on her lap, and she continues reading about the hippopotamus. It's now being fitted for a tutu.

"Nora?"

My voice is rusty, unpracticed. Nevertheless, Nora drops the book to the floor with a clunk and tries to wrap what she can of her arms around me. Her willing nearness is a welcome surprise.

"Alon! Oh, I'm so glad you're awake! How do you feel?"

Little by little, I stretch and flex my limbs. There's still pain, but it's a mere trickle and not the cascading falls from before. My lungs still wheeze a bit and my ribs are tender, but it's a vast improvement from where I began.

"More...normal. There's some pain, but better. Can I have...water?"

"Of course."

Nora doles out a healthy serving from a pitcher on the small bedside table and helps me sit up enough to drink. My throat is still sore and swollen from the last attempt, but thankfully this time there's just a tight pain that slowly relaxes under the flow of water. I'm honestly just glad I've managed to avoid another coughing fit.

"Do you want to lay back down?"

"No. Thank you. I'd like to sit for a little while." I readjust the blankets slowly. "What happened?"

A shadow crosses Nora's face and it's not from the tree outside the window.

"Are you sure you want to know?"

"Yes."

Nora takes a breath. She won't meet my eye. "Teddy met me when I first returned to the palace. He convinced me to meet him in the gardens and then staged an attack. We fled to Moore Hall and he went back and forth to the palace under the guise of trying to find who attacked us. I know now it was just to make sure Father wouldn't catch on to what was going on. They probably would have gotten away with it if you hadn't shown up."

Nora fiddles with her hands, twisting her skirts into tight knots and then halfheartedly trying to smooth the wrinkled fabric. She's so nervous and uncomfortable I almost take pity on her and reassure her she doesn't need to tell me it all. But I also know I *really* need to know if they did anything to her. If that bastard hurt her in any way I'm going to –

"I forced the issue of going home and —" Nora takes a shaky breath. She's fighting back tears "— Teddy showed me who he really is. He held me prisoner for several days until I managed to escape and walked back to the palace. It took me all night. That was the same night you were brought there. As a guest."

I flinch. The spasm reminds my body of earlier pain, and the memory runs deep. I take slow breaths through my mouth to offset the starbursts flashing behind my eyes. After a few moments, my body relaxes again.

"What happened next?"

"I told Mother and Father what happened when I made it back. We put all the pieces together and made a plan to rescue you."

"That's why you told them you wanted to join them?"

Nora nods absently. "That was Father's idea. They told me their plans while Father and the guards moved into position around Lord Moore's study." She gives a half-hearted snort. "Teddy was so excited thinking that he had won it was easy to get information out of him. Once Father heard enough to make sure the courts would find them guilty, he and the guards moved in. There was a fight, but it was over quickly. I just wish...I wish we had gotten there sooner."

I can read Nora's guilt as clearly as the tides. She feels responsible for what happened to us. To me. I don't want to keep pushing, but I need more answers. I cautiously reach out a hand. Nora grips it carefully, clearly not willing to let go.

"What did Teddy mean about finding a witch? Why did he say you were cursed?"

Nora really does begin to cry now. Her tears run quietly down her face as she sniffles next to me. If only I could reach far enough to touch her shoulder, her face. To offer some sort of comfort.

"Father made a deal with a witch before I was born. He agreed to the cost without hearing what it was. When I was four, she came back to collect." Nora lifts her tearstained face to mine. "The payment she wanted was me."

Wracking sobs take the place of the quiet tears. I just hold Nora's hands as she weeps beside me. I curse my inability to move and attempt to murmur some soothing words to Nora. Eventually, she quiets. Taking a sip of water, Nora continues.

"Mother and Father refused to pay so the witch considered their deal broken. She told them that if I was not wed by my twenty-first birthday that she would come back to claim me. If I did marry, then she would claim the soul of my partner instead."

My heart falls out of my chest deep into the pit of my stomach. "Is that why I died on our wedding night? Why didn't you tell me before, Nora?"

"I don't know." The simple confession hangs between us. "Mother and Father forbade me from saying anything to you in case your parents tried to annul the marriage. They were just trying to protect me."

"Did you actually find her? The witch I mean?"

"Father did. Kind of." Nora has mostly composed herself now, blowing her nose on a handkerchief before tucking it away again. "After we left for Korala, Father renewed his search. He couldn't find Belladonna – that's her name – but he did find a woman claiming to be her daughter. She said Belladonna passed on several years ago."

My heart begins to make its slow climb back into my chest. "Does that mean your curse is lifted?"

"We don't know." Nora shrugs helplessly. "Her daughter could only hedge vague guesses as to whether the curse was still in play. Especially because you did technically die on our wedding night and fulfilled the requirements laid out."

We sit in contemplative silence. My thumb traces an absent path along the back of Nora's hand. Who would have thought that the girl who was destined to have her partner die by her twenty-first birthday and the boy who couldn't die would be brought together. *Tutu* really was right. We really are *Anima Mate*.

"You know you can always tell me anything."

A small ghost of a smile crosses Nora's face. "I know that now."

"What does this mean for us?"

"Us?"

"You and me."

"I know the definition, thank you." Nora fills her cheeks with air and then blows it out sharply. "I came back to Sephiroth to talk to Teddy. To end it — us — he and I."

Warmth spread through my body. "Why?"

"Because I choose you, Alon."

My heart is back in its rightful place in my chest and it's going to burst. I grip the blankets with my free hand, trying to steady myself. As quickly as my excitement rises, however, it falls again under a wave of doubt.

"Are you only choosing me because Teddy turned out to by a scheming psychopath?" My words are shaky, unspoken emotion resonating from deep within them. "Nora, I love you as I have never loved a woman before. There is a space behind my heart that calls for you, that *craves* you. I want you to be with me because you love me. I want to be your first choice."

"You feel it too? The space behind your heart? I thought it was just me."

Nora looks stricken, absently rubbing at the space above her heart. With my free hand I rub the same place on my chest. Nora casts her eyes around the room and seems agitated.

"I don't know how to make you understand that you *are* my first choice. I would say trust me, but I know you haven't had much of a reason to do so. Wait!"

Nora digs frantically through her skirts. She dips a hand into a hidden pocket and pulls out a pale pink checked handkerchief. Shoving the chair out of the way, Nora half-kneels, half-crouches next to the bed and unwraps the handkerchief.

"Alon, I have not treated you with the respect you so clearly deserve. From the moment we met I have been drawn to you in a way I cannot explain. I was so focused on what I thought I wanted that I missed you standing in front of me asking for nothing more than what I was willing to give you. I will never forgive myself for the lost time we could have had together. You have become my trusted companion and a dear, dear friend. So, I guess what I'm trying to say is – Alon will you marry me?"

Smiling shyly, Nora presents me with a ring. The gold band catches the afternoon light with a sparkle. I can just make out the etchings of leaves curling around the edges and a small sunflower made of the same gems as her pendant inset along the top. The light reflects off the stones into a small spray of starbursts onto the ceiling above us.

I can't help it. I laugh. A deep belly laugh that shakes through my ruined body and leaves me coughing and trembling. Nora helps settle me and goes to tuck the ring away, clearly fighting back more tears. I stop her with a gentle hand.

"Of course I'll marry you, Nora. As long as we get to do it my way this time."

Nora's smile lights her face like the full moon coming out from behind the clouds. She carefully slips the ring onto my finger, and I pull her down next to me onto the pillows. We fit so perfectly together, like I've held her this way my entire life. Her familiar scent surrounds us like a hug, and I close my eyes. There's finally peace in my world.

"Hey Alon?" Nora's voice is quiet. I make a sleepy sound in return. "What does your way mean?"

Chapter 44

In Which Vows are Exchanged

Nora

"Nora, darling, are you still here?" Queen Ululani's – no *Mama's* voice stutters to a gasp as she rounds the corner. "You look absolutely radiant."

There's a rush of heat to my face and I just know my neck is a matching crimson. Abigail secures the last few pins into my hair and pronounces me done.

"I think we may want to give the blushing bride a few moments alone," she says with a smile in her voice.

"Quite right." Mama's voice is thick with tears. "Let's go check to make sure everything is ready, shall we?"

The two breeze out of the room together, herding the remaining maidservants out the door ahead of them. I'm so thankful for the brief moment of quiet in an otherwise hectic day and I inhale a few deep breaths to steady myself. Turning back to the full-length mirror, I inspect Abigail's work.

She has done a truly magnificent job with my hair. Abigail managed to coax my curls into soft waves down my back, a half crown of braids studded with flowers and ivy circling my forehead. A few loose curls escape here and there to frame my face. My gown is a pale silver satin, the same color as the full moon at its zenith. I had insisted on wearing an embroidered Sephiroth wedding gown, but instead of the traditional flowers and leaves, I wanted to have stars ring my skirts and bodice. The gold and pale blue threads shimmer as they catch the early evening light and, when I move, they blur together into a rich constellation of movement. Everything feels perfect.

When Alon had insisted on having a wedding his way I had not expected that to mean we have it back in Korala. Or that it would take significantly longer than we had thought it would. His recovery after being tortured had been slow and needed much patience. We learned through the experience that although Alon may return from the dead, he heals the same way I do. Slowly.

So, we waited. We waited through the winter and Alon got to experience Sephiroth during Yuletide. Mother and Father rang in the New Year with their masked ball, as was tradition, and we were welcomed as the guests of honor. Alon, Atlas, and Hanale, the only brothers that had stayed at court when the weather turned cold, got to experience a true Sephiroth winter and what it meant to dream of spring.

Once Alon was strong enough, he began to work with Hayden and Father to root out the dissenting voices on the High Counsel. Thankfully, the rebellion really was focused more on their sons, and the Counsel was more or less unaffected. Several members did choose to step down for various reasons and proper replacements were found to ensure the voices of the people were still heard. Father even made the decision to allow the working unions to elect representatives to fill some of the empty seats. The High Counsel now boasts three members of the working class who bring a different perspective to the Counsel chambers.

Mother and I also established her own Queen's Counsel to act as liaisons between the Queen of Sephiroth and her people. We were not nearly so strict in our requirements of rank and nobility to join and instead focused on ensuring several women from every economic class were able to take part. Already our Counsel has produced much fruit, and Mother is becoming quite revolutionary, pushing the boundaries of growth and development for the people. Even Father admitted that she had become a bit radicalized.

Winter melted into spring and with it returned the soft earth and spring shearings. Alon had improved greatly, and the doctors allowed him to truly rejoin the world with no restrictions. He took advantage of Father's requests for help and spent much time with him touring the fields, reading about agriculture and animal handling in the library, and overseeing the traditional road maintenance that springtime heralds. I often joined him in the libraries in the afternoons, but more often than not found myself reading books on Korala or the occasional novel.

As the tree buds unfurled into new leaves, we began to talk of returning to Korala. Alon missed his home and wished to return to the sea and to his family. We asked Mother and Father to join us on our journey, but they regretfully declined with promises to come see us after the harvest when the weather turns cold. With Hayden stepping up more as Crown Prince, Father can step back a little and take small moments of rest.

As such, we set off just before Maytide and spent several leisurely weeks at sea. Alon taught me about sailing, and we sparred almost daily. I was able to beat him most days, but his strength is fast returning, and it won't be long before he will again have the advantage of size. I can already feel how our sparring has changed my body. The softness has smoothed into taut lines, my shoulders and upper back wider than before.

It's not just my body that has grown stronger either. The bond Alon and I share has grown with time and bloomed with the spring crocuses into something familiar and exciting. We remain whole unto ourselves even though it was difficult at times to resist. Once Alon had recovered enough to move back into the palace for the remainder of his convalescence, we had many discussions about our relationship with each other and what we thought our next steps should be.

One very awkward afternoon hangs sharply in my mind when I asked Alon that we not give ourselves over completely until after our wedding in Korala. To my relief he wholeheartedly agreed. He confessed he had been nervous that I would want to take things further once he was healed. In his words, he wanted to make sure he honored me the right way and wait until we had a wedding worthy of our union and not one arranged for us.

All that changes tonight. My blush deepens even further at the thought. *I wonder what he has planned...*

My musings are cut short as Mama and Abigail return.

"It's time, Your Highness," Abigail announces as she curtsies deeply.

Mama straightens one last flower and gently ushers me out the door. The Manor House in Korala doesn't have a true bridal suite, but Mama had overseen the preparation of a small suite of rooms overlooking the western coast for us to use instead.

Together, Mama and I link arms and walk side by side through the almost deserted Manor to the front door. An elegant carriage adorned in rainbow hued flowers and white ribbons is parked at the bottom of the stairs. Handsome chestnut horses whuffle to each other, eager to stretch their legs and get on with it.

A coachman helps Mama and I into the carriage and we set off. As we descend further into the port town, Koralan's throw flowers and call out blessings and good wishes. I'm struck again by just how much the people love Mama and Baba and their seven sons, how integrated they all are together. Without one, the other wouldn't survive.

We pull to a stop at the top of the stone stairs leading down to the beach. The crowd offers their arms and their support as they help us down from the carriage and dance us to the steps. Flower wreaths are wrapped around my neck and hair, bathing Mama and I in their perfume. We carefully descend the black rock stairs towards the beach below.

At the bottom, I stop to catch my breath and almost lose it again. As the evening sun dresses itself for its final curtain call, it illuminates an image I hope I won't ever forget. Alon stands barefoot on the hard packed sand near the water's edge. His hair reflects the sunlight in a halo and his white shirt and simple pants a stark contrast to the deep blues of the water beyond. His smile is so wide I can see it from all the way back here. I can't help but smile in return.

"Are you ready?" Mama asks quietly.

"I don't know if I'll ever be."

"Trust me, my dear."

Clasping my hand and looping her arm through mine, Mama pulls me gently forward. My steps are awkward at first, but a few more strides and my toes sink confidently into the shifting grains underfoot. A year ago today I was walking a much different aisle in a church. It was wrong. Stilted. This one feels like I'm walking home.

All around me are the smiling faces of the people I have grown to love. All six of Alon's brothers reach out in blessing as Mama and I pass them. While my family lacks women, Alon's has aunties and cousins in abundance. Many I only met a week prior when they traveled in to attend our wedding, but they have already accepted me wholeheartedly and welcomed me as one of their own. Now their smiling faces radiate such joy at the prospect of gaining another member of the family it makes me slightly teary as I move through the crowd.

The walk down the aisle somehow takes forever, but also just mere minutes. The loose sand is left behind as I step up next to Alon and face him. He carefully dries a tear from my cheek and clasps both his hands around mine.

"You look..."

"Stunning?"

"Like the Moon Goddess Herself."

Fresh tears threaten to spill over, but I manage to keep them in check. Together we walk the last few steps to the water's edge and stand underneath an archway of flowers. We had decided to forgo an official ceremony and simply exchange vows and rings surrounded by the people we love.

"Are you ready?" Alon asks.

I nod and pull out the sunflower ring I had used to propose to him all those months ago. Taking a deep breath, I straighten and recite the same words I did a year ago. This time, though, I actually mean them:

"Alon. In front of our friends and family, I give you everything I am and everything I will grow to be. I vow to be your truest friend, to share your hopes and dreams, and to work beside you to achieve the goals that you hold dear. I promise to always be by your side and to listen with an open heart. With this ring —" I fumble briefly before sliding it onto his finger "— I pledge to you my fidelity, honesty, compassion, and forgiveness. I vow to love you always, no matter what our future holds. To be your loyal confidant, friend, and wife. You are my kindred soul, my heart, now and forever."

Alon sniffles and casually wipes his cheek.

"I didn't mean to make you cry!"

He just grins at me. "You started it."

From behind us come the sounds of sniffled laughter. I look out into the crowd and most have their own handkerchiefs out, trying to cry into them discreetly. Mama and Baba are watching with such love and pride it makes my heart swell. Alon clears his throat, and I turn back to him.

"I, Alon, receive you, Nora, as my partner and my love. Beside me and apart from me, in laughter and in tears, in sickness and in health, in conflict and serenity, asking that you be no other than your one true self. Loving you in what I know of you and trusting what I do not know in all the ways our life together may bring. Nora, with this ring —" Alon carefully slides a matching sunflower band onto my left hand. It sparkles in the golden evening light. "— I promise to grow with you, to build our love, to speak openly and honestly, to listen to you and cherish you for all the days ahead. From this day forward you shall not walk alone, but together with me as an equal. My heart will be your shelter, and my arms will be your home."

My heart sings out in response, and I can no longer stop the tears when they come. Alon and I stand there, sand under our feet and saltwater licking at our heels. Our hands are clasped, our eyes locked. We are finally together. Whole.

"Kiss her already!"

I laugh as the spell breaks. Alon gives me a devilish smile before twirling me out and then back, swirling my skirts and letting the setting sun sparkle off me. He catches me as I come back in and dips me down, my arms wrapping around his neck.

"I love you."

Alon presses his lips to mine in a gentle kiss. My arms tighten briefly around him before relaxing as he stands me up. A fire sparks deep in my body, and I try to soothe it back to its restless slumber. *Not yet. Soon, but not yet.*

From high above us comes the resounding cheers from the townspeople, crowding the cliff sides so they can watch our ceremony. Laughing now, Alon grabs my hand and twirls me again. We race back through the sand as our family throws flowers over us.

I collect my skirts in one hand and begin the climb back up the rock steps. By the time we reach the top I'm out of breath and my heart pounds in my chest like a drum. Alon and I are swept up into the current of well wishers and safely deposited back into the carriage Mama and I had arrived in earlier.

The horses turn their faces towards home, and we set off back to the Manor House for our celebratory dinner. Alon hands me a bag of coins and together we toss them out into the crowds, sharing our wealth and blessings with the people around us.

My cheeks hurt from all the smiling. My heart is full and happy. This is the wedding that I was always meant to have. This is the wedding that Alon and I deserved.

Chapter 45

In Which a Union is Made

Alon

Nora carefully pulls all the pins from her curls, letting them fall around her shoulders like a halo. My heart is a contented cat purring in a sunbeam, basking in the knowledge that I finally have her. She's finally mine.

We're in the main bedroom of my family's holiday home in the mountains. Mama and Baba surprised us with an impromptu second honeymoon to make up for the disaster that was our first wedding night. Heat floods my body and sets me at high alert. It really is our wedding night. The quiet sounds of the house echo around us and it's easy to pretend we're the only ones here.

"There. I think I got them all."

Nora gives her curls a final shake and I stare, mesmerized as they cascade down her back. Rising from my place at the end of the bed, I stand behind her at the vanity. She meets my gaze in the mirror and smiles at me. I want so badly to lay claim to her, to have her devour me as I devour her, but I know I need to go slowly. More than anything, I want Nora to enjoy this.

The urge to touch her overwhelms me and I do something I've wanted to do since I first saw her. I bury my hands in her hair and gently comb through her ringlets. They're even softer than I thought possible. Carefully sweeping her hair over her shoulder, I bend down and kiss the silky skin at the nape of her neck.

"Now tell me, dear wife," I murmur as I kiss up her neck and gently tug on her ear with my teeth. "Was our wedding everything you wanted?"

A small, contented sigh slips through Nora's lips, and her heartbeat skip briefly as I leave a trail of kisses back down to her shoulder. She leans into my embrace ever so slightly.

"It was better."

That same lazy cat rears back its head and snarls. I tilt her chin towards me, unable to hold back any longer, and guide her lips to mine. The kiss is gentle, sweet. It lingers between us full of hope and promises and longing and desire.

I pull away briefly. My own cravings are mirrored in Nora as her eyes bore into mine. She stands, turning completely towards me, pulling me into her. We collide in heat and friction and lips and tongues. She sucks on my bottom lip and a groan rises from the depths of my soul to hang around us like a veil. She's not going to make this easy for me.

Wrapping my arms around her waist, I lift Nora up and over the low bench she was sitting on and stumble backwards until my knees hit the bed frame. We fall together onto the blankets, her hair in my eyes and my arms holding her close, keeping her with me. Nora effortlessly straddles me, kissing me like she is in the middle of a drought, and I am the rain.

Her need calls to me in an aching cry and twin flames spark between us. Each one antagonizes the other, tempting it to grow bigger, to grow louder. I slide my hands along her frame, cupping every inch of her I can reach, until I find the closures of the dress at her back. The damned clasps are so small and the satin laces slippery enough that my hands just fumble uselessly, unable to find a hold.

"Wait!" Nora gasps, chest heaving with the effort of removing herself. "Let me help."

She slides off me and her sudden absence is crippling. I want her with me. Next to me. On top of me. Around me.

Groaning, I roll over and sit up to find her. Nora is sitting along the side of the bed, watching me in the mirror again. She pulls her messy hair over her shoulders and just waits for me to help her.

"It would be a shame to ruin such a beautiful dress."

"Trust me," I growl, "your dress is the least of my concerns."

A pale pink tinge flushes the back of her neck and shoulders. I can't help it, I kiss it. Nora's blush deepens and I kiss down her spine to the top of her dress.

Now that I'm able to see what I'm doing, I make quick work of the fastenings. The corset top loosens inch by inch down her back to reveal a simple white chemise beneath. Nora rises from the bed and unties her skirts herself, placing them and the corset on the bench in front of the vanity.

I can read her hesitation at revealing herself in every line of her body. Every tense muscle and uncomfortable fidget betrays her uncertainty. I just wait, lazily taking in each and every bit of skin I can see and imagining what I can't. Eventually, Nora turns and stands before me in her chemise, hair wild and eyes heavily lidded and sparkling.

I slide off the bed to stand facing her. With measured movements, I pull my own shirt above my head and drop it next to me. Nora's intake of breath as she half reaches out her hands to touch me sends a delicious shiver tingling up my spine.

Nora's hands hover between us, a question in her eyes. I almost laugh at the absurdity of the moment. How can she not know I want her to touch me? That I *live* for her touch, her want, her need. My hands wrap around her wrists, and I gently guide her hands the rest of the distance between us until they rest against my chest.

I stand perfectly still, eyes closed, as Nora runs those same soft hands across my shoulders, along my arms, down my chest and stomach. I bask in her touch while she explores the planes of my body. Her fingers trace the very outline of my soul across my skin as she gently caresses every piece of my being she dares touch.

The primal need to hold her, to have her, overwhelms me and I crush Nora to me. Our bodies collide in heat and need. Without breaking our embrace, I reach down and pull on the backs of Nora's thighs to lift her. Her legs effortlessly wrap around my hips, the skin of her inner thighs brushing against my stomach and driving me wild.

Turning so Nora is next to the bed again, I carefully place her along the edge. Her legs part to let me in closer and I take full advantage of the space she makes. I can feel Nora's heat calling out to my own and I groan into her. Her answering cry sets me ablaze.

Slowly working my hands under her again, I try to untuck Nora's chemise from where it's trapped beneath her. Her arms slide around my neck and Nora arches herself against me, moving forward enough to let me free the flimsy fabric the rest of the way. My hands slip beneath to brush her bare skin, and I pull her as close as I can while our mouths collide with a new sort of frantic need.

Resting a hand on my chest, Nora pulls back, and we break apart. Bright patches of color are high on her cheeks, her breath coming out in uneven pants. I'm sure mine is just as irregular, but I can't be bothered to focus on anything other than her.

Watching me, Nora hooks her hands under the pooling fabric at her waist and pulls it up and over her head. The offending garment is unceremoniously dropped to the floor with my shirt. Nora's body is stiff as she presents herself to me, letting me take her all in.

My heart stutters. I'm only vaguely aware that I'm staring and I don't even care. Nora tries to discreetly hide behind her hair, and I reach out to stop her, to push it back out of the way. I want to see her. *All* of her.

The creamy skin of Nora's neck cascades down her breasts, over her navel, and to her hips. She lacks the traditional hourglass figure that so many of my brothers and peers claim to want in a woman, but Nora is the most beautiful creature I have ever seen. I can see the tension and strength throughout her body that our days of sparring have created. The hard-earned muscle is ever present just beneath the surface and I long to run my hands along her. She is so much more than I could have ever imagined, traditional figure be damned.

"Is it —" the flush I'm used to seeing on Nora's neck spreads down her chest and she tries to cover herself again "— is everything okay?"

"I can't tell you," I say, my voice reduced to a husky shadow of its usual sound, "how much I wish you knew that this is more than okay. That *you* are more than okay. Nora you are irresistible to me in a way that no other woman has ever been. You've driven me crazy ever since I first saw you in that garden."

I carefully pull her arms away and drink in every inch of her like a dying man. I drawn her to me again and trace a path with my lips from beneath her chin down to the heat of her core. She moans and sighs in turn under my ministrations, slowly collapsing back until she's lying on the bed again. I lean over top of her, gently kissing from her inner thigh to the inside of her knee.

"I'll be right back."

Nora props herself up on her elbows as I pull away and struggle out of my remaining clothes. We at least had the good sense of not wearing shoes earlier, but these pants must be one of the single most restrictive pieces of clothing I own. After managing to open the waistband enough, I yank them down and kick them off my feet.

I stand before Nora, completely naked, and present myself to her. Just as she did for me, I let her look without the pressure to do anything more. Her eyes widen for a second, but not with fear. No, definitely not fear. If anything, it's pure lust dripping from her gaze as she takes in every inch of me finally bared for her to see.

She opens her arms, beckoning for me to return, and I fall into her again. We are heat and lust and want and desire. There is no place for awkwardness or hesitancy as we give in to the need and surrender to its depths.

We sink further back into the bed and explore each other. My own hardness gets between us only briefly but is easily managed with a quick shift in our position. With more willpower than I thought possible, I pull away and move back down Nora's body. I want to kiss her, to taste her. To lavish attention on every bit of her I can see and everything I can't.

Nora's murmurs grow louder as I trace a path down her body with lips and tongue. I make sure to be attentive to her breasts, caressing the flesh and nipping at her peaked nipples in tandem to ensure they receive equal attention. She buries her hands into my hair, moaning as she arches beneath me and pulls me closer.

I kiss lower still until I am kneeling between Nora's knees. Moving carefully so as not to scare her, I gently massage the muscles of her inner thigh. I work my way up along the inside of her right leg first, paying special attention to the connective spaces along her pelvis, before moving in reverse. Then I switch and do the same for her left leg.

I make another pass and can feel as Nora relaxes even more, becoming nothing more than putty in my hands. A quick check shows me that her eyes are closed, the ghost of a satisfied smile on her lips. It takes unbelievable effort to move so slowly.

From my vantage point, I can already see how wet Nora is. I inhale the scent of her arousal and feel myself twitch longingly. The snarling lust I've held at bay for so long won't wait forever.

A few more minutes of massaging her legs and I kiss my way back up her body, carving patterns with my tongue. Nora welcomes me with open arms, open lips, and open legs. I sink between them and devour her again, our nakedness slipping against each other.

"Are you ready?" My question hangs there, unsure both of itself and Nora's answer.

"Yes."

"It may hurt, but only for a moment."

Nora bites her bottom lip and nods. Her body begins to tense back up and I kiss and caress until she relaxes again. Lining myself up, I slowly enter her and practically burst right then and there. She feels even better than I thought possible.

I move further in until I feel her natural barrier in place. It's surprising it hasn't already broken with how much time Nora spends on horseback. Pulling myself back briefly, I give a sharp thrust and break through. Nora cries out and I force myself out of her again, every muscle in my body thrumming with the effort to give her a moment to collect herself.

"Are you okay?"

"Yes." Nora's eyes are shut and her face unreadable, but her answer is confident. "Keep going."

As slowly as I can manage, I enter her again and push forwards until I am fully within her. Nora's muscles flex and tighten around me and I force myself to stop and breathe again. Watching Nora's face for signs she needs me to stop, I fall into a steady rhythm of thrusts.

Nora tangles her hands through my hair and pulls me down to kiss me with the fierceness and passion of fire. Her body arches to meet mine and our hips move together like a dance. Our breath comes out in achy gasps, our heartbeats stuttering together faster and faster.

Wait. No. I'm building too fast. I want Nora to experience her release with me. With a groan of regret, I pull out completely again. Nora needs to enjoy this too.

"No," she pants, eyes glazed, "don't stop."

A smirk slides across my face. "Don't worry, love. I'm not going anywhere."

I clasp her to me and flip onto my back, pulling Nora on top of me. She settles across my hips and, with a little help, takes me again. A guttural moan tears from me as I slide inside her again. Nothing will ever feel better than this.

Nora begins to move against me, cautiously at first and then faster as she learns what makes her body sing. I watch as she dances and writhes above me, her breath coming out in sharp cries as her breasts heave with her rocking. I grasp her hips and together we move as one.

Nora is nearing her climax and the anticipation of my own is sending uncontrollable shivers through me. Holding onto Nora's hips with one hand to help keep her seated, I grab one of the pillows near my head and shove it under my hips, elevating them to give Nora more leverage. She leans back and grinds even harder against me. We both shudder as I slide just that bit deeper into her and she clutches my arms, raising my hands to her breasts. I knead her flesh and pull on her nipples. Nora reacts like I lit her body on fire and moves even faster.

Removing a hand from one of her breasts, I slide it down her body and use my thumb to caress her sensitive nub. It's firm against my hand and I stroke it in circular motion, a lazily slow pace that quickens as we hurdle towards our finish. Nora's groans reach a new guttural pitch until, finally, together we release and become one.

I startle briefly from sleep, unsure of my surroundings. Nora is curled next to me, her back pressed against my chest. She slumbers peacefully under the blanket we had pulled over ourselves earlier. The fire in the hearth has died low and moonlight streams through the uncovered glass of the windows.

Moving slowly so I don't wake up Nora, I slip out from under the blanket and stretch. I carefully pick my way through the half-illuminated room and go to stand before one of the open windows. The cool night air dances across my nakedness and sends goosebumps crawling along my skin and prickling through my hair.

The moon hangs low in the sky above me. It's just days away from reaching its full strength before its light will begin to fade again towards the darkness of a new moon. I bask in its glow, sending up a silent prayer of thanks for the blessing the Moon Goddess bestowed upon me all those years ago. Without Her, I would have never survived this long to meet Nora. I would never have found my way here.

"Alon?" Nora's sleepy voice calls through the partial darkness behind me. "What are you doing?"

"Don't worry, *Ku'u Lei*. I'm coming." I take one last look at the moon, and I swear it almost looks as if it winks back at me.

Turning from the window, I return to the bed and curl around Nora. I reach for her and pull her close, sharing her warmth. My breathing slows to match hers and together we fall into a peaceful sleep.

In Which it All Ends

Prince Alon wanders through the halls of the house his Mama and Baba had gifted to him and Nora on the eve of their wedding night. The stately manor has served them well – housing not only their own four children, but providing a home for their twelve grandchildren and three great grandchildren. History is woven into every rug on the floor and every tapestry on the wall. Love waters the gardens and warms the fireplaces on chilly evenings. It pains him to see it witness such suffering.

Nora started to decline several years before, growing old as so many do. Little by little, her strength faded and her body began to fail. Even now, however, her mind remains sharp and her wit unmatched as the day they met. She spends most days bedridden and a shadow of the woman she once was, but does what she can to remain cheerful for her family and hide her pain from those around her.

Alon felt the changes to his own body as he grew older as well. He continued to age the same as Nora, but his gift keeps him from serious harm. There is still something wrong, though. Something he can't seem to place.

Every morning with the dawn he wakes feeling renewed, but by the time the last rays of the sun sink in the evening skies that feeling of wrongness plague him again. An ache behind his heart tells him that his time with Nora is nearing its end. Refusing to accept this truth, he roused himself from their marriage bed to take one last journey alone.

On the east side of their manor stands the library with its accompanying balcony overlooking the sea. It's there he goes, pausing only to retrieve a small silver dish etched with the phases of the moon. Opening the balcony doors, he inhales the sweet scent of the moonflowers growing along the arbor, well out of reach of small hands. The flowers are in full bloom. Their faces rise to drink in the warm silvery light of the moon shining down upon them.

On one of their pilgrimages to the Elders to readdress the treaty, Alon was granted the privilege of bringing back some of the seeds of the moonflower with him. Nora tended the flowers as dutifully as she oversaw the changes to the treaty to reintegrate the Koralans and the Elders back together. As the moonflowers grew and thrived on the arbor, so did the relationship between the two peoples. They live as one family again, celebrating both the moon and the sun in turn.

Alon carefully selects one of the delicate white blooms and gently plucks it from its vine. Setting it on the balcony next to him, he uncaps a small flask and pours seawater into the basin. It swirls and eddies, turning as silver as the bowl. Alon places the moonflower into the water and raises it to the heavens as an offering. Taking a deep breath, he repeats the words Aurelia had taught him so many years before:

"With the moon this blessing was given. With the moon it shall be returned."

The moonflower glows silver for a moment and then fades to brown as it slips down below the surface. Weariness falls over Alon like a heavy blanket on a cold winter day. It won't be long now.

Returning the bowl to its shelf, Alon makes his way back through the halls to the room he and Nora shared for their life together. She's huddled under the covers, so much smaller than he remembers her. Careful not to wake her, he slips beneath the blankets and curls around her. Even in their advanced age, Nora still fits perfectly against him. They remain a matched pair to the very end. Nora's breathing is shallow, labored. Alon's heartbeat slows to match hers and he falls into a deep slumber.

As one they entered the world under a *Perigean* moon. Their destiny was written for them before they even had words to share their stories. Now they leave this world as one, twin candles guttering out with the same gentle breeze that welcomes them home.

Acknowledgments

Well. Here we are at the very end. It's crazy to think that if you're reading this then you have read my book and that is one of the weirdest and coolest feelings ever. I guess the biggest question is whether you're someone like me who finds it weirdly enjoyable to read the Acknowledgments section in a book or if you just skip right over and move on to the next book on your TBR list. Honestly, no shade if you skip it. If your TBR is anything like mine, you can't stop reading for a second or it'll somehow end up in the triple digits...

This book has been an incredible experience to create, and I definitely couldn't have done it without some help along the way. I want to give a thank you and a shout out to Emily for helping me with the title. Apparently, I can write the thing, but naming it was a struggle I was not prepared for. I very much appreciate your help.

A big thank you to Amy Biancoli for reading an earlier draft and helping me find the confidence to look into publishing my story. Your encouragement means the world. Amy is also an incredibly talented writer, author, musician, and now playwright in her own right so y'all should go check her out as well.

I couldn't even dream of writing an Acknowledgments section without mentioning you, Cooper. You have been a godsend throughout this entire process, and I can very confidently say that this book would not exist without you. You have been my biggest cheerleader and supporter. You saw me through bouts of low confidence and high emotion and never stopped encouraging me to keep going. Your insight into helping me fix my plot-holes was absolutely instrumental. I mean it from the very depths of my heart when I say *thank you*.

And finally, dear reader, I want to thank you. For choosing my book over all the other incredible stories and authors out there. For giving this small, indie author a chance to share her story with the world. For sticking it out and reading to the end of my rambly Acknowledgments. I hope that this is just the beginning for us.

About the Author

When Olivia Richardson isn't finding words to bring her stories to life, she can most likely be found with her nose buried in a book or adding more titles to her ever-growing TBR list. Olivia lives in Vermont with her husband, son, and their brat of a tuxedo kitten named Stella. When she is not building apartment buildings out of blocks for her son or working on the never-ending pile of home projects around the house, Olivia spends time in the kitchen creating delicious concoctions to send into work with her husband. She has ruined many a diet at his workplace and plans to continue to do so as long as she can. *Under the Perigean Moon* is her first novel.

www.ingramcontent.com/pod-product-compliance
Lightning Source LLC
Chambersburg PA
CBHW021133260626
47169CB00005B/1595